THE BELL
BETWEEN WORLDS

IAN JOHNSTONE

THE BELL
BETWEEN WORLDS

HarperCollins *Children's Books*

First published in Great Britain by HarperCollins *Children's Books* in 2013
HarperCollins *Children's Books* is a division of HarperCollins*Publishers* Ltd,
77-85 Fulham Palace Road, Hammersmith, London, W6 8JB.

Visit us on the web at
www.harpercollins.co.uk

2

978-0-00-749122-3
Printed and bound in the United States of America

For Emily, who shares my worlds

PART ONE

The Bell

1
Gabblety Row

"Their voice is clear and true, yet it is not breathed, nor carried upon the air. It echoes like thought inside the skull, speaking words where none are spoken."

GABBLETY ROW WAS QUITE the most peculiar and ramshackle building in town. Its undulating walls, higgledy-piggledy red tiles and winding iron drainpipes all showed an utter disregard for straight lines. The frontage of four shops with three floors above rose in an astonishing disarray of red brick and dark brown beams, leaning here and lurching there until it reached the garret rooms at its top. These chambers teetered outwards on a forest of wooden brackets, such that they loomed over the pavement below in a manner quaint to behold from a distance, but utterly terrifying to those walking beneath.

The long passage of time had added to the chaos, bending beams and bowing walls to form a miraculous collection of angles, bulges and crannies. In recent years the entire structure had slumped sideways and backwards away from the two main roads that crossed at its corner, as if the whole building was shrinking from the incessant noise and pollution of the traffic. And yet,

9

while it seemed to cower from the twenty-first century, Gabblety Row clung to the slick, hard edges of modern life like a barnacle to a rock. Years came and went, but Gabblety Row remained.

The terrace also had a curious way of settling into the hearts of all of its residents. Sylas Tate, for instance, was often woken by loud, unearthly groans that seemed to issue from every wall, floor and ceiling, as if the tired old structure was easing its great weight one more inch into the earth for a few hours of rest, or perhaps heaving one more straight line into crookedness. Being a boy of extraordinary imagination, Sylas loved these weird sounds. A creak of the building's old joints would transport him to a swaying bough in the highest reaches of an ancient tree; the groan of a beam would take him to a hammock in a storm-weary galleon; and the sharp crack of a splitting timber would have him at the sights of a musket, firing into the massing ranks of some terrifying and brutal foe. And these moments of escape, these tricks of imagination, were now the happiest moments of his young life.

It was not only the noises that Sylas loved about Gabblety Row. He adored the baffling passageways that ran the length of the terrace above the shops, darting left and right and up and down for no apparent reason, leading to some doors that he'd never seen open and others behind which lived his only friends in the world.

And perhaps, most of all, he loved his room.

Like any good sanctuary, it was extremely difficult to reach. The only way to it was a narrow staircase that led upwards from an undersized door on the third-floor passageway to a creaky trapdoor that opened in the furthest, darkest corner of the room. As the old building had heaved and slumped over the years, so the door and the passageway had become both low and narrow, such that they were now almost impossible for an adult to negotiate. This meant that, in his room, he could be sure to be absolutely alone: a situation that suited him well, for he was not the most sociable boy. He mixed with people perfectly well when it was necessary, at school or on the bus, but kept himself to himself when it was not. Sylas's uncle sometimes said that his mother's death had turned him into a moody and melancholy boy — "far too serious for a twelve-year-old" — but Sylas didn't agree: as far as he was concerned, he simply knew his own mind and found it company enough. Whatever the truth, Sylas was used to filling his life with his own kind of cheer.

This was just what Sylas was doing at four o'clock on that peculiar Friday afternoon. He was lying in his room turning his favourite kite over and over in his hands, imagining it thousands of feet in the air, carving its beautiful path above the distant hills at the edge of town, gliding over caves and waterfalls, forgotten bowers and crevices, great hollowed-out oaks and lakes carpeted with lilies. He pictured it among the great birds that he sometimes saw from his window soaring above the town — eagles, owls, falcons, ospreys — playing with the wind and surveying all the beauty of the world.

Suddenly the grating voice of his uncle brought him crashing back to earth.

"Sylas!" came the voice through the old trapdoor. "Mail!"

Sylas sighed, drawing himself reluctantly out of his daydream. He lowered the kite carefully to the floor and pushed himself up from the mattress.

"Coming!" he shouted.

He took down his tatty old rucksack from the shelf, walked to the corner of his room and, as was his habit, kissed his fingers and touched the smooth, worn edge of a photo frame suspended above the trapdoor before heaving it open and descending into the darkness below. As it fell closed, the old picture rocked on its nail, briefly animating his mother's faded face, her warm, smiling eyes still bright beneath the glass.

The short, dark stairwell led to a not-quite-straight oblong of light in which Sylas could see the silhouette of his uncle.

Tobias Tate was an exceptionally tall man — a fact that was only made more apparent by his thinness. His legs and arms were so long and slight that one might fear for their safety as he swung them up and down the narrow staircases and passageways of Gabblety Row. Even his face was long and narrow, and his hair stood up on end in a manner that suggested that just as gravity pulled him down, some other invisible force tugged at his upper extremities. And yet, perhaps in an attempt to fight this upward tendency, Tobias Tate had developed a graceless stoop — an arching of the shoulders and a thrusting forward of his head — which gave him an ugly, almost predatory appearance. When he entered a room, it was his sharp nose that appeared first, followed by the black plumes of his eyebrows and his furrowed brow, then his long, sinewy neck. A bookkeeper by trade and passion, he spent most of his days in his study poring over piles of papers and tapping on his many computers, all of which made his stoop more pronounced, his face more pallid and gaunt, and his character more unutterably miserable.

"Tardy!" he barked. "Tardy, Sylas, that's what you are — and if you don't know what it means, look it up, because on account of your tardiness I don't have time to explain."

The voice was dry and expressionless, but Sylas could tell from the unusual length of his uncle's sentence that he was in an especially irritable mood. A large, thin white hand thrust a pile of letters into Sylas's chest.

"Sorry, uncle, I'll post them straight away," he said, pushing them into his rucksack. He stepped around and over his uncle's stray limbs and into the corridor beyond.

"Tardy! Look it up!" Tobias Tate shouted after him.

Sylas walked quickly down the meandering grey passageway. Someone less experienced in the curious ways of Gabblety Row might trip over an unexpected rise in the floor or bruise themselves against a bulge in the wall, but these corridors were Sylas's domain. Small of stature and deft of foot from his many errands, he moved with an assured ease past the many apartment doors on his left and right, until he turned on to the staircase. He took the stairs in twos — a feat of considerable skill given that each pair varied in height and angle — and soon bounded off the bottom step and through the large oak door.

It opened at the end of the terrace, directly opposite the Church of the Holy Trinity. The majestic spire soared above Gabblety Row as if trying to teach a lesson in uprightness, but that was perhaps the church's last salute to the world: the main roof had fallen in and the grounds were now an overgrown jungle of trees, bushes, ivy and broken stone.

Sylas hesitated — he had not had a chance to lay flowers for his mother this week, and it was already Friday. He looked at his watch. There should be time after the post office.

Suddenly he was assailed by a blast of screeching, honking car horns, and the acrid smell of fumes as the lights on the corner changed to green. The two roads that met at the corner of Gabblety Row were the busiest in town, each four lanes across and jammed with steel and noise and agitated people. These were serious roads, roads that did not like to be interrupted, and they growled irritably at one another each time the traffic lights changed.

Sylas turned the corner and began the familiar walk along the frontage of shops: the sweet, doughy-smelling Buntague's

13

Bakery, the ominous undertaker's Veeglum & Retch, and finally Sam Clump's, the locksmith. Then something very odd caught his eye. It was a movement somewhere ahead of him, inside the dusty window of the final shop in the row, the one that had been empty for years.

He approached the filthy, arched panes that made up the shopfront. Each dirty section of glass had been set into carved wooden frames as crookedly as the rest of the row and bent the light in a unique way, making it almost impossible to see into the dark room beyond. All Sylas could make out was the usual darkness flecked with dust and cobwebs.

He shrugged and was about to turn away when something unfamiliar made him look up. To his surprise, he saw that there, nailed over the dilapidated nameplate that had always been blank, was a new shop sign. The lettering was like none he had ever seen, a dance of outlandish arcs and curves in reds and purples and blues.

He read out loud in wonderment: "The... Shop... of..." He blinked and frowned, "...Things."

"*Yes, indeed.*"

Sylas jumped and looked about him, trying to find the owner of the voice. There was no one. The voice had sounded so clear and close, even over the drone of the traffic.

"*Do come inside.*"

A shiver ran down Sylas's spine. It was inside his head.

The voice was accented and strange, like none he could remember. Surely, if he was imagining it, it would seem more familiar. He found himself stepping backwards towards the edge of the pavement.

"*Careful!*"

A horn screamed wildly and Sylas felt the wind of a passing

14

car tearing at his clothes. He threw himself forward, gasping with fright, and steadied himself against a window frame. When he had gathered his wits, he found himself standing right next to the doorway.

"*You have nothing to fear.*"

He peered again through the dirty glass, but could see nothing but darkness. For some time he stayed rooted to the spot, glancing nervously from side to side. Finally his nerves got the better of him and he turned and started to walk away.

In a few steps he had reached the corner of Clump's locksmith's and he heard the sound of Sam Clump chatting cheerfully to a customer as he prodded a screwdriver into a misbehaving lock. Sylas paused and looked out at the busy road and the endless throng of faces peering over steering wheels, then across to the harsh lights of the supermarket, and finally he looked back at the mysterious dark window.

What harm could come to him so close to Sam and to all these people? Surely he had just imagined the voice – after all, he had imagined stranger things before.

He felt the sting of a raindrop against the side of his face and looked up to see the sky darkening. As the heavens rumbled, he drew himself up and walked briskly across the pavement to the Shop of Things.

$$S$$

The rain fell in sheets that moved like silvery curtains across the town. A warm wind caught the drops and hurled them this way and that, so that there was nowhere they did not reach. They swirled into bus shelters and blasted into doorways; they curled beneath umbrellas and danced between the leaves of trees. Soon the town had become a world of shabby greyness, its dull buildings framed by pendulous, smoky clouds above, and murky pools and rivulets below.

The stranger turned out of a lane on to the main road, gathering his loose-fitting coat about him and drawing down the hood so that his face could not be seen. He cursed as a gust threw up spray from a passing car and he quickly slid the black holdall off his shoulder, tucking it under his coat. Even with this awkward burden he moved quickly, pausing only once or twice to look at road signs and to wait for cars as they turned into side roads. He seemed agitated, casting his dark eyes left and right and sometimes muttering under his breath, but his strides were sure and powerful and he moved swiftly past other pedestrians.

As he neared the traffic lights, his attention was drawn to a strange, ramshackle building on the opposite corner of the junction. He put the holdall down and leaned against one of the traffic lights, peering out from under his hood at the peculiar arrangement of beams, drainpipes and brickwork that lay before him.

"And thus at this our journey's end," he said in a weathered voice, "is another, just beginning."

Then he stepped out in the direction of Gabblety Row.

2
The Shop of Things

*"When the sun sets, it merely sleeps, to rise another day; a path
that ends, ends not, but leads back from whence it came; and thus
at this our journey's end is another, just beginning."*

THE DOOR CREAKED ON its old, dry hinges, but opened easily. Sylas
heard the half-hearted ring of the rusty shop bell above his head as
he stepped into the gloom.

He was immediately aware of the strong odour of decaying
wood and damp walls, which hung heavily in the air and caught
the back of his throat. The front of the shop was relatively clear,
containing a few empty cabinets whose doors hung off their hinges
and vast grey spiders' webs that hung wall to ceiling like drapes.
But within, all he could see were stacks of crates and parcels
that ascended from floor to ceiling like weird postal sculptures,
arranged in long lines stretching the full length of the shop. He
glanced at one stack and saw that each parcel and crate carried
a shipping label stamped with the city of origin: *Beijing... Addis
Ababa... Rio de Janeiro... Alexandria... Khartoum...*

"Welcome."

It was the same strange accent, the same deep, gentle voice, but this time it was not inside his head, it was in the room. Sylas became aware of a dull glow in the dark interior of the shop, at the end of one of the stacks.

"Thank you," he blurted, his heart pounding.

"It is said that the greatest endeavours have modest beginnings," said the voice, this time with some humour. "So I must ask you to use your imagination."

Suddenly Sylas saw the sparse light in the shop shift slightly, and a shadow moved. His eyes darted from left to right trying to find the owner of the voice, but there were so many dark corners and strange objects that he was at a loss where to look. He was about to turn and retreat back to the door when the silhouette of a small stooped man appeared against the dusty light at the far end of one of the stacks.

As Sylas walked to the back of the shop, the figure paused and seemed to bow slightly before reaching for something from a shelf. A sudden flare of orange light made Sylas squint and look away, but when he turned back, he saw the room gradually coming to life. The dark figure was lighting a row of candles on what had once been the shop counter, but was now a broken expanse of rotten wood.

The man stepped forward and leaned on the counter, bringing his face into the halo of light.

It was a fascinating face, quite unlike any Sylas had seen before. The pale skin was wrinkled around the mouth, eyes and the wide brow, showing him to be a man of great expression and animation. His bright, oriental eyes were calming and gentle, like nothing could surprise them, as if they had seen much of most things. His white beard was flecked with bluish-grey hairs around the edges, which lent him a distinguished but outlandish appearance, an effect that was only heightened by the way in which it drew to a point below his chin. He wore a grey, foreign-looking velvet cap upon his head, like a crumpled pot that had slumped to one side, and a dishevelled grey suit made of some coarse material that showed the myriad creases of too much wear. Even his shirt, which had apparently once been white, was now turning grey in sympathy with everything else. His tie, which was a rich dark green, provided the only colour.

His most distinctive feature was his warm, welcoming smile, for his eyes twinkled and his features creased into a pleasing, amiable expression of kindness. Sylas found himself smiling back — a broad, bold smile that brightened his spirits and dispelled his nerves.

The old man lit the last of seven candles and sighed, making the flames dance slightly.

"I believe in a certain amount of gloom," he said, and with a wink he blew out the match. "What your eyes cannot see your imagination must discover. And your imagination is very important, young man."

Sylas looked at him quizzically. "Important?"

"Yes, for a great many things… and you will put it to very good use in my shop," said the shopkeeper. "Now, let us dispense with the formalities. They call me Mr Zhi."

He stepped around the counter and held out his hand. It was covered in a beautifully embroidered velvet glove of the same dark green as his tie. Sylas only had a moment to look at it, but he saw that the stitching on the back of the hand glittered slightly in the candlelight.

As they shook hands, the old man straightened and looked at him expectantly.

"And how should I address my very first customer?"

"Oh… Sylas. Sylas Tate, sir — Mr Zhi, I mean."

He felt flustered, but almost at once he felt Mr Zhi's eyes soothing and reassuring him, as though telling him in some silent language that all was as it should be.

"You are very welcome, Sylas Tate," he said, pronouncing the name with care. He raised himself up. "Now, where shall we start?" He looked into the darkness and seemed to ponder for a moment, then he tapped the side of his nose and his eyes twinkled. "Follow me," he said.

He grabbed a candle from the counter and set off with surprising speed between some of the stacks. Sylas had to run to catch up. They turned left, then right, then left again, passing opened parcels of what looked like peculiar musical instruments.

"What *are* all these things?" asked Sylas.

"Ah well, that is a very good question to which there can be no good answer," said the old man, without turning. "But you have found the right word. I collect and sell *Things*. *Things*, by definition, are objects we find hard to explain. Were I to explain them, I think I might have to close up shop!"

At that moment they arrived at a wall of crates. Some had been taken down and opened and the floor was strewn with straw and shredded paper. Mr Zhi turned to Sylas and smiled.

"As you can see, I have many thousands of Things in my shop," he said, his eyes now peering into one of the crates, "but I consider it my particular talent to know which Things will interest which people. That is why I have never taken to having my wonderful Things displayed on shelves and in cabinets. That would take away all of the mystery, which is the greater part of any good Thing, and a good deal of the discovery, which is much of what is left!"

The shopkeeper bent low over the crate and very gently lowered his gloved hand into the straw.

"This you will like," he said.

He rummaged for a moment and then, with great care, he raised his hand. He was holding a fragile wheel, made of some kind of metal, from which hung a number of silvery strings. Sylas half expected to see a puppet dangling below but, as Mr Zhi lifted the wheel still further, he saw that each string was tied to a tiny silvery bar, from which were suspended three more strings: one at the centre and one at each end. Each of these additional strings was connected to a further bar and thereby to three more strings, and so on, and so on, until Sylas could see a vast and wonderful structure of silvery twine emerging from the crate. Just as he began to wonder how such a complicated thing could have remained untangled in the straw, Mr Zhi drew himself to his full height and raised the wheel above his head.

Sylas gasped in amazement.

There, on the end of each of the hundreds of strings, were tiny, delicate, beautiful birds, each with its wings outstretched in some attitude of flight. Their feathers shimmered like rainbows in the candlelight and, as each bird turned on its string, they seemed to throw out more light than they received, so that the surrounding walls of crates moved with colour.

"It's wonderful, just wonderful," said Sylas, letting his rucksack fall to the floor.

"It is, is it not?" said Mr Zhi, with evident pleasure. "Of course, such wonders are created in part by your very own imagination," he said, moving the great flock of birds slightly closer to Sylas. "To some, this is a beautiful object that must have taken several years for many careful hands to create. To others, to those with true imagination, it is a marvellous flock of magical birds carried by a wind we cannot feel, calling a cry we cannot hear, united by a purpose we cannot know. To them, each bird is as alive as you or I, because in their imagination they see them soaring, climbing, swooping, turning…"

Sylas found himself staring ever more intently at the delicately balanced parts of the mobile, watching closely as they moved around each other on the gentle currents of air in the room. He saw how each bird was finished with astonishing detail, showing the individual feathers, the tail fan, the precise angle of the wing as it manoeuvred in flight. He marvelled as they glided past each other without ever colliding, as if aware of one other.

And then, perhaps in a trick of light, he thought he saw one of them twitch.

A wing lifted slightly and a long neck turned. Then a crooked wing seemed to straighten as one of the birds turned in a wide arc around another. He blinked in disbelief as he saw another bird beat its wings, change its path in the air and then resume its endless circling. He let his eyes drift from place to place within the multitude, watching as every one of them seemed to take on a life of its own.

At first they beat their wings at random, but soon every bird was flapping in time with the others. And then, without warning, they broke from the circle below Mr Zhi's hand and moved in one great flock, banking left then right, their wings catching the light in unison, forming a breathtaking display of colour. The gossamer strings seemed to have disappeared altogether. Moments later the birds turned their heads upwards and rose as if carried by an updraught of air. Sylas gazed in astonishment as he watched them soar over the top of Mr Zhi's hand in a beautiful arc of light and colour, before swooping downwards to the floor. At the very last moment they turned upwards and sped through the air towards him, their wings beating rapidly now, their feathers ruffling and shimmering. As they circled round his head, Sylas laughed out

loud, wanting to reach out and touch them. His heart thumped —
not from fear, but from a wild, intoxicating excitement.

"So now you see it!" came Mr Zhi's voice from the dark.

Sylas caught his breath. "I see it!"

Then, abruptly, the flock of birds wheeled sharply above
his head and streamed towards Mr Zhi's gloved hand. As they
reached the glove, they turned again, so tightly this time that the
leading birds met those at the rear of the flock, forming a circle. As
the last joined formation, Sylas could again see the occasional glint
of the silvery strings in the darkness, and then he saw that the tiny
bars were supporting their weight once more, as though they had
never been gone. The birds circled more and more slowly until
they were drifting gently on the air currents. Their wings moved
no more.

Mr Zhi began lowering them back down into the straw. Sylas
wanted to ask him to let them fly some more, but had the feeling
that they had done all that was intended.

He cleared his dry throat. "What *was* that?" he asked.

Mr Zhi simply patted Sylas cheerfully on the shoulder, picked
up the candle and started back along the passageway of parcels.
Sylas paused for a moment, glancing down at the pile of straw, but
then picked up his rucksack and scrambled after him.

"There's much to see!" he heard Mr Zhi say up ahead. "Please
keep up!"

He moved so swiftly that, as Sylas turned one corner, the
shopkeeper had already turned the next and the only way to keep
pace was by following the dying traces of candlelight that flickered
against the walls of parcels ahead.

"But what *was* it?" asked Sylas breathlessly.

"Ah well, the most wondrous Things show themselves only to
those who are supposed to see!" shouted Mr Zhi ahead of him,

without turning. "So it was with you and the mobile. When you saw it, at first you saw just a beautiful object, a thing of gossamer strings and silver bars and bright-painted feathers. But then you brought it to life. It stirred without any draught to carry it, the wings moved without any plan or design. You made the birds *fly*," said Mr Zhi, turning to Sylas excitedly, "fly like I've never seen before!"

Sylas looked puzzled. "But wasn't that just in my imagination?" he asked. "You told me to use my imagination."

"No, I saw everything you saw, but that is not to say that your imagination didn't bring it to life. You made the birds fly as you dreamed they might, and in doing that — in putting your imagination to work — you showed that you are able to use it like few others. You are able to see the world as it is promised to us."

Sylas laughed. "I'm pretty sure I see the world like everyone else."

"Certainly you do, but the mobile is a sensitive Thing. It shows what you are *capable* of seeing, not what you already see." The shopkeeper cocked his head on one side. "A little confusing, isn't it? But don't worry, I have more to show you!"

With that, he turned and set off into the gloom of the shop. Sylas screwed up his face. "*The world as it is promised to us?*" What could *that* mean? He knew he had a good imagination — his uncle was for ever telling him that he lived too much in his head — but there was nothing unusual about *that*. He jogged after the strange shopkeeper, wondering what he was getting himself into.

As he went, he saw that the giant stacks of parcels were packed so tightly that the shop had become a maze of little corridors, which gave the impression of a room much larger than it actually was. Sylas was just starting to become a little worried that he might not be able to find his way out again when he sped round a corner and almost charged headlong into Mr Zhi.

The proprietor caught him by the shoulders. "I think this shall be our next stop, young man," he said, with a wide smile.

He turned about and stepped on to a small upturned box. He reached up to the topmost shelf and took down a large flat parcel from the top of one of the piles.

"This Thing is at once very different from the mobile, and very similar," he said, grunting as he lowered himself back down. "Like the mobile, it uses your imagination to show what is possible, not what you already know to be true."

Sylas watched with excitement as Mr Zhi carefully tore open one end of the parcel, then pulled out a large flat object, and cast the wrapping on the floor.

"The mobile told us that you can see what *the world* may become," said the old shopkeeper. "With this Thing — this set of mirrors — we will show something else: that you can see all that *you* are able to be."

At first the object looked like a leather-bound book, but as Mr Zhi laid it carefully on the box, Sylas saw that it was not made of leather but of two pieces of wood, joined along one edge by tarnished but ornate brass hinges. The top piece was black and the piece beneath white. As he leaned forward to look more closely, Mr Zhi took gentle hold of the black panel and lifted. The hinges creaked slightly and the black panel swung open.

What was revealed seemed unremarkable. Both panels comprised a simple mirror framed by an ornately carved border. The old man lifted them up and adjusted them carefully in front of Sylas until he was looking at himself in both mirrors, each showing his reflection from a slightly different angle, the white one from the left and the black one from the right. The effect was interesting at first, but no more so than looking at a reflection in a bedroom dresser.

As he glanced between the mirrors, Mr Zhi peered at him, taking in Sylas's wide brow and small stubby nose; his high arching eyebrows and dark brown eyes that seemed a little sad and old for his age; his thick, dark, wavy hair, cut crudely so that it fell in a tousled mass about his face. The proprietor smiled quietly to himself and shook his head, as if finding something difficult to believe.

"I just see myself," said Sylas with a shrug.

Mr Zhi chuckled. "I'm afraid this will not be easy. You would not need money in my shop, but my Things still come at a price: the struggle to understand." He moved the mirrors a little closer to Sylas. "The trick with these mirrors is not to look—"

Suddenly there was a noise at the back of the shop: the clunk of a door closing, the snap of a latch. Mr Zhi frowned and quickly closed the mirrors, pushing them into the nearest pile of Things.

"Please wait here," he said, then set out quickly towards the back of the shop.

There was something about the way he had hidden the mirrors that alarmed Sylas. It was clear at once that whoever had entered by the back door was not expected. Instinctively he took a few paces after Mr Zhi, but when he saw a large shadow move across the candlelight on the ceiling, he stopped.

Mr Zhi turned. "Stand very still," he said. "I'll be straight back."

A shiver went through Sylas. All of a sudden, Mr Zhi sounded worried. Very worried.

3

The Third Thing

"Here miracles rise from the earth and awe is in the air; here wonder flows over and, like a mountain spring, never runs dry..."

SYLAS STOOD STILL, AS he had been told, and listened.

At first he heard nothing but Mr Zhi's footsteps, but then came the sound of voices. Low voices, speaking quickly in urgent tones. He could not hear what was being said, but one of the speakers was Mr Zhi. The other voice was deep and masculine, speaking in murmurings that resonated through the shop but were impossible to make out. There was a quick exchange between the two men, and then suddenly the strange voice boomed loud and clear.

"No! It must be now! Today!"

Then, for a long time, the voices were a mumble.

Finally, after Sylas felt like he had been standing there for hours, Mr Zhi came back into the room.

"My apologies!" he said as he strode back towards Sylas. His face bore the same calm, amiable expression as before, but Sylas noticed that he was walking even more quickly. "That was my new assistant — I had quite forgotten that we had arranged to meet, so much was I enjoying your visit!"

"That's fine," said Sylas. "Is everything... all right?"

"Oh, quite all right, though I am sorry to say that we will not have as much time as I had hoped." The shopkeeper blew out his cheeks and fingered his little beard, eyeing the pile of Things where he had deposited the mirrors. "In fact... yes... yes, sadly I think we must leave the mirrors for another time..."

He turned on his heel and marched back towards the rear of the shop. "Come on, young man! The second Thing must wait, but the third Thing is by far the most exciting of all!"

Sylas shook his head in bewilderment and set out after him — this shop was getting stranger and stranger.

When they reached the back of the shop, there was no sign of the assistant, though Sylas noticed that the back door was slightly ajar. Meanwhile the shopkeeper had dropped to his knees behind the counter. All that could be seen of him was the very top of his odd little hat, which bobbed and danced as he scrabbled around on the low shelves.

"This third Thing is marvellous in its own right," mumbled Mr Zhi as he threw unwanted Things over his shoulder, "but it will also help you to understand..." He grunted as he paused to look at something. "...To understand the others. This is it!"

He murmured with satisfaction and stood up, dusting the creased lapels of his jacket. He gave Sylas an excited wink and then lifted something above the broken surface of the counter.

It was another parcel, but different from all the others. It was an oblong about the size of a novel, covered with some kind of leather, which was folded over neatly on all sides and fastened with twine, tied in a bow at the top. The old man had placed his gloved hand on top of it, as though part of him didn't want his most special of Things to be seen. He turned it over and ran a finger over the wrinkled leather.

The candles crackled and spat, the dancing flames making the shadows shift. Mr Zhi held the parcel for another moment with both hands, running his thumbs over the leather wrapping. Then he squeezed it fondly as if bidding it farewell and pushed it across the counter.

"Take a look at this."

Sylas's eyes ran over the neat folds of worn leather and the carefully tied twine that bound it. As he took hold of it, he felt the same stirrings of excitement that he had experienced when he had first entered the shop. It was surprisingly warm to the touch, the leather soft and yielding against his skin.

With a glance at Mr Zhi, he took hold of one end of the twine and pulled. The knot untied itself instantly and both the twine and the soft leather wrapping fell away as though they were made of silk.

Sylas's eyes widened. "Wow..." he whispered.

Between his palms lay the most exquisite book he had ever seen. The cover was made of mottled brown leather that had seen better days, its once smooth finish now dented and grazed by its many years of use. But into this drab leather had been laid the most beautiful decorations of gold, silver and dark red stones. Sylas turned it so that it caught the candlelight and saw that they formed a pattern: a row of gems, seven on each edge, placed on the outside of a stitched, golden zigzag that ran along the four sides, the thread sewn so tightly that the stitches could hardly be seen. Within this border a superbly adorned symbol had been laid into the leather: a large snaking S made of gold at the top and silver at the bottom. The back cover was beautiful too, with the same zigzagging border around its four edges, this time in silver.

He looked back at Mr Zhi and saw that the old man was also transfixed by the book. It took a moment for their eyes to meet.

"It's beautiful," said Sylas in a whisper. "Is it old?"

"Very old."

"And what does the S mean?"

"Most people who know about this book call it the Samarok, and it is thought that the S comes from that name. Aren't you going to open it?"

"Yes — yes, of course."

Sylas allowed the book to fall open. The pages turned in a flurry of paper until they settled on what must have been the weakest part of the binding, towards the end of the book. The first thing to strike him was the wonderful woody, rich aroma of old books — much more intense than he had smelt before — like dry oak leaves on a forest floor. Then he saw the words, written in black lettering that marched a little irregularly across the page, the lines undulating slightly as they went. It was not a printed book, but one written by hand.

He looked up at Mr Zhi, who was placing some spectacles on his nose.

"Someone wrote this by hand?"

"Not one person, Sylas, many," replied the shopkeeper, clearly enjoying Sylas's amazement. He leaned over and peered through his spectacles at the open book. "Have a look."

Sylas turned the page with great care and saw that the next was written in strange looping tails and graceful lines. The page opposite was written in another crowded, huddling scrawl. He flicked through towards the front of the book and, sure enough, almost every page was written in a new hand, with smudges here and crossings-out there, giving the appearance of some sort of collected journal. But when he reached a point around halfway through, the style changed and it was written in one measured, unremarkable hand in almost perfectly straight lines. There were still errors, and parts of pages were faded and illegible, but it looked far more like a normal book.

"There are two parts to the book," explained Mr Zhi. "The first part is a copy of an ancient text that has now been lost. These few pages are all that remain of many volumes, which were written to provide answers to some of the questions we have spoken about. The second part is a collection of writings by many people, each of whom followed a path not unlike the one that lies ahead of you."

Sylas frowned and looked up. "What *path*?"

Mr Zhi simply smiled. "We'll come to that. Read me a line or two," he said.

Sylas shrugged, pressed down two pages and ran his eyes along the first line. The shapes of the letters and even the words seemed familiar, but they made no sense. He started at the beginning again, but for some reason the letters did not form words.

"Strange..." he mumbled.

He turned to a page at the back of the book, which was written in an old-fashioned, slanting hand. Again, he stared at the first line, trying to make sense of it. He shook his head, turned the page and began running his finger over the first sentence of another entry, but after a few moments he stopped and let out a sigh.

"I don't get it," he said. "The words look familiar, but they don't make sense. Is it another language?"

"Not a language," replied Mr Zhi, smiling once again. "A cipher. A code."

Sylas's eyes leapt back to the page. "A *code*?"

"Yes. Time is short, but let us just try one final thing before you go. Close the book."

Sylas pressed the ancient covers shut.

"Now, clear your mind, and remove all thoughts of what you have just seen in the book. When I say so, I want you to open the book again, but this time don't expect to be able to read what you find. In fact, I want you to think of something else entirely — anything, as long as it is not to do with books or writing of any kind."

Sylas knew that he would find that very easy. He closed his eyes and the image of his mother's face instantly filled his mind.

"When you have that thought in your head, you may open the book," said Mr Zhi in a whisper.

Sylas clung to the image of his mother, then quickly opened his eyes and picked up the book. He turned to a page somewhere in the second part and cast his eyes over the strange, carefully drafted script.

It looked as it had before, written in a strange hand in a dark ink, but as his eyes focused on the first word, he saw to his amazement that it was not made up of letters as he had previously thought, but strange symbols. They were not familiar — they were not even similar to those in the alphabet, but were much more complex, forming patterns that rose and fell from each line. Sylas looked up at Mr Zhi in astonishment.

"But... the words didn't look like this a minute ago."

"What did they look like?" asked Mr Zhi, clearly enjoying himself.

"I'm not sure..." said Sylas. "Like normal words, I suppose."

"That's right, because that is what you *thought* you would see. The brilliance of this cipher is that it tricks your eye into seeing whatever you expect. You thought you would see words written in English, so that is what you saw. But they were meaningless. In truth you were looking at one of the world's most ancient codes: a cipher known as *Ravel Runes*."

Sylas repeated the words under his breath.

"The problem for anyone trying to read Ravel Runes is that

they must first learn to see the symbols as they really are, before they can even begin to work out what they might stand for."

Sylas looked back at the book and, sure enough, the writing once again looked encouragingly familiar and easy to read. But it made no sense. He blinked hard.

"That's *weird*," he said, shaking his head and laughing. "Just weird!"

"Weird is one way of putting it," said Mr Zhi with a smile, "and wonderful is another. Ravel Runes are difficult enough to read, but just *imagine* how hard they are to write. Think of the *time* it takes." He leaned over the counter and for a while they both stared in silence at the writing, admiring the hand that wrote it.

"Time!" cried Sylas suddenly. He scrambled for his wristwatch. "The time! I'll miss the post! My uncle will kill me!"

To miss the post was unthinkable. His uncle had two major topics of conversation: the importance of timeliness and the *supreme* importance of his correspondence. He would see a failure to catch the post as a conspiracy to overturn all that was good in the world: a capital offence punishable by interminable lectures on both topics for at least a week.

Sylas snatched up his rucksack and in a blind panic started off down one of the dark corridors of Things. As he left the sphere of candlelight, he found himself peering into the darkness of several passages, none of which looked familiar.

He heard a kindly chuckle behind him.

"Calm yourself, Sylas," said Mr Zhi, walking up. "I'll show you out, but first, take this."

He pushed the Samarok into Sylas's hands.

Sylas looked at him in surprise. "You mean... to keep?"

"To keep. You have much more use for it than I."

"But I... I can't!" cried Sylas as he followed Mr Zhi towards the front of the shop.

"But it's already yours, Sylas, I've given it to you."

Sylas hesitated for a moment, but then shook his head. "Thank you," he said, "really, but I don't know what I'd do with it! I don't understand the code."

"You will," replied Mr Zhi.

As they emerged from the warren of parcels and stepped into the light, the shopkeeper turned and smiled.

"I have a motto, young man, one that has served me very well: 'Do not fear what you do not understand.' You have much to learn about the world you live in, but most of all about yourself — about who you are and where you are from. The Samarok will help you on that journey."

"That's the second time you've said that — *what* journey?" asked Sylas, more confused than ever.

Mr Zhi took hold of the door handle and let the great din of the passing road into the shop.

"The Samarok is yours, and its journey of discovery will be yours too. Only you will know when that journey has begun, and where it is taking you. All I can offer you is this." He pulled a small white envelope from his pocket and held it out to Sylas.

"What is it?"

"It will help you to decipher the runes," said Mr Zhi. He held out his gloved hand and grasped Sylas's in a handshake. "Now, you must go."

"I don't know what to say."

"Then say nothing," said the shopkeeper.

Sylas paused for a moment and looked into Mr Zhi's kindly eyes. He felt he had made a friend and he wanted to say that he would be back, but somehow he knew that Mr Zhi had shown him the Things that he wanted to show, and that was the end of it.

He walked through the doorway and peered into the street beyond. It looked even colder and gloomier than it had before. The sky was bleak and threatening and the blanket of cloud seemed to brush the top of Gabblety Row. Rain lashed the passing cars, which threw it angrily back into the air to form a silver-grey mist above the road. The noise was a shock after the quiet seclusion of the Shop of Things: the hiss of tyres on the wet road, the growl of ill-tempered engines and the splatter of rain on the pavement. Sylas could hardly bring himself to step outside.

"Go now." Mr Zhi's voice was gentle but firm.

Sylas pushed the book inside his jacket and stepped into the street, gasping slightly as the first cold raindrops splattered on his face. He turned to look one more time at the old man in the half-darkness of the doorway. The shopkeeper was leaning against the door frame in a way that only emphasised the untidiness of his dishevelled grey suit.

"Thank you, Mr Zhi," said Sylas. And then with sudden determination he added, "I'll try to understand. I will."

Mr Zhi smiled broadly and gave a low bow. "That is all that I can ask. And that is all your mother would ask."

With one last wink, he let go of the handle and the old glass door swung closed.

Sylas stood stock-still for some moments, dumbfounded by Mr Zhi's final words.

Then something made him glance back up at the shop sign.

The new wooden board above the door had been repainted entirely in a dark green. It was as if 'the Shop of Things' had never been there.

4

Sundown

"Of beasts they spoke, of feral servants chained;
Born to the yoke of man, yet sent forth untamed."

TOBIAS TATE SAT BACK in his leather chair watching the rain pouring down his grimy office window, reflecting on his day. He found it impossible to imagine a worse one, though, as he was unusually short of imagination, that was not particularly surprising. He had decided to devote the day to visiting his clients in Gabblety Row, which was a task so disagreeable to him that he forced it upon himself but once a year. The problem was that such visits demanded contact with *people* and, even worse, with people who considered that they *knew* him.

But what had made this day quite unbearable was that he had been subjected to a long and heated encounter with Herr Veeglum, his oldest client. The problem arose because the undertaker claimed that he had embalmed two more dead bodies than appeared in the accounts. Tate had pointed out that this was quite impossible. Veeglum had replied that one does not *imagine* embalming one corpse, let alone two, as it is a very vivid affair. The conversation had become increasingly strained until, with some irritation, Tate had suggested that perhaps Veeglum had inhaled too much embalming fluid.

And so the meeting had ended on a very sour note.

This was his dark mood as he sat back in his old office chair, large hands clasped behind his head and eyes fixed intently on the dripping windowpane. At that moment there came a soft knock on one of his two doors: the one that opened into the corridor.

Tate expelled all the air from his lungs in a blast of exasperation. He closed his eyes as though to shut out whatever it was that threatened to intrude, but only a moment passed before he heard the knock again.

Sweat pricked his brow.

"What is it?" he barked.

There was a brief silence. "Uncle, it's me," came the reply. "Can I come in?"

Tate's shoulders and head slumped into a stoop of depression. "That door's for customers," he sighed. "Come through the apartment!"

There was a brief pause as Sylas obediently let himself into the apartment via the next door along the corridor and made his way across the kitchen and finally tapped on the other door to the office. It was a rule that made so little sense that he never remembered it.

"Yes! Yes!" snapped his uncle. "Come IN already!"

The door opened and Sylas slid into the room. It was clear at once that something was wrong. He was drenched from head to foot: his hair plastered to his face, his clothes baggy and misshapen. As he stood staring up at the darkening face of his uncle, drops of water fell around his feet.

Tate lunged for some papers that lay just inches from the gathering pool. "You're raining on my documents! Back! Back!"

He pushed Sylas to the wall in an attempt to contain the damage. Sylas waited with a look of resignation until the floor around him had been cleared and his uncle had removed his bony hand from his chest.

"So? What do you want?" demanded Tate, still caressing one of the stacks of ledgers.

"Well," began Sylas, slowly bringing his eyes up to meet his uncle's. He swallowed hard. "It's just that…" He drew a breath and squeezed his eyes closed. "I'm very sorry, but I missed the post."

Time stood still.

Tobias Tate stared at Sylas without changing his expression and Sylas winced, waiting for the inevitable explosion. The first sign of the impending storm came when his uncle's face began to twitch in an alarming manner, pulling his features into entirely new and unbecoming shapes. Then his right eyelid closed and his head began jerking to one side as if gesturing to something outside the window. Sylas knew better than to look. He pressed himself back against the wall and braced himself.

"You…" Tobias Tate swallowed hard and took a deep breath. "You fool! Idiot! Imbecile! Are you some kind of vegetable? Is there… How…"

There was a pause while he gathered himself. He clutched a spike of his hair and pulled at it until Sylas thought it might come clean out, then marched away towards his desk, turned and began pacing up and down, muttering to himself.

"Never have I… never… such incompetence… fool… *moron*…" and so on, and so on, until Sylas wondered if he might be able to slip away without being noticed. But suddenly his uncle whirled about, marched up to Sylas and thrust his face squarely into his.

"What were you doing instead of posting my mail?" he snarled, raising one eyebrow.

"I — I went into the new shop, the Shop of Things," ventured Sylas. "And uncle, it was so wonderful, so magical... I saw such amazing Things that I just lost track of the time..."

"Shut up!" roared Tobias Tate. "SHUT UP! You *dare* to make excuses when you have shown absolute disregard for the trust I placed in you? When you have possibly cost me my good name with valuable clients? When you have quite probably cost me..." he paused to emphasise the scandal of this final crime, "... MONEY!"

"I know, it was stupid and I'm really very sorry, uncle, but..."

"But? *BUT?* No buts! You must say nothing further to me! You — must — not — speak!" He banged the wall as he spat out each word. "You're as bad as your mother! A dreamer — a careless, foolish, deluded—"

"Leave her out of this!"

Tobias Tate stood up to his full height and an amused sneer passed across his face. He crossed his arms and scowled down at the boy for some moments before he spoke.

"I always knew you were an insolent, wilful child, for all your 'yes sirs' and 'no sirs' and 'pleases' and 'thank yous'. You need to be taken in hand before you turn out like *her*. Yes, that's right — firmly in hand!"

Sylas set his jaw. "I WANT to turn out like her!"

"Oh, really? You *want* to be mad?"

Sylas reeled back against the wall, his eyes burning with tears. He wanted to say something — scream something — but words escaped him.

"Thought not!" shouted his uncle, marching to his chair. "Back to your room. You will not leave that room until seven o'clock, when you will come down, prepare dinner and help me with my files. Now, give me the letters and go." He fixed Sylas with a glare. "Go!"

Sylas felt a surge of rage. He rummaged in his bag, found the letters and threw them on the floor, then let himself out of the office. He slammed the door of the kitchen beyond, stormed out into the corridor and clattered up the dark staircase to his room.

As the trapdoor fell closed, he dropped his rucksack and turned to the faded photograph of his mother, reaching out and touching the glass. Tears streamed down his face, but he did not sob or wipe them away. They were the silent tears of one who had shed them before, and who knew they did no good.

His uncle's cruel face surged into his mind and his snarling voice echoed in his ears:

"...as bad as your mother... deluded... mad..."

He flinched at the dark, cruel significance of these words.

It had been five long, lonely years since he had last seen his mother. Or at least since he saw her as he liked to think of her: her tender face, slightly old for her years; her long dark hair drawn back in a ponytail, which he used to play with as she worked in their small front room, her delicate hands tapping on her computer or scribbling formulae in her many laboratory notebooks. He could hardly remember her soft, soothing voice, which had always been the last sound he heard at night and the first he heard in the morning.

That part of his life was now only a distant memory.

Everything had changed the day he had watched them take her away. He had looked on helplessly as she scratched and clawed at them as though battling for her life – and although he would never have believed it, that was exactly what she was doing. He remembered the man with the large thick glasses and the too-cheerful smile.

The one with the needle.

He could still see the stout, sallow-skinned woman whose beady eyes took in the whole room, peering into their life until nothing was private any more. But he remembered no sounds. He knew that his throat was sore afterwards, he assumed from screaming, and he remembered his mother's face contorting as though she was crying out — but his memories of that day were like an old silent movie: white faces speaking but making no sound, their movements jerky and unnatural, everything depicted in shades of silver and grey. And he struggled to see past that movie into the rich colour of the life he had had before, when it was just the two of them. Somehow that day had made that vivid life seem unreal, like a precious dream that dissolves in the hard, cold light of day.

How hard and cold that final day had been, when finally it came a year later: the day his uncle told him she had died. He had said it so abruptly, in a matter-of-fact bluster of words, though Sylas remembered the tears in his eyes, the way he had drawn him into his bony body, just for a second or two — just in the first brief agony of that truth. He remembered the phrases: so inadequate, so trite and trifling given the horror and pain they conveyed.

"Disease of the mind... deteriorated so quickly... nothing to be done..."

"Nothing to be done," he murmured. It was the most devastating phrase, because he would have done anything to save his mum. He would have brought the world crashing down for just another day with her.

And yet he was not even allowed to go to her funeral.

"Too young," he was told. "A brief, formal affair, given the lack of family... given the... circumstances."

And so Sylas had chosen his own quiet, secluded spot in the churchyard opposite. It was not her actual grave, which he knew to be somewhere far away, but the place he went to remember her, to be with her, to give her some flowers. The window seat in his room that overlooked that graveyard had become his favourite place to sit, because that way he felt that in some small way he was closer to her.

He wiped his face, picked up his rucksack and walked over to the seat. He wanted to think about something else, but even then the window seat was where he needed to be. He pushed himself back into the corner, one shoulder up against the ancient glass, and pulled the Samarok from his bag. He rested it on his knee and for a moment gazed out at the once-great stone arches of the church, now glowing pink in the dying rays of the sun. There was something beautiful in this twilight display, but to Sylas the sight was gaudy and unnatural. He saw nothing of the midsummer sunset unfolding in the wide sky; heard nothing of the great chorus of birds in the churchyard as they celebrated the end of the day. Instead he stared at the ruins, reflecting on their loneliness and slow decay. He gazed at those great broken windows, now emptied of their colourful glass, framing instead a jungle of weeds and ivy that spilled out on to the graves.

He sucked in a breath and looked down at the Samarok. He had to turn his mind to something else.

He stared at the cover, his eyes drawn to the embroidery and inlaid stones glittering in the twilight of the fading day. He ran his finger along the length of the large S that adorned the cover, then opened the book to a random page and looked at the sea of beautifully crafted runes.

His thoughts turned to the piece of paper Mr Zhi had given him and he took the now damp, crumpled envelope from his pocket, examining the rain-blotched scrawl on the front. It read simply "Sylas" in a hand that he recognised: the strange oriental hand that had painted the sign of the Shop of Things. His excitement grew and he tore it open.

Inside was a single slightly yellowed piece of paper that had been folded in half. It was not a letter as he expected, but a single paragraph. The writing was so distinctive and flamboyant that at first Sylas thought it was yet another language or code, but, to his surprise, it was written in English. Although the rain appeared to have blotted some of the letters, it was perfectly readable. He read it aloud to himself.

"They came from the cool of the sand-scented temples: from the long dark of the coiling passages and the oily flicker of many-columned halls. They rose as leaders of men in that ancient land, men of words and vision whose mystery brought hope to the squalor-born. But while the people lifted their eyes upon the gentle countenance of these blessed men, they saw not the cool and dark of their hearts, nor the oily flicker behind their eyes."

He gave a low whistle. What did *that* mean?

He read it over again, taking his time to pronounce and understand each word, but when he reached the end of the passage, he was just as confused. The piece assumed that he would understand who "they" were and what the "ancient land" was, but no matter how much he racked his memory, he could think of nothing. Even if he could guess at the real meaning, he had no idea how it would help him to understand the runes. He sighed and ran his hand through his hair — this wasn't going to be easy.

He picked up the Samarok and closed his eyes, trying to clear his mind. Not wanting to be clouded by thoughts of his mother, he pictured Mr Zhi himself, standing behind his crooked old counter in the Shop of Things, winking and stroking his beard to a point.

He turned to the title page, blank except for three lines of runes a third of the way from the top. It was clearly an inscription or dedication of some sort, as it was too long to be the title. Sylas allowed his eyes to pass slowly along the lines, taking in the intricacies of the runes. Each had its own form, its own unique shape and line, which was sometimes complex in its own right, but — even more wonderfully — also related to the runes around it. Within a word, each separate character was interlaced with two others, sharing its space with the curves or inflections of the symbols on either side, so that a rune rarely looked the same twice. The collection of characters formed a tangle of dashes, strokes, arcs and dots that ought, by any logic, to look crowded or haphazard, but instead fitted together with astonishing grace. Sylas's art teacher had once talked about the great calligraphers of the Far East who could create writing of sublime beauty and meaning, but he had never dreamed of anything as beautiful as this.

But it still didn't mean anything.

He yawned as he stared at yet another page, now difficult to see in the fading light. He widened his eyes to fight back the tiredness and glanced out of the window. The sun had nearly set behind some clouds, plunging the churchyard into near-darkness, and rain was once again clattering against the windowpane.

He was about to turn back to the Samarok when he thought he saw a movement in the churchyard. He paused, wiped his bleary eyes, then swept his hand across the glass to remove the condensation. The streaks of water distorted the light, stretching the lines of the darkening church. The few passing cars cast beams of yellow and red light on to the ruined walls and the overhanging branches of trees. Sylas looked for some moments, but there was nothing: just rain and trees swaying in the wind.

"Deluded," he muttered under his breath.

Then he saw another movement.

He leaned forward and wiped the window dry with the sleeve of his sweater, his eyes trained on one particular arched window in the old church.

There, beneath a large overhang of ivy, something was creeping through the undergrowth.

Sylas shrank back into the shadows.

A gargantuan black hound emerged from under the ivy, walking under the archway towards the end of the church.

It was truly massive, the points of its shoulders standing proud of the rest of its dark figure, rolling as it moved lithely through the undergrowth. The head was hidden in the shadows, hanging low beneath the matted mane of its neck. The sloping back gave way to powerful haunches that stood lower than the shoulders, giving it an ugly, predatory profile.

Sylas was transfixed. He wanted to retreat into his room, but something made him stay.

The beast stopped.

For a moment it was entirely motionless, but slowly its shoulders braced and its thick neck rose. Its huge head emerged from the darkness until Sylas could see its crumpled brow and long canine snout that seemed scarred and disfigured. Beneath, its gaping jaws lolled open, revealing a cruel mass of ragged teeth.

Without warning, the beast's powerful neck swung sharply and it looked directly up at his window.

Its small eyes seemed to catch the twilight and they burned in the shadows. The nose twitched, sniffing the polluted air. Sylas pushed himself as far back on the window seat as he could, hoping that the shadows would hide him, but their eyes seemed to meet. The rest of the world faded and he was filled with a new, creeping terror.

5
The Lie

"This is a life-giving journey. It is a bitter-sweet elixir that restores my spirit, strengthens my heart and, most of all, opens my eyes."

SYLAS GRIPPED THE EDGE of the seat, willing himself to climb down into his room, but his limbs were frozen. The pale yellow eyes of the hound penetrated deep inside him, calmly peeling away the layers until they saw weakness and loneliness, until they glared coldly at a boy's thoughts of his mother.

"Sylas!"

It was Tobias Tate's grating voice, coming through the trapdoor.

"Sylas! Come down!"

Sylas glanced at his watch. Five past seven – he was late.

He glanced back out of the window in time to see the beast drop its head and resume its stooped prowl along the ruined remains of the aisle, passing quickly out of sight.

"Come here AT ONCE!"

Sylas peered down into the churchyard until he was sure that the hound was gone, then sighed, heaved himself off his seat and walked over to his trapdoor.

He found his uncle standing in the corridor, hands on his hips, peering at him as if he was an account that would not balance.

"Well?" he squawked, his voice echoing down the passageway. "Where've you been?"

"Sorry I'm late," said Sylas dismissively — he was in no mood for another lecture from his uncle. "I saw something really strange from my window... something in the churchy—"

"Daydreaming, I knew it!" growled his uncle. "Well, I have no interest in your nonsense. And there's no time for dinner now — you can daydream about that!"

"Fine!" sighed Sylas, pushing past his uncle into the flat.

Tobias Tate watched him go and frowned, seemingly a little disappointed to have had the wind taken from his sails.

Dinnertime was spent sifting, trawling and rummaging through endless mountains of paper. What made this task especially infuriating was that everything was already in the right place, filed properly into the many piles about the office. But, as an accountant of great care and attention, Tobias Tate had to be convinced of this. Sylas would make helpful observations and suggestions while being chastised, corrected and mocked; a torture that only came to an end when his uncle had dissected and exploded every sensible suggestion put to him, and Sylas had been duly reminded of his dull wits, poor instincts and low birth.

On this particular evening Sylas found this task more frustrating than ever, not only because of his anger about their earlier clash, but also because his thoughts kept turning to the hound in the churchyard and the strange Shop of Things. His mind was filled with images of the dark hound and, more excitingly, the endless warren of parcels and packages, the amazing flight of birds beneath the mobile and the peculiar runes of the Samarok. But he knew it would be some time before he would get back to its pages: the filing would take as long as it would take. Tobias Tate's old grandfather clock tick-tocked its way through the endless minutes and chimed the passing of interminable hours.

Finally, as the clock struck nine, his uncle sat down in the chair in his favourite corner, ate a quick dinner (which he reserved entirely for himself), put his hands behind his head and fell asleep. He drew breath in long, deep snores of rasping snorts that built to a crescendo of clucks and splutters and then began again at the bottom of the scale.

Sylas could not believe his luck – this was his chance to escape. But he must not be hasty – his uncle's finely tuned ears might hear him leave. He replaced the pile he was sifting through and edged closer to the desk, then picked up some papers by the window and rustled them loudly. His uncle snorted and spluttered, but his eyes stayed closed and the metronomic drone of his snoring resumed. Sylas smiled quietly and replaced the papers, taking care to leave them exactly as he found them – his uncle had not asked him to check this pile.

As he drew his fingers away, he froze.

He blinked, certain that his eyes were playing tricks on him.

In the header of the topmost letter was a logo: a stark, black-and-white fern leaf coiled into an almost perfect circle, with the words *Winterfern Hospital for the Mentally Ill* emblazoned below in silver lettering. Sylas had seen that logo before, on the white coats of the doctor and nurse who had taken his mother away. But it was the date on the letter that had made his blood run cold.

Two weeks ago.

His stomach turned. He picked up the letter, seeing as he did so that there was another beneath it dated three months before. A cold sweat formed on his brow. Now he could see the letterhead of another jutting out further down the pile, bearing a date of a year before. He turned his eyes back to the one in his hand – the one from just two weeks ago — and began to read, his heart racing. The room receded — all he could see was the stark black type.

Ms A. Tate: Clinical Report

Dear Mr Tate,

Amelie has shown some continued improvement under the revised regime of sedatives and occupational therapy and is responding particularly well to her new surroundings in the garden room. She has developed a keen interest in botany and spends extended periods reading and walking in the hospital grounds. Nevertheless she continues to experience severe psychotic episodes throughout the night and some hours of the day.

We recommend a continuation of the current course of treatment. As we have indicated previously, while her guardian's visits are extremely helpful, we feel that family visits would also be beneficial.

Yours sincerely,

Dr Adrian Kopenhauer
Supervising Psychiatrist

Sylas's hands began to shake. He took up the next letter and the next. Each was another Clinical Report, each dated three months before the last. He turned slowly to the sleeping form of his uncle and stared at him, his chest heaving, tears in his eyes.

Tobias Tate continued to snore, oblivious.

Sylas shook his head in disbelief. How could this be? His mother, still alive? And his uncle knew all along?

He grabbed the pile of papers, whirled about and rushed from the room.

6
The Chime

"... we wake to sounds that assail the senses and crowd the mind, like dreaming that will not end."

SYLAS SAT LISTLESSLY ON his mattress, papers strewn about him, tears pouring down his face. His wonderful room, his sanctuary from the world, was suddenly cool and dark, hollow and soulless, for surely it was part of this great lie, the sham that lay in scattered pieces around him, typed in hard black letters for anyone to see. It too had hidden the truth from him, for had he not lived in it every day of the past four years? Had he not grieved in it? Had he not looked down from its window into the churchyard and thought of his mother? Given her up? Let her go?

His eyes shifted back to the mattress, to the scores of Clinical Reports, Review Meeting Reports, Annual Statements, and then finally to the document in his trembling fingers, the Order of Committal, the document that gave the doctors the right to take his mother away against her will, the document that had started it all.

At the bottom were two signatures. One of these he knew all too well.

It was his uncle's.

Sylas felt nauseous. He forced himself to look away, but everything he saw around him seemed to be part of the lie: the familiar walls of his room, his meagre furniture, the crooked beams of the old building, even the picture of his mother. Even that. It was no longer what it had been to him — a piece of her, a way to feel close to her. Instead it was just a snapshot, because it was not how she was today, not how she looked in her 'garden room', or walking around the hospital grounds, or how she would look at him if he was with her now.

He sat like that for some time, he had no idea how long. Eventually he stirred, his eyes slowly finding focus. They drifted around the room until they fell on something that could be no part of the lie, had no place in the conspiracy. He saw his flock of colourful, bird-like kites hanging on the wall: meaningless but also innocent — things that he himself had created.

When he had first moved to Gabblety Row, he had yearned to be far away, far from his uncle and the news he had brought. From his windows he had watched the distant birds flying above the hills at the edge of town and they had become his dearest dream, his favourite escape. Inspired by their beauty and freedom, he had become a creator of his own birds: an ever-growing squadron of kites, all painted in the brightest colours arranged in odd but beautiful designs.

And they were more than just works of art. When he finished one of his kites, he would clamber out of the window on to the roof, where he could sit with one leg on either side of the ridge and launch his kite into the air. It would soar over the town as he yearned to do, escaping normal life, dazzling the residents of the housing estate over the road and brightening the day of those caught in the endless traffic jams below. He dreamed that one day he might create one so beautiful that it might even tempt its sisters to journey from the hills and across the grey town to fly over Gabblety Row. But so far the only visitor he ever received on that breezy rooftop was Herr Veeglum the undertaker, who would often lean out of his garret window at the other end of the row and raise his sallow face to watch.

Sylas had no real urge to move, to do anything, but the sight of his kites made him think of something. He ran his sleeve over his face, pushed himself up from his mattress and went over to his only piece of furniture — a three-legged dresser with many ill-fitting doors and drawers. He pulled the top drawer off its runners and carried the whole thing back to his mattress, laying it down on top of the papers.

Inside were the most important things in the world.

This is where he kept the gifts his mother had given him when he was young, before she went away. Most of it looked like bric-a-brac: a jumble of worn and threadbare toys, an old glove, birthday cards, half a plastic tiara ("broken, but magical," she had told him with a girlish smile), faded photographs, the key to their old cottage. And nestled among all these things were his most beloved possessions of all. First, a large pigment-stained wooden box, containing two rows of small glass jars set snugly into a felt base, each with a little cork stopper. Inside every jar was a dazzling paint: red, the colour of molten rock; orange, like tongues of fire; silver, like fish scales in water; green, like the forested hills, and many, many more. Each was labelled in silver ink by his mother's own measured hand: *Orivan Red*, *Grysgar Orange*, *Girigander Silver*, *Mislehay Green*; names that meant nothing and yet everything, for their mystery fed his imagination.

It was with these strange colours that Sylas painted all of his kites, and somehow, through these outlandish pigments, he shared his creations with her. His painting was never planned, the design coming to him only as he placed each colour on the canvas; but then, as the wondrous design started to take shape, it would create an elaborate maze of colour: swirls, curves, angles, shapes and symbols. With the paints, he would transform his kites into living things, with glistening eyes, gorgeous crests, plumed feathers and powerful arching beaks: all picked out in a unique display of tiny dots and lines.

For a moment he looked up at the flock of multicoloured kites and felt warmed and consoled. These, at least, remained constant and true: their colours as bright — their designs as beautiful — as ever before.

He laid the box of pigments on top of the papers and took his other prized possession from the old drawer. A large hardback book, on whose cloth cover was a simple, gold-foiled title:

REVELATIONS: A BOOK OF SCIENCE

He turned to the title page and read the inscription written in an elegant hand across the bottom corner:

Learn all that you are, my dear Sylas, learn all that you are able to be, M

He paused. There was something strangely familiar about those words, and not just because he had read them so many times. He thought back to Mr Zhi's words in the Shop of Things, as he was unpacking the mirrors:

"*... you can see all that you are able to be.*"

He frowned and ruffled his untidy hair. A coincidence perhaps? But then he remembered the shopkeeper's parting remark:

"… all your mother would ask."

He stared blankly at the page. Could it be that all this was connected in some weird way? The arrival of the Shop of Things, his strange meeting with Mr Zhi, and then — straight afterwards — this discovery about his mother?

Surely not — that was impossible. But then nothing really seemed impossible when he was with Mr Zhi...

Sylas shook his head. His mother would laugh at him. She had been a woman of science and facts — that was why she had given him this book. *That* was what she had meant in her inscription: learn, read, find out about the world.

He settled back on the mattress, tried to clear his mind of all this nonsense and turned through the dog-eared pages. This was unlike any boring science book he had come across at school. Its gloriously jumbled pages were filled to the brim with beautiful drawings and quirky explanations of all manner of animals, plants and things of the cosmos; of medicines, engines, machines, contraptions, theories and inventions. These pages told a story that was at once science and magic, a story that was almost as much an escape for him as his wonderful kites.

He stopped at the first page of the chapter he loved most of all, the one about the wings of birds and the flight of aeroplanes. Soon he was lost in the fascinating, freeing world of the skies: in clouds and thermals; in the endless migrations of birds and the beautiful shapes of their wings; in inventions that reached into the void — kites, hot-air balloons, gliders, planes...

And the more he read, the more the exhaustion of this strangest of days started to wash over him. His eyes became heavy and the print faded and blurred. Slowly the marvellous book of revelations slid from his chest and his eyes closed.

Sylas slept, comforted by the weird lullaby of Gabblety Row: the endless growl of traffic making the windows rattle and the trapdoor leap on its hinges; the ancient walls sighing and grumbling into the cool night air. Even the occasional yellow beams from passing headlights served only to brighten the depths of his dreams, dreams that now filled his mind with a new image. It was an image that warmed him, drew him close, consoled him. It was a delicate, female face, a face that he knew.

Then for a moment everything was silent. The sound of traffic stopped, the windowpanes rested in their frames, the floorboards ceased humming for the first time in decades. Even Sylas held his breath, the vapour from his lips hanging in the air.

As the dust began to settle on the windowsill, it began.

The room shuddered with a sound of such power that the dream was shattered in a moment. It tore through the walls, hammered on the ceiling, crashed through the floor. It shook the kites from their fittings, sent the Samarok skidding across the floorboards and threw the window wide open.

It entered Sylas through his chest and pounded his lungs until his heart missed a beat.

It was not a definable sound, but one so immense and terrifying that it swamped the ears and confused the mind. It was a moaning, aching howl that drowned everything and consumed all.

He threw himself upright in bed and found himself gasping for breath. The very air seemed to have rushed from the room. He pushed the eiderdown back and at once felt a piercing chill. He looked around desperately for the source of the noise, hoping that in some way he might silence it, but he realised that it was everywhere, in everything, and there was nowhere to hide.

7
Flight

"The thoughts that brought me here are forgotten. My dreams are lost to me. My one hope is that I might survive."

SYLAS HESITATED FOR A moment, unsure what to do, then flung himself back on to the mattress, drawing the pillow over his head. Even that resonated with the deep, low moan and the mattress shook beneath him.

He thought the world was coming to an end: that some great earthquake had struck the town or some gigantic volcano was at this very moment pouring rivers of lava into the streets and pelting the town with a downpour of rock.

"Stop! Please stop!" he shouted into the mattress, but he couldn't even hear his own voice.

For what seemed like a minute the noise continued relentlessly, tearing at his eardrums. But then it seemed to ease slightly. And then a little more. The wail was definitely fading now — becoming more bearable.

As it eased, Sylas realised that it was not a horrifying sound, the sound of war cannons or buildings crashing down. Rather it was a solitary, immense, dolorous chime. Its voice was metallic and hollow and it rang rather than screamed. The more the noise faded and his ears recovered, the more it came to resemble the single dying note of an enormous bell.

Sylas pushed his bedding away and sat upright again. As he tried to control his fear, he became sure that the noise was coming from outside, from the window. He stood up and edged slowly towards it, dragging his bare toes over the comforting, familiar roughness of the floorboards. The curtains were blowing wildly in the wind, flashing bright in the passing headlights, and he found himself wondering why the cars hadn't stopped.

As he reached the sill, the sound of the phantom bell once again reached a deafening pitch. He closed his eyes, fearing what he was about to see. Gripping the base of the window frame in his cold hands, he swallowed hard, then drew himself forward.

Everything looked normal. The traffic still sent shafts of light into the sky and thick, acrid pollution into the air. The road bustled with cars: a jostling mass of white, red and blinking orange lights. Rain was falling, and Sylas could see it glistening on the black street below. But the chime of the bell pervaded the night — immense, unstoppable — drowning out any other noise.

He searched for the source, looking past the road and the housing estate on the other side, out to the pinprick lights on the towering chimneys at the edge of the town. He looked through the fog of gases that they spewed into the sky.

Finally his eyes rested on the dark hills in the distance.

"Impossible," he said to himself, "that's miles away."

There seemed no way that a sound could pass so far across the hubbub of a town, with its clamorous factories and riotous roads, but Sylas was certain. He squinted towards the dark horizon and listened to the chime slowly fading away, transfixed by its mysterious power.

Finally the noise of the road became audible and brought with it some sense of normality. His earlier thought came back to him — why had nothing stopped? Why was everything carrying on as normal? His eyes turned to the cars that flew past, the drivers apparently unaware of anything extraordinary; to the occasional person rushing along the street, huddling under an umbrella; to a tramp in dark, ragged clothes standing in a puddle. No one seemed to have heard the sound.

It was as if the bell was ringing only for him.

Suddenly the room shook and the curtains flew into the room. His ears felt as though they were being pierced with needles and a blast of rain hammered into his face. He wanted to scream, but the air had rushed from his lungs.

It was happening again.

Sylas threw his hands over his ears, but that had little effect — it was as though his very bones were vibrating with the sound of the bell. He shut his eyes and tried to focus his mind, but the aftershock hummed in his skull and shattered his thoughts.

He slid down below the window and wrapped his arms round his head, rocking backwards and forwards. He wondered if he was going to die, or worse, if this was the end of all things.

But slowly, too slowly, the noise began to subside. He had no idea how long it took, but finally the timbers beneath his feet ceased their shuddering and the wall at his back became still.

Frightened as he was, Sylas pushed himself up and leaned out of the window to see if anything had changed. He looked along the length of the street, across to the houses and over them to the town, but again the world seemed unaware of the strange chime.

And yet he had the inexplicable sense that something was out of place, as if he was looking at the world through a distorted windowpane.

Then he saw it. His eyes were fixed on the sphere of orange light around one of the electric streetlamps. He could see thousands of tiny raindrops falling from the dark night sky, but there was something wrong. The rain was not falling straight down, but at a steep angle to the ground, as though being carried on a high wind.

There *was* no wind.

His eyes shifted from one streetlamp to the next all the way up the street and, sure enough, the rain was the same everywhere: it was being drawn towards the source of the sound. As he watched and the sound gradually waned, the rain returned to a normal, vertical path. As the noise died, its hold over the tiny drops weakened and fell to nothing.

Then the chime struck again.

He recoiled and covered his ears, but forced himself to stand at the window and watch. As the shock hit his room, the rain was driven back, away from the hills, sending another cold, painful blast into his face. He tried with all his might to keep his eyes open and after the impact of the chime he saw the rainfall gradually swing about, once again sweeping towards the source of the sound. The long note of the bell was drawing it in.

Drawing it towards what?

His thoughts came to him in fragments, but somehow he managed to piece them together: something magical was happening. His mind went to the dark corridors of the Shop of Things, the beautiful birds flying without strings, the strange shifting runes of the Samarok. He turned and peered across the room at the Samarok glistening on the trapdoor. Suddenly Mr Zhi's words came rushing back to him.

"The Samarok is yours, and its journey of discovery will be yours too. Only you will know when that journey has begun, and where it is taking you."

Surely he couldn't have meant *this*? But then Sylas thought about the street outside – everyone else just carrying on as though they could not hear the bell...

"Only you will know..." he murmured.

Could it be that somehow the bell was calling to him, drawing him in, like the rain? But even as he started to believe that it might just be true, his thoughts returned to his mother – surely he should be looking for *her*, not following some bell? *That* was the only journey that mattered now.

But Mr Zhi had made it sound as though this 'journey' had *everything* to do with her.

"I'll try to understand," Sylas had said.

"... that is all your mother would ask."

He looked around the room, at the papers strewn across the floorboards, at the kites scattered and broken. The empty shell of his sanctuary seemed even more lifeless than before, now riddled with questions and deceits. There was nothing here to keep him, nothing that made sense to him any more. All that lay ahead of him now was his search for his mother and the journey to understand the Samarok. Somehow these journeys were one and the same. And the bell was the beginning of it all.

He picked up the Samarok and put Mr Zhi's message between its pages, then snatched the rucksack from the shelf and slid the book inside it, followed by a bottle of water from his sink. He pulled on a sweater and his trainers and hesitated, looking back at the papers on the floor.

He ran over and rummaged through the documents, picking out the Order of Committal. He checked for the name and address of the Winterfern Hospital, then slipped it into his bag. Seconds later he was clambering down the dark staircase towards the corridor.

The chime had almost faded away. He could hear the rain lashing the outside of the building and the flutter of a moth against one of the wall lamps. The corridor seemed darker and more ominous than usual — a few of the bulbs had burned out at the other end, leaving it in blackness. But Sylas felt a surge of excitement as he took his first steps towards a destination he could only guess at.

As he picked his way along the corridor, he looked warily at his uncle's apartment door and then at the next one, the one leading directly into the office. He willed them to stay closed, and to his relief he was soon past them.

He was about to breathe a sigh of relief when the bell sounded again. The din was almost unbearable, seeming to reverberate between the walls and ricochet along the length of the passageway. He held his ears, expecting his uncle and the other residents to burst out of their apartments in a blind panic, but the doors remained closed. He continued, reminding himself to step carefully over the loose floorboards — if no one else could hear the bell, they would surely be able to hear a clumsy step. He looked carefully from board to board, planning his way ahead. Finally, when he was nearing the staircase, he began to relax.

He looked ahead into the passageway, into the darkness, and felt the blood drain from his face.

A surge of adrenalin charged through his body. There, suspended in the darkness at the end of the corridor, were two pale yellow eyes. As Sylas watched, they blinked slowly, coldly, and moved towards him.

The monstrous jaws of the wolfish hound emerged into the lamplight. For a moment the two faced each other. The beast stood with its head and shoulders in the flickering light, its long body disappearing into the blackness. Its head moved slowly up and down as it drew long, rasping breaths. The sound of the bell was fading once more and Sylas could hear the air hiss between its teeth and a growl as it exhaled. It blinked lazily and its tongue curled upwards to the fangs that protruded below its wrinkled snout. Its eyes were fixed on his in a way that left no doubt of its intent.

Sylas was motionless: breathing deeply, trying to steady his nerves, his eyes avoiding the beast's drooling jaws and lolling tongue. He glanced towards the first step of the staircase. It was about halfway between him and the beast. There was no way he would make it, and if he did, the hound would pounce on him from behind. When he looked back, it too was looking at the staircase and he had the unnerving feeling that it was willing him to try. He swallowed hard and drew in another long breath.

As a chime crashed through Gabblety Row, Sylas whirled about and threw himself forward, charging back down the corridor. He could hear nothing but the bell, but he could sense that the beast was already in motion. He pictured its sinewy muscles tightening as it launched itself out of the darkness. He thundered down the corridor, his fists pumping the air. He passed the door to the office and then hurled his full weight against the main door to the apartment, turning the brass handle. To his relief the door opened and he staggered inside the kitchen, turning in time to see the dog's massive head careering towards him, its eyes wide and its teeth bared in a hungry snarl.

He leaned his body against the door and slammed it shut. The latch fell into place and he threw a bolt across.

The beast hit with incredible force, bending the wooden panels and cracking the plaster around the frame. Somehow the door held. As Sylas stepped back, it struck again and he saw a crack of light appear between two timbers. A splinter of wood flew off and nicked his cheek. It would give way all too soon.

He turned and ran through the doorway into the adjoining office, pulling it closed behind him just as he heard the beast smashing its way into the kitchen. Breathlessly he skirted the desk, praying that his uncle had left the door between the office and the corridor unlocked. He reached for the cold brass handle and turned it. The door held firm. He hurled himself against the wooden panels, but still it held fast. He heard a crash and turned to see the kitchen door bulge and splinter and the hound's ghoulish head forcing its way through, its jaws biting at the shards of timber. In desperation he wrenched at the handle, rattling and twisting it from side to side. Suddenly he felt something smooth and cold brush against his fingers. He bent down and saw the old brass key still sitting in the keyhole. With a surge of relief he turned it and shouldered the door open, almost falling into the dim light of the corridor. He ran as fast as he could towards the main stairwell, hearing snarls, growls and crashes behind him.

In seconds he was there.

As he turned on to the first step, he looked behind. The massive figure of the hound smashed through the door in an explosion of plaster and splinters, hitting the opposite wall and falling to the floor. It lowered its head and glowered through reddened eyes, then threw its glistening snout high into the air and let out a blood-curdling howl that almost drowned out the chime of the bell.

Sylas launched himself off the top stair, taking them three at a time, forcing himself to keep his eyes ahead. He heard the clatter of the dog's claws on the floor above as it gave chase. He reached the second floor and saw a crowd of residents gathered round the stairwell, peering up at him with frightened faces.

"Run!" he cried. "Get inside!"

Most scattered as he passed, but the more curious remained

and as he continued his descent he heard their shrieks and shouts behind him. He thundered on to the sound of plaster shattering and wood snapping close behind. Finally he leapt off the bottom step and flung himself through the outside door.

He skidded to a halt on the pavement, gasping for breath, then turned to close the door.

It was already shut.

A tall, dark figure stood to one side, stooped over the lock. He heard the bolt click into place and then the figure slowly rose and turned. He found himself looking into the sallow face of Herr Veeglum.

"In a hurry, are vee?" asked the undertaker, leaning forward to peer into Sylas's face. His voice was as grey as his features: monotone and dry.

Sylas had never actually heard Herr Veeglum *speak* before. He was about to attempt a reply when the dog struck the door. The thick oak panels shuddered, but didn't move.

"Built for ze job," said Herr Veeglum, glancing over his shoulder as though he needed reassurance of that fact. "But it vill not hold for long."

Sylas stared at him, utterly confused. "But how did you...?"

Herr Veeglum raised a gloved hand and put a finger to his lips.

"Zer is more here zan meets ze eye, young man. But zer is no time to explain. You must go."

He spoke firmly, but his manner was altogether warmer and his eyes livelier than Sylas would have expected. He so much wanted to know why Veeglum was there, but the undertaker was already leading him round the corner of the row.

As they came to the front of Buntague's Bakery, the old man stopped and pointed across the street.

"Run as fast as you can," he said. Then he put his mouth to

Sylas's ear and hissed: "Ze bell is calling *you*, Sylas!"

With that, he gave the boy a firm shove between the shoulder blades and Sylas found himself in the road. He heard the wail of a car horn and he turned his head to see three cars bearing down on him. He threw himself forward, darting left and then right to avoid them as they slammed on their brakes, sending up plumes of spray from their tyres. His heart was in his mouth, but somehow he danced between them and got safely to the other side.

As he stepped on to the pavement, he chanced a look back across the road. Herr Veeglum was still standing there, his hands at his sides, his face peculiarly calm, bearing an expression not dissimilar to Mr Zhi's at the moment he had said goodbye. The undertaker raised one hand in a brief wave, then motioned furiously for him to go.

Sylas glanced quickly in the direction of the Shop of Things. Somehow he knew that Mr Zhi would be able to explain everything, but he could see no light through the window and there was no sign of the old shopkeeper. He summoned all his courage and turned his back on Gabblety Row.

Veeglum watched as Sylas sped off down the pavement towards the supermarket and then disappeared down a dark alley at its side. He shook his head wistfully, turned and walked round the corner of the row. When he reached the door, he stood some distance away and watched it shudder and vibrate as the beast charged at it from behind. The timbers held, yet around the frame tiny clouds of dust were curling into the night air and small pieces of mortar were falling to the floor. Then the great wooden beam above the frame shifted and an entire brick fell out of the wall.

He unfastened the buttons of his greatcoat and pulled it from his shoulders, revealing an immaculate black suit, a crisp white shirt and a pressed black tie. He laid the coat neatly on the pavement, folding the arms tidily over the top.

At that moment another smaller figure appeared from the lane behind Gabblety Row. This man also wore a suit, but of an ill-kempt, crumpled sort, and his appearance was all the more curious on account of his odd little pot-like hat and one ornately decorated glove.

Veeglum didn't acknowledge him as he approached, but pulled on a plain green glove of his own.

Then they turned to face the door.

Sylas ran down the alleyway into the housing estate, the noise from the road quickly giving way to the near silence of the sleeping town. He emerged into a cul-de-sac and swung right, following his normal route to the shops. For once he was glad of the many errands he had run for his uncle, for he knew these roads well. He took a twisting, turning path down little-known lanes, across private gardens, allotments and tiny streets: he would be almost impossible to follow. He headed for the Hailing Bridge, which crossed the river in the centre of town. It lay directly in his path to the bell.

The bell struck again and he saw the rain around him change direction sharply, then slowly swing around as the sad, long note drew it towards the hills. He glanced in disbelief at the darkened windows of the estate, the curtains firmly closed and the occupants oblivious to the drama that was unfolding around them. Every unexpected splatter of rain in a puddle, every random crunch of a stone underfoot made his heart race even faster, but he fixed his eyes ahead and ran for his life.

He negotiated a warren of darkened pathways and finally he saw the bridge ahead. It was a simple structure of steel girders fixed at crude right angles to one another, most of which were emblazoned with graffiti colours. The centre of the bridge was unlit, but the two lamps at either end shone brightly above the oily black river.

Sylas's heart sank.

There, barely visible in the very middle of the bridge, was a man leaning on one of the railings, looking in the opposite direction.

What was he doing there at this time of night?

Sylas stopped — this felt wrong. He thought of turning and running back through the estate to the other bridge, but retracing his steps would be dangerous. He considered waiting to see if the man moved away, but by then the dog might be upon him.

There was no option: he must cross the Hailing Bridge, and do it now.

He gathered his courage and slowly climbed the steps to the span of the bridge.

As he reached the top, the man became more visible. He wore a loose, torn black coat and seemed unusually tall and muscular.

Sylas was uneasy, but he kept on walking. The chime of the bell was waning now and he could hear the sound of rushing water beneath him, the black surface sending up distorted reflections of the distant streetlamps on the other side of town. As he passed out of the light, he walked close to one of the railings and tilted his head to see the man's face, but it was covered by a large hood.

He controlled his nerves and strode on. Soon he was walking past the stranger. One, two steps beyond. He braced himself to run.

"Hello, Sylas."

He froze, heart racing.

"A curious place to meet — don't you think?" It was a deep, accented voice.

Sylas eyed the far end of the bridge — he would have no chance of reaching it if the man gave chase.

"I— I don't know you... do I?"

"The middle of a river, I mean," said the man. "It's neither here nor there."

Sylas turned and saw that he hadn't moved, but was still staring out over the river.

The stranger sucked in a deep breath. "What did the Greeks say about rivers? A border between worlds, was it? Or was it something about fate... I can't remember. Your world, not mine."

Sylas started to back away. "I don't... I don't know," he stammered, "but I have to..."

"And where do you think you're off to?" said the stranger sharply, stirring for the first time and standing to his full, towering height. He peered down from the shadows of his hood. "I'm afraid you won't get very far without my help."

"But who *are* you?" asked Sylas, still poised to run.

The man seemed to consider this for a moment.

"Call me Espen," he said. He lifted his hands to his hood and pulled it back.

Sylas took a step back. The stranger's youthful features were terribly disfigured. His burnished mahogany skin was riven by a cruel tear that ran from just below his hairline, over the bridge of his nose and cheek to his neck, where it disappeared under the folds of his coat. The wound was still red and inflamed and he winced slightly as he attempted a smile.

"Take this as the mark of a friend," he said, waving his hand towards his face. "I've already met the abomination that chases you."

Sylas was suddenly struck by the stranger's voice. He had heard it before. It was the voice from the back of the Shop of Things.

Mr Zhi's assistant!

His panic began to subside. "Are you... do you know Mr Zhi?"

The stranger smiled briefly. "Yes."

Sylas felt a wave of relief. He glanced in the direction of the estate. "So you know what that thing is? The thing that's chasing me?"

"Answers breed questions, Sylas," said Espen, "and we're already out of time. I don't wish to meet that thing twice in one day. We must go."

"Where?"

The man was looking back towards Gabblety Row. "You know where," he replied in a vacant voice, still looking away. "To the bell."

"Can you hear—"

Suddenly a mournful howl rose from somewhere on the housing estate, in precisely the direction Espen had been looking. The soulless baying hung in the air, echoing from walls, trees and rooftops. The lights of the estate began to flare into life.

"It's already close," said Espen. "How fast can you run?"

"Pretty fast," said Sylas. He knew he was quick — it was the one compliment his uncle ever paid him. "Follow me."

He turned and sprinted to the end of the bridge, leaping down the steps in threes, disappearing in a trice.

A smile passed over Espen's face as he set out in pursuit.

As they ran across the town square, the walls and windows about them echoed their steps and Sylas glanced nervously in all directions. But as quickly as they had entered the square they left it behind, charging into another darkened lane. They ran along overgrown alleys and behind shops, down lanes, over walls and into parks. They charged through a skate park, under a railway bridge and across a builders' yard, never once pausing for breath.

The bell chimed several more times as they ran, battering Sylas's ears, urging them on, challenging them to run faster.

Finally they found themselves in a small street bordered on both sides by the low, huddling houses of factory workers. Sweating and panting, they came to the end, where a great chimney stack loomed above them.

Espen slowed to a walk and called ahead: "Stop! Let's rest for a moment."

Sylas slapped his feet down on the tarmac and leaned his weight on his knees while he caught his breath.

"See!" he panted with a grin. "Pretty fast!"

Espen raised an eyebrow.

"I don't know why you're doing this," said Sylas, "but thank you."

"Maybe someday you'll return the favour," said Espen with a brief smile, but then the levity left his face. "Your shoulders bear us all, Sylas." The stranger spoke under his breath, almost as though he didn't want to be heard.

Sylas frowned quizzically and there was an awkward silence.

Espen shook his head as if annoyed with himself. "Give me the book," he said, holding out his hand.

Sylas instinctively took a step backwards, surprised to hear the stranger speak of it.

"The Samarok?"

Espen nodded and turned his palm up expectantly.

"What do you want it for?"

"Give it to me, Sylas," demanded the man impatiently. "I'll give it back, but I must show you something."

Sylas eyed him carefully. He didn't want to show the Samarok to anybody, let alone to someone he had just met. But then again Mr Zhi had obviously trusted him. He fought with himself for a moment longer, then set his rucksack on the ground and took out the beautiful book. He turned it over in his hands for a moment, feeling the touch of the sharp stones and cold metal against his skin, then handed it over.

Espen took it and looked thoughtfully at it for a moment, then glanced about him as if looking for something. He walked swiftly to the edge of the pavement, lifted the Samarok high into the air and, summoning all his strength, brought it crashing down against the kerb.

8

Passing

"As we leave the light, we enter darkness; as we pass from warmth, the cold creeps about us; as we depart from one, we enter the Other."

SYLAS CRIED OUT AS the book collided awkwardly with the concrete. There was a sharp crack and a piece broke away from it, spun in the air and clattered across the hard surface, ringing metallically as it came to rest on the wet pavement.

"What are you doing?" yelled Sylas, rushing after the two pieces.

Espen said nothing, but watched quietly as Sylas picked up the book and tucked it under his arm, then went in search of the other piece. He found it lying in the gutter, a torrent of rainwater washing over it. It was the beautiful S symbol from the cover, now bent utterly out of shape.

Sylas wheeled round in a rage.

"Look what you've done!" he bellowed, holding up the twisted piece of metal. He could hear the blood rushing in his ears and felt his cheeks burning red.

The stranger was unmoved. He looked down at Sylas and held out his hand.

"Give it to me," he said calmly.

"You must be joking," said Sylas and made to put it in his pocket.

"Give it to me now!" boomed Espen, his deep, gritty voice echoing up the street.

Sylas took a step back. Part of him wanted to take the book and run, to take his chances on his own. But he still saw no reason why Espen should wish him harm. He looked at the piece of metal in his hands. It was useless anyway — what more could he do? The stranger waited expectantly with his hand outstretched. Finally, with an attempt at a look of defiance, Sylas reached out and handed him the broken symbol.

Espen took it with one hand, and with the other he seized Sylas's wrist. Sylas shouted in protest and tried to pull free, but the grip was vice-like. He saw that the stranger was manipulating the piece of metal in his free hand. It pivoted round the point at the centre of the S, where the gold of the top curve met the silver of the bottom. He realised that there was a hinge in the join, allowing the two parts to swivel around one another.

The symbol wasn't broken: it had just rotated out of shape.

Espen twisted his hand a little further and it once again formed a perfect S.

Sylas ceased his struggle. "Why does it—"

"So that it can do this," said Espen.

The symbol rotated at its centre until it formed a broken circle, with the silver and gold forming its two halves. Then, before Sylas could pull away, the stranger slid it over the boy's narrow wrist and adjusted it slightly so that it formed a complete ring. There was a barely audible click.

Sylas snatched back his arm and looked closely at his wrist, which now bore a perfect bracelet. There were no faults or cracks

— the gold met the silver in an invisible join.

"How did you do that?" he asked.

Espen shrugged and smiled.

Sylas turned his eyes back to the bracelet and ran his fingers over the metal, marvelling at its smoothness. He gripped the new join and tried to prise it apart, but the metal held firm. He tried the pivot, but that too was solid. Finally he attempted to pull the band off his wrist, but as he slid it towards his hand, it seemed to tighten and fit snugly against his skin.

"It won't come off," he said, looking up.

"I should hope not," said Espen, still smiling. "You don't want to lose it, Sylas. It's there to protect you."

Sylas looked from the stranger's earnest face to the bracelet, which had now closed tighter than ever.

"Protect me from what? From the animal?"

"In a way, it protects you from yourself."

Sylas looked up in surprise, but the stranger had already turned and set off in the direction of the vast chimney stack.

"Come!" shouted Espen.

Sylas took the book from under his arm, glancing at the cover, now marked by a highly decorated S-shaped groove where the symbol had been. He crammed the book into his rucksack and ran on.

The bell chimed again. Once more he was hit in the chest by a shockwave of sound and he saw the rain dance in the air. But there was something unexpected about this toll of the bell. Even though they were nearer its source, it seemed quieter than before, less forceful. It still had great power, but Sylas was sure that it had weakened: he did not have to hold his hands to his ears as he had when he first heard it; it was not impossible to think as it was before. It dawned on him that none of the chimes had been as powerful as the one that had woken him in his room. The bell was dying away.

"I think it's stopping!"

The stranger turned and nodded, as if this was to be expected. Then his dark eyes looked back down the street and widened.

Sylas felt the skin prickle on his back and neck. Without slowing his run, he turned his head.

He saw it straight away, emerging from some shadows into the lamplight. The beast was at full sprint, bounding high into the air with each stride, its jaws hanging open to reveal its white teeth glistening cruelly in the yellow light. As it caught sight of its quarry, it raised its head a little and howled into the night air. It was muffled by the sound of the bell, but its misty breath rose from its jaws and its tongue rasped visibly against its teeth.

Sylas turned and collided with Espen's broad chest. A powerful arm curled about his waist and hoisted him into the air, over the chicken-wire fence that bordered the factory complex. Just as he seemed to be clear, he caught his knee on the metal bar that formed the top of the gate and he cried out in pain.

Espen didn't pause. "Brace yourself!" he growled.

Sylas gasped a lungful of air and flailed around him, hoping to grab hold of something, but he felt himself pitched into nothingness. A moment later he landed and fell backwards. He was winded and in shock from the pain in his knee, but he forced himself up on his elbows. Espen took a step back on the other side of the gate and with a quick glance behind him he launched himself into the air, vaulting over the top of the gate. His leather boots crashed into the gravel next to Sylas.

He crouched down to look at Sylas's knee, which was already bleeding through his jeans.

"Can you run?"

"I think so."

Espen hoisted him on to his feet and pushed him ahead. At first he limped, but soon he was running, his fear overcoming the pain. He peered over his shoulder and his eyes widened as he saw the huge figure of the black hound behind Espen, charging towards the gate. It bounded into the air, its jaws gaping in anticipation of its prey, its powerful limbs propelling it to an astonishing height. It was sure to clear the top of the gate.

But then two things happened at once. Espen slowed his run and turned slightly, raising one hand into the air with its palm facing downwards; and the dog's path through the air seemed to falter, as though it was meeting with some kind of resistance.

The effect was only momentary and Sylas thought his eyes were playing tricks, but an instant later the dog crashed headlong into the wire mesh of the gate, its teeth and jowls tangling with the criss-cross of chicken wire, sending a spray of rainwater and drool into the compound. The massive weight of its body followed, crushing its head against one of the metal bars. It whimpered, then collapsed to the ground in a heap.

"Did *you* do that?" gasped Sylas in disbelief.

Espen turned to him and winked. "I've given it something to think about. Go on — to the bell!"

Sylas felt a new thrill of excitement. The Shop of Things, the bell, the hound, all of these had seemed magical, but in a confusing, mystical way. This was *real* magic.

The factory had three huge chimney stacks that belched black, grey and white gases into the air, each crowded about with concrete laboratories, warehouses and offices. Vast steel pipes wound across the compound, crossing one another many times before finally arriving at the base of the chimneys. Sylas ran swiftly among these perilous structures, ducking under them, leaping over them, never straying from the direction of the bell. As they ran, spotlights began flicking on all around them, sending powerful beams of white light across their path. Security lights, triggered by their passing.

They mounted a gangway and were plunged back into darkness. Sylas looked to the front and could just see that the gangway came to an abrupt end at some low railings not far ahead. Just beyond them he could see a high wire fence under a dark overhang of trees.

The forest. He looked upwards at the night sky and he could see the silhouette of the hills looming over them.

He turned back to the gangway, which disappeared into the dark courtyard behind. Then he saw a faint movement beyond, like one shadow moving over another; a definite, pounding, repetitive motion that became clearer and clearer as he watched. Then it tripped one of the security lights and the white beam lit up one side of the hound's giant frame, catching its ragged jaws and wild eyes. Another beam was triggered, then another and another, each giving a snapshot of the beast in an attitude of pursuit: crouching, lurching and bounding towards them, maddened by the chase. It skidded every few steps and collided with pipes and metalwork, but shrugged them off, undeterred.

Sylas vaulted over the handrail at the end of the gangway and landed as best he could on his bad knee, staggering and sliding over the wet tarmac until he caught hold of the fence. As he turned, Espen sailed over the metal bar and landed firmly on both feet, then turned to look back. The beast was almost halfway along the gangway, devouring the small distance between them with its huge bounding strides.

Espen braced himself ready to fight and then raised both arms in front of him in a wide V-shape. He held them there for a moment with his palms facing downwards and then he slowly dropped them in front of him, gradually bringing his palms together. Suddenly the great plumes of smoke from the chimney stacks above twisted in the air, turning away from the night sky, plummeting towards the ground.

Sylas stepped backwards until his back was against the fence. The three clouds of smoke collided, spiralling round each other to form a seething column of black, grey and white. A second later the deluge of billowing gases engulfed the gangway and the beast, splaying outwards and then collapsing back on themselves in one vast, suffocating, swirling cloud. Sylas held his breath, waiting for the hound to come charging through it, but all he could see was the great wall of churning smoke. Moments passed, and still there was no sign. Finally he threw his fist in the air in celebration and looked over to Espen, a wide grin on his face.

But the stranger was grim-faced.

"We're out of time!" he shouted, running up to Sylas. "It's too strong. You must go on alone."

Sylas's heart fell. "Surely..."

"The bell is calling *you*, Sylas, not me. I'm here to keep you alive. I must stay here and fight."

Sylas opened his mouth to object, but Espen strode up and without hesitation hoisted him into the air, guiding him over the fence.

Sylas braced for a shock of pain, but he landed in leaves and long grass. He picked himself up and looked through the chicken wire at Espen, who met his gaze.

"Thank you," he said.

Espen nodded and gave him a brief smile. "Onwards, Sylas," he said. "There lie the answers, about who you are... about your mother."

Sylas drew a sharp breath. "What...?"

Just then his eyes were drawn to a dark shadow in the grey wall of gases.

Suddenly the beast erupted from the cloud and sprinted along the final yards of the gangway, not bounding as before, but still moving at a pace, swaying slightly as though it was struggling to control its limbs. Then, as it drew fresh air into its lungs, it surged forward, descending on its quarry.

Espen swung around, his arms in the air again, this time with his palms turned inwards. He brought them together in a sharp clap and at that instant the railings on each side of the gangway buckled, twisting and crumpling under a devastating magnetic force. The beast staggered as it was struck on the flank by a folding rail, then it slumped, momentarily pinned down by one of the supporting bars. As it raised its head to howl, the bell tolled again, its primal, resonant note drowning out the cries of the black beast. The chime forced the cloud of gases backwards and then drew them in until they engulfed Espen's motionless figure.

Sylas forced himself to turn and set out into the darkness, running ahead of the gases, crashing through the undergrowth beneath the canopy of the trees.

He squeezed between trunks and climbed over fallen trees, slipped into hollows and clawed his way up banks. The darkness pressed in on him and his imagination started to play its usual games, conjuring pale yellow eyes blinking somewhere far off in the undergrowth and dark shadows shifting in his path. He thought he felt the scrape of claws as he brushed against tree trunks — then the bite of razor teeth at his heels.

"Just keep running," he told himself. "*Keep running!*"

He thought about Espen and the beast fighting behind him. He tried to picture his new friend crushing the dog under piles of twisted steel and rubble, then turning and running after him to join him at the bell. But soon his mind became crowded with

80

images of a bloody fight, of Espen and the beast locked together, tumbling across the compound, the beast's vicious jaws closing about his neck, and then it was the beast that he saw leaping over the fence in one mighty bound and setting off into the forest, its snout lowered to find his scent, gaining on him, hunting him down.

He shook his head.

"Run!" he grunted through gritted teeth.

He pushed on through the thick undergrowth, thundering through fallen leaves, twigs and saplings, feeling the path ahead with grazed hands. He had been climbing for several minutes now and he told himself that he must be near the top of the hill. Sure enough, the ground soon started to level out and his way became a little easier. He did not slow down, but glanced about wildly, gasping, looking for some sign that he was near the bell.

And then he saw it.

It was not an object, nor was it a movement: it was an absence of something. There, directly ahead, the meagre moonlight pooled where there were no trees. It could have been a clearing, but when Sylas turned his head, he saw that it was not only the area in front of him: all of the forest as far as he could see simply stopped a few paces ahead.

He slowed to a walk and put his hands on his hips, drawing long, deep breaths.

Where the trees ended the ground was littered with broken foliage, branches, boughs. He could see the paleness of splinters and crushed pulp and the raggedness of broken limbs. He inhaled the sweet, wholesome scent of fresh wood. As he drew level with the very edge of the forest, he saw that these limbs were not just branches but entire trunks — whole trees that had been felled by some unimaginable force. But the path of this destruction was very narrow, for not far ahead he could now see another wall of trees where the forest began again.

Suddenly he realised what he was looking at. He turned his head and looked to his left to see a long, perfectly straight pathway of obliterated forest. He had no idea how far it went because it disappeared into the darkness. He looked to his right and the scene was exactly the same: a narrow path of broken wood disappearing into blackness. But where was the bell? Sylas stepped into the graveyard of timber and stared out into the blackness. He looked at the horizon in both directions and could see nothing, but then he lifted his eyes above the canopy of the trees.

There, some distance away and suspended high above the forest, was an immense bell.

It was tilted away from him and was entirely motionless, at one end of a giant swing. But there was nothing to carry its weight: no rope, no cord, no chain. It seemed to float in the night air. It was hard to guess its dimensions because there was nothing around it to compare it to, but to Sylas it looked about the size of a house. It was a pale colour, perhaps brass or gold, and it seemed to reflect light that was not there, as though it had been polished to such perfection that it was stealing all the light in the sky. There was some kind of design around its rim and he squinted and craned forward and felt a new stirring of excitement. He could just make out symbols, and soon he could discern the shapes clearly, carved with perfect precision into the metal.

Ravel Runes.

He felt a slight movement of air, a gentle motion that wasn't even a breeze, blowing from the direction of the bell. It seemed to bring him to his senses, for as he blinked and looked again, he realised that it was moving — moving towards him. It was becoming larger and larger with every passing second, and the slight shifting of air was now a breeze, a mounting wind moving down the channel between the trees, ahead of the swinging bell. He gasped and stepped backwards, glancing towards the trees.

His gaze fell on two large pale eyes.

They peered out at him from the blackness of the forest, just paces away. There was a rustle of leaves and a shifting of shadows and then the cruel snout of the beast emerged into the clearing. It had wide gashes across its face and Sylas could just make out that it was carrying one of its paws off the ground as though injured. Nevertheless its huge frame looked more powerful and terrifying than ever. Its greasy fur flew up around it as the breeze became a wind that whistled between the broken limbs of the trees.

Sylas felt a chill in his bones, but, to his surprise, there was no panic. He turned his eyes from the hound to the bell, which was now crashing through the forest, gathering pace as it went, sending twigs, leaves and branches flying through the air in all directions. And suddenly, as the wind became deafening and swept the air from his lungs, he felt entirely calm.

He was only dimly aware of the hound crouching back on its haunches, preparing to pounce; he did not see the forest buckling under the raging power of the bell; he saw only the bell itself – its radiance, its perfect glistening surface; its vast mysterious message depicted in runes about its rim. As it glided towards him and the wind became a hurricane, its beauty filled his vision and stirred a new emotion in him, an emotion that was so unexpected, so out of place that at first he did not recognise it.

Joy. A pure, overwhelming, wonderful joy that filled his heart, grew like a sob in his chest and made him want to cry out.

And, as the wind ripped at his clothes, as the beast launched into the air, he reached out to touch the approaching bell.

Then he heard Mr Zhi's voice in his head.

"You have nothing to fear."

PART TWO

The Other

9

The Groundrush

"It seems that Nature welcomes their very touch, bending to their will not because it must, but because their will is its own."

Her palm was warm on the back of his hand, and he could feel her fingers pressed between his. He looked down and saw their hands clasped together: her delicate white skin a sharp contrast to his own grubby wrist. He had always loved her hands. They were so fine and gentle that he sometimes felt he should not touch them. When they were at work, moving in confident sweeps across the paper as she drafted graphs, equations, diagrams, they had all the elegance of her creations, all the beauty of her brilliant mind.

He pulled his eyes away and looked ahead at the sunlight that danced brightly on rippling water and in that moment he was aware of a warmth that he had forgotten. He tried to look beyond the beautiful radiance, but the light dazzled him. He tried to shift his feet, but they seemed distant and numb. All he could see was the light, and all he could feel was her hand on his. He wanted more than this – he wanted to speak with her – so he turned to look into her face.

Sylas woke with a start. The warmth that had felt so real just moments before disappeared and in its place he felt the dull ache of a chill in his limbs. His arms were splayed wide and he pulled them across his chest to try to warm himself, but they only pressed his damp clothes to his skin, making him gasp. All that was left of sleep disappeared and his mind began to clear.

His first thoughts were of the beautiful bell, tearing through the forest towards him, sending branches flying in its path. Then he recalled falling backwards, unbalanced by the great wind that had risen before it. But he could not remember landing, or the bell reaching him, or anything since, except his dream. Something else filled his thoughts: a growing unease that gradually formed a picture in his mind – a picture of the beast. He could see it clearly: its glaring eyes, its jaws gaping wide, its filthy claws outstretched as it launched itself towards him.

He forced his eyes open and saw a blackness so complete that he would have thought them still closed were it not for the dim light at the very edges of his vision. Ignoring the stiffness in his neck, he turned his head and saw that, sure enough, there was a line of blue-grey light through which he could just make out the angular shapes of broken branches and twigs, some silhouetted, some dimly lit. He turned his head the other way and there too was the strange strip of light. As he craned to see more, his rucksack pressed into his back and he shifted to ease the discomfort, but a sharp pain ran across his shoulders, making him groan.

The groan echoed back.

His heart quickened and he held his breath. "Hello?" he said in a husky voice.

The word echoed back to him, then again, and again. The voice was his own, but the sound was cold, metallic and hollow. His mind flew back to the chase, the factory, the woods, the clearing – and the bell. Pushing himself up into a sitting position, he glanced around at the wide circle of light and for the first time he understood.

He was under the bell.

He seemed to be lying at the very centre of the bell's massive black shadow. The light at its edge, which he had at first thought to be a thin strip, was in fact a gap of at least his own height between the bell and the ground. The darkness made him uneasy and, glancing about for signs of movement, he heaved himself to his feet among the broken branches, wincing as his weight fell on his sore knee.

He began to make his way towards the light, choosing the easiest path through the undergrowth. The sound of snapping twigs and crunching leaves echoed eerily around him, setting his nerves on edge. His eyes scoured the darkness for any sign of the beast, lingering on ragged silhouettes that looked all too much like angular shoulders or crouching haunches. But nothing stirred beneath the bell.

Sylas drew near the light and he paused, squinting into the gloom. Ahead of him he saw the pathway of mangled trees stretching off into the distance, bordered on both sides by the forest. It was as he remembered from the previous night, but there was one difference: it bore a strange, wintry cloak that was quite wrong on a July morning. Many of the trees had lost their leaves and were dusted with a white frost; a cold mist hung low over the ground and his breath formed clouds in the air, which drifted upwards to join the featureless grey sky. Everything was still and silent — there was no wind, no chime of the bell, not even the call of birds in the trees.

Sylas peered left and right, then stepped out from under the bell and into the light. A new edge to the chill made his teeth chatter, and he gathered the collar of his jacket round his neck as he picked his way through twigs and branches. He stopped next to the stump of a great old oak, which now sent spears of broken wood into the sky where its canopy had once been. He turned and leaned back against it, slowly raising his eyes.

There, just paces away and rising to a point high above the treetops, was the perfectly smooth polished surface of the bell.

It was an unusual shape for a bell, resembling a gigantic golden teardrop. It had a dark circular opening at its base, bordered by a fluted lip bearing the runes that he had seen the previous evening. Above, its great curving sides bowed outwards in gleaming arcs and soared to an astonishing height before tapering inwards at the top. Here the bell narrowed and narrowed until, at the highest reaches, it came to a bright ring of gleaming metal. Sylas found himself peering above to see what supported the great weight of the bell, but there was nothing. It was as if it was suspended in the air itself.

He looked back down at the band of vast Ravel Runes etched deeply into the shiny surface. He stared at them long and hard, moving his eyes from one to the next, hoping that in some way they might work together to form a message: something to explain what was happening. As he gazed at them, he had the strange sense that they were familiar, that he may even have seen this sequence before.

A pheasant suddenly crashed through a bush to his right, launched into the air and flew across the clearing, clucking with each beat of its wings. He glanced in the direction of the bush, which swayed from side to side.

He saw a movement behind it, in the shadows of the wood.

A human figure emerged from the darkness, stepping nimbly over some broken branches.

Sylas held his breath. At first he thought it was Espen and

his heart rose, but he saw quickly that it was not a man's frame, nor even a boy's: it was far smaller and its lines were much more slender.

It was a girl. But her slight figure and her disobedient mass of red hair were the only signs that she was not a boy, for her movements were robust and masculine, her skin ruddy and tanned and she wore a coat that was almost comically oversized, made of a brown, crudely woven material. She took three steps into the clearing, throwing her shoulders back and her head high as if to defy her smallness, then she stopped and stared at Sylas, looking him up and down.

Her narrow face bore a bold expression, but the way she carried her elfin body betrayed her caution: her knees were bent as though poised to run and she held her grimy hands slightly out from her sides, ready to defend herself.

Her eyes fell on the bracelet around his wrist and suddenly her eyes met his. Sylas saw for the first time that beneath the streaks of mud on her cheeks she had a pleasant, even pretty face, with lively, smiling hazel eyes.

"Who are you?" She had a husky voice and a rich accent.

He was almost surprised at the question. He had become accustomed to everyone seeming to know more than him, and he had assumed that the girl would be no exception.

"I'm Sylas," he replied, "Sylas Tate."

She said nothing, as though she expected him to say more.

"And you?" he asked.

"I'm Simia," she said. There was a brief silence, and she shifted her weight from one foot to the other and played nervously with a stray lock of her fiery hair.

"Are you... a Bringer?"

"A what?"

She cleared her throat and repeated herself more loudly: "A Bringer."

He was baffled. "No," he said, "I'm not."

The girl frowned and nodded towards his wrist. "So what's that?"

He looked down at the silver and gold bracelet. "If I'm honest, I don't know what it is," he shrugged. "It was given to me."

"*Given* to you?" said the girl, in a tone of disbelief. She narrowed her eyes as though to detect a lie. "But you *are* from the Other, aren't you?" she probed.

"The other what?"

Simia exhaled loudly, sending out a cloud of mist, and looked around her. "The *Other*. You're from the Other, aren't you?"

Sylas shook his head despairingly. "I'm from Gabblety Row. In town," he said, deciding that any kind of answer would be less irritating than another question.

"Gabbity-what? There's no Gabbity-*whatever* in town," she replied suspiciously. She eyed him for a few moments, staring into his friendly, open face. "Listen. We haven't got time for games. Just tell me this: did you come from the bell?" She pointed to the vast golden teardrop that loomed above them. "Did that bring you here?"

Sylas gave her a cool look that told her straight away that he was not playing games. He was not aware of having been *brought* anywhere, but her questions made him start to wonder. He looked around. He was in a forest as he was last night, but it *was* strangely cold and the trees were bare, as though it was winter. Then he remembered how Espen had talked about escaping to the bell, as if it would take him somewhere safe. Finally he looked at this oddly dressed girl with her strange accent and nonsensical questions. Perhaps this really was somewhere... else.

"I guess so," he said, without conviction.

"You... *guess* so," said Simia, putting her hands on her hips. She gave Sylas a long, steady look, then began to laugh. It was a light, cheery giggle and Sylas found himself smiling with her.

"Well, I *guess* that'll have to do," she said. Her face straightened. "If you *are* from the Other, and you *did* come through by the Passing Bell, you really need to get out of here."

"Suits me," said Sylas. Then he added, almost to himself: "I've got to start looking for—"

"Forget looking for anything!" said Simia incredulously. "You need to—"

"I *need* to find my mother," said Sylas firmly. "That's why I'm here. Well, at least that's—"

"Whatever... right now all you need to worry about is what *they'll* do when they know you're here."

"*They?*" repeated Sylas.

Simia let out a sigh of exasperation. "You really don't know anything..."

She stopped mid-sentence. Sylas was staring past her towards the bell. She turned and saw in an instant what he was looking at: the bell was moving. They both instinctively took a step backwards as its huge mass tilted slightly and then began to sink very slowly towards the ground.

"What's happening?" asked Sylas in a whisper.

"It's leaving."

The rim had reached the highest of the broken branches and Sylas expected to hear them splintering and cracking under its weight, but there was no sound. It continued to sink towards the earth, its great form moving through the tangle of wood as if the branches were made of air. The mist in the clearing rolled away sluggishly towards the trees. The bell reached the point at which it should have struck the frost-hardened ground, yet it continued to sink out of view, into the earth itself. The only sign that it had made contact was a very low, almost inaudible chime. Soon its base had entirely disappeared and the runes had reached the level of the broken limbs. Sylas watched the beautiful symbols gradually sinking from view.

Before long, half of the massive metal structure was embedded in the ground and he could clearly see the ring as it slowly descended from its place above the treetops. The deep chime was fading now, and it became less and less audible with every passing second. As the top of the bell drew level with his eyes, he glanced over at Simia. She too was watching, leaning back against a stump with one hand shoved deep into her pocket and the other twirling a lock of her hair. When he looked back, the bell had almost completely disappeared. Finally the last glimpse of bright metal slipped out of sight, the last strains of the chime died away and the clearing was once again shrouded in absolute silence.

Sylas looked hard at the place where it had disappeared, but there was no sign of the bell: branches still lay strewn across the ground and even the mist was now drifting slowly back into the clearing. It was as though it had simply melted away.

"Well," said Simia with a tone of finality, "looks like you're here to stay." She tucked her unruly hair behind her ears. "Now follow me."

She gathered the great folds of her coat about her, tied them tightly round her middle with a rope belt and darted off through the undergrowth.

"Follow you *where*?" Sylas shouted after her.

She stopped on the fringe of the forest and looked over her shoulder. "Somewhere safe."

"But I don't even know who you are!"

"I'm one of the Suhl," she said. "And I'm all you've got."

She dashed into the undergrowth.

Sylas looked back at the place where the bell had disappeared and saw only a dank wasteland of broken trees disappearing into grey mist. Without the golden light from the bell, the surrounding forest looked darker and more threatening than ever. Not even a ray of sunlight penetrated the blanket of cloud above. He had no idea why he was here, what was happening or what to do about his mother, but there was no going back now. He turned and ran after Simia.

Despite her size, she moved at great speed and Sylas found it difficult to keep up with her, especially with his bloody knee. He could see her bright hair bobbing up and down and side to side ahead of him as she avoided trees, leapt over gullies and vaulted rotting logs. She moved as though she lived in the wilds: certain of her way through the labyrinth of trees. They were running downhill so he assumed that they were heading towards town, though he was no longer sure that it would be there. He willed himself on, forcing his injured leg through the undergrowth and over the many obstacles that lay in his path. But he was falling behind.

"Wait!" he shouted irritably.

She slowed her pace and glanced back. Her shoulders slumped in her huge coat and she started to jog back up the hill towards him.

"We have to keep moving!" she said impatiently.

"I know, it's just my knee," said Sylas. "You'll have to slow down — or go on without me," he added reluctantly.

Simia looked down at his bloodied trouser leg. "What a mess," she said, sucking her teeth. "Why didn't you say?"

"You didn't really give me a chance."

She arched a ginger eyebrow. "If we slow down, we'll almost certainly run into them, and that would be *bad*," she said, with heavy emphasis. "I can't believe we've even got this far. You'll just have to keep up as best you can..."

Her voice trailed off as something seemed to occur to her. She turned and looked back down the hill. "Unless..." She glanced at Sylas. "I'm going to try something, but it may not work." She looked unsure of herself. "Just... well, just... stand back."

He took a step back.

"No," she said, flapping both hands. "Further back."

He eyed her warily and limped several paces backwards.

She turned her back to him, facing directly down the hill. She took a deep breath, pulled up the heavy sleeves of her coat and stretched her arms in front of her. Sylas looked at her tiny figure dwarfed by the vast tangled arches of the forest, wondering what new miracle he was about to witness.

Precious moments passed, but nothing happened. The forest fell silent.

Simia shook her hands and lifted herself up on her toes, as though a couple more inches of height might increase her chances, but still there was nothing. Her arms dropped to her sides and she shook her head. She adjusted her stance and her shoulders seemed to heave as she took in a lungful of air, then she raised her arms again.

"Come on, Simsi," she muttered under her breath. "*Concentrate!*"

Once more Sylas looked out into the dense forest, waiting for something to happen. At first he saw nothing, but then something peculiar made him squint. Slowly he became sure that the forest ahead of them was shifting and changing. He blinked his eyes, but the shapes of the trees continued to alter and warp. It was as though he was looking through a lens that was distorting the light, blending the lines of one tree with another, stretching them and morphing them until he was unsure which was which. The ground too was shifting. Leaves blurred with moss and roots until the forest floor was a mass of melding browns and greens. All of this motion was focused directly ahead, between Simia's outstretched arms: to the left and right, the forest looked as it had before.

Sylas started to feel a little dizzy as he watched, but he found it impossible to look away, so beautiful was this display of colours, so strange the spectacle. And the longer he looked, the more there seemed to be order in the chaos: the vertical lines of the trees seemed to be drifting left and right, leaving an open pathway in the centre. There, where the trees had stood, the battle between the colours of the forest floor was being won by the brightest of all the greens. Soon the movement slowed and, as it did so, Sylas began to understand what he was looking at: it was a pathway, bordered on both sides by the trees that had stood in their way, its floor carpeted with soft, verdant moss.

But Simia had not finished. She moved one of her arms out towards the passing stream and moments later the silvery flow of the water started to veer from its path downhill and turn towards the long line of moss. Before long it had reached her feet, where it turned again and started flowing over the bright green surface. Sylas watched in amazement as the stream gathered pace on this smooth, slippery channel and became a shallow film of water, cascading between the trees.

Simia's hands fell to her sides and she gasped for breath.

"It's called a Groundrush," she panted. "It's for..."

There was a noise somewhere further up the hill and a bird nearby launched itself into the air. They looked sharply in its direction, their eyes scanning the skeletal trees and the shadows between. A wood pigeon sped upwards towards the grey sky, slapping its wings together as it darted through the branches.

Sylas glanced nervously at Simia. Her bold grin was gone and for the first time there was fear in her eyes.

They heard footsteps pounding through the forest somewhere far behind. The sound was heavy and resonant — whatever was making them was huge.

In the next moment the silence of the forest was shattered by a blood-chilling howl.

Even as the terrifying sound met their ears, Simia was in motion, grabbing Sylas by the collar and dragging him to the edge of the streaming water.

"It's them! The Ghor!" she hissed in his ear. "Do exactly what I do!"

Then, without warning, she leapt into the air, throwing her legs out in front of her. She travelled some distance with her giant coat flapping about her before landing with a great splash in the icy water. As the water rushed about her, she lay back and wrapped her arms round her chest. She began to slide forward, carried with ease over the slippery, spongy surface. She quickly picked up pace and in no time she was careering down the hillside away from him, swiftly passing out of sight as she fell away into a dip in the forest floor. Seconds later she was thrown into the air some distance beyond and he heard her cry out to him as she landed back on the slide somewhere entirely out of view.

Just then a great chorus of howls echoed through the forest behind him and he heard the footsteps — closer now — crashing through the forest. They were on his trail. He pulled the rucksack from his shoulders, clutched it to his chest and leapt into the air.

He splashed into the freezing stream and gasped as the cold made its way quickly through his clothes. There was a gentle jolt as he went over a rise, then suddenly his heart was in his mouth as he accelerated downwards. Tree trunks flew past him faster and faster and, when he looked upwards, he could see a flurry of bare branches silhouetted against the grey sky. On both sides a blur of rocks and roots whisked past his face and he felt a growing excitement. He tucked in his elbows and allowed the surge of the stream to take him. He went over a bump and was thrown up in the air — suddenly weightless, hanging some distance off the ground — and in that moment everything went strangely quiet: the sound of rushing water faded; the wind stopped roaring in his ears. As he turned through the air, he was able to look back up the slide, and his blood ran cold.

Where he had been standing only moments before were two gargantuan black hounds, sniffing the air and prowling through the undergrowth. He saw in them the features of the beast that had pursued him the previous night: the cruel jaws bearing rapier-sharp teeth; the immense, powerful shoulders; and the long, sloping back.

But there was one difference. They seemed almost twice the size.

Before he saw any more, the ground hurtled up at him and his pursuers disappeared from view. He hit the slide face first and water splashed into his mouth and nose, but he was quickly flipped on to his back as the mossy path banked left and then right.

Trees, leaves, bushes, rocks whisked past him in a stream of colour. He looked down between his feet and saw the bright green slide below him, turning this way and that, sometimes rising, the force pressing him down into the ground, other times falling away so that he was thrown into the air. The sound of wind and water became deafening and the Groundrush swerved ever more quickly from side to side, throwing him against its mossy banks.

Then, as quickly as this strange journey began, it was over. Sylas looked ahead of him and saw that the green of the moss came to an abrupt end. He just had time to brace himself before shooting off the slide into a pool of water that sent up a wall of spray around him. Gasping for air, he slid on to an expanse of brown leaves that flew up in a blizzard around his tumbling limbs, tearing at his hands and face. There were several painful jolts as he bounced off mounds and roots, but finally he came to a halt, face down against a row of bushes.

He lay panting and spitting out soil. Everything was quiet except for the flutter of leaves gradually settling on top of him.

The thought of the dark figures running through the woods made him push himself up. He saw Simia standing a few paces off, drenched from head to foot, but already on her feet, staring back up the Groundrush. As he watched, she steadied herself, held up her head and lifted her arms into the air. He looked back up the slide, which he could see writhing and turning through the forest, sometimes clearly visible as a long green line, sometimes falling out of view into a dip or twisting out of sight behind a clump of trees. As his eyes followed its curves, rises and falls, he realised that he was once again looking at a confusion of colours and lines. No longer was the slide a distinguishable shape, but a drifting slurry of colours like paints in a mixing pot. Soon the outlines of the trees were shifting again and he could no longer see any sign of the path that the slide had taken. Seconds later the trees were once again standing in their rightful places on the hillside.

It was as though the Groundrush had never been there.

10
The Ghor

"What rule is there, what law
But gnashing teeth and grasping claw?"

SIMIA FLEW ACROSS THE forest floor, moving even faster now that the ground was flattening out. Sylas winced each time his knee twisted beneath him, but somehow he kept up with her, turning this way and that to avoid trees, logs and bushes. He listened for sounds of their pursuers, but heard only the wind in his ears and the leaves and twigs under his feet.

"They'll know now that we're heading for town," panted Simia, "but we'll be safer once we're there — more places to hide. It's not far."

He looked up, expecting to see the familiar factory looming above the treetops. There was no sign of it, but the further they ran, the more he became aware of the scent of smoke in the air, and it soon became visible, hanging in long grey clouds among the branches of the trees. As it thickened, its odour became more distinct — not the acrid, artificial smell of the factory, but the soft, rounded scents of woodsmoke.

Simia vaulted over a fallen tree and pushed her way through

the thick dark green leaves of some bushes, soon disappearing from view. Sylas clambered over the log and then forced his way into the dense mass of leaves that slapped at his face and pulled at his clothes. He squeezed his eyes shut and struggled on until his hands met the back of Simia's coat.

He opened his eyes and took an involuntary gasp of the thick smoky air.

Ahead of him, at the bottom of a bank of rubbish, lay a town — but it was not the town that he knew. The great towering chimney stacks of the factory were nowhere to be seen. Neither were the houses, the rooftops, the roads. The streets were not straight and regular as he remembered them, but narrow, meandering and paved with dirt, forming a muddy labyrinth that twisted and turned into the distance. They were bordered on both sides by a great disorder of low wooden dwellings unlike any that he had seen before: a muddle of pyramidal rooftops, arranged at befuddling angles to one another, stretching off into the distance until they finally disappeared into the smoke. Some were higher than others, seeming to tower over everything around them, but almost all of them were exactly the same shape: square at the bottom, pointed at the top.

The only exceptions were far away in the centre of town: great rectangular structures that dwarfed the pitched roofs around their base; and an immense, curiously shaped tower with sides that bowed inwards and rose towards what looked like a pair of platforms at its top, arranged one above the other.

The narrow streets bustled with people, some scurrying quickly from building to building, others bearing heavy loads and making their way slowly to or from the centre. Many of these travellers drew simple carts behind them, some helped by donkeys or ponies, some using their own tired limbs to haul their wagons over ruts in the road and between the throng of pedestrians. Even from this distance Sylas could see that their clothes were oddly drab and cheerless — like those that Simia was wearing — and that most wore hoods or hats of a variety of shapes. The scene seemed altogether foreign and of another age. Yet there it all was — right there — where his home should have been.

"What *is* this place...?" he murmured.

Simia turned to him briefly, seemed about to say something and then changed her mind.

"I'm taking you to some people who'll explain," she said. Before he could reply, she set off down the slope, picking her way through the rubbish and towards the nearest lane.

"Who?" Sylas called after her. "Will *they* know anything about my mother?"

But she was gone, already halfway down the refuse-ridden slope.

He shook his head in frustration, but set out after her. His progress was slowed by piles of splintered timber, broken bottles and jars, empty crates and rotting sacks whose contents he did not like to guess at, but soon he drew level to Simia, who waited for him next to a muddy ditch that bordered the lane. She pointed at it.

"Get your clothes as dirty as you can," she said in a low voice. "And that weird bag thing — roll it in the mud."

Sylas looked down and saw that his dark jeans and colourful rucksack looked decidedly odd compared to the drab clothing of the other people in the lane. He slid the bag off his shoulders and splashed into the centre of the ditch, sinking up to his shins. He staggered sideways and pressed the bag into the sludge, then he squelched his way to the other side.

He looked at himself with satisfaction: both his clothes and his bag were now covered in mud and he blended into the sea of brown and black.

"Hoy!" came an urgent cry from his left.

Sylas turned to see a mule-drawn cart bearing down on him. Simia yanked him out of its path as the three animals stampeded past, sending up a spray of muddy water. Then came the huge wagon, piled high with a mountain of boxes, chests and crates that leaned over precariously as the driver steered clear of the two children. It skidded on the mud, but soon steadied and the imposing, dark-skinned driver took the opportunity to shake his fist angrily at them, shouting something in a language Sylas had never heard before.

He looked about him and saw an endless stream of wagons swerving this way and that to avoid one another and the many people on foot. The pedestrians walked along the edge of the road by the ditch, watching the carts and carriages warily and stepping aside to avoid being crushed. By contrast to the forest the noise was deafening: the hollering of voices, the stomping of hooves, the splashing of wheels through the mud. There were no cars, no engines, no horns, but it seemed just as noisy and confusing as any road he had ever seen.

When he looked back at Simia, she was eyeing the edge of the forest.

"Come on," she said nervously, "let's get out of sight."

She pointed across the lane to a narrow passageway. They set off at once, weaving between wagons and carts to the other side, then running into the shadow of the alley.

"Stop a minute," panted Sylas. "I don't understand any of this. Just tell me what's going on!"

She put her hands on her hips and turned to face him. "Didn't you get any — I don't know — training, or whatever you people normally get before you come here?"

"You're not listening to me!" he snapped in frustration. "There is no 'us people' — it's only me. I'm not a 'Bringer' or whatever it is that you think I am. No one's trained me or given me special powers. I just live with my uncle somewhere," he waved across town, "somewhere over there — at least, that's where it was... God knows where it is now. I'm here because the bell brought me here, and because something about all this might explain what's happened to my mother. That's all I know about any..."

"OK, OK!" said Simia, raising her hands in mock surrender. She eyed him for a moment and then glanced anxiously towards the forest. "Listen, I'll tell you two things. First, just over there, on the other side of town, there are some people called the Suhl. Good people. People who know a lot about where you're from and the bell and plenty more besides. Perhaps even about your mother. I want to take you to them so they can help you." She pointed into the forest. "And behind you, in those trees, is a nightmare. It's called the Ghor. They're definitely *not* good people, they're monsters. They won't help you, they'll tear you limb from limb. And they're not all the way on the other side of town, they're just out of sight and running this way." She threw her hands out imploringly. "Now can we please *leave*?"

She started to turn around, but Sylas caught her shoulder.

"What are they? The Ghor?"

Her shoulders slumped. "They were created to do one thing above all else," she said curtly. "Hunt. Hunt people. They were born for it — literally *made* for it. Give them a trail, or even a scent, and they're pretty much unstoppable. They'll search out the smallest track, smell the faintest trace and then run you down. They are faster than anything and they'll almost never lose your trail."

"And those are the dog things that I saw?"

"Not quite," she said impatiently. "They were the Ghorhund. The Ghor and the Ghorhund are two kinds of the same thing. Sometimes they're more like men — upright, on two legs, clever, cunning — we call those the Ghor; and sometimes they're just like dogs, but bigger, faster and stronger — those are called the Ghorhund." She glanced back towards the lane and the forest. "Hang around here much longer and you'll get to meet them face to face — would you like that?"

Sylas saw the fear in her eyes. "No," he said, "let's go."

"Right then."

She whirled about and darted off up the passage, weaving between the townsfolk, leading them deeper and deeper into the warren of wooden buildings. The further they went, the stranger and more unfamiliar everything became. It was not just the peculiar pyramid-like buildings on each side of the passageway, nor the curious little shops and stalls selling a bewildering array of objects whose purpose Sylas could only guess at, but also the strangeness of the people who strolled, chattered and worked around them. Their clothes were simple, made almost exclusively from a crudely woven cloth that many of the men wore wrapped round their waist like a skirt or a long kilt. Some women also wore headdresses, adorned with coloured stones and symbols, and many of them had tattoos of similar symbols on their hands and temples. Some wore thick, starkly coloured make-up around their eyes, accented with sharp black lines. The effect was altogether alien, and yet something about them seemed familiar to Sylas, but he could not think why. While many spoke a language he could understand but had a thick accent, like Simia, others — particularly those wearing the most splendid clothes and headdresses — chattered to each other in a foreign language. It really was as though the bell had transported him somewhere — to a place or a time very far away from the Gabblety Row that he knew so well.

They passed a huge shop frontage that was packed to the ceiling with pots, pans, containers, cauldrons and all manner of glass objects: globes, jars, phials, measuring jugs, beakers, flasks, straight tubes, coiled tubes, winding tubes, tapered tubes, bulging tubes. Some of these strange items looked a little like devices he had once seen in his mother's laboratory or in his book of science. But they were also somehow different: more delicate, more natural-looking and organic, almost as though they had been grown rather than shaped or made. He glanced up at the richly inscribed nameplate above the window:

THE PECULIORIUM

PURVEYORS OF PECULIAR PARTICULARS FOR THE PRACTICE OF THE THREE WAYS

He saw that the window was divided into three sections, each with an ornate sign hanging above; one read *Kimiyya*, the next *Urgolvane* and the last *Druindil*. Sylas frowned and turned to ask Simia what all this meant, but she was already far ahead, darting through the crowds. He lingered a moment longer, mouthing the strange words under his breath, then set out after her.

They rushed on and on, further and further into the warren of lanes and passageways. As they lost themselves in the bustle of the town, Sylas thought less of whatever was behind and took more notice of the strange buildings that rose around them. All were built from rough-hewn rock and timber and none had the straight lines and hard edges of the town he knew so well.

Instead they seemed to have borrowed from Gabblety Row some of its odd shapes and crookedness, its undulations and waywardness, so that each and every structure was entirely unique. Nevertheless the majority shared two features: low doors that people had to duck through to enter and whose frames were carved with curious symbols and hieroglyphs; and great sloping roofs that began low to the ground and soared on four triangular sides towards a single point, forming an irregular but perfectly proportioned pyramid. More than once he caught himself staring upwards at these strange structures, and more than once Simia turned and yanked him on, muttering at him to stop gawping and being so conspicuous.

Finally, as they reached the end of a lane that opened out into a square, Simia stopped to catch her breath and pulled him into the shadow of a shop awning.

"Let's rest here for a minute," she panted, pushing her bright hair behind her ears.

Sylas leaned gratefully against a wall, his chest heaving. He remembered the bottle of water in his backpack and lowered the bag from his shoulder.

"Water?" he asked, opening the drawstring.

Simia glanced down and screwed up her nose. "I'll stick to water from my own world, thanks very much."

"What do you mean, 'your own world'? Why do you keep saying stuff like that?"

"Because that's the way it is," she said, brushing at her coat. "You're from the Other and that means your water's from there too. I'd rather not mix worlds up inside me, if it's all the same to you."

Sylas stared at her and was about to ask again what she meant by the 'Other', but she was looking at his rucksack. She crouched down by it and pulled it wider open.

"Is that—" she cleared her throat, —"is that... *the Samarok?*"

Sylas looked down and saw the ancient volume, with its glistening stones and the deep S-shaped groove catching the light.

"Yes," he replied, surprised that she knew what it was.

Simia reached in and touched the supple leather of the cover. "I can't believe this is the real thing... the *actual* Samarok."

"You know what it is?" asked Sylas. "To be honest, I don't know much about it. Someone gave it to me."

Simia scoffed. "Someone just *gave* you the Samarok?"

He nodded. "A man called Mr Zhi just showed up at the row and..."

Simia's mouth fell open. "Mr Zhi? You know Mr Zhi?"

"Do *you?*"

Simia laughed incredulously. "Of course I don't *know* him, but everyone's *heard* of Mr Zhi."

"Well, I'd never heard of him until yesterday."

"Why aren't I surprised?" she said with a sigh.

Someone shouted nearby and her eyes rose to the passing throng of traders and townsfolk. She pulled the drawstring sharply closed.

"We've got to be careful," she whispered. "We can talk about all of this and drink some *proper* water when we're safe. It's not much further."

"Sure, fine," said Sylas, smiling at her sassiness. "Where to next?"

"Not far now, but first we need to cross Scholar's Square," she said over her shoulder as she plunged into the crowd. "Try not to gawp."

Sylas sighed and set out after her.

They pushed through a queue of shoppers at the end of the

lane and emerged into the wide plaza beyond.

It was a curious scene. Around the edges, hordes of people milled about buying and selling goods from a gathering of ramshackle stalls and open carts, while the space in the centre was almost entirely taken up by three large timber structures consisting of a latticework of legs and supports to about chest height, topped with a flat expanse of boards, like gigantic stages.

What was even more peculiar was that on each of the three stages was a group of children wearing matching gowns like a sort of uniform, some sitting at desks and others moving about in some or other activity. They seemed to be working under the direction of three teachers, one on each stage, whose authority was clear to see not only in the children's obedience, but also in the size and style of their headdresses, which were extravagantly designed and ludicrously large.

But what made the picture utterly bewildering was what these classes were doing.

On the nearest of the three stages, for instance, the children stood with their arms at their sides while their teacher faced them and, in a rapid motion, pointed at various places beneath their feet. As she extended her finger, a trapdoor fell into the void beneath the stage exactly where she had pointed. Even before the teacher's finger had reached its full extent, the children standing on the trapdoor shifted position, stepping one pace left or right, forward or back, almost as though they had known where the teacher was going to point next. As though they had read her mind. Such was the speed and fluency of the teacher's movements and the students' responses that the class appeared to be performing an elaborate, silent dance, weaving effortlessly between one another as the trapdoors fell away, leaving them with less and less safe ground upon which to stand.

Despite the apparent danger, they remained entirely calm, never looking at one another, never colliding, never glancing down at their feet, but instead gliding around the stage, stepping closer and closer to one another until all of them had moved on to the last remaining island of solid flooring. Even when they were pressed in tightly against each other in this tiny space, they remained entirely focused, arms at their sides, eyes fixed on those of their teacher. Only when the teacher clapped her hands did they emerge from their apparent trance and, along with the watching crowd, erupt in a round of applause, congratulating one another on their apparent success.

"You're gawping," hissed Simia in Sylas's ear.

Sylas blinked. "Well, of course I'm gawping! What are they *doing*?"

"Learning Druindil," said Simia, as if it was abundantly clear what they were doing. She pointed at each of the three stages in turn. "Druindil, Urgolvane, Kimiyya — one for each of the Three Ways. They're from the local schools — this is where they come to show off what they've learned." She pulled sharply on his sleeve. "Now *come on*."

She led him out across the square, past the second stage. Sylas followed but continued to gawp, for the scene on the next stage was no less strange. Here all of the students were seated at their desks, listening to their teacher as he strutted up and down at one end of the platform beneath a banner that read 'The Memorial Academy of Urgolvane'. While at first the class appeared to be entirely normal (excepting of course their strange gowns and the comical headdress of their teacher), Sylas soon found himself staring at the chairs and desks, convinced that something was not quite right. Then he realised what had caught his eye: parts of the furniture were missing. Some of the chairs and tables were missing a leg, some two, and others were suspended in the air by a single leg in one corner. He squinted, thinking that perhaps his eyes were playing tricks, but they were not — the legs and supports had been deliberately sawn off.

Yet the chairs and tables remained upright.

The entire class was being supported by some invisible force.

Some of the classroom furniture wavered a little, but none showed any signs of falling as Sylas knew they should. Indeed some of the children were so confident that they rocked backwards and forwards as though swinging on their chairs, supported by absolutely nothing.

Sylas's eyes followed those of the children to the teacher at the front of the class and again he blinked in disbelief. He had thought that the old man was walking to and fro on some kind of raised platform for he looked down upon his class from some height, but he saw now that there was no such platform. The teacher was suspended several feet in the air by the same unseen force. His clogged feet seemed to touch down upon something firm so that he was able to walk as normal, but as far as Sylas could tell, there was absolutely nothing there. At that very moment the teacher stopped in his tracks, turned to his class and bellowed a command in a language that meant nothing to Sylas. The students who were rocking on their chairs ceased at once and the entire class bowed their heads in concentration.

Suddenly one of the students, along with her chair and her desk, rose into the air, reaching the same height as her tutor before starting to drift slowly round the stage. Soon all of the students were doing the same, sailing up into the air with their weird furniture, then drifting between and around one another until the entire class was in motion, forming a great swirl of students' chairs, desks and gowns. The surrounding crowd burst into wild applause and a group of very proud parents began shouting the names of their loved ones as they drifted somewhere overhead.

Sylas was about to leave Simia's side to take a closer look when the sound of a commotion behind him made him turn. He saw a flurry of activity back across the square, near where they had entered. Then a new, awful sound pierced the air.

Screams. Screams of unbridled terror.

Suddenly everything was in motion. Simia took hold of the back of his sweater and heaved him with all her might in the opposite direction. At the same moment the crowds around them also broke into a run, scrambling desperately towards the exits on the other side of the square. The students suspended somewhere high above suddenly lost their concentration and fell out of the air, crashing down on to the stage amid a hail of splintering wood and shouts of pain and fear. Above this thunder of noise came a new sound, a sound that had become all too familiar: a haunting, canine howl. It rose from somewhere behind them, but then echoed from the walls of the surrounding buildings, resounding from every surface, filling the air.

"They're on to our scent!" yelled Simia at his side as they reached a full sprint.

Sylas caught a glimpse of the terror in her eyes and felt a new surge of panic. They were moving as fast as they could between the mass of bodies and flailing limbs, turning this way and that to avoid capsized stalls and the clattering carts of fleeing traders. But they both knew that in these crowds they were moving too slowly. Far too slowly.

Their eyes darted everywhere, looking for a way to escape, but all they could see was a mass of bodies, frightened eyes, broken stalls, careering wagons.

Suddenly Sylas lunged to one side, grabbing Simia's coat and pulling her along with him.

"What are you doing?" she protested, trying to pull away.

He headed directly for one of the rattling carts, which swayed under a heavy load of sacks filled with fruit. He pointed frantically.

"Get in!" he hissed in Simia's ear.

He knew that in the cart the Ghor might not be able to follow their scent, especially if they surrounded themselves with the strong-smelling fruit. It seemed hopeless, but at least it was a chance. Simia seemed to understand. She quickened her pace, caught up with the cart, and then vaulted over the low wooden side and dropped to her knees between two sacks of apples. Sylas heard some yelling behind him, but dared not look round: he launched himself forward off his good leg, caught hold of the rear of the cart and hauled himself into position next to Simia.

He was struck by the harsh, acidic scent of rotting apples and he saw that they were squatting in a mulch of crushed fruit that had fallen from the sacks. He pressed himself down as far as he could and they busied themselves pulling the sacks into a small circle around them – the perfect hiding place. Sylas looked up, wondering if the hunchbacked driver might have seen them, but he was too busy lashing his mules, trying to make his own escape.

"Ghorhund!" hissed Simia suddenly, staring back across the square.

Sylas's blood ran cold. There, in a clearing where the commotion had begun just moments before, were two gargantuan black beasts, sniffing the air and prowling through the wreckage of a stall. He saw in them the features of the black hound that had pursued him the previous night: the cruel jaws bearing razor-sharp teeth; the immense, powerful shoulders; and the long, sloping back.

To his relief they seemed to have lost the trail of scent, for as he watched, one of them let out a howl of frustration, its breath clouding the air, and then launched itself at an abandoned cart. It crashed into the cargo of boxes and crates, sending the entire load flying, some high into the air, some off the opposite side of the wagon and on to the plaza. Most of the boxes were smashed into pieces, and lengths of timber and splinters of wood flew in all directions. The beast erupted from the cart amid a cascade of debris, leaving it rocking precariously from side to side on broken axles. But before it could settle, the second Ghorhund struck from behind, propelling the rear of the wagon high into the air until it slewed to one side, tipping its remaining contents on to the paving. There was a sharp crack as the yoke twisted and snapped. The ponies broke free of their harnesses and ran screaming, the whites of their eyes flaring as they galloped through the fleeing crowds.

The Ghorhund tore at the sides of the cart with their huge jaws, pulling away great mouthfuls of timber and metal, then hurling it away with a sharp flick of their powerful necks.

"That could have been us," murmured Sylas.

Their cart was accelerating towards the edge of the square and they could hear the driver shouting at people to get out of the way and cracking his whip at the mules, trying desperately to make them run faster. The sight of the fleeing ponies had now set them at a full gallop so that the cart was swaying dangerously on the slippery surface. The two children clung on to the sacks, desperate to stay hidden.

"Look!" hissed Simia, her face betraying a new fear.

Sylas followed her frightened eyes and saw three huge figures entering the square, then jogging towards the Ghorhund. They bounded lightly in a way that seemed unnatural in men so large, taking huge strides with ease. He recoiled in horror as he saw why:

their powerful legs bent backwards at the knee like the rear legs of an animal, giving them an aberrant, predatory stance. In truth they seemed as much beast as man, with dark, matted fur rising from clawed feet up sinewy legs and appearing again above their black tunics in patches across their shoulders and down their arms to long, hooked fingers. Bristles gathered around the back of their necks to form a thick mane that covered most of their massive heads, which hung low between their shoulders as they ran. Their faces were difficult to see, but even at this distance Sylas could make out areas of pale human skin covering parts of an elongated jaw that rose to what looked almost like a snout.

Almost, but not quite, for there was not one thing about these creatures that was neither man nor beast, but rather a mixture of the two: they moved with the agility and power of an animal, but with the precision and intent of a man; they had the stature and gait of their human cousins, but their manner was of threatening, rapacious hunters.

"The Ghor," murmured Simia, her voice full of dread.

They drew near the Ghorhund, slowed and then, with a single purpose, fanned out across the square, one loping along each edge, the third jogging into the centre, stooping low at times to examine the paving. Suddenly, just a short distance past the Ghorhund, it stopped and lowered its head to the ground. It paused there for a moment as though sniffing the stone, then raised itself up and looked directly towards the fruit cart.

Sylas could feel its keen eyes searching among the sacks.

Then, in one swift movement, the hunter threw its head back in the air and to his horror it let out a bloodcurdling, canine howl. Moments later it started forward and began sprinting at an astonishing speed towards them. The others changed direction and fell in behind, soon moving as one, striding perfectly in time, their massive claws beating out a single terrifying rhythm. Just moments later they were overtaken by the two Ghorhund, which flew across the square, baying lustily as they rejoined the hunt.

At that moment the fruit cart skidded round a corner into a busy road lined with shops and stalls. The smell of smoke became more powerful and Sylas could hear the chatter and bustle of crowds, but he was hardly aware of his surroundings. Instead his eyes were fixed on the corner that they had just turned, watching for the first sign of their pursuers. Simia pushed herself up on her hands to peer cautiously over the top of the sacks.

"We've got to get out of the cart," she said. "Wait for me to move, then do as I do."

Sylas nodded and eased himself a little off his haunches to make sure that he was ready. They passed a hanging sign bearing the words *The Mutable Inn* written in large ornate lettering.

"Now!" exclaimed Simia, and she stood up and launched herself into the air, falling quickly out of sight. He hauled himself to his feet and saw her land some distance away, staggering slightly and bracing herself against the wall of the inn. He heard the cry of the driver from behind and saw a number of faces turn in the street, but dared not look: he braced himself against the side of the cart and threw himself into the air. He cleared the muddy road and landed next to Simia on the stone terrace of the inn, grimacing from the pain in his knee.

Simia drew close to him. "Follow me inside," she said under her breath. "And, for the sake of Isia, cover up your trinket!"

He glanced at the bracelet shining brightly on his wrist and, with a glance up and down the busy street, he covered it with the muddy sleeve of his jacket. He saw Simia disappear through the large wooden door of the Mutable Inn, and he quickly followed her.

As he pulled it closed behind him, he heard a noise in the street. He was tempted to ignore it, but could not resist peering out through the small glass panel mounted in the door. Once again people were running, screaming and shouting as they glanced anxiously back down the road. Soon their cries were drowned out by the vicious howls of the Ghorhund: and then they came, their massive paws pounding into the dirt with such thunderous force that the door rattled on its hinges. People threw themselves to the ground, against walls and through doorways, as the two black beasts streaked past the inn, crashing through abandoned stalls and boxes, knocking those who moved too slowly to the ground and tearing the road into a shower of mud and grit that splattered the window. They sped on, driven wild by the hunt, oblivious to the pale face peering out at them from the inn.

Sylas watched as the poor people in the road stared fearfully after the Ghorhund, then slowly turned and looked the other way — their faces filling with a new terror. Those who had been thrown to the ground roused themselves and scrambled to the side of the road, heads lowered as if fearing a blow. He heard the Ghorhund reach the fruit cart in which they had escaped, announced by the crash of splintering wood followed by a chilling howl of triumph and the screams of the unfortunate driver.

Then, as a woman whimpered outside the inn door, three silent shadows moved in front of the window.

11

The Mutable Inn

"… such is their power to change the very fabric of the world."

THE DARK, ALMOST-HUMAN shapes were stooped forward, their heads sweeping low as they bounded lightly along the street, making so little sound that, were it not for the gentle fall of their feet in the mud, he would have thought them ghosts or apparitions. Sylas knew instinctively that even as they ran they could hear the slightest noise, and he found himself holding his breath as he watched. Their movement was wolfish and hungry, but they moved with remarkable control, striding in perfect unison and in precise formation. They took no notice of each other, their disfigured heads swinging from side to side as they took in the pale, fearful townsfolk at the sides of the street.

For the first time Sylas saw their faces and he felt his stomach turn. Their pendulous, hooded brow and monstrous jaw and cheekbones were almost canine, yet amid the patchwork of pale human skin and dark matted fur were quick, intelligent human eyes, seeing everything with a deliberateness and menace that was far from animal-like. They were both the handler and the hound: measuring the situation, scrutinising every detail of the street and all the while hunting as a pack. He felt the same creeping terror that he had seen in Simia. His chest tightened, the blood drained from his face and he took an involuntary step away from the door.

None of them seemed to see him at the window, or hear his short breaths, or sense his fear. As quickly as they had come, they were gone.

Sylas exhaled, his breath clouding the glass.

"What are you doing? Come on!"

He turned and saw Simia standing in the inner doorway. She beckoned to him urgently, then disappeared into the room beyond.

He gathered his nerves and followed her, leaving behind a distant sound of splintering wood, shouts and wails issuing from a neighbouring street.

The strong scent of smoke filled his nostrils as soon as he walked into the dimly lit interior of the inn. It was not the smoke that he had smelt on the street, or the smoke of cigarettes or pipes, but one with a weirdly sweet and fresh aroma. So strange was the scent that it took him a few moments to identify it as that of common, freshly cut green grass, spiced with burning tobacco. He looked about the gloomy room to try to find its source and saw scores of men huddled low over tables, most smoking long pipes, others gulping from metal tankards. Some raised their heads as he entered and stared at him steadily for a moment, but they soon lost interest and returned to their conversations. The low drone of voices was broken only by an occasional cough and peals of laughter from a table at the end of the room.

He looked for Simia and soon saw her balancing on the first rung of a stool at the bar, talking excitedly to a tall barman, who looked with interest over her shoulder towards Sylas. He had an odd appearance, with massive, clumsy-looking limbs and a long, doleful face that was made even longer by an overly long nose, a narrow mouth and a redoubtable chin that hung far below. But his most striking feature was the great shiny dome of his head, which at first seemed to bear some sort of hat or skullcap but, on closer inspection, revealed itself to be emblazoned with a vast array of tattoos: shapes, symbols and markings that encircled his crown to astonishing effect.

The barman leaned his large frame forward and rested his elbows on the bar, his piercing green eyes taking everything in. Sylas could feel them interrogating him, exploring his every feature until he had the distinct impression that they could even see what he was thinking. The strange man seemed to be looking into him, layer by layer, peeling them away like the pages of a book. Sylas shifted uncomfortably and, not knowing what else to do, smiled. The man held his gaze without responding, then turned back to Simia, said something and walked quickly to a door at the rear of the inn. As he opened it, he glanced back at Sylas and gave him a brief nod that looked almost like a bow, then disappeared into the darkness beyond.

Relieved to be freed from the man's penetrating gaze, Sylas turned to see Simia beckoning him to join her at the bar. To his surprise, she looked almost as cheerful and relaxed as she had before the chase: her cheeks had regained their ruddy colour and her eyes some of their lively sparkle. As he drew close, she leaned forward and whispered in his ear.

"We're safe, for now at least. Thanks to the cart we've broken the trail," she said with reassuring confidence, but without acknowledging that it had been Sylas's idea. She nodded towards the door at the rear. "Bowe is a friend. He's gone to check that the way is clear."

"Strange... it was like he could see right through me," said Sylas.

She laughed. "Oh, don't mind that — he just has a way of seeing things. It's what he does."

"What he... *does*."

"Yep," she said matter-of-factly, pushing herself up on to the barstool to peer out of the window to the street. "Now we should have some time for a *real* drink, if you fancy?"

He looked at her, bewildered by her calm — only moments ago they had been fleeing for their lives. But he could not deny his thirst.

"Sure," he said, heaving himself on to a neighbouring stool.

Simia reached over to an abandoned tankard on the bar and peered into it with interest, then held it out to him. Sylas looked at the dark green contents doubtfully, sloshing them around and sniffing at them, then raised the tankard to his lips. Carefully at first, then with increasing abandon, he drank down the contents. The flavour was decidedly odd but delicious: a mixture of lemons, rhubarb and woodsmoke. The combination was surprisingly sweet and refreshing. He finished it in large satisfying gulps, then set down the tankard with a loud belch. He was dimly aware of Simia watching him with keen interest and a suppressed smile.

"'Scuse me," he said. "That's great — what is it?"

He clamped his hand over his mouth.

With each word, clouds of pungent, sweet green smoke billowed between his lips. Simia shrieked with laughter and banged the counter with glee. He stared at her with a mixture of alarm and embarrassment, then parted two of his fingers and spoke quietly, trying in vain not to exhale as he did so.

"What *is* this stuff?" he mumbled, breathing out a succession of smoke signals depicted in glorious greens and yellows.

Simia was still heaving with laughter. "Oh, it's... sorry... *your face!*" She let out another shriek of delight, then worked hard to gather herself. "It's called Lemon Plume," she said, drawing a long breath. "It's a favourite with this lot — the Muddlemorphs."

"Muddlemorphs?" repeated Sylas with interest, seeing to his relief that the smoke was growing thinner and less noticeable.

"Pretty much everyone here is a Muddlemorph," she said. "They can change things — play around with stuff — change it from one thing into another. It's a weird kind of Kimiyya — the Third Way. They come here to work on the farms: making the soil better, cleaning the water, that kind of thing. Problem is, they love their tricks so much that they spend all their time showing them off to each other in taverns like this."

She jumped off her stool and pointed to the wooden seat. "Here, touch this."

Sylas hesitated, wondering if he was to be the butt of another joke, but reluctantly reached forward and touched the seat. He pulled his hand away sharply, and looked up at Simia who was beaming with delight.

"Weird, isn't it?" she said with a giggle.

He touched the seat again. To his amazement the wood bowed under his touch as though it was a cushion. He pressed his finger deep into it, and the grainy surface yielded; then he released it and it sprang back.

"Yes," he said, his broad face breaking into a smile. "Very weird."

He jumped off his own stool and found that it was the same. He walked over to a bench nearby and pressed on the wooden seat to find that the entire panel gave under the pressure of just one finger. "Magic..." he said quietly.

Simia walked over, her head cocked on one side. "But you have stuff like this in your world, don't you?"

He laughed. "You must be joking."

"But you *do* have magic," she said with a frown. "They told us so in school. What do you call it — sci... scient?"

Sylas frowned. "*Science?*"

"Yes, that's it."

"Well, there's not much magic in *science*," he said with a grin, thinking of Mr Prendergast, his befuddled science teacher at school.

She looked a little affronted. "Well, it always sounded magical to me," she said defensively. "Buildings that touch the sky, light that turns on and off, things that fly..." She flicked her fiery hair back off her face. "What's that if it's not magic?"

He looked at her for a moment and straightened his face. "You know, I hadn't seen it that way before," he said. "You're right, it *is* magical."

Simia still seemed a little put out.

Sylas had an idea. "If you like, sometime I'll show you how to make one of those things that flies."

Her eyes widened with excitement. "Really?"

"Sure," he said. "Your very own bird of paper and string."

She drew a sharp breath. "You know how to do that?"

"Your friend Bowe sees things... I make birds out of paper and string," he said with a wink. "It's what I do."

She clapped her hands in delight and looked about as if she wanted to tell someone straight away. Her eyes came to rest on the table from which there had been so much noise as they entered the inn and suddenly she seemed to be struck with a thought.

"Wait here," she said, jumping down from her stool.

She walked off at a pace and disappeared into the crowd that had gathered round the table at the rear of the inn. Sylas could hear her voice among the gathering followed by a brief silence, then he saw her fighting her way back towards him, weaving between arms and legs. She bore a triumphant expression as she marched back to her stool accompanied by a rather strange-looking young man. He was young and lean and had a huge crop of curly blond hair as unkempt as a wild hedge, with golden tufts erupting in all directions and great twirls and whirlpools formed in its centre. His clothes were of the same fashion: a threadbare shirt with several buttons undone, one sleeve gathered about his elbow and the other loose about his wrist, and a collar that stood to attention on one side. But while his hair and clothes were comically haphazard, his pale, angular face was quick and intelligent and he had a bold, decisive manner. He walked with long, ranging steps and, even as he first glimpsed Sylas, he fixed his narrow eyes upon him as though examining his every feature. His gaze was not as penetrating as that of the barman, but travelled swiftly over Sylas's face, his odd-looking, muddy clothes, his bloodied knee and the bag containing the Samarok, so that by the time he reached the bar he seemed to know Sylas's story.

"So are you going to introduce us?" he asked Simia in a sharp, youthful voice.

Simia waved her hand towards the stranger. "Sylas, this is Ash, one of the finest Muddlemorphs I know."

Ash gave a solemn bow.

"And Ash, this is Sylas, who has just had his first taste of Plume."

Ash raised his 'head and cocked an eyebrow. "Indeed?" he exclaimed. "Your very first taste? Rather a late starter, aren't you?"

Sylas smiled and shrugged. "We don't have Plume in... where I'm from."

"Is that so?" said Ash, looking intrigued. "A place without Muddlemorphing and without Plume? '*Whereimfrom*' sounds *very* interesting." He glanced at Simia and grinned. "This'll be fun."

He leapt up on to a stool, drew some stray strands of hair off his face then, with a quick glance over his shoulder to check that no one was looking, reached over the bar and helped himself to a tankard of Plume from a nearby keg. The strange fluid drained into the metal cup with a hiss and a fizz and puffs of green smoke rose from the brim, disappearing quickly into the air.

Sylas shot Simia a wary look. "What's this all about?" he whispered.

"Don't worry," she said, squeezing his arm. "We're just going to show you a bit of *our* kind of magic."

Ash held the tankard aloft like a trophy and lowered it in front of Sylas's face. "Let's play a game, Sylas," he said, handing him the cup. "Do you know how to blow shapes?"

"No," said Sylas, peering at the greenish surface of the Plume.

Ash looked questioningly at Simia. "He doesn't know much about much, does he?"

"Tell me about it..." she muttered.

Ash took a deep breath and thought for a moment, then seemed to have an idea.

"Right," he said, rolling up his sleeves. "Let's start simple. Take a swig of Plume."

Sylas looked doubtfully into the tankard then, with a wary glance at Simia, took a draught of the sweet, pungent fluid.

"Good. Now I want you to blow out — not too hard! — gently, that's right..."

Sylas exhaled slowly and his eyes widened as he saw a trail of bright green smoke drifting into the air, gradually forming a small cloud that hung above the bar.

"Yes, very good. Now this is the difficult bit. I want you to imagine the cloud turning in on itself, getting smaller and smaller.

Imagine the particles of smoke getting closer together, meeting up with each other..."

Sylas thought the whole thing rather strange, but there seemed no harm in trying, so he looked intently at the vivid green cloud — which even now was starting to disperse — and began to imagine its shape changing. He thought of the tiny particles of smoke and tried to hold them in his mind, then he thought of them pulling together, drawing inwards. He imagined the wispy, trailing edges of the cloud curling back until the puff of smoke became smaller, denser, less like a cloud than a floating ball of vivid green.

"I thought you'd never done this before."

So intent was Sylas on the task in hand that he hardly heard Ash's cry of surprise. His eyes were still fixed on the cloud, which was already shifting and changing, rolling and churning. It had begun to diminish, drawing into itself, curling back towards its centre. Before long, it was half its original size, its colour had become intense and it had formed a clearly discernible sphere of colour.

"That's it!" cried Ash, glancing at Simia and then back at Sylas and the ball of smoke. Then he whispered, "Now watch!"

He raised one hand and cupped it beneath the peculiar cloud.

Almost immediately Sylas saw the orb of smoke starting to change again — a slight deepening of colour, a coarsening of texture or perhaps an alteration in the light. But soon the metamorphosis was clear to see. The colour of the sphere began to drain out at the bottom, releasing a bright green powdery cascade like sand from an egg timer, which fell directly into Ash's waiting hand. Sylas could hardly believe his eyes as he saw a pile of green building in the centre of the young Muddlemorph's palm, no longer smoke but tiny particles of sparkling powder: *granules* of Plume. He looked up to see the final traces flowing out of the orb and beyond, Ash's face creased in an enigmatic smile.

"That," he said, "is Muddlemorphing."

Simia clapped enthusiastically and patted Ash on the back. Sylas leaned forward and stared in bafflement at the powder.

Ash raised his hand. "Take a pinch."

Sylas hesitated, unsure what might happen next.

"Go on — put it on your tongue."

He glanced doubtfully at Simia, but she nodded with enthusiasm, so he reached over, pinched some of the sugary substance between his fingers and dropped it on his tongue. The effect was instantaneous: a crackle and a fizz, a sharp tang on the taste buds, then a great torrent of flavour flowing down his throat and up his nose. It was exquisite but bewildering at the same time. Despite his best efforts, he found himself struggling to breathe, then he coughed and spluttered.

"And so here it is again!" cried Ash, pointing with pride to the puff of green smoke that Sylas had exhaled. Sylas looked up with watering eyes and saw Ash beaming with delight as the cloud drifted up to the same spot as the original, directly in front of Ash.

"Now quick, before it disappears!" cried the Muddlemorph. "You try to shape it this time — try something difficult... something like... like the tankard you drank it from!"

Still trying to catch his breath, Sylas turned his attention to the thinning cloud. He pictured a cone in his mind and then imagined the smoke filling it, taking its shape. Nothing happened for a moment, but then the cloud swirled, shifted and took the shape in his mind. There, hovering just above the bar, was a perfect tankard made of bright green smoke, no longer drifting but holding steady in the air.

Ash looked at Simia and Simia looked at Ash. They both seemed astonished.

"How did you do that?" asked Simia in a whisper.

No one was more surprised than Sylas. "I don't know," he said, clearing his throat. "I did what you told me."

Ash gazed from the cloud to Sylas and then back to the cloud in bewilderment, then seemed to find his presence of mind.

"Yes, well... I didn't know I was such a good teacher..." he said distractedly. "Anyway, back to the trick!"

He snatched Sylas's metal tankard from the bar and held it beneath the one made of smoke, then waved his other hand above it. Again the change was barely discernible at first: a slight shift and shimmer, a darkening in shade, but then there was a definite movement: the tankard of smoke tipped in the air. At the same moment Sylas saw to his astonishment that a green liquid was flowing from the lip, falling in a thin stream directly into the metal cup below. It drained away as quickly as it had formed and, as the last of the liquid fell, it simply disappeared.

"And there you are," said Ash, handing Sylas the cup. "Back to where you started."

Sylas peered over the brim and saw, to his surprise, that it was once again full almost to the top with churning, smoking Plume. He laughed and looked back at his companions.

"Great!" he cried.

Ash still seemed preoccupied by what he had seen. "You say you'd never made Plume shapes before?" he asked in a low voice.

Sylas shook his head. Again Ash and Simia exchanged a look.

"Do something for me," said Ash, gesturing for him to drink a little more Plume. "Try a few more shapes. I just want to see you do it again."

Sylas shrugged and took another swig of Plume, enjoying the intense aromas and flavours as it slid down his throat, then exhaled slowly, creating a billowing cloud of green smoke in front of him, larger than any of the ones before.

"Try something really difficult," said Simia excitedly, "like a ship, or — or a face or something."

Sylas's imagination was already at work, summoning the tall masts, bulging sails and webbed rigging of a galleon, its mighty prow rising and falling, heaving and yawing on conjured waves, and in the same moment the wisps of smoke gathered and joined to form those same shapes and motions: turning, twisting and drifting with Sylas's mind as if he was commanding it.

And then, as soon as the beautiful galleon had formed, his imaginings moved on again, leaving Simia staring in disbelief as sails, timbers and ropes dissolved into a cloud, which in turn started to take new shape: an oval — no, something human — a face, a female face with long flowing hair, traces of a brow, cheeks and an elegant neck formed of greenish trails of smoke. Then, impossibly, the face opened its mouth as if to speak...

There was a loud bang as a huge hand slammed down on the bar.

"Stop this!"

Sylas blinked as if from a trance and looked up to see Bowe glowering at his companions.

"You draw attention to yourselves like this? You must be mad!" growled the barman. "The Ghor are searching every building in the street! Now they're sure to be told that you've been here."

Only then did Sylas look past the thinning cloud of smoke into the room and see a wide circle of faces, all of them staring at him in wonderment. Beyond were more pipe-puffing, Plume-swilling Muddlemorphs jostling for position, trying to catch a glimpse of Ash and his strange companions. Instinctively he reached down and checked that his sleeve was covering the bracelet.

"The *Ghor* are after them?" hissed Ash.

Bowe nodded.

"Is that so?" murmured Ash, glaring at Simia. "You didn't tell me *that*!"

"You should know better anyway, Ash," said Bowe darkly. "You shouldn't be drawing attention with your childish tricks. And what are you doing playing around with Kimiyya anyway? You know that's not our way."

Ash dropped his eyes and mumbled something under his breath.

Bowe glared at him for a moment longer and then placed his massive hands behind Sylas and Simia, heaved them off their stools and ushered them towards the rear door, clearing a path in the crowd as he went.

Ash watched them go, still perplexed. "I'm not entirely sure that it was *me* doing the tricks..."

He raised a hand to bid them farewell.

Sylas entered a dark, damp hallway that sloped downwards towards a flight of stone stairs lit by a single oil lamp. As soon as the door closed, Bowe seized his hand.

"Sorry about that," he said, in his deep, slightly ponderous voice. "It's a pleasure to meet you." He pulled his face into an amiable smile and pumped Sylas's hand up and down. By contrast to his rather cumbersome manner, his deep green eyes were lively and moved quickly over Sylas's face, tracing every line and form. A slight frown seemed to pass over his face, as though something about what he had seen confused him, but it was gone in an instant.

"And you," said Sylas, nodding a little formally. "Thank you for helping us."

"You're with friends now," said Bowe, leaning in a little. "Though trust no one but Simia until she gets you safely to the river. No one — understand?"

Sylas nodded, his gaze lingering for a moment on Bowe's eyes, taking in their deep, watery green and the great sadness etched in the heavy brow above and dark rings beneath. As before, there was something deeply magnetic about his gaze, as though his dolorous eyes were looking beyond what most could see.

Sylas suddenly became aware that he was staring. "What's at the river?" he blurted.

Bowe smiled, as if reading his mind. "Friends," he said. "Friends and a place of safety. If anyone knows anything of this journey of yours, or what it has to do with your mother, then you will find them at the river."

Sylas's eyes widened. "My mother? How did you—"

"One thing at a time, my young friend. For now, just concentrate on getting to the river, for many perils lie between here and there." Bowe smiled his wide, gentle smile, and patted Sylas on the shoulder.

"Is the coast clear?" asked Simia, starting to descend the stone staircase.

Bowe glanced at her. "Before your antics in the bar it was," he grumbled. "Now I'll have to double-check."

As they clambered down the stairs, Sylas stared at Bowe with new interest. The strange tattoos on the dome of Bowe's bald head looked oddly like concentric rings of eyes, each worked in perfect detail, some looking up, some down, some left and some right, some half concealed beneath an eyelid, others wide open and staring straight back at him. There was also a word tattooed in a different, lighter ink on the back of his skull... *NAEO*.

Sylas stepped off the bottom stair and entered a room stacked high with beer kegs and racks of wine and lit by a row of lamps on the far wall. The hubbub of the inn had faded and now all that could be heard was the drip of water from the dark ceiling, which echoed across the chamber. Simia was already halfway down a long aisle between two racks of wine and Sylas caught up with her at the other end, where she had paused next to a small oak door.

"I'll go first," said Bowe, striding up from behind.

He turned a lock in the door and pulled it open. Beyond, there was a long stone ramp, leading upwards to a trapdoor. He climbed it in a few steps and knelt down on the damp flagstones. To Sylas's surprise, instead of lifting the trapdoor and peering outside he simply lowered his head as if to listen and closed his eyes: silent and brooding.

"He's a Scryer," whispered Simia, seeing Sylas's confusion. "He doesn't need eyes to know what's going on. He senses the things that connect people — thoughts, feelings, stuff like that. If anything's out there looking for us, he'll know."

Sylas looked up and watched with renewed interest as Bowe squatted with his head bowed and his eyes firmly shut. "So can he... tell what I'm thinking?" he asked, running over his thoughts since they had entered the inn.

"Not really. But he can tell what you're thinking about *people*, and what they're thinking about you. It's strange. You never quite get used to it." There was a short silence. "So think of my good points, all right?"

Sylas smiled. "You'll have to let me know what they are."

She gave him a sharp jab with her elbow and grinned.

As they waited in the darkness, Sylas thought about Bowe's strange gift and what he must have seen — he had not even been aware of thinking about his mother, which made him feel a pang of guilt and frustration. How could he think of anything else? He really should be trying to find her. What if all this was just taking him further away from her? But Bowe had said that he might find answers if he—

"Come! Now!" hissed Bowe from the top of the ramp.

As they climbed, Bowe stood to his full height and hoisted the trapdoor back on its hinges, letting in a shaft of bright light. They squinted but kept moving out on to a muddy lane.

They found themselves looking at a row of abandoned carts and a long line of stable doors, from which peered the long faces of mules and donkeys. The lane ran parallel with the road on the other side of the inn, leading to the back doors and stores of the many shops and taverns. It was deserted but for some workmen loading boxes and cloth bags into a cart.

"You should be all right as long as you move quickly," said Bowe, still flicking his eyes up and down the lane. "Go via the Lord's Chamber — it's risky but they won't be expecting it."

Simia nodded and stepped out into the lane.

"Thanks, Bowe," said Sylas with a brief smile, turning to leave.

Bowe reached out and caught his shoulder with his free hand. The Scryer fixed him with his large green eyes and his face creased with a slight frown of confusion. He seemed about to say something, but then changed his mind.

"Don't forget, Sylas, you have many friends."

Sylas looked quizzically into Bowe's eyes and smiled. "I won't."

They turned and ran as fast as they could down the lane. The grey canopy of cloud parted a little and rays of sunlight fanned out across the town, touching the alley ahead of them as though to light the way. The golden beams drove away the greyness, glinting off wet rooftops and shining brightly off the puddles.

As they darted down another small alleyway, the rays caught the bracelet on Sylas's wrist, sending out a glorious shower of silver light, which for a moment gave Bowe's eyes new fire as he stared after the running children. A frown passed over his face as he pondered what he had just seen.

Then, to his surprise, tears welled in his eyes.

12
The Lord's Chamber

*"His empty eyes search tirelessly for what drives us on; but
they see nothing, for what can the soulless see of a soul?"*

THE ALLEYWAY LED BETWEEN two large houses and Sylas tried to
peer in at windows as they ran, keen to see a little more of this
strange world. But the rooms were usually dark, and when he
saw a fire or a lamp, it never showed anything of the interior. He
longed to stop and look more closely, but Simia ran as swiftly as
ever on her short legs and he found it difficult enough to keep up.

They turned left and then right and he found himself running
a little downhill on a stone pathway between more houses, then
clambering up a number of stone steps past some stables.

Suddenly his senses were assailed by the sights and sounds
of a busy street market. Mules, carts and people thronged its
centre while the pavements, such as they were, heaved with
stalls displaying a baffling array of goods. From where he stood
Sylas could see vegetables, dried meats, cakes, pies, eggs, flour,
coloured powders and bottles filled with liquids that he could
only guess at. But, despite the variety of colours and shapes and
smells, there was no doubt about what type of market this was.

The silvery flanks of fish dripped from lines above every other counter and carpeted almost every stall, and the stench caught in his throat as he made his way between the crowds of shoppers. Tables brimmed with trout and perch, heaved with pike and eel, and groaned under the weight of salmon. It seemed to him that all the fish were larger than he had encountered before and their scales somehow cleaner and brighter.

Simia slowed her pace to whisper in Sylas's ear. "Not far now," she said, "but this bit's dangerous. Keep your eyes down and don't run. Whatever happens, don't run."

He nodded and fell in behind her, forcing himself to keep his eyes ahead, despite the bustle and noise around him. Soon he became aware that there were no longer any stalls on his left and in their place were great white marble steps. The noise from the street market altered, echoing from the mass of stone that now loomed above him. Out of the corner of his eye he saw a vast white pillar rising high above his head, so thick at its base that it took him several paces to walk past. Beyond there was darkness: a shady recess that shrouded the rest of the building from view. Moments later they were passing another immense pillar made of the same smooth, white stone and he was desperately tempted to turn his head to see what he could of the great chamber. Very slowly he allowed his eyes to drift from Simia's back to the lowest of the steps.

Suddenly a shifting shadow made him hold his gaze.

As he drew closer, it moved again — only slightly, but enough to convince him of a figure standing just a few paces away, at the top of the steps. He held his breath and moved his head slightly so that he could see a little more. His skin crawled. Standing almost completely still next to the nearest pillar was an immense stooped shape that looked almost human, but even without looking up he could make out dark, fur-clad, muscular legs that were so distorted, so horrifyingly malformed with their swept-back knees and gigantic hooked claws that Sylas was glad he could see no more. He drew his eyes back to Simia and saw that she was walking faster, seeming even smaller and slighter than normal.

Then the creature spoke. It was a mixture of low growls, wheezing breaths and the harsh raspings of a long, canine tongue. Sylas imagined unseen eyes watching him from above and half expected to feel the grip of a large hand or claw on his collar. But the figure did not reach for him, or shift from its station. Soon he was past it and drawing close to the next pillar. The reply came moments later: a gravelly snarl that reverberated in the dark recesses of the building. Again Sylas shrank away, expecting to see a gigantic figure emerging from the shadows to seize him and drag him away, but nothing happened. He walked on, head still lowered, and soon the pillars and the sounds and the white steps disappeared behind him. He released his breath and allowed himself to look up just in time to see Simia stop in the entrance to a small lane. She flashed him a triumphant smile.

He walked up to her. "Were they the Ghor?" he asked breathlessly.

Simia looked past him back towards the building and nodded. "But those ones weren't looking for us, they were just guards. They're only around when something important is going on."

"What's happening?" asked Sylas.

She raised her eyebrows. "You," she said. "*You're* happening."

Sylas pressed his hand to his chest. "Me? They're all here for *me*?"

"Yes, I think so." She looked at him steadily. "It's not every day that the Passing Bell rings, you know."

He looked nervously back down the street towards the

138

building. It was a vast, white, blockish structure with six huge columns along its front, supporting a gigantic flat stone roof. The edge was decorated with inscriptions and symbols, the most striking of which was at the very centre, between the two middle pillars: it was a huge empty face with no features except two hollow, staring eyes. Sylas found his gaze drawn to it, captured by its ghoulish glare that somehow seemed to look straight back at him, spying him in his hiding place. He recoiled and looked away, turning instead to the long inscription depicted in giant red lettering. He tried to read it, but the alphabet was strange.

"What does that say?" he asked, nodding in its direction.

Simia took a cursory look. "It says, 'Stop gawping and get moving'."

He glared at her.

She sighed. "It's the Devotion to Thoth. It says, 'Our Dream, Our Fullest Joy, Our Second Soul.'" She gave a snort of derision. "Or something like that. Anyway, it may mean something to that lot —" she nodded out into the busy street — "but it doesn't mean anything to us."

"Thoth — is he like... a king?"

"Thoth isn't *like* anything — he's just Thoth." She glared hatefully at the inscription. "His name is Thoth, but they call him stuff like 'the Dirgh' and 'the Priest of Souls'. They don't mean anything. They just hide what he really is."

"Which is?" asked Sylas, noticing that her fists were clenched tightly at her sides.

"A murderer," she said, and then looked away. She was silent for a moment and then added abruptly: "This isn't the place to be talking. Especially about him. Let's get going."

Sylas took a final look at the strange inscription and the empty face of Thoth. The thrill he had felt after passing the Ghor had now completely left him: in its place was a hollowness, a slow and creeping dread.

He blew out his cheeks. "I don't like this…" he muttered to himself.

Simia threw her hands wide. "*Now* do you see what we're—"

Just then there was a commotion on the street and they both turned to see what was happening. Among the drab clothing of the crowds they saw a flash of bright crimson flanked by the towering figures of six Ghor guards, which growled and lashed out as they forced a path through the throng. They reached the steps of the Lord's Chamber in a few strides and then parted to let someone pass. The tall, elegant figure climbing the steps was clad in shimmering crimson robes that flapped and billowed in the gentle breeze. Sylas could see little at this distance, but he could make out her dark skin and her proud, confident gait: the way she brushed imperiously past the attendant guards and, when she turned, the way she commanded silence over the crowd without a word.

"This is worse than I thought," whispered Simia. "That looks like Scarpia, the most vicious of Thoth's Magrumen."

Suddenly the crowd murmured and parted as another figure emerged, this time dragged by two of the Ghor guards, his head hanging between his hunched shoulders and a gaping wound in one of his legs.

They both stiffened. It was the driver of the fruit cart.

Sylas covered his mouth. "Oh my God…"

Scarpia gave a small gesture with one hand and suddenly one of the guards lunged at the poor captive, grasping his neck between its jaws and heaving him up into the air, crushing him against one of the columns. The poor wretch let out a desperate scream and struggled weakly, but his efforts only enraged his captor, who threw him even more viciously against the stone. Scarpia turned to the crowd and shouted some kind of pronouncement while pointing at the wagoner.

"She's making an example of him," muttered Simia, shaking her head.

The Ghor guard swiped at the face of the driver with a claw, which was enough to knock him unconscious, his head slumping to his chest and his arms falling to his sides. Scarpia gesticulated at the guard, who dropped him in a heap on the floor.

Her point made, Scarpia turned with a flourish of her robes and, kicking the wagoner's arm out of her path, strode into the shadowy recesses of the chamber. The guards followed her in formation and the last one grasped the poor wagoner's skull and dragged him inside.

"*That's* what happens when they catch you," said Simia, turning to Sylas.

He felt sick. He looked at Simia palely for a moment, then nodded. "Let's go."

They turned and broke into a run.

He followed her over the rough, cracked paving stones into the gloomy backstreets of the town. They ran and ran, grateful to be leaving the horrifying scene far behind. Sylas kept replaying the awful image of the poor captive falling limp against the column. *Because of me*, he thought. *Because of me.*

The further they went, the more pungent became the smell of fish. Fishing nets lay drying in the lanes and discarded fish heads and tails lay in piles next to open doors, from which issued the clatter of knives against chopping boards. Just as Sylas started to wonder whether they would ever leave this foul-smelling maze of lanes, they rounded a corner and emerged into the light.

Suddenly they were surrounded by open space. Ahead lay a

wide expanse of mud that sloped steeply towards a granite-grey river. It snaked past them, turned sharply and disappeared behind the houses that crowded its banks.

Sylas's eyes were drawn to a flurry of motion to his left. There, on the near bank of the river, casting a broad shadow over much of the muddy slope, was a gigantic waterwheel. It rose perhaps three storeys above the surface of the river, almost as tall as the mill house to which it was attached and towering above the houses at the top of the bank. It turned with remarkable speed given its size, powered by a fierce torrent of water that churned at its base. Its huge blades plunged deep into the passing current and erupted in a cascade of froth and foam to soar high into the air, trailing silvery curtains of water beneath. He could hear the thunderous maelstrom even from the top of the bank.

"Impressive, eh?" Simia looked at him with a proud smile, twisting a lock of hair between her fingers.

He nodded. "What's it for?"

"It's a Gristmill. You know, for milling wheat, corn, that kind of thing." She leaned over to whisper in his ear. "Except it's not. It's not that at all."

She flashed him a grin and walked off at a pace towards the mill, swinging her arms confidently at her sides. Sylas stepped out on to the mud and followed her, hoping that this might be the end of his journey: his knee throbbed and he was all too aware of a gnawing hunger in his stomach and a heaviness in his arms.

"Is this it?" he called after Simia.

Simia frowned and put her finger to her lips. "Yes," she whispered. "Don't worry, there's a lot more to it than you'd think."

They reached the bottom of the bank and mounted the stone platform at the base of the mill, heading for a staircase that led up to an arched door. The platform and steps were made of large blocks of white stone so neatly finished that the cracks were hardly visible, giving it the appearance of a single piece of rock. When Sylas looked up, he saw that the towering sides of the mill house were made in the same way and to his left he could see another similar high wall winding off into the distance, which looked as though it bordered a garden.

Sylas expected to start climbing the steps to the door, but before they reached them, Simia changed direction. She walked confidently through the spray, leading him towards the river's edge and the great wheel. He watched the raging torrent as it rushed past where they stood, its boiling surface forming great standing waves as it flowed out into the main stream of the river. The only other noise he could hear was the groaning of the vast limbs of the wheel — each the size of a tree trunk — emerging from behind the wall of the mill and sweeping through the air, climbing upwards at dizzying speed.

Simia turned. "It's OK, just follow me!" she shouted, barely audible even though she was only inches away.

He watched doubtfully as she walked to the edge of the platform, let her foot drift out over the side and then dropped down directly into the path of the gigantic wheel. He was about to exclaim when she seemed to find her footing and was soon descending steadily out of view. He stepped to the very edge of the platform and peered over. There, leading directly down to the foaming water, was another small stone staircase that could not be seen from the bank. A metal ring was set into the last step, to which was tied a rowing boat that danced and bucked on the waves. Simia jumped into it, regained her balance and busied herself fixing a pair of oars in the rowlocks.

Sylas cast his eyes warily up at the passing blades, then

lowered himself carefully down the steps, taking care not to slip on the wet, mossy surface. When he reached the bottom, he stepped into the boat and quickly nestled down among some empty sacks, glad to take the weight off his legs. The blades of the wheel passed terrifyingly close to their heads and the timbers of the boat trembled as they were pounded by the waves, but Simia seemed entirely unconcerned as she prepared the boat. After a few moments she leaned fearlessly over the side, untied the rope from the metal ring and pushed off.

The boat was whisked downstream in an instant, but she pulled on one of the oars and turned it out into the river, away from the main current. She then began heaving them through the water, drawing the vessel back towards the water mill. The sight of her rowing was both marvellous and comical to behold, for the oars were far too long for her tiny frame. At the top of each stroke she had to stand to her full height, leaning backwards to draw the oars through the water, and then she would sit down with a thump on the seat, gritting her teeth and yanking them out of the water to begin the cycle again. All this she did with an expression of fierce determination, which brought a quiet smile to Sylas's lips.

She propelled them in this fashion until they were alongside the wheel, just an oar's length from where its huge blades plunged into the water. They were pounding the surface of the river so violently that he began to get alarmed, but Simia remained reassuringly calm. She seemed to be waiting for something. He followed her eyes back to the wheel's slicing blades and thought that he saw them slow a little. Moments passed and he became certain: the wheel was gradually coming to a halt. He could now see between the sweep of each beam that formed the spokes of the wheel and although they still dropped sheets of water he could make out the mossy stone of the mill house. The more he looked, the more he realised that there was something strange about it. There was a small rectangular opening at its centre — a door that led into the depths of the mill, flickering dimly with torchlight.

"Is that the way in?"

"Yep," said Simia, her eyes still fixed on the wheel.

Sylas looked at the thundering waters. "So how do we get to it?"

She flicked her red hair back. "Like this!"

She stood up and yanked on one of the oars, spinning the boat in the water, then with two swift heaves, she propelled them directly between two of the passing beams. He threw himself down into the bottom of the boat and was drenched by a deluge of water. The boat rose and fell alarmingly on the waves and he felt the firm clunk of the bow striking something.

But there was no shuddering jolt or crash of splintering wood.

When he opened his eyes, he saw that they were already through. Above him was the baffling latticework of the wheel and the great axle spinning at its centre; to one side the blades still plunged past making the boat leap and twist on the surface, and on the other the solid, mossy stones of the mill house towered above him.

He looked around for Simia.

"Up here!"

She grinned from the dark opening above, already tying the mooring rope to a ring. She held out her hand and helped him to clamber up on to the slippery doorstep.

He found himself in a cool, dark passageway that disappeared into shadows a few paces ahead.

"Welcome to Meander Mill," she said.

"Thanks, can we use the front door next time?" he grumbled.

She laughed. "It has to be like that to keep it a secret. Of course, the others slow the wheel down a lot more... but where's the fun in that?"

He saw the white flash of her smile in the gloom. She leaned to one side and grasped a large iron lever in the wall, then pulled it down. There was a loud clang of metal against metal somewhere above his head, followed by a sound like sliding chains or gears falling into place. Then the floor began to move.

The glassy black eyes squinted as though they would peer through the very stones of the mill. For some time they were motionless, fixed to the place where the children had disappeared, now shrouded in curtains of water. But, as a beam of sunlight moved across the waterwheel, changing the drab scene into a dazzling display of glistening wood and shimmering water, so the eyes moved. They took in the perfectly crafted stone walls of the building, lingered on the odd-looking red-tiled roof that seemed to glint and scatter the light as though it was inset with metal or glass, and then they fell slowly past the top of the wheel, back down to the flurry of water and foam.

"Come, we can't do any more," came a gruff voice from somewhere behind.

The creature blinked away some spray, which fell like a tear on to pallid skin, then dripped on to the snout below. There was a brief nod and the oily eyes flicked towards the opposite shore.

The canoe surged away, the bow gliding effortlessly through the waves.

13
Sanctuary

"... all thoughts must turn from great to simple things: instead of glory, survival; instead of all that was promised, sanctuary."

THE SHAFT WAS UTTERLY black — a thick, disorienting blackness that closed in on them as they left the passageway far below. Deprived of sight, Sylas's other senses sharpened: the clanking of chains in some unseen part of the mill seemed unbearably loud, the smell of damp and oil in the air became overpowering and he felt as though the lurching motion of the platform would throw him off balance. But he was curiously calm as they climbed through the darkness, almost glad that his tired eyes would see no more wonders, at least for now.

As the clanking of the chains faded, a new and unexpected sound echoed down the dark shaft.

It was a solitary singing voice.

The tune was carefree and playful like a nursery rhyme, but the voice was old and dry. The more he listened, the more he began to hear distinct sounds and words. To his surprise, they were not joyful and childish as was the tune, but full of sorrow:

"And so we change as change we must,
When standards rot and sabres rust,
When the sun is set and night is come,
When all is lost, when naught is won."

When the voice reached the end of this verse, it started again at the beginning, repeating the words exactly as before, but this time they seemed more poignant and simpler. The melody became more haunting, as if in sympathy with the words. As the platform rose through the darkness, it grew louder and the effect became more powerful, as though new sorrows were added to the heartache. Simia started to hum the simple tune, and the melody was soon echoing about them and resonating in the depths of the shaft below.

Sylas began to see a vision forming in his mind. To begin with it was a blur of meaningless shapes formed in shades of grey and brown, but in moments the bleak image became clear — it was a rotting purple flag bearing a single silver feather, fluttering limply over a misty battlefield. The image did not stay solid in his mind and soon the grey mist engulfed the standard, at the same time rolling back to reveal a long line of dishevelled, bloodied men staggering, limping and crawling towards a dark horizon. Near at hand and against the backdrop of a mighty sea, he saw women crying in despair, crying for their fallen fathers, brothers and sons.

As these imaginings became too real to bear — as he began to feel his spirits fall into a deep melancholy — there was a loud rattle above his head and the singing stopped.

An instant later he was bathed in sunshine.

Shielding his eyes, Sylas looked up and saw two doors sliding back to reveal a large perfectly circular opening that glowed with golden light. As his eyes adjusted, he found that they were ascending between the great doors and leaving the darkness behind.

The platform came to an abrupt stop, making him totter forward. He felt Simia's steadying hand on his arm.

"This," she whispered in his ear, "is where we hide."

He rubbed his eyes and looked about him.

They were standing in the centre of a great round chamber that towered above them, soaring to an astonishing height. The platform upon which he and Simia had been standing formed a kind of stage, surrounded in all directions by row upon circular row of wooden seats, each higher than the last. It was like a theatre with the stage at the centre. All of the fittings – the chairs, the stage, the steps that ran up to the highest benches at the back – were constructed from a great confusion of driftwood: cracked planks, broken rudders, mildewed deck timbers, nameplates and gangplanks. The entire hall was heaving with detritus from the river. The air itself carried a pungent but pleasant scent of its waters, so that all in all it was as though they had once flowed through this ancient room and, over the years, deposited the river's bounty of wrecks and maritime waste.

And amid these choice prizes there was one feature that truly stood out: each and every seat sported a quaint canopy of wood, tall enough so that someone could sit within it, but not so high that it would obscure the view from the row behind and, as Sylas looked more closely, he saw that these odd alcoves were in fact the upturned prows of small boats, pointing directly up towards the ceiling. The effect was to create – from a graveyard of simple wreckage – a theatre fit for kings.

But his eyes did not linger on the strange woodwork, or the high stone walls hung about with fishing nets, or the many ceilings far above; instead they dwelt upon the vast space in its middle, for it was criss-crossed by countless shafts of light. The beams bounced off large porthole-like mirrors mounted on the stone walls, each placed with precision to catch the light and pass it on to the next. The result was a latticework of sunlight that only became more and more beautiful and intricate as he raised his eyes. The chamber seemed to narrow above his head where it met a circular balcony supported on columns constructed from sawn-off masts: the first of a series of such structures built one above the other. All of them left a round space at the centre through which the beams could pass. Finally, at the very top of the mill house, there was a ring of blinding light, which seemed to be the source of all the light in the room. Sure enough it dimmed slightly as the sun passed behind a cloud and at the same moment all of the beams in the great round hall faded. A moment later it brightened again and the hall was once more bathed in wondrous golden sunshine.

"We take it for granted, but light can be so beautiful, don't you think?"

It was the singing voice.

Sylas first saw her at the top of the steps behind the rear circle of seats, standing with her back to him and looking into a dark, glassy panel that circled the hall. She was slight of stature, standing little above Sylas's own height, but she carried herself with an unmistakable authority: straight-backed in her long burgundy robe. It was decked with glittering insignia and the braiding shimmered around her cuffs, tracing a radiant line down one arm. But it was her bright silvery hair that was her most distinctive feature, for it fell in a long ponytail all the way down to her waist, and in it was a braid of the same colour as the gown.

"It's very beautiful," said Sylas. His voice echoed loudly around the hall, making him flinch.

The woman turned away from the panel and smiled. Her face

was lined with age, but her pearly skin glowed in the golden light and her dark eyes sparkled.

"Yes, indeed," she said with a slight nod of the head. "We may have to hide, but it will not be under a rock! Isn't that right, Simia?"

Simia laughed lightly and nodded.

"You are from the bell?"

"Yes," replied the girl, rocking on her ankle.

"And it was the Passing Bell? You're sure?"

"Yes. It was just like you said it would be."

The woman turned her eyes back to Sylas and looked him up and down with interest.

"And were you followed?"

"Chased, but not followed," said Simia. "We came through the inn — Bowe helped us."

The woman nodded, seeming satisfied. Her eyes moved back to Sylas and the hall fell silent.

He shifted nervously, glancing about the room. He looked at the dark, glassy panel into which the woman had been staring and for a moment he thought that it altered a little as he watched, as though something was moving inside.

Simia started fidgeting next to him as if she too found the silence more than she could bear and suddenly she spoke in a flurry of words.

"He says he isn't a Bringer, but he's wearing a bracelet that looks just like a Bringer's and he seems to know absolutely nothing about anyth—"

The woman raised her hand and frowned.

"Simia! I'm sure our guest will speak for himself."

Simia made a point of pursing her lips as though gluing them together.

The woman turned back to Sylas and smiled warmly.

"My name is Filimaya."

He smiled nervously. "I'm Sylas — Sylas Tate."

"Welcome, Sylas. I trust you're well after your journey?"

"I'm fine, just tired."

"But of course you are," said the woman. "And that's to say nothing of your knee." She moved swiftly down the steps and motioned them towards the bench nearest to the platform. "Come and sit down at once!"

Sylas frowned. "How did you know about my knee?" he asked, sitting on the nearest of the seats.

Filimaya smiled enigmatically and sat down on the platform to face him.

For the first time he saw her face in detail. She had elegant, kindly features, with the fine bones and pretty, tapering eyes of a woman who, although handsome to this day, had once been a great beauty. Despite her amiable features and the kindness in her eyes, he also saw an unmistakable sadness: a sadness that blended so well with her smile that it seemed almost an illusion.

She raised her eyebrows. "So it seems that you're not familiar with our ways." She looked down and took hold of his ankle, then tugged at his trouser leg. Sylas drew a sharp breath as she pulled the material away from the dried blood around his wound and peered at a cut that ran all the way down the side of his knee. "That is rather strange for a Bringer."

"But I'm not a Bringer. I don't even know what a Bringer *is*. I keep telling Simia that all this is an accident — all I really want to do is to find my mother!"

Filimaya looked at him quizzically. "Your *mother*?"

"Yes. That's what I'd be doing if I wasn't here," he said,

sounding more frustrated than he intended. "I should be trying to find her."

"Well, we must speak about her. But all in good time."

She pushed his muddy trouser leg further up to the knee exposing a large graze. He reached down instinctively to stop the pain, but she caught him by the arm.

"You are not a Bringer," she said, glancing at his wrist, "and yet you are wearing the Merisi Band."

Her fine fingers ran over the smooth metal surface, first on the silver half, and then on the gold.

"But I don't even know what that is — it was given to me."

Filimaya looked astonished.

"Strange, isn't it?" exclaimed Simia eagerly, taking the opportunity to join the conversation. "But that isn't the best bit — tell her what's in the..."

"Simsi, I shan't tell you again," said Filimaya sternly. "I want to hear what Sylas has to tell me."

Simia flinched and snapped her mouth shut, looking a little wounded.

"Who gave it to you, Sylas?" asked Filimaya.

"A man called Espen — the man who helped me to reach the bell. I was being chased by a dog or — or something like a dog."

"A Ghorhund?"

"Yes, I suppose so."

"And it came to find you?"

He shrugged. "I think so — it was just waiting for me when the bell started to ring."

She put her hand over his knee. He expected her hand to hurt, but it felt soft and soothing. "You heard the bell ringing?" she asked, pulling something from a pocket in her robe.

"Yes — from my room."

"And you were the only one? The only person to hear it?" She raised a small bottle and began pouring a green fluid between her fingers.

"Yes," he replied. The ointment felt pleasantly cool as it trickled over his wound. "But other people seemed to know about it — like Espen, and Herr Veeglum, and I think that Mr Zhi must have known…"

He stopped mid-sentence. Filimaya was looking at him in utter consternation.

"I *told* you it was all very strange," said Simia, clearly enjoying her reaction.

"You know him, Sylas?" asked Filimaya. "Mr Zhi?"

Sylas looked up from his knee and lifted his chin. "Yes, I do," he said.

A smile curled the corners of her mouth. "Then we have a *great* deal to talk about," she said, "but not here — we must go upstairs."

She pulled her long train of silver hair over her shoulder and then rose briskly to her feet and held out a hand to him. He took it, but continued to stare in bewilderment at his knee.

It was healed.

There was no blood, no wound, no graze — not even any of the green fluid that she had poured between her fingers.

Filimaya simply smiled and drew him forward.

They walked briskly up the aisle towards the outside of the hall and then turned sharply behind the great sweeping row of upturned boats, following a curving walkway covered with a thick green carpet. It seemed to run round the entire circumference of the hall, bordered on one side by the jutting prows of launches and rowing boats and on the other by the dark, glassy panel that rose from the floor to a point high above Sylas's head. He found himself leaning as far as he could from this strange surface, for on more than one occasion shadows seemed to gather, change and move somewhere within. When he turned his head towards it, he could see nothing but a greenish blackness and his own dishevelled image staring back.

However, soon he saw an area where the zigzagging beams of light fell directly on to the glassy panel, illuminating the murky greenness. As they approached the patch of light, there was a sudden rush of movement. He blinked and peered hard into the gloom, but it had disappeared. Seconds later he saw it again – by Filimaya's shoulder – a rapid swirl of silvers, oranges and reds, and then again in another halo of light at her waist.

The colours had shape and form. It was a shoal of fish, gliding silently behind a panel of glass.

He turned to Simia with wide eyes. She grinned back.

"Filimaya," she said, tugging the old woman's sleeve. "Can we show Sylas the Aquium before we go up?"

Filimaya slowed her step and smiled. "You're quite right, Simia, we're forgetting our manners." She turned to Sylas. "You really haven't seen Meander Mill until you've seen the Aquium."

She raised one hand to the centre of the great hall and, very slowly, dropped her arm. As it fell, so the great lattice of light above them moved and stretched as each and every beam shifted in unison – not greatly, but subtly so that Sylas wondered if he was seeing things. As he lowered his eyes back down to the panel, he saw that all of the beams were now moving towards it, bathing it in pools of light. Soon a great arc of light was moving over the glass, making it glow a deep, rich green.

Simia squeezed his arm. "Isn't it wonderful?" she whispered.

He was looking at something of astonishing beauty. Behind the panel, which he could see now was made entirely of glass, was an expanse of green water that in places churned and shimmered with the silvery shapes of hundreds of fish. They moved in huge shoals: gliding, turning, spiralling and darting into and out of the green wall of water. Some were long and sleek, others round and broad, some had orange fins, some red, and others still were silver all over, but all moved together in a breathtaking dance of light and colour. He watched as one large shoal swam swiftly from one side of the hall to the other, rising and dipping to avoid others as they went. The fish moved so effortlessly and yet so perfectly in unison that they reminded him of the flock of tiny birds that he had seen in the Shop of Things.

"It's amazing," he said quietly.

"Look behind you," said Simia.

Sylas turned slowly and looked. He retreated into one of the upright boats.

Simia giggled with delight. "Beautiful, isn't it?"

He nodded slowly without taking his eyes from the panel. He was looking at an entire wall of fish, their glittering flanks teeming against the glass from the floor to the very top. The sight was wondrous: a vast, glorious work of art depicted in life itself, its colours, shades and forms shifting and changing constantly. Each and every fish was in motion, moving between, beneath and above those around it as if searching for the perfect position in the teeming shoal. Although their efforts at first seemed random and disorganised, Sylas soon saw that they had a purpose: they were trying to stay close to Filimaya. At her shoulder a great vortex of fish turned in endless circles as they seemed to take their turn to be the closest to her. She appeared entirely unaware of this commotion, looking instead at Sylas, enjoying his delight.

"What…" he blurted after another long silence. "Why are they here?"

Filimaya looked a little surprised. "Well, that *is* an odd question," she said, cocking her head to one side in puzzlement. "We hardly need a *reason* to surround ourselves with beautiful things. But I suppose, if they have another purpose, it is to remind us of our place."

Sylas furrowed his brow. "Your *place*?"

"Our place in the world," she replied, as if this should be obvious. "Our place in Nature. Now come, for we may have only a short time to talk."

She turned and set off along the green carpet, her robes billowing about her. The vast shoal of fish shifted behind the glass and then began gliding in the same direction, rolling and turning as it went.

Soon they had reached a wooden staircase that partially blocked the way ahead. It climbed beyond the top of the Aquium, then twisted with the curve of the wall to the first balcony high above. Filimaya danced lightly up the steps with the ease and energy of a young woman. Simia scrambled to keep up, but Sylas lingered for a moment on the bottom step, letting his eyes drift back to the great shoal of fish at his shoulder.

He bit his lip and then drew his hand across its cool surface of the glass. Instantly the fish turned and began teeming beneath his fingers. He gasped and drew his hand away. In the same moment the shoal calmed and once again slowed to a gentle churning motion. He glanced up the steps and, checking that no one was watching, threw his arm out across the glassy surface of the tank. Even before his arm was outstretched, the great shoal had responded, wheeling about and, with a flurry of tails, setting out in the direction of his sweeping hand. However, they did not stop beneath his palm, but darted onwards with breathtaking speed around the huge arc of the Aquium, rising and falling, rolling and weaving as they went.

"Are you coming?"

It was Simia, blinking irritably on the top step.

Sylas's heart was thumping and he realised that he hadn't been breathing. What had just happened? Was it the fish acting on their own or was it *him*? Surely not, and yet something had made him fling out his arm: something had made him think this would happen. He shook his head as he saw the shoal rounding the last of the arc, completing an entire circuit of the room and once again drawing close to his shoulder.

With some difficulty, he drew his eyes away and continued to climb.

He soon reached the top step where Simia was waiting for him. Without saying a word, she set off along the balcony as he drew near. He paused to look around. To one side and over a wooden railing were the same beams of light that he had seen from the hall, but they were closer together here, and the pattern that they made in the air was far more complicated. He walked to the railing and peered over the edge. The magnificent latticework of light poured down into the hall below and from this vantage point he could see everything: the circular platform, the many concentric circles of seating and the impressive sweeping circle of the Aquium that still swirled with life.

"These are the galleries," said Filimaya somewhere ahead.

He saw the old woman's elegant figure standing on the far side of the circular balcony, beyond the beams. He turned and began skirting the void towards her, trailing his hand along the banister and casting his eyes about him. At every few paces he passed a large wooden door set into the outside wall, each leading to some sort of chamber beyond — he counted ten such entrances in total and he was only halfway around. When he looked the other way, he could see two further floors above, and although the beams of light made it hard to see any detail, he thought he could see more doorways leading to more rooms. It looked more like a hotel than a mill.

Filimaya was standing in front of one of these many doors. As Sylas approached, she pushed at it, leaving it to creak open. He craned his neck round the door frame and looked inside, but the interior was pitch-black. Filimaya raised her hand and drew a finger towards the door, and at the same moment one of the beams of light beyond the railing changed its path, lifting from its downward angle until a pool of light moved across the floor and through the doorway. It advanced further and further from the opening and then, as it reached the far wall, the entire room suddenly glowed with its bright light. The beam had fallen on another porthole-shaped mirror on the far wall, then bounced off to another out of sight, which in turn had sent the light on to mirrors scattered around the walls, creating another web of beams.

"This will be your room while you are with us," said Filimaya, smiling warmly as she ushered him through the doorway.

He glanced around him and saw a stone wall at the far end, with wooden panelled walls on the two sides. There was a large green sofa, a leather armchair, a small desk and a cosy-looking bed in the corner, which held his eyes for some time, such was his longing to rest.

Filimaya followed his gaze and laughed. "I'll not keep you for long, then you can rest," she said. "But first, let us see if we can discover why you are here."

14

The Other

"Can there be any greater discovery than the fact
that we are not alone?"

FILIMAYA WALKED BRISKLY OVER to the armchair and sat down, gathering her long silver ponytail so that the glistening braid trailed down at her side. She gestured to Sylas to take a seat on the sofa.

He moved stiffly across the room, took off his rucksack and flopped down on to the soft cushions, letting out a long sigh of satisfaction. Simia was about to fall gratefully on to the sofa next to him, but Filimaya held up her hand.

"Not you, Simia. Sylas, I assume you'd like something to eat and drink?"

Sylas nodded eagerly, trying to ignore Simia's scowl.

"But I want to hear everything!" she complained. "I *deserve* to hear everyth—"

"You do indeed, young Roskoroy," interrupted Filimaya sternly, "but you know we're on our own here at the moment and Sylas must have something to eat and drink. So must you."

Simia whirled round and stomped across the wooden floor,

mumbling under her breath: "Find the bell... save the Bringer... make the tea..."

She heaved the door closed with a loud clunk. Sylas was surprised that the room had not been plunged into darkness, but when he looked up he saw that the beam of light now passed through a perfectly round window above the door frame.

"Don't worry about her little tantrums, Sylas," said Filimaya, leaning forward confidentially, "she's a spirited girl but warm-hearted too. Quite astonishing, given all that she's been through..." she added, as an afterthought.

"Why do you call her that? Roskoroy?"

"Oh, it was her father's name, though here your father's name is what you call a 'surname' — like Tate, for example. But for Simia, her father's name is a matter of especial pride... but that's a whole other matter."

She drew in a breath and patted her knees. "Sylas Tate, I believe we both face much that we do not understand and we have to piece things together quickly. If the Ghor are so interested in your arrival, our hideout will not stay a secret for long."

Sylas leaned back into the sofa. "But we were very careful. We..."

"They have ways," said Filimaya with chilling certainty. She cleared her throat. "I must begin by telling you that your arrival is something of a surprise to us. It's not a bad surprise by any means — indeed it may be a very good one — but it is a surprise nevertheless."

Sylas looked confused. "But you sent Simia to *meet* me."

"I *was* expecting you, but only once the bell had chimed. Those who know how to listen can hear the bell, even if it is not ringing for them."

"And you know how to listen?"

"I do."

He thought for a moment. "And the Ghor — would they have heard it?"

Filimaya shook her head. "No. But those whom the Ghor follow almost certainly would."

"Thoth?"

She nodded.

"Now your arrival was a surprise because the chime of the Passing Bell is a summoning. It rings only at someone's bidding."

Sylas shifted uncomfortably. "But who would summon me?"

"*That* is the mystery," said Filimaya. "For there is only one group of people who use the Passing Bell, and they are all but destroyed."

"So it was them who…"

Filimaya shook her head. "No — it couldn't have been them."

"Why?"

"Because 'they' are us. The Suhl." She gazed earnestly into his eyes. "This place, the mill, is one of only a few sanctuaries that we have left. There are just a handful of people still alive who are capable of raising the bell, and I know them all. Sylas, none of them conjured the bell. *We* didn't bring you here."

She settled back in her chair and looked at him steadily. He dropped his eyes. He had hoped that when he reached the mill he might start to understand what was happening to him, but now he was more confused than ever.

"So you don't know why you are here any more than I do?"

"I have no idea," he replied. "I don't even know where 'here' is. Is this some kind of other—" he paused, still finding the idea quite ridiculous— "a kind of other *world*?"

Filimaya raised one of her slender eyebrows, but did not laugh. "Yes, in a manner of speaking," she said lightly, "though it is best to think of it as something a little different, something a little more complicated. I'm afraid there's no easy way of explaining it, so I'll do my best to show you."

She started pointing at objects in the room. "You will already have seen how the things around you seem strange, but at the same time familiar: the wooden panels, the sofa, the floorboards — all of them look like the things of your own world, do they not?"

Sylas shrugged. "Yes, of course."

"That's because your world is not as different from ours as you may think. Now take a look at the mirrors on the walls."

He turned and looked at one of the mirrors mounted on the wall to their side. He squinted into the beam of light and even as he watched it dimmed slightly, then shapes and forms became visible in the brightness. At first they seemed random, but they soon started to form a picture — a picture that moved. He glanced in astonishment at Filimaya, but she too was staring at the mirror with one finger outstretched. When he looked back, the picture had taken shape. It was one that he recognised: on one side was the broad sweep of the river as it travelled round the meander, and on the other was part of the huge waterwheel, its massive blades flicking swiftly across the corner of the mirror. But, as he looked more closely, he could see that although it was familiar it was also quite different from the view that he knew, for it was looking down at the river from a great height.

His eyes widened. "This is the view from the roof of the mill!"

"Of course!" said Filimaya matter-of-factly. "That's where we harvest our light, so all of our views come from there. Now look more closely. Look beyond what is strange and unexpected, and see what you *know*."

Sylas glanced at her quizzically, then shuffled forward on the sofa until he was close to the mirror. He gazed at this strange window on to the world. He tried to ignore the weird, pointed roofs of the houses and the dark smoke lying over the town; he made an effort to imagine it without the distant tower, the vast waterwheel and the long lines of fishing nets along the riverbanks; and he did his best to look past the numerous strangely dressed figures he could see stooped over them and the curious little canoe paddling across from the far shore, its two occupants huddled over their oars. As these details faded in his mind, so he began to see the shape of the river and the form of the hills above the town. He saw the dark, shaded fringe of the forest and then, catching his eye and drawing his gaze upwards, the high, graceful circles of eagles in the sky.

He knew these things.

He felt the blood draining from his face as his eyes passed over the contours of hills that he remembered seeing from his window in Gabblety Row, and valleys filled with trees that he had gazed at when dreaming of places far away. When his eyes moved back to the river, he realised that he knew all too well these wide banks and this sweeping expanse of water. There, by a collection of fishing nets stretched across the mud, and there, where the little canoe was drawing close to a mangled jetty, were the places where the Hailing Bridge should have met the shore.

"Do you see?" came Filimaya's gentle voice.

Sylas nodded, his eyes still fixed on the mirror. "It's all just like home!"

Instinctively he peered across the river and over the town to a point in the distance — to the point where Gabblety Row should have been. He saw more pointed roofs and more bluish smoke, but no crooked chimney stack, no slanting walls, no Gabblety Row. Instead of the misshapen roofs and odd slumping walls he saw a strange-looking building of about the same size, flanked at both ends by tumbledown towers, each topped with its own pyramidal roof.

He let himself slip back on to the sofa and slowly lifted his eyes to Filimaya's face. "So this world is in the same... *place*... as mine?"

"That's right. Your world — which we call 'the Other' — occupies the very same space and the very same time as our own, but for some reason it is separate. Not only is it separate, it is different — like the other side of the same coin."

Sylas shook his head and looked about him at the wood-panelled walls and the sofa and the door, as if doubting that they were really there. "You call my world the *Other*?"

She nodded.

"So what's this place called?"

Filimaya smiled. "Well, most people know nothing else — to them it is simply the world. But to you and people of your world, ours has the same name: 'the Other'."

Sylas pondered this. "So 'the Other' is just the world you're not in?"

"That's right. It's rather appropriate when you think about it, given that the worlds are a reflection of one another."

There was another long silence. He wanted to ask more, but he had no idea where to start.

"It doesn't seem real, does it?" she said.

"No," he murmured, his eyes fixed on the mirror. "But after the last few days I'm not sure what real *is* any more."

"It is indeed a strange twist of reality. And what is even stranger is that we, the Suhl, should be the ones who understand it best — for we believe in togetherness, the oneness of all things. To us this separateness is quite... wrong."

"Well, it doesn't seem *right* to me either."

She gave him another of her sad smiles, seeming pleased with his remark.

"None of us finds these darker truths easy to accept — there are times when I still find them hard to grasp." She drew a long breath. "But now I think we must at least try to understand more about you and what brought you here. Do you agree?"

Sylas drew his eyes away from the mirror, which still glimmered on the wall. "Yes," he said, with new excitement. Perhaps this was finally the moment he would find out why all this was happening to him. Perhaps, he thought, casting his mind back to Espen's last words, perhaps he would hear what it all had to do with his mother.

"So let us do this: tell me everything that led to you coming here — people, places, anything that you think may be of importance — then I will tell you if I can explain any of it for you. How does that sound?"

"Fine," he replied. Yet, as he turned his thoughts to the past few days, he hesitated. "But so much has happened... Do you want to hear *everything*?"

"Let's get as far as we can," said Filimaya, settling back into her chair, drawing her legs up beneath her like a young girl.

And so Sylas began to tell his strange story. Filimaya listened intently, her sad eyes narrowing at times and widening at others. She was transfixed as he described Mr Zhi and asked him to explain every detail of his appearance and to recount every word that he had spoken. Sylas did his best to remember, telling her about his visit and ending with the moment he had been given the Samarok.

"Where is it now?" asked Filimaya, interrupting Sylas part-way through a sentence.

He leaned over the side of the sofa and lifted up his rucksack.

"It's in here," he said. "Do you want to see it?"

Filimaya eyed the bag keenly for a moment, but then drew her eyes away. "No. We can look at it later. Please continue."

He replaced the bag by the side of the sofa, noticing how her eyes followed it until it was out of sight. He resumed his story with his awakening in the middle of the night, the awesome chime of the bell and the terrifying encounter with the black dog. He told of his meeting with Herr Veeglum as he left Gabblety Row, his flight through the estate and his encounter with Espen on the bridge. Again Filimaya wanted to know more about these two men — how they appeared, how they spoke, what they said — and Sylas did his best to remember.

He had no difficulty recalling Espen's last words as he had fled into the forest: "*There lie your answers about who you are... about your mother.*"

He recounted every word and then paused, hoping that they might mean something to Filimaya.

For a moment she simply regarded him with the same warm, sad eyes.

"You hope that I know something of your mother, don't you?"

He nodded eagerly.

"I'm afraid I do not," she said, leaning forward and placing a hand on his.

Sylas's heart sank. He had felt sure that, if anyone he had met would know something of her, it would be Filimaya. "Of course," he said, dropping his eyes. "There's no reason you..."

"Tell me about her," she said, squeezing his hand.

He hesitated. He *never* spoke about his mother. That was his rule, his defence: his way of keeping her close, of keeping his memories intact and untouched.

"It's all right," said Filimaya, leaning back in her chair. "Simia will be a while yet, and we should save something of the rest of your story for when she returns. Tell me about your mother."

To his surprise, Sylas found himself wanting to speak about her. Filimaya's beautiful, kindly face somehow reminded him of her and he felt unexpectedly at ease. He knew he could trust her.

He began to describe his mum as he liked to remember her, when they had lived together in that lovely, warm little house in the country, the one next to the ruined mill and the angry little stream, where they had both been so happy. He talked about her important job as a biologist, of her love of learning, of her rooms full of books and laboratory equipment and charts and models. He talked excitedly about their walks in the woods when his mum would show him all of its wonders, and tell him what things were called, and explain how things grew and lived and died. And then, reluctantly, he described how it had all changed.

"It was just at night," he said, "At first, that is. I remember hearing her from my room. The bedrooms were right next to each other and the walls were paper-thin. She really didn't mean for me to hear. She hated me to hear. I just thought she was talking to someone... but it was the wrong tone. Her voice was quiet, as if she was speaking to someone very close. And then other times I would hear her singing quietly: so softly that it was as though she was singing a lullaby or something. But whenever I went in I found her on her own, curled up with her eyes closed as if she was talking in her sleep. And I'd think she was asleep, only... it was strange... every time — when I got near — she stopped."

He looked at Filimaya. He saw none of the judgement in her eyes that he so feared.

"And then it got worse," he said. "Much worse. Sometimes

she'd wake up shouting… screaming. And she was so frightened. She'd come through to my room and sleep in my bed. Often she was shaking so much that she kept me awake. And she'd cry. She didn't think I knew because she didn't make a sound, but I could feel her when she hugged me… you know, sobbing… shaking."

Filimaya leaned forward again, focused on everything he was saying, her eyes glazed with tears.

"And it just got worse and worse," he said. "It started happening during the day and people stopped visiting. And then, one day, some people came and spoke with her, and showed her a lot of paperwork, and they had a big argument. Mum told me it was nothing to worry about, but—" he winced and swallowed hard— "but the next day they came back… and this time they came to take us away. And there were doctors there. For Mum. With needles and drugs and—"

His voice wavered and he pushed himself back in the sofa, keeping his eyes away from Filimaya's, knowing that he might cry.

"And that was it. The last time I saw her. She was taken to some kind of hospital and I went to live with my Uncle Tobias in Gabblety Row…"

"Your uncle?" prompted Filimaya gently. "Your father's brother?"

Sylas nodded. "I didn't know him well at all — my dad died when I was a baby and we weren't close to his family, but my uncle's the only one still alive now. It was him who told me that—" the words caught— "told me that she had died."

Filimaya reached forward and took him by both hands.

"Oh, Sylas, I'm sorry."

"It's OK," said Sylas, drawing away a little. "It turns out it was all a lie anyway. That's what I found out just before all this happened. That my uncle's been lying to me. That she's still alive."

Filimaya sat up straight. "He *lied* to you about something like that?" she said incredulously. "Are you sure?"

"Absolutely. I found the letters from the hospital. That's why what Espen said was so strange. All this has happened at the same time — almost like everything is tied to this—"

Suddenly the door flew open and Simia entered, announced by a fanfare of clattering crockery. Sylas wiped his sleeve over his face.

Simia did not see his tears because her tiny figure was almost completely lost behind a tray of formidable proportions, upon which was a spread of enticing refreshments: a large jug of water topped with some kind of flower petals; a silver teapot that left a trail of steam as she walked; a loaf of brown bread, carefully sliced; a large block of yellow cheese; and best of all a rich, dark fruit cake that Sylas could smell halfway across the room. All this had been so well prepared that, despite the severe expression on Simia's face as she turned to position the tray between them, it was clear that she had taken great care over the task.

"Thank you, Simia," said Filimaya, smiling at Sylas apologetically. "You're very kind."

Simia's face remained set and unsmiling as she quickly poured three glasses of water and three cups of tea. As soon as she had finished, she slid Sylas's feet off the sofa and sat down next to him.

"So," she said, her face suddenly breaking into an excited grin, "where have we got to?"

Filimaya and Sylas looked at one another and laughed.

"You're in time to hear about the bell," said Filimaya, leaning forward to take up her tea. "That's right, isn't it, Sylas?"

Sylas smiled and nodded. He did not mind Simia's intrusion; in fact, he was glad of the change of subject. What more was there to say? Besides, the sight and smell of good food had reminded him that he was starving. He helped himself to a piece of bread, some cheese and a large slice of cake, then sat back and continued his story. Between mouthfuls he described the bell in the forest, how it had passed above his head and the next thing he remembered was waking up in its shadow.

When he had finished, Filimaya leaned back in her chair, absorbed in her own thoughts while he turned eagerly to another piece of cake and bit off large mouthfuls of moist, sweet fruit, still warm from the oven. Simia looked excitedly from Filimaya to Sylas and then back at Filimaya.

She could contain herself no longer. "Isn't it just so thoroughly... gorgeously... *weird*?"

Filimaya looked at her distractedly and then turned back to Sylas.

"And Mr Zhi didn't explain *anything* about the bell?"

"No, nothing at all," replied Sylas with his mouth full of succulent cherries, "but then I only met him once. The first thing I knew was the—"

"He didn't give you a message?" interrupted Filimaya.

He shook his head.

"Well, this is all very peculiar. Very strange indeed..." she said, again consumed by her own thoughts.

"Didn't I say!" cried Simia, rolling her eyes. She clapped Sylas on the back and, not knowing what else to do with her excitement, devoured an entire piece of cake in a single mouthful.

Filimaya was silent for some time, staring over Sylas's head into the dim corner of the room. Then she shook her head and turned to Simia.

"And you were chased by the *Ghor*?" she asked.

"Yep," she replied rather proudly. "Three Ghor and two Ghorhund. And then Scarpia turned up — at the Lord's Chamber. They tore the town apart trying to find us, but we were too quick." She grinned at Sylas, but he could not bring himself to smile — he was remembering the poor wagoner.

"*Scarpia...*" repeated Filimaya, looking perplexed.

Simia seemed about to launch into a more detailed account of their death-defying flight across the town, but all of a sudden Filimaya sprang to her feet and walked to the door.

"Sylas, you must forgive me," she said, turning in the doorway. "I was enjoying our conversation and I know I said I would explain some of what has happened to you, but I find that I cannot. I can tell you only two things for certain: that something very unusual and unexpected is happening, which you already know; and that I believe your arrival to be of the utmost importance. More important than any of us can know."

Sylas choked down a piece of cheese and looked from Simia to Filimaya.

"So... what now?" he asked.

"Yes, indeed. Well, this is too momentous to keep to ourselves," she said. "I must call a Say-So..."

"A Say-So?"

"A gathering of the Suhl. They may be able to help us, but even if not, they should hear your story. It may affect us all."

With that, she gave them an apologetic smile and then disappeared from the room, drawing the heavy door closed behind her.

S

"And remember, you mustn't be seen." The whisper carried traces of a deep, hoarse voice.

"Tell me once and I'll remember; tell me thrice and I may just forget on purpose…"

The words were formed with great effort, as though gurgled rather than spoken, shaped by a tongue not designed for speech. The speaker exhaled loudly through a glistening snout.

"Then you'll not live long, friend," was the quick reply.

The hunched figure shrugged its sloping shoulders beneath its cloak, but did not risk another quip. With a last look both ways, it stood from its crouch and ran quickly from the hiding place. Its movement was fluid and swift, but it stooped low to the ground, as though its limbs were jointed strangely amid the folds of its cloak, drawing it along on all fours. When the creature met the mill wall, it paused again, flicking its head from side to side, and then it began to climb. It did not look for purchase on the smooth surface of the wall, but crawled lizard-like, without grips or footholds.

Moments later it was peering into the garden of the mill and then, seeming certain that the coast was clear, it slid on to the top of the wall. Drawing itself up, it looked quickly left and right, then pulled the cloak from its shoulders. The body beneath was thin and pale grey, glistening with moisture. It was almost human, but not quite: the shoulders were too narrow, the chest too flat, and the hands and feet far too large. A fibrous ridge ran along its spine, parted at the back of its neck, ran up behind its gills and met again across its brow, giving it a perpetual malevolent frown.

The creature set out along the wall, heading for the mill house. In two lurching paces it was there and — with another darting look to its side — was climbing again, heaving its weight up the almost vertical wall at an impossible speed.

Its companion watched quietly from the shadows, glancing

occasionally along the banks to check that no one was approaching. Then, seemingly satisfied that all had gone according to plan, the figure turned and retreated further into the bushes, emerging moments later with a canoe and sliding it over the muddy bank towards the water's edge.

15

The Say-So

"They mean so well and yet, alas, a meeting of men so rarely involves a meeting of minds…"

The sun dappled the forest floor: here, lighting the browns, reds and yellows of a confusion of leaves; there, falling upon a mossy stone, making it glow greenly. Her figure moved in silence between the arching trees, her white gown a stark contrast to their wintry limbs. The only sound was of leaves rustling on a light wind.

She faced away from him and made no gesture, nor any attempt to turn, but he knew that she wanted him to follow. And that was what he yearned to do, for to stand with her in the light would be to banish all of his cares into the shadows and instead to be at home, to be safe, to be loved. He sensed that all this lay but a few steps ahead – just there, where she now walked slowly across a sunlit clearing, her path strewn with gossamer, sparkling with pearls of dew. But as hard as he tried his feet would not carry him through the forest. With every step, she moved further and further away from him and, as she did so, the shafts of winter sunshine drifted with her, drawing long shadows across his path.

"Mum! Wait!" he cried desperately, but his voice was just a whisper, like the leaves in the breeze.

He cried out again, but still he could not find his voice. She walked on across the clearing, moving slowly towards the thickening woods. Before she reached the first of the trees, she stopped and, turning her head slightly, she spoke. Sylas could not make out her voice as it was only a whisper, but somehow her words formed in his mind, so clear and true that it was as though her lips were at his ear.

"Know me, and you will find me," she said.

SYLAS WOKE GASPING FOR air as though he had been suffocating. His muscles were tense and sore and he could feel a trickle of sweat running down his neck. There was no voice, no forest, no sunshine, indeed there was no light except for a meagre strip of flickering orange leading from the door, which stood slightly ajar. He pushed himself up on the sofa and sat for a moment, waiting for his head to clear.

He thought he heard the sound of leaves in the wind again, drifting from the door, but the more he listened, the more he became sure that the sound was not leaves at all: they were whispers, murmurs and stifled voices. He lowered his feet to the floor and felt the rough floorboards on his toes: his mud-caked shoes and socks had been removed and laid to one side. He stood and stretched, finding his limbs surprisingly refreshed, walked over to the door and pulled it open.

A bright orange light poured into the room; the whispers became a hubbub of chattering voices and the air was filled with a medley of smoky scents that made his head swim — honey, blackberries, plums, fresh grass and sprouts.

"You're awake! Just in time!"

It was Simia's voice.

She was sitting on the floor of the gallery, with her legs hanging down below the banister. She had retrieved her coat and was once again lost inside its folds of crude cloth. She grinned over her shoulder and patted the carpet next to her.

"Come and sit here," she said. "Best seat in the house!"

Still yawning, he stepped forward and peered over the railing. To his astonishment the hall was transformed from the vast, bright, airy space that he had seen earlier in the day. Now the mirrors no longer reflected bright beams from one to the other, but instead were empty and dark. Their light was replaced by flickering lamps hung from countless brackets on the wall, so numerous that the walls and ceiling looked almost like a starlit sky.

The hall was alive with a bustle of people: young and old, women and men, many bearing the traits of some far-flung or foreign place, with dark skin or broad features, high brows or wide eyes, long, slender necks or stout, rounded shoulders. Most were sitting on the circular benches talking agitatedly to their neighbours, but some were still gathered in groups around the outside, in front of the Aquium. All were wearing the same burgundy robes that he had seen on Filimaya, though none seemed to Sylas quite as impressive as hers.

The guests showed signs of great excitement, forming tight huddles where they sat or stood, jabbing at the air and waving their hands about as they made some unheard point or answered some unheard question. Many puffed feverishly at pipes of different shapes and sizes, issuing clouds of flavoured smoke into the towering space above. There was a great confusion of voices, some loud and agitated, others whispering and secretive, many using strange languages and accents, a large number of them elderly, with greying hair.

And below, just visible between Sylas's feet, a younger congregation of guests gathered round a figure whom he could not at first see, but as the group parted, he saw, to his surprise, that it was none other than Ash, smiling enigmatically as he showed his audience a glass in the palm of his hand, which appeared to be full of pebbles. His incongruous green robe was a confused rumple of creases and his hair looked if anything more untidy than it had been in the inn: now an extraordinary explosion of blond curls.

"Why's Ash here?" whispered Sylas. "I thought he was a Muddlemorph."

Simia followed his eyes and shrugged. "He is and he isn't," she replied, poking her head between the bars to get a better look. "We're good at pretending to be whatever we need to be — you know, blending in. Ash is *really* good at it, though. In fact, sometimes I think he likes being a Muddlemorph more than he likes being one of us."

At that moment there was a gasp of wonderment from the little gathering as Ash raised the glass into the air. Sylas saw to his amazement that the pebbles had turned into crystal-clear water. The young man lowered the glass, drank down the contents and smacked his lips. "And that," he cried, "is the perfect cure for gallstones!"

There was a loud chorus of laughter from those around him and they began to applaud, but they were quickly silenced by an older man who turned and snapped at Ash. Sylas noticed that most of the older people standing nearby were also looking at him disapprovingly.

"What did he do wrong?" asked Sylas.

Simia sighed maternally. "He used Kimiyya."

"One of the Three Ways?"

"Yes, and it's also a big no-no here. The Suhl are only meant to use Essenfayle."

"What's that?"

"There you go again with all your questions," she sighed, nudging him in the ribs. "Essenfayle is *our* way. The *Fourth* Way."

Just then he saw a slight movement in the shadows further around the gallery. It took his eyes a moment to adjust but, as they did, he saw a large figure standing next to the banister and then the glint of large eyes staring directly at him. A flicker of torchlight illuminated a long face and glinted brightly off a bald head. It was Bowe.

"Why's he up here?" he asked Simia, pointing. "Shouldn't he be with the rest?"

She looked up. "Oh no, he always skulks about in the shadows at these things," she said. "Meetings are difficult for Scryers. Too many feelings and thoughts — connections between people. He says it's like looking into a blinding light — or everyone shouting at the top of their voice. Too much to bear."

Sylas looked thoughtfully at Bowe's stocky figure, his arms crossed in front of him, his sparkling eyes turning slowly about the hall, and for a moment he wondered what it must be like to see the world in that way: all the myriad thoughts and feelings of daily life, one moment admiration, affection, goodwill and the next mistrust, fear, hate — all around him, all the time. A blessing and a curse. He looked at the Scryer with new interest, taking in the deep lines of his face, the heavy brow, the downcast eyes.

"He looks sad," he said, thinking aloud.

Simia sucked a breath through her teeth. "He has plenty to be sad about. He's lost more than most of us: his wife and all his brothers... even his daughter. They say she was taken on the last day of the war."

"Taken prisoner?"

She nodded. "Her name was Naeo. She's probably dead, like everyone else."

Sylas shook his head. So that explained the tattoo on the back of Bowe's head.

His eyes travelled back to Bowe and, to his surprise, he saw that the Scryer was still looking at him. His gaze had the same strange intensity as in the Mutable Inn, his expression quizzical, as though he saw in Sylas something he could not quite understand, or perhaps believe.

A loud clunk reverberated through the hall followed by a metallic rattle.

The many speakers fell silent. All eyes turned to the centre of the chamber, where the two great circular doors in the floor were already sliding back to reveal the darkness of the shaft below. As they shuddered to a halt, a lone figure rose slowly out of the shadows on the platform. Sylas recognised Filimaya's flowing silver hair straight away, looking even more beautiful in the shifting lamplight. As she ascended, she turned and nodded politely to various people in the room and all smiled warmly and bowed in greeting. The weave of purple strands in her hair shimmered and glistened, lending her an ethereal appearance.

Simia followed his eyes. "They say those are the last threads of the Suhl standard — the flag carried by Merimaat herself."

The platform came to a sudden halt with a sharp clank. Filimaya paused for a moment while the sound died away and then raised her head to speak.

"Come close and hear me," she said in a strong but lilting voice.

There was a general commotion as those still standing made their way to various parts of the hall to sit down, jostling one another for the best positions.

Simia leaned over. "That's how all Say-Sos start. When someone says that, everyone has to shut up and listen."

She rifled through her coat and brought out a tatty-looking

notebook, a pot of ink and a quill.

"What's that for?" whispered Sylas.

"It's where I write *important things*," said Simia, turning through pages of handwritten scrawl to a clean page. "And this is going to be *important*."

Gradually the great hall came to order and Filimaya moved for the first time, turning on the spot so that she could see everyone in the congregation. Seeming satisfied that they were ready to listen, she cleared her throat and began.

"First of all, my good friends, an apology for my dramatic entrance," she smiled and pointed down to the platform. "I was outside because I had to be sure that we are not being watched. I fear that we now face a greater threat from our enemies than ever before."

There was a general murmur in the hall, but Filimaya continued without pause.

"By now you will all know my reason for gathering you here. The Passing Bell has brought us a visitor. A Bringer."

There was another rumble of excitement and a general nodding of heads. Filimaya waited until the hall had fallen silent.

"But that is not all. This Bringer is a boy."

Suddenly the congregation erupted with cries of disbelief.

"A *child* Bringer – surely not!" shouted one woman.

"A boy? Nonsense!" bellowed another.

Sylas shifted nervously and glanced at Simia, who muttered something under her breath.

"If I might finish!" boomed Filimaya suddenly, her voice surprisingly resonant in the large hall. "It seems certain that this boy is a Bringer and perhaps even more special than that. He was aided in his journey not only by the Merisi, but by Mr Zhi himself."

At this the clamour in the hall rose to a new pitch despite Filimaya's raised hands and calls for calm.

"You can't believe children's stories!" cried a man with a shiny bald head and flame-red beard. "Not on matters of this importance!"

"Well, I disagree," said Filimaya calmly. "But it isn't just what he says. He wears the Merisi Band."

There was a collective gasp. The man stared at her long and hard. "And I suppose you know that it's not a fake?"

"I do."

"How exactly?"

"Because, Salvo, I can tell that he is a boy who speaks the truth," said Filimaya. "But if we need proof, I think this will suffice."

She reached down to a small bag almost hidden beneath her cloak and stood holding her hand aloft. Between her fine fingers she held the Samarok. The entire gathering gasped.

Sylas felt a surge of panic — an overwhelming fear that the book had been taken from him and that he had been foolish to tell these strangers that he had it. The blood was draining from his face as he heard Simia's voice in his ear.

"She's only borrowed it. She needed to see it for herself — and she knew that the others would have to see it too."

Salvo was back on his feet. "Well, all of these Merisi trinkets are very impressive, but he could have been given them by anyone! If this boy really is a Bringer, surely he should be here, now, speaking for himself!" Sylas looked anxiously at Filimaya, praying that she would not look up at him. But already the room was mumbling its agreement and Filimaya seemed to be considering the proposal.

She hesitated, then glanced up with an expression of apology.

"Very well," she said. "I had hoped to avoid this, but I can see why you need to meet him. Just remember this: he is a boy, and he is our guest." She looked meaningfully round the room until her eyes rested upon Salvo and then, apparently satisfied that everyone had heard her, she raised her hand and beckoned to Sylas.

"Come down, Sylas," she said with an encouraging smile. "I'm sure that everyone will make you very welcome."

§

The creature lay entirely still, its body pressed against the smooth grey stone with limbs spread wide, its face against the glass. The only movement was the slow opening and closing of the gills beneath its angular jaws. Its slimy body had taken the colours of the mill wall — granite-grey with a speckled, slightly bluish pigment — making it almost invisible from below. The black orbs of its eyes peered down into the chamber, watching contemptuously as the assembled Suhl talked and gesticulated, rose and retook their seats. It paid Filimaya scant attention, instead searching among the faces, peering into the shadows.

Only when Filimaya looked up into the gallery did it turn back to her, pausing on her for a moment and then following her gaze. It saw the wide circle of the balcony, the banisters and, just visible to one side, a small shaggy-haired boy climbing to his feet. It flicked its tongue across its yellowed, pointed teeth and shifted its head slightly to one side, letting out a low, rasping purr. Its brow furrowed as it took in every detail of its quarry, who now walked nervously to the staircase and began to descend into the chamber.

The creature lifted its reptilian head and sucked in a triumphant breath, turning its eyes to the sprawling town below. For some moments it watched the smoke curling up from chimneys to the evening sky, forming layers of murky bronze in the dying light. Then it looked down to the bank and along the riverside path, checking for prying eyes. There was no movement nearby, but its attention was drawn to a gathering of figures walking along an alley some distance away. It recognised their smooth, effortless gait at once: it was a small group of Ghor, their necks swinging from side to side as they searched doorways and peered in windows. Then it saw another group in the street beyond, moving slowly and deliberately, scouring every alcove and porch, window and opening.

Gradually it became aware of the same silent, creeping motion in every lane and alley, every street and square: hundreds, perhaps thousands of Ghor stealing through the shadows of twilight, swarming through the town. Its frown deepened as it looked up to the hills, to the winding roads, and saw that they were black with a flow of dark figures streaming towards the lights.

Fluttering high above the distant hordes was a regular line of gigantic flags glowing blood-red in the failing light. At their centre, a black, empty face glowered across the open fields and huddling homes. The eyes were hollow and skeletal, but they seemed to see all. As the fabric snapped in the wind, so the deathly visage seemed to flicker with life, scowling at the final glimmer of day.

"Thoth," gurgled the creature, a shiver running down its protruding spine.

16

The Chosen Path

"The well-lit path so often leads us to what we already know. We must have the courage to turn from the light — to choose the darker, more dangerous path..."

THE HALL REVERBERATED WITH excited voices as Sylas took his place next to Filimaya and everyone retook their seats. He looked out at the sea of faces and for the first time he realised just how many there were. There was not a space free in the entire chamber, and the congregation were pressed in upon one another, sitting with their shoulders hunched forward to give themselves more room in the upturned boats. But the most disconcerting thing of all was that, no matter how he stood, the largest number of them was always behind him. He could feel their eyes burning into his back and he heard many making comments about his strange, filthy clothes and his shaggy, unkempt hair. When he turned, that part of the hall would fall silent and nod at him politely, but at the same moment similar discussions would strike up behind him. It was an odd and humbling arrangement.

No doubt that was the idea, he thought.

To his dismay Salvo rose from the crowd a little in front of him and stood stroking his ginger moustache, waiting for silence. Eventually the hall became silent and he turned his flushed face to Sylas.

"Welcome," he said in a dry, abrasive voice.

"Thank you," said Sylas, rather more loudly than he had intended. The words echoed alarmingly around the hall and they seemed to cause a great buzz of excitement among the onlookers.

"Rather bold, isn't he?" muttered a woman behind him.

"I am Salvo, son of Salasar," said the man in a beguilingly amiable tone. "Might I ask you who you are and where you're from?"

He cleared his throat. "My name is Sylas Tate. I'm from here — this town, but in... in the Other. I live in a building called Gabblety Row with my uncle. It's not far from the town centre, on the junction of Via Road and Grebe Street."

Salvo continued to nod when Sylas fell silent, as though wishing more words from his lips. When the boy said nothing further, he frowned and scratched the glistening dome of his head.

"You know Mr Zhi?"

Sylas nodded. "I do. But I only met him a couple of days ago," he said.

Salvo began shaking his head and looked at his colleagues as if for support. "This is quite ridiculous... a boy Bringer who only met the Merisi a few—"

"Whatever it is, it's *his* story!" barked another man at the far side of the hall. "Let him tell it in his own words!"

Salvo hesitated, then threw his hands in the air and returned to his seat.

Filimaya placed a hand on Sylas's shoulder and whispered in his ear. "Go on now, Sylas, just tell them what you told me."

And so he told his story. His voice was dry and hesitant at

first, but the more he spoke, the stronger it became. As it unfolded and he heard murmurs of excitement and interest from his audience, he gained confidence. The crowd were attentive, particularly when Sylas mentioned Mr Zhi (when they seemed fascinated by every word the old man had spoken) and when he pulled up his sleeve and showed the Merisi Band. It was at this moment that the majority of the Suhl seemed to be convinced of his story.

From that point onwards many of them sat back in their seats, turning their minds to the mysterious matter that now lay before them. As Sylas finished his tale, the great gathering of the Suhl was entirely silent.

Sylas breathed a quiet sigh of relief, not only because he had reached the end of his long narrative without faltering, but also because his audience seemed to have believed him. Even Salvo was subdued and sat hunched forward, with his bristled chin resting in his hands and his head shining with perspiration.

Filimaya stepped forward and put her hand on his shoulder. "Thank you, Sylas," she said. "You have given us all a lot to think about." She turned to the gathering and raised her fine eyebrows. "Perhaps there are some questions?"

The entire congregation rose to its feet at once.

There was a brief silence while everyone looked at everyone else, and then someone started laughing.

"By the time you answer all these, Sylas, the bell will have rung again and it'll be time for you to go home!" shouted someone in the front row to another peal of laughter.

Sylas smiled. Looking around him, he saw for the first time how amiable and friendly the faces in the crowd were: no longer fearful, but open and warm.

Gradually they all came back to order and everyone took their seats, with the exception of one man with a large grey forelock and a pencil moustache, who remained standing, puffing prodigious quantities of smoke from his pipe. Soon all eyes were turned on him.

"Might it be helpful if one of us takes the lead?" he enquired of the crowd, peering over his glasses. When there was no objection, he turned to Sylas.

"Sylas, my name is Grayvel: I am honoured to meet you," he said with a low bow. "Yours is a remarkable story, and it was even more remarkable for the excellence of its telling."

"Quite so!" shouted some others among the crowd.

"But now we find ourselves in a tricky spot. You see, you are not at all what we have come to expect from a Bringer."

"But I'm *not* a Bringer — I don't even know what a Bringer is!" objected Sylas.

Grayvel's grey eyebrows furrowed and he breathed forth a torrent of smoke. "Yes, so you say... so you say. But that is part of what makes you so — if you will forgive me for saying it — so peculiar. While we were not expecting the Passing Bell to ring, we cannot ignore the fact that it was forged for the sole purpose of summoning Bringers — or at least that is all it has ever done until now. Therefore, to us, the very fact that you came here as you did makes you a Bringer. And then, to add to our confusion, you are carrying the very things we would expect a Bringer to carry: the Samarok and the Merisi Band."

"I know — none of it makes sense," said Sylas, "but surely, if I was a Bringer, somebody would have *told* me that I was one?"

"Quite! It really is very confusing! Not only have all other Bringers been quite aware that they were Bringers, they have been prepared by the Merisi over a period of many years. When they arrive, they know exactly what they are here for and precisely what to expect."

"I don't know who the *Merisi* are either," objected Sylas.

"But you do, Sylas, you do!" cried Grayvel, throwing his arms wide. "You have met the most eminent of them all — Mr Zhi himself!"

Sylas shook his head and sighed. "But he said he was a shopkeeper! He didn't even mention the Merisi!"

Grayvel frowned thoughtfully while taking his spectacles off to rub them on his sleeve. "Yes, as I say, it is quite inexplicable. Given all that Mr Zhi knows as leader of the Merisi, it is hard to understand why he would allow one so young to make this journey so ill prepared."

"Unless he had no time, Grayvel," boomed a new voice from a different part of the hall. It was a giant bear-like figure with a voluminous mantle of bushy brown hair that gathered about his face in a prodigious beard. But it was his sheer physical size that was most impressive: broad, slightly rounded shoulders; a mighty chest that strained at the confines of his tunic and a slightly bulging waist that was clearly not as lean as it once had been. The impression of strength was heightened by leather armour strapped around his torso and shoulders, emblazoned with buckles and buttons of brass that had been polished to a shine.

"I think we just have to accept what Sylas has told us," he continued. "He is no Bringer, nor was he intended to be. Look at the facts: Bringers have always been accomplished scholars with a knowledge of the runes and the Samarok. They're schooled in at least Essenfayle and one of the Three Ways. Most importantly, they know exactly what their purpose is: they have information to share with us and they're ready to learn what we teach them. Sylas may carry the Samarok and the Merisi Band, but he's no Bringer. He's something different. Perhaps something more... After all, even as a boy, he's worthy of Mr Zhi's protection and the call of the Passing Bell. I agree with our sister, there's something miraculous in this!"

There was a mumble of agreement from many in the crowd.

"With respect, Bayleon," protested Salvo, rising quickly from his seat, "you speak of miracles when the circumstances demand facts." He spread his arms out to the chamber. "We all need to ask who summoned the boy. You assume he is here for our benefit, but without knowing who *brought him*, how can we be sure? What if Mr Zhi was deceived? Remember the Ghorhund near his home — and Scarpia herself is here in town! Thoth has his hand in this!"

"Salvo," implored Filimaya, "you must remember that the beasts were trying to *kill* Sylas, not help him!"

"Yes! And they nearly killed us good and proper on the way from the bell!" shouted Simia, standing up so that she could glare at Salvo over the heads of the crowd.

"Sit down AT ONCE, young Roskoroy!" hissed Filimaya. Simia opened her mouth, but then thought better of it and threw herself down into her seat.

A silence fell across the great hall as everyone retreated into their own thoughts. Sylas turned slowly on the platform, seeing expressions of apprehension and concern. Some smiled at him as he glanced in their direction, but they soon passed back under a shadow when his eyes had moved on. He could sense that these people feared something terrible, something he could not even imagine — like Simia when they had first seen the Ghor on the hill.

"Can I say something?" he asked Filimaya, drawing the eyes of everyone in the room.

Filimaya nodded. "Of course," she said, looking pleasantly surprised. "That might be very helpful."

Sylas cleared his throat and tried not to look as nervous as he felt.

"It sounds as though something terrible has happened to you," he began, "something that has made you hide, and meet like this in secret, and fear what you can't explain — even me. Well, I can understand that, I really can. Until two days ago I was living a normal life with my uncle. But that's all changed now. I don't know why I'm here, I don't even know where here is, and it's definitely not where I want to be — I should be looking for my mother somewhere in my own world. I've been hunted and nearly killed, and now I'm as far from home as I've ever been. I think I have as much reason to be doubtful and scared as anyone. But the thing is, I haven't got a choice — I'm here now, and whatever is going to happen will happen."

He swallowed hard and took a deep breath, suddenly aware that the great chamber was deathly quiet.

"I said before that Mr Zhi hadn't given me a message — anything to tell you. Well, maybe I was wrong."

Many in the congregation leaned in, intrigued.

"Before I left him, he said one thing: that I must not fear what I do not understand. Maybe that message was as much for you as it was for me."

He heard his final words echoing about the hall and set his teeth, waiting for cries of "Impudent boy!" or "Insolence!" or some other phrase that his uncle liked to use. But nobody spoke. Some turned and looked at one another enquiringly, but none seemed to know what to say.

A very elderly man rose unsteadily from his seat, bracing himself on the shoulder of the man next to him. He had flowing locks of white hair and a long moustache of the same colour, and it was clear from his beautifully decorated robes that he was senior in some way. The congregation turned to look at him.

"It's Fathray!" whispered someone in the first row. "He's going to speak!"

The old gentleman peered at Sylas from beneath tangled grey eyebrows. "Thank you, Sylas." His voice was dry, but full of authority. He formed his words very slowly and precisely, seeming to choose each one with great care. "I think your comments — and those apposite utterings of Mr Zhi — were just what we needed to hear."

He gave a slight bow of his head and then turned to the crowd, sweeping his fading eyes across the whole congregation.

"Sisters and brothers, I think we have heard enough. Any more prittle-prattle and tittle-tattle and we would quite deserve to be thrown to the Ghor. I for one am convinced that Sylas is on a portentous path that may be exigent..."

"Fathray," interrupted Filimaya with a broad smile. "As ever, we value your wise words greatly, but it is always helpful to understand them. Could you please use plainer language?"

Fathray blinked at Filimaya in astonishment, as though he thought his words to be quite plain enough already, but then he chortled good-naturedly.

"Ah yes..." he said. "Quite so. I *should* have said I believe his path to be important to us. It seems evident that this is why our old friends the Merisi have tried to help him and the Ghor have tried to hinder him. But, whether or not he can help us, he is in great danger and he has entered our house. He is our responsibility, and we must not fail him. To my mind, the only question is, *how* do we help him?"

The crowd mumbled agreeably. Fathray paused, as if reluctant to continue. "In my view, there are only two options open to us. The first is to hide him — to protect him and hope that somehow his purpose here will become clear. But that is the fearful way,

192

the way of which Mr Zhi would certainly not approve. The second—" he hesitated again— "the second is to take him to the Magruman."

The room was suddenly filled with loud chatter and excitement, and it seemed to Sylas that everyone started speaking at once, some with expressions of excitement, others alarm. Salvo rose from his seat with a flushed face.

"That could be the end of us all! We would be leading him to the last real power that we have!"

"And what alternative do we have?" interjected Ash, sweeping back stray locks of blond hair in frustration. "Should we wait until the Ghor find him and kill him as surely they shall? I'm sick of simpering and hiding. This may be our very last hope! Mr Zhi was right — we mustn't be frightened just because we can't see the end of this. We're better than that!"

This stirred the hearts of many, for there was a rumble of support and some took to their feet to shout their approval.

"We are the last of the Suhl!" cried Ash.

There was a crescendo of applause.

"That's right!" shouted Bayleon, raising his bulky figure from his seat and punching the air.

Filimaya raised her arms and called for quiet. The Say-So quickly came back to order.

"Friends, it seems we are coming to an agreement: that Sylas should be taken to the Magruman."

"No! There is no agreement!" cried Salvo, throwing his arms in the air. "And Filimaya, you of all people should want to keep Paiscion from harm!"

A complete hush fell over the room as though Salvo had said something unthinkable. Filimaya seemed taken aback and her cheeks coloured a little. She turned slowly to look at him.

"Salvo, whatever I may wish for myself or for Paiscion is quite irrelevant." Her voice trembled a little with emotion and she paused before continuing. "It is the majority that we must consider, and the majority that must decide — that is the purpose of a Say-So."

She held Salvo's stare until he lowered his eyes.

Ash rose from his seat. "Sylas should travel to the Magruman. I say it is so!"

A moment later Grayvel too rose from his seat. "I say it is so," he said. Fathray then stood and spoke the same words, followed by those around him. Soon the entire congregation were taking to their feet in support of the motion.

"I say it is so!"

Finally, begrudgingly, even Salvo rose and mumbled the words.

"Then it is decided," said Filimaya with a smile of relief.

"But if this is our course we must consider another matter," said Grayvel, turning to the congregation. "Sylas cannot be taken to the Magruman by road: it is controlled by Thoth and his spies. There is only one route that is passable, and that is across the Barrens." There was a murmur of concern and an exchange of worried looks. "As we all know, this is not to be attempted—"

"I will take the boy," said Bayleon, rising to his feet. He touched his fist to his armoured chest. "He'll need a tracker. He'll need a Spoorrunner."

"And if Bayleon is going," said Ash, standing and grinning at his friend, "so am I."

The congregation voiced its approval.

"Me too!"

This final voice was rather insubstantial and it took some moments for the congregation to realise who had spoken. Finally their eyes fell on the small red-headed girl now clambering up on to the stage.

"I'm going too," repeated Simia proudly. "Sylas needs me."

There was a loud chuckle somewhere in the back row and then slowly, amiably, everyone began to laugh.

Simia put her hands on her hips and glared.

17

The Water Gardens

"How can a people thus steeped in the joys and perfections of Nature fall at the hands of those She so detests?"

"I SAID WAKE UP!"

Sylas flinched and his breath quickened. He must have dozed off in his room.

He forced his eyes open. Simia was standing at the end of the bed, her hair fiery in a shaft of sunshine, her tanned face wearing a broad grin. He hadn't just dozed off; it was the next day.

"Come on!" she said. "I don't know what people get up to in your world, but in mine sleeping in the afternoon is just plain lazy. And boring. Anyway, Filimaya wants to see you in the gardens."

Sylas pushed himself up on his elbows and squinted at the criss-crossed beams of light. "What time is it?"

"Late! You'd better get a move on. They want you to leave tonight to go to the Magruman, just to be safe."

"About that," said Sylas, "what exactly *is* a Magruman and what—"

"Not for me to tell you," said Simia smartly. "They don't even think I should come along."

She glanced around only to see that Sylas was still in bed.

"Are you going to lie about all day?" she asked in a matronly tone. "Get up! Filimaya's waiting!"

Sylas groaned and slid his stiff limbs out of bed. He saw that there were fresh clothes lying on the sofa and he walked over to inspect them. They were very coarse and crudely dyed in browns and greys like Simia's, but they seemed to be the right size. He dressed as quickly as he could, finishing with a simple but warm coat, then tapped Simia on the shoulder. She turned around and inspected him.

"Big improvement," she said, cocking her head on one side. "But then that wasn't difficult."

"You can talk!" retorted Sylas, pointing mockingly at her giant coat, which still swamped her tiny frame. "Why do you always wear that thing? It's way too big."

Simia looked down and smoothed some of the folds with her hands. He saw that she was a little lost for words, and he immediately regretted saying anything.

"I like it," she said with a trace of hurt in her eyes. "It was my father's."

He winced. "Oh," he said, "I'm sorry, I didn't..."

"We have to go," she said briskly, throwing her head back. She pointed over to the Samarok on his bedside table. "Don't forget your precious book."

He walked sheepishly over to the book, put his hands round the leather cover and tucked it under his arm, enjoying the velvety sensation on his palms.

Simia led him out of his room and round the gallery to the staircase. As they walked, he noticed that many of the large wooden doors leading off the landing now stood slightly ajar and occasionally he thought he heard someone moving inside. Simia saw him trying to peer into one of the rooms.

"Lots of them stayed last night," she said still a little tetchily. "Longest Say-So I've ever seen. A lot more 'Say' than 'So' if you ask me," she added, rolling her eyes.

They clambered down the steps into the great hall, which showed little sign of the meeting the previous evening. The vast shoals of fish were once again twisting and turning through the dark green water of the Aquium, disappearing here only to reappear there a few seconds later. Sylas slowed to watch them swimming, yearning to reach out to the glass as he had done the previous day.

Simia turned and tutted. "Come ON!" she insisted.

He took a last look at the glorious maelstrom of silvery bodies, then with a sigh of frustration followed her down the steps to the platform.

As they stepped on to the circular stage, she reached down and pulled a wooden lever concealed in its rim and he heard the familiar clunk and grating of gears somewhere below, and then it started to move, lowering them slowly into the darkness. The doors were soon drawing closed above their heads and they were plunged into the gloom of the shaft.

"Filimaya's going to teach me to control them," said Simia as the platform continued to descend.

"Control what?"

"The fish," she pronounced proudly.

Sylas bit his lip, remembering how they had seemed to react to his hand. "Really?" he murmured. "That'd be great."

Moments later the great platform shuddered and, with a deafening clank, it halted in front of a dimly lit opening.

"This way," said Simia, stepping off. She took a few paces

forward, then descended a long staircase towards a glimmer of daylight somewhere below. Sylas edged forward through the darkness and followed. There were no railings and he had to trail a hand over one of the slimy walls to keep his balance. After a while they stepped into a short passage and then emerged into bright sunlight. He shielded his eyes and gazed out at the astonishing scene before him.

"Wow," he whispered.

They were looking out across the gardens of Meander Mill. Immediately in front of him was a shower of bright red and yellow leaves that formed a perfect frame to the beautiful display beyond. Through them he saw vast eruptions of life and colour: here, a giant plant with dark, finger-like leaves and huge tubular flowers made of a single white petal spiralling round a deep blue stamen; there, a mountain of grass-green leaves arranged into great fans, rocking and tilting in the breeze; to one side, a display of fine drapes made from the tendrils of a weeping willow that bowed down to a mossy bank; and nearby, a patchwork of amber, scarlet and gold formed by great swathes of dappled leaves. All this despite the chill of winter. But what made the sight truly breathtaking was the constant motion of silver-white water frothing over pebble-strewn waterways, bubbling down mossy banks and cascading down rocky channels. The entire garden glistened and shimmered, making the sun's rays dance among the leaves.

"Are you coming?" called Simia impatiently.

She was standing on a bank of moss and grass at the bottom of another short flight of steps. Sylas bounded down to join her, landing with a pleasant thump on soft, spongy moss. They set off along a faint path that led round the base of a tree towards the nearest of the waterways. As he walked, he became aware of the strong aromas rising from the plants around him, some fresh and green like new-cut grass, others rich and fragrant like fine perfume. They were like none he had ever smelt before: somehow purer and more intense.

"It's so beautiful," he said, raising his voice so that Simia would hear him.

"Hmm," she grunted, without turning.

He stopped. "Listen," he said. "About the coat — I'm really sorry. It was a stupid thing to say. I didn't know it was your father's — it just didn't occur to me."

"It's fine," she retorted sharply.

"I... I guess it didn't occur to me that you *had* a father."

She whirled about. "What's *that* supposed to mean?"

He shrugged. "It doesn't matter."

"Yes, it does matter," she protested, hands on hips. "Everyone's got a father — why shouldn't I have one?"

"Well, I don't," he said flatly.

She frowned. "Of course you have."

"No, I don't. He died before I can remember. Never met him. So no father, not really."

She looked at him long and hard and her face softened. "Oh," she said.

"It's OK. You didn't know," he said meaningfully, but with a smile. "I'm a bit of a lost cause really — I don't know where my mum is either. She could be here for all I know."

Simia lowered her eyes. "I'm sorry I snapped," she said, sounding ashamed. "You didn't know about my coat. Or about my father. It's just that... he died too."

"I'm sorry," said Sylas softly.

There was a moment's silence. "Call me Simsi," she said, looking away.

He drew a deep breath. "I will. And let's start today again, shall we?"

She raised her eyes and smiled. "Good idea."

"So where's Filimaya, Simsi?"

"Not far now."

They walked in silence through veils of leaves and over carpets of thick, luxuriant grass, and soon reached the edge of the stream. They crossed a series of stepping stones, and at the other side Sylas stopped to take a better look at the tumbling water, curious to see where it was coming from.

To his surprise, he saw a great cascade falling from a carefully crafted opening halfway up the garden wall. The torrent crashed down on to rocks below, then muddled between them and formed a stream over the grassy bank.

"It all comes from the great wheel."

It was Filimaya's voice.

He turned around to see her standing next to him, dressed in a long white gown with a beautiful silver feather stitched high on the breast. She had appeared without making a sound and was now looking up at the waterfall as he had been, admiring its beauty.

"It's not an ordinary waterwheel," she continued. "It lifts water almost to its very top and sends it into channels within the walls of the mill house, which then flow down to the Aquium, then inside the garden wall and out into the garden. The waterways are some of our finest creations."

"So is the garden!" exclaimed Sylas.

"Well, that *is* our finest creation," she replied lightly, "although of course we must share the credit with Nature. We must always remember Her role in things." She took a deep breath of the scented air and looked over at Simia. "Thank you, Simia, you can leave us now. Please go and help Grayvel with the preparations.

He's expecting you on the top floor."

Simia pushed out her lower lip and seemed about to protest, but Filimaya frowned, which silenced her before she had even begun.

She looked over at Sylas. "See you later," she said. "And don't do anything exciting without me!"

"I won't," he said, but he wondered if he would be able to keep that promise.

She turned and, with a surly glance towards Filimaya, stomped off over the stepping stones, her voluminous coat flapping about her. When she reached the other side, she skipped off through the trees, humming a tune and twirling a finger through her hair.

Filimaya watched her go, smiling quietly to herself. "Such a spirited child," she said, almost under her breath. "And such a comfort to us..." She drew a breath. "Did you sleep well?"

He nodded. "Strange dreams, but yes, thanks."

"All this is like a strange dream, is it not?" she asked, with a smile.

"The strangest."

"Well, I hope I can help you to make more sense of it. I'm very grateful to you for speaking so honestly yesterday, particularly about your mother – I know those things were not easy to talk about. I'm just very sorry that I wasn't able to tell you anything about her. At least the Say-So reached a conclusion, though: we will take you to Paiscion, the Magruman."

He cleared his throat. "Yes, though... I don't really know what that means."

"Of course! I apologise. Paiscion, the Magruman, is the most powerful and the wisest among us. If there's anyone who can help you – help *us* to understand why you're here, who you really are – then it's Paiscion."

Sylas nodded. Powerful and wise sounded good.

"But that's not to say that we can't use your time here well," continued Filimaya. "You and I should try to improve our understanding in a different way. I would like to spend a little time telling you something of ourselves, and there is no better place to do that than here, in the Water Gardens. They'll help to explain both who we are and what we believe in, because working with Nature is something of a talent of ours — a very particular talent. We call our talent Essenfayle."

"Simia said something about that," said Sylas excitedly. "She said it's the 'Fourth Way'."

Filimaya nodded. "Indeed it is. It's *our way* — the way of the Suhl. Most people are taught that there are only three ways, or to use the languages of your world, three kinds of magic. They are Urgolvane, the way of force; Druindil, the way of communing; and Kimiyya, the way of transformation. But although each of those kinds of magic seems very different, they have one thing very much in common: they change the natural order of things. They change what things are made of or how things behave. They leave the world a different place, and normally not in a good way. Essenfayle is not like that. It changes nothing. Instead it works with the natural connections between things: connections like the rain and the stream that carries it away, the roots and the earth that feeds them, the sun and the leaves that bask in it. A garden is woven together by millions of these connections, and when you know how to work with them, you can make a garden like this."

"Even in winter," said Sylas, looking around him in wonder. "So is this what Essenfayle is for? For making things grow — that kind of thing?"

Filimaya laughed. It was a bright, beautiful laugh.

"Well, yes, in part. But there are many other things one can do

203

with Essenfayle, such as light a dark building with a single beam of sunlight." She gestured towards the mill house. "You have already seen that. But it's most powerful in the outdoors — here, where we're surrounded by Nature. Here we can do so many things, like connect with other living things..."

As she was speaking, she turned and waved her hand out over the stream. At first nothing happened: the dancing water continued to flow as before. But then, to Sylas's astonishment, the surface broke in one place and then two, then three and four, until soon it began to boil with froth and foam. Moments later it erupted as dozens of tiny fish launched themselves out of the water towards Filimaya's hand, flapping in the air for a moment before splashing back down into the stream. As the moments passed, more and more fish joined the display, leaping out of the water only to fall into it again a few paces further upstream, then drift with the current and launch themselves upwards again, forming a silvery arc beneath her hand.

She gave him a brief smile, then raised her other hand. "... Or change the way the wind catches the leaves..."

He looked excitedly across the stream and saw a large bronze-coloured bush swaying as Filimaya spoke, its beautiful leaves leaping and twisting under a new breeze. Filimaya moved her hand slightly and several fallen leaves flew up into the air high above the bush and then fluttered downwards, where they were caught up by another gust. She shifted her hand again and they began moving slowly around the garden, all the while rising and falling on currents of air. They drifted around Sylas so that he could feel the gentle wind against his neck, and then they moved back to the bush where they were joined by others, until he and Filimaya were entirely encircled by fluttering leaves, dancing on an invisible wind.

"... Or change the way light plays between the clouds," said Filimaya, lifting her eyes to the sky.

At that moment the light in the garden altered as though a patch of cloud had moved away, and suddenly they were bathed in warm winter sunshine. The bronze leaves glowed more brightly as they continued their dance. The flurry of leaping fish glistened as they flew through the air, the droplets of water about them sparkling like diamonds. Sylas wanted to cry out with excitement, but he found himself speechless, so beautiful was the great circus of light and colour around him. In that moment, with her arms tracing invisible lines through the air and her face brightened by her creation, Filimaya looked like a great conductress, directing a symphony of leaves and light beams.

All at once, she lowered her arms and everything altered. The leaves were no longer carried on the breeze and they drifted down to the ground. One by one the fish stopped jumping, and soon the stream babbled its way towards the river as it had before. Finally the light changed as a cloud moved overhead, casting a new shadow across the garden.

"Now do you see?" asked Filimaya expectantly.

Sylas looked up and grinned. "I see..." he said, taking a very deep breath. He thought for a moment. "But you said that Essenfayle doesn't change natural things — surely that's what you just did? Change things."

"It might seem that way, but I didn't. All I did was change the *connections* between things. The fish were in the stream already, I just made them aware of me. The wind was blowing, I simply changed how it played across the leaves. And the clouds were drifting across the sky all along — I just changed where they went. The most important thing about Essenfayle is that it works *with* Nature, it does not alter it. It cannot create clouds, or wind or fish, but it can change how they behave towards one another."

Sylas nodded slowly, beginning to understand.

"Is that how the Passing Bell works — connecting this world with the Other?"

She smiled broadly. "Good," she said, putting a hand on his shoulder. "You'll make an excellent student of Essenfayle. Now if we look at Kimiyya, for example, it is an entirely different picture. Kimiyya changes the very essence of things, the make-up of them. It alters the way substances behave and combine, forming entirely new creations, some of them harmless enough — even useful — but many of them utterly monstrous and dangerous. The Ghor themselves are a product of Kimiyya, as are many of Thoth's creatures. It is a powerful magic, but do you see how different it is from Essenfayle?"

"Yes, yes, of course," said Sylas, horrified by the thought that the Ghor had somehow been planned and grown — farmed like some hellish kind of crop.

Filimaya turned, parted a curtain of willow leaves and walked into the green shades beyond. "Walk with me," she called from beyond the canopy.

Sylas found his eyes drifting back to the stream. With a quick look both ways, he extended his hand towards it, then a little more. Nothing happened. He felt slightly foolish and his hand wavered in the air, but in that moment he thought of the fish leaping in the sunlight, of the bright, silvery arc of flapping tails and glittering scales. Suddenly two fish leapt from the dancing surface of the water, rising high into the air, seeming to reach towards his hand.

"Sylas?" called Filimaya.

He dropped his hand and, with another quick glance around him, pulled back the green veil and stepped under the willow tree.

The riverside was still. The boats rolled quietly in the ebb and flow of the stream. For some moments all that could be heard was the chatter of birdsong, the gentle lapping of the water and the soft clunk of the jostling boats.

But then, almost imperceptibly, one of them seemed to drift a little away from the others, against the flow of the current. It stopped in its new position and for a few seconds it seemed as though it would drift back among the other boats, but then a long bluish-grey arm slid noiselessly out of the water and reached over the side. Three wart-ridden fingers closed round a stack of papers, snatched them into a fist and dragged them down into the murky waters.

The surface stirred, betraying a powerful movement below, and a dark shadow snaked away through the water. Its fish-like motion propelled it swiftly along the bank until it reached an overhanging willow, where it paused. Two bulbous eyes broke the surface first, then a snout that rose a little above the water and sucked in the air. It stayed there for some moments, turning its head to sniff in different directions, and finally it gave out a gurgle of satisfaction before once again it was on the move.

It swam quickly to another low, overhanging tree where it stopped again and lifted its entire grotesque head, the water dripping silently down its scaly neck. It reached forward with its long fingers and parted some leaves so that it could see into the garden. The protruding eyes searched for a moment, then it bared its rotten teeth in a grin. It made an odd clucking noise in its throat as it watched Sylas reach out towards the stream, but just then, as his sleeve fell away to reveal a glistening metallic band, the Slithen recoiled.

Its grin faded and it shuddered, hissing through its teeth.

A look of puzzlement came over the loose, scaly features and it turned away from the bank, looking out into the river as it considered what it had seen. Then, as it lowered itself back into the murk, it slid its pointed tongue across the pink curl of its lips and a sneer passed over its face.

18
The Two Worlds

"And now darkness gathers — a quiet, contagious darkness, rooted in the history of our two worlds."

SYLAS STEPPED INTO THE warm sunlight. They were on the grassy bank of another small stream, which flowed haphazardly between rocks on its way towards the river. Beyond it, another gushing rivulet emerged from between the lustrous leaves of a giant ivy plant, which lay like a cloak over rocks and stones and scaled the garden wall to its very top. Further ahead flowed another stream and then another, each carving its own unique path between bright mossy banks, green rocks and beautiful plants, bushes and trees. Occasionally two streams would meet and form a deep, slow-moving brook or a rippling pool, only to part again further down the slope and resume their playful journey through the garden. Between the leaves and trunks Sylas could just make out the river's edge, frothing under the deluge of water.

"This is Mr Zhi's favourite part," said Filimaya over the sound of rushing water.

Sylas looked at her in surprise. "He's *been here*?"

"Oh yes, but many years ago, before the war," she replied,

starting to walk up the bank towards a piece of thick, mossy timber that bridged the first stream.

Sylas walked hurriedly behind her. "So was he a Bringer too?"

"He may be the most important of them all."

"Why?"

She laughed. "Well, that's difficult to say. I suppose when he looks at our two worlds he sees connections where others see barriers and differences. That's a very marvellous thing, particularly in someone from the Other. No doubt it's partly because he has spent so much time in both worlds, but it's also more than that — it's a special... vision that he has."

Sylas frowned. "In what way?"

"Well, Mr Zhi would say that the connections between the worlds are all about you," said Filimaya, sweeping her hand across the garden. "Look at these plants, these trees, these streams — aren't they like those you know from the Other?"

Sylas looked around him. "Yes... but there is a difference. Everything's brighter and — I don't know — fresher."

"Well, yes, certainly there are differences, but only the ones you'd expect. We don't have machines or cars or factories and we never have — just imagine what a difference that has made to the living things in our world. What you see are simply your own plants, fish, trees — all natural things — allowed to grow as Nature intended."

He looked again at the broad leaves and the thick, lush undergrowth. It was hard to believe that these bounteous plants were those that he knew from his own world, but they *were* all oddly familiar. Larger and greener, yes; but he knew their shapes and scents.

"OK, so the machines then — surely that's a difference between the two worlds, not a connection?"

Filimaya stepped off the mossy log and started to walk towards a pool of water, beckoning to Sylas to follow her.

"Yes, they are a difference, but Mr Zhi would say that there is a connection at the heart of that difference. Where you have machines and technology, we have magic. Not the magic of your storybooks and fairy tales, but magic that is as important to us as your technology is to you: magic that warms us at night and brings in our crops; magic that raises buildings and powers towns; magic too that forges nations and then brings them down. Magic in our world, as technology in yours, is used by some to communicate, to educate and to heal, and by others to increase their power and to vanquish their enemies."

Sylas had reached the edge of the pool and he stood staring into the crystal-clear water, trying to absorb what Filimaya was saying. A shoal of silvery fish entered from one of the streams and swam slowly round the bank, finally circling in the shallows at their feet, drawing as close to Filimaya as they could.

"Well, I can't think of anything in my world that's as wonderful as this garden, or the Aquium, or the light in the mill house."

Filimaya raised an eyebrow. "That's only because you are used to your kind of miracle, Sylas. To us, cars are carriages with invisible horses, light bulbs are lanterns without flames and aeroplanes, well, they are magic indeed. Don't you think that your mother would call her science a thing of wonder, a kind of magic?"

Sylas thought for a moment. "Yes, she would."

"And the two are more closely linked than you might think. Kimiyya is the foundation of alchemy, which in your world has been developed into chemistry — the science of substances and how they react to each other."

He frowned. "But you made Kimiyya sound like such a bad thing — are you saying chemistry is bad?"

Filimaya smiled. "Well, it certainly can be bad. There, in the Other, science is used in ways that are good and useful, but also in ways that can be harmful and destructive. It's the same here with the Three Ways, but they are perhaps not used with the same care. Too often, far too often, they are used for evil."

Drawing her silver hair over her shoulder, she leaned a little over the pool and peered down at the fish, which swam excitedly beneath her gaze. Sylas leaned in too, watching the fish of many different kinds, all swimming together in a shoal.

"Mr Zhi used to say that we were quite wrong to refer to your world as the 'Other'," continued Filimaya. "He said we should think of it more as a reflection of our own world. Like your face staring back on the surface of this pool — you know it's yours, but you also accept that it's different from the one you can touch. Have you ever noticed that things in Nature often fall into two complete opposites? Light and dark; hot and cold; life and death?"

Sylas thought for a moment. "No, I hadn't, but it seems kind of obvious."

"It's obvious because it's natural to us — it's the way the world works: good and evil, male and female, fire and water. Essenfayle teaches us about the connections between all things, and even these things — these opposites — are no exception. Just as winter cannot exist without summer, and there can be no death without life, there's something that connects all opposites. Indeed the connections between these things may be the most important of all. When your world is asleep under the moon, ours is awake under the sun; when your world is in the full bloom of summer, ours is paling in its winter."

Sylas blinked. "So it's night-time in my world *right now*?"

Filimaya nodded.

"And when the bell brought me here... I didn't sleep until morning — but it was *already* morning?"

"Yes," she said, smiling. "That's why you were so tired last night."

He puffed out a lungful of air. "That's... weird."

Filimaya laughed. "Weird, yes, but wonderful too," she said. "The discovery of the Other led to an age of wonder, a time when the true nature of the world seemed to be within our grasp. There was not one way into the Other, but hundreds. There were not only Bringers, but travellers from our world too. It was a time when your world learned much of what it knows about magic, and our world — or at least our part of it — learned so many things about yours."

Sylas shook his head as he tried to imagine what he was hearing. "But if there were loads of people going this way and that, surely we'd know about it? I mean, not everyone's going to keep quiet."

"I'm not sure that everyone *did* keep quiet in those early years. Certainly some of our magic was seen by people who shouldn't have seen it. A number of unscrupulous displays of magic passed into your myths and legends and, in some cases, they led to entire schools of magical study in your world. I've already mentioned your world's alchemy, which developed from Kimiyya and later became your chemistry; and what you call telepathy and necromancy are probably a corruption of Druindil, the way of communing. But those indiscretions soon died out when the Merisi appeared."

She stood up and gestured for him to follow her to the edge of the clearing. They emerged on to a gravel pathway that led towards a small wooden building in the dimmest, most shaded corner of the garden.

"What did the Merisi do?"

"They were wise, and restrained, and careful. They followed a great Eastern philosopher named Merisu, who first taught of the two worlds. While our ancestors were excited by their discoveries in the Other, from the very beginning the Merisi were cautious, warning of the dangers of too much haste. At the heart of their beliefs was a conviction that it was up to them to ensure that the way between the worlds was used wisely. They shared their texts with us and offered us their teachings, and in return they asked that we strictly control our explorations of the Other. Indeed soon it was ruled that no one from your world — no one other than a member of the Merisi — was to be brought into ours. It was left to them to choose those best suited to make the journey, to ensure that they were properly prepared and to make sure that their findings were properly recorded. And so the first true Bringers came to us. From that point on they were to be summoned every ten years on the summer solstice."

A flooded woodland meadow lay in their path and Filimaya stepped on to a raised walkway, that passed over the glistening surface. She moved lightly, as though the grass and earth beneath her feet and the wind playing about her robes were aiding her every motion, easing her passage through the garden. At that moment, with all that she had told him flooding his mind, revealing things of mystery and possibility beyond anything he had dreamed about, Sylas thought that she looked truly magical. He followed closely behind, keen not to miss a word.

"And what did the Bringers do when they were here?" he asked.

"They were brilliant researchers for your world and teachers to ours. Bringers were honoured members of our society, lecturing in our schools, speaking to our communities, giving counsel to our leaders. And while they did all this they learned from us, studying our beliefs, our customs, our magic; noting their most important findings in their book of learning..."

Sylas's eyes widened. "The Samarok?" he asked breathlessly.

Filimaya smiled. "Yes, the Samarok."

Sylas pulled the book from under his arm and stared at it with new wonder. This was it? The single record of all that learning? How could Mr Zhi have entrusted him with something so important?

"Let us stop here, Sylas."

Filimaya had paused at the end of the walkway. Ahead of them stood the wooden building, which Sylas could now see was little more than a ramshackle hut, accessed by some crooked stone steps. At first he thought it had no windows, but as he looked up, he saw two panes of glass set into the sloping roof, one on each side of a smoking chimney.

"I think you have heard quite enough of my voice for now," she said, her eyes lingering on the Samarok. "But I hope I've answered some of your questions."

Suddenly they heard the slow creak of a door swinging on aged hinges. A set of long white whiskers emerged from the doorway of the hut. It was Fathray, the ancient gentleman from the Say-So.

"Ah, there you are," wheezed the wizened old man, squinting into the light. "Come on then, Filimaya, hand him over — he's mine now!"

Filimaya smiled fondly at him. "Of course, Fathray. But just remember, watch your language."

"Why, what can you mean?" retorted Fathray with a twinkle in his eye.

She raised her eyebrows. "Just choose your words with a mind to your audience," she said. "We're not all scribes, you know. If you can't count the syllables on the fingers of one hand, don't say it!"

Fathray raised his great fluffy eyebrows. "Ah, my dear Filimaya, always so par-si-mon-i-ous," he said with a mischievous grin, counting out the syllables with his long fingers. "Well, if Sylas listens as pers-pic-a-cious-ly as I expect, we'll be just fine, no matter how lengthy our con-fab-u-la-tions!"

Filimaya laughed. "Your thumb doesn't count, Fathray."

He knitted his eyebrows. "Ah well, that's why I'm a man of words and not numbers!"

He gave a grin of very few teeth, then turned on his heel and disappeared into the darkness.

Filimaya put a hand on Sylas's shoulder. "Go on," she said encouragingly. "Fathray's going to show you a whole new world."

Sylas glanced doubtfully at the ramshackle building. "Another world? In *there*?"

She smiled. "Oh yes," she said.

§

The Slithen shifted from shadow to shadow through the deserted streets, slithering beneath canopies, through nets and between crates until it reached the fish market. There it crawled under an empty stall and waited, scanning the desolate street, sniffing the air.

A horrifying, bloodcurdling scream shattered the silence, echoing from the walls, ringing from the cobbled street. The Slithen shuddered and eyed its source: the vast pillared building with stone steps at its entrance and, above, a giant inscription in red lettering and a black, skull-like face, its eyes glaring down, seeing all. Slowly, reluctantly, the Slithen climbed out from its hiding place and rose on unsteady legs. Drawing a long, rasping breath, it stepped out in the direction of the Lord's Chamber.

It had taken no more than five steps when it saw the first movement. Silent but swift, two large shadows glided from the rear of the dark edifice and prowled out on to the white stone. The creatures launched themselves off the steps and landed on all fours on the cobbles. With a chilling snarl, they rose to their full height, looming above the cowering Slithen.

One of the Ghor lowered its grizzled head and glared at the stinking creature with its half-human eyes. "You *dare* approach the Lord's Chamber?"

It shrank into itself, pulling its webbed hands into its chest, lowering its head between its sloping shoulders. "I have information," it gurgled between clenched teeth. "Information about the S-S-Suhl."

The other guard closed its huge black claw round the Slithen's neck and tightened it until the creature began to gasp, its gills flaring wide.

"What could a snivelling trail of slime like you tell us that we do not already know?" it snarled, extending its neck until its sharp, discoloured teeth grazed the Slithen's cheek.

The Slithen tried to straighten, lifting its head a little. "I know lots-s-s," it rasped proudly, opening a clenched hand to reveal the creased, grimy remains of the documents it had stolen from the boat.

The Ghor leaned in and peered at them, then let out a loud, scoffing bark. "They could be anything! There's more filth on them than ink!" It slapped them out of the Slithen's hand.

The creature yelped with pain and then cried: "I know where they're hiding the boy!"

The two dark figures shifted. The grip around the Slithen's neck loosened.

"What do you know of a boy?"

The Slithen pulled itself up still further. "I'll not be telling mutts-s-s like you," it hissed. "I want to s-s-speak to Thoth. Take me inside."

The two guards exchanged a glance, then let out a low, growling chuckle.

"As you wish…" grunted the larger of the two.

It grasped the wretched creature round its neck and dragged it towards the steps. It took the entire flight in one bound while the Slithen's spindly legs slapped the sharp edges of the stone, making it squeal. The guard simply closed its grip until the shrieks died away. It drew the miserable beast through the imposing doorway of the Lord's Chamber, then trailed the limp body down a long, torch-lit corridor. At the end it paused next to two gigantic bronze doors.

It gathered itself for a moment, then knocked.

"What is it?" came a smooth, female voice from beyond.

"An informer, my Lady," barked the guard, glancing down at the dying Slithen in its claws. "It claims it knows where the child is."

There was a brief silence.

"Enter," called the woman.

The guard pushed on the door and it swung open to reveal a huge chamber with high ceilings, supported by rows of columns like those on the front of the building, though these were beautifully decorated with symbols and hieroglyphs. The majority of the marble floor was filled with long lines of chairs, leaving a single aisle in the centre, which stretched from the doors to the far end of the hall. There, a giant red banner hung from the ceiling and from between the folds of the fabric glared an immense empty face, its hollow eyes seemingly fixed upon the strange scene beneath.

A bloodied figure knelt on a raised dais of stone, whimpering quietly. It was the wretched wagoner who had unwittingly driven Sylas and Simia through the town. He was flanked by two black, hunched Ghorhund bearing thick silver collars, their bared teeth just inches from his neck. Behind stood a woman, resplendent in her black and crimson gown, the whites of her beautiful tapering eyes clearly visible against her ebony skin.

"Bring him here," she purred.

The guard strode forward, lifting the prisoner high into the air so as not to dirty the polished marble. When it reached the dais, it dropped the Slithen unceremoniously on the floor.

"It says it'll only speak to Thoth..." it growled.

The Slithen's eyes widened in terror and it shook its head, trying in vain to speak.

"Will it indeed?" said the woman, arching a narrow eyebrow. She tilted her pretty oval face to one side and smiled. She leaned over the cowering Slithen. "Well, I *am* sorry to disappoint you, my dear creature, but Thoth is not here."

She waited for it to respond, but it was still struggling to find its voice. When it said nothing, she lowered herself still further, extended one of her small hands and lifted its slimy chin.

"Though I suppose that, as I *am* Scarpia, Magruman of Gheroth, I could almost be said to speak for Thoth." Her mouth widened into a gentle, beautiful smile. "Indeed *some* would say that you are as good as looking at him right now. They would say that this is his voice; that this—" she reached down and began stroking its grime-coated head — "is his hand, comforting you; that this—" she motioned to the nearest Ghorhund, which immediately stepped to her side — "is his dear pet. And I am quite certain that they would say that these are his teeth that you feel about your neck."

The Ghorhund seized the terrified Slithen round its throat.

Calmly, Scarpia rose, wiping her hand on the Ghorhund's ruffled mane. Her face suddenly hardened and her black eyes flared.

"Now tell me everything you know."

19

The Den of Scribes

*"Even as the threads of history are unpicked by meddling hands,
we shall gather them up and on these very pages weave them into a
new, most glorious design."*

As THE DOOR CLOSED, the little hut was plunged into a gloomy
half-light. The corners were shrouded in darkness, but the centre
was bisected by two sloping beams of light from the windows in
the roof. As Sylas looked down their length, he saw, to his surprise,
that they descended far below where the floor should have been
into a deep chasm at his feet.

"Do keep up, young Master Tate, time is not our friend!"

Fathray's voice echoed about him, and then he saw the little
old man's white locks some way below him, bobbing downwards
as he descended a spiral staircase. Soon the only evidence of him
was the sound of him humming a tuneless melody: a collection of
notes that had absolutely no business being together.

Sylas found a metal railing to his right and started to follow.

As he descended, he could sense the closeness of the walls
around him and smell the mustiness of the earth.

"What is it with these people and dark places?" he muttered

under his breath.

Fathray's footsteps stopped. "Oh, I'm afraid you must forgive us our love of the shadows," he called up from the darkness. "We have had to become quite accustomed to tunnelling like rats and living like moles!"

Sylas bit his lip. "I'm sorry, I didn't…"

"Not at all!" came the cheerful reply.

The footsteps resumed and the old man struck up his peculiar tuneless humming once again.

As he followed, Sylas was relieved to find that soon a new light began to penetrate the gloom. After just a few more twists of the staircase he could see a definite glow rising from below his feet and moments later he had to squint as he looked into a strong white light. He saw a long, narrow chamber criss-crossed by a network of bright beams, just as he had seen in Meander Mill, though here the beams seemed to fulfil a different purpose. They zigzagged across the chamber several times, bouncing between mirrors fixed to the walls, then rose to the ceiling, where they turned sharply downwards, falling on to a series of large, brightly lit wooden desks arranged along the centre of the room. Each of these strained under the weight of great piles of books, scrolls and parchments, and a number of people in white gowns were hunched over them, poring over some or other document. A handful of other people worked feverishly at the rear of the room: stacking, sorting and tying together large heaps of paper and books, then carrying them to a growing mountain halfway along the room.

"Welcome to our burrow, young Master Tate."

As these words echoed up from the bottom of the staircase, all activity in the room stopped and everyone looked towards the new arrival. Sylas hesitated, then gave a nod of his head. Everyone in the room gave a courteous bow and continued to look at him expectantly for some moments, but when he said nothing, they turned back to their work.

"I'm afraid our little Den of Scribes isn't much to behold," continued Fathray, "but it has served us well these twenty years. Come — let me show you around."

He let Sylas off the bottom step and started to guide him along the row of desks. The floor was made of uneven, hard-packed earth and Sylas had to choose his footing carefully for fear of stumbling. He looked up at the arched ceiling and saw that it too had been carved out of the earth, supported here and there by simple braces of timber. However, the walls on either side were lined with books, documents and papers that had been arranged neatly along shelves that ran the full length of the room. At the top of each panel of shelving was a plaque, upon which was engraved a quotation. The one nearest to them was credited to Paiscion:

"Forgetting is a merciless foe. He offers no second chance."

The next he looked at seemed to have been written by Fathray himself:

"There is no such thing as too much knowledge, or if there is, that is more than we wish to know."

Fathray swept his hand in front of Sylas's face. "Here, on this side, we keep the originals and there, on that side, are our labours of love: the transcriptions. The lower shelves—"

"Originals of what?" interrupted Sylas.

"Oh, heavens!" said Fathray, whirling around. "Did Filimaya not tell you what we do down here?"

Sylas hesitated, not wishing to embarrass Filimaya. "Well, no, not... exactly," he said.

Fathray simply chuckled and wheezed. "Out of sight, out of mind! We tunnel rats are used to it! Eh?" He clapped Sylas heartily on the shoulder.

Sylas smiled quizzically, wondering how he had suddenly been made a fellow rat.

"Well, I'm afraid I haven't got time for a proper tour," continued the old Scribe. "That would take days." He extended his ink-stained finger and drew it along the nearside wall. "See here, these are all of the old documents. Up there—" he pointed with a flourish to the top shelf — "are the histories; below them are the works of learning, particularly on the subject of Essenfayle; below those are journals; then there are government papers and the works of fiction, and finally, down there—" he pointed to the bottom shelf, which brimmed with papers and folders — "are the registers of births and deaths. Rather important, those," he muttered reflectively, "if we are to remember who we are."

Sylas looked at the vast collections of registers for a moment, but then his gaze travelled back up to the top shelf, where something had caught his eye. Nestled in among the drab brown histories were three much larger black volumes, embossed with beautiful silver designs. Each of the spines bore the same inscription, marked out in ornate silver lettering:

The Glimmer Myth

He frowned and mouthed the title under his breath. He was about to ask Fathray what it meant, but the old Scribe pulled him further down the hall, pointing his crooked finger at the long line of desks, which glowed under the beams of light.

"Here is where we scribble — transcribing each and every one of the original documents into new volumes, which are then stored on those shelves." He pointed to the other side of the room, where long lines of identical brown leather volumes stretched the full length of the room.

"But why are you *copying* everything?"

Fathray looked down at Sylas, his eyebrows arching over the rims of his spectacles. "To keep them safe! We aren't just copying them, we're *encoding* them! We're transcribing each text into one of scores of scripts — secret ones — special ones — *beautiful ones* — ones that only we know. We call them Veil Scripts. Most have been around for centuries, but we are fairly certain that we are still the only ones who can decipher them. That way we know that they can be of no use to anyone but us. Come — I'll show you some."

He led Sylas down the length of the room past Scribes writing frantically at their desks, each of them seeming to compete with the next to write faster and in stranger and stranger scripts. Their heads were so low to the tables that they seemed almost to be sniffing at the ink as it met the page and they only raised their eyes to throw an occasional prying glance at each other's work.

At the far end of the earthen hall they came to a wall shrouded in shadow. With a tiny movement of his hand, Fathray drew a beam of light from the nearest table across the floor and on to the very centre of the wall. Suddenly the entire surface writhed with symbols, shapes and runes, each one carefully inscribed in one of a rainbow of colours. Sylas gasped. Everywhere he looked curves, strokes, designs and characters were entwined with one another, forming a great glistening tapestry of impossible complexity.

"This is our record of every symbol, character and rune available to us," said Fathray with some pride. "Quite apart from being the prettiest wall in all Gheroth, it's a wonderful tool. You see, the scripts are arranged in groups of similar types so that we can choose which we need more easily. The colours are absolutely precise, because the colours are just as important as…"

He trailed off. Sylas had taken several steps backwards and was staring open-mouthed at the wall.

"Impossible…" whispered Sylas. "It… can't be."

"My dear boy, what's wrong?"

With some difficulty, Sylas drew his eyes away from the wall and looked into Fathray's face. "I've seen these symbols before."

Fathray looked puzzled. "Surely not. Where?"

Sylas felt the hairs prickling on his neck.

"In my own paintings."

There was a silence as Fathray frowned at Sylas as he stared back, both hoping for an explanation.

"But these ciphers are only used by the Suhl," said Fathray finally. "I'm certain that you are mistaken."

"I'm not mistaken," said Sylas firmly. "I've been painting them for years — on my kites."

There was another silence as Fathray glanced from Sylas to the symbols.

"Did anyone teach you?"

Sylas shook his head. "No, no one understood why I painted them. My mother helped me, but she never did any painting. She just taught me to use the brushes and she…"

He paused as something seemed to occur to him, then he walked to the wall and peered closely at some of the symbols. "What do you call this colour — this green?"

"Why, I believe we call it Mislehay," said Fathray.

"And this red?"

"That's Orivan. Sylas, what's this about?"

Sylas turned back to the wall and pointed to a large ornate rune depicted in silver. "And this is Girigander, isn't it?"

Fathray was startled. He stared at Sylas for a moment, stroking his long moustache.

"How did you know?"

"My mother gave me a set of paints…" said Sylas, putting his hands to his head as he struggled to understand, "and they were labelled with those names — labelled in her own handwriting…"

Fathray's features suddenly became animated and he threw his hands in the air.

"Well, Master Tate, I can assure you that there is no other place she could have learned of these colours than here, from us! They are names that only we use!" He took Sylas by the shoulders and, in his excitement, shook him rather too hard. "This confirms it! You *are* one of us after all!"

But Sylas felt no such excitement; he felt sick. His mother *knew* about all this? How could she have known?

Fathray began pacing up and down. "Where is your mother now?"

"In hospital," muttered Sylas.

Fathray slowed his steps. "She's unwell?"

"She's… yes, I mean… I'm not sure."

"Indeed…" murmured Fathray, frowning.

"It's just a family thing — my granny was the same… dreams — vivid dreams, that's all."

The old Scribe looked intrigued. He regarded Sylas keenly for a moment, then turned his eyes back to the wall. For some time they were both silent, looking intently at the symbols. Finally Fathray drew a long breath and spoke.

"Young Sylas, we know at least one important thing: that for whatever reason you and your mother were connected to us long before you heard the Passing Bell. You certainly *were* meant to come here. I am now more certain than ever that we are right to help you reach the Magruman. Only he will know what must be done."

Sylas did not reply. His eyes moved over the great mass of lines and colours on the wall as he thought about the kites and the paints and his mother. None of it made any sense. He had always painted whatever had come into his head — no one had ever taught him. And then there were the paints: where did his mother get them? And how had she known the names of the colours? He stared into the great labyrinth of runes, tracing their intricate lines with his eyes, wondering if she had seen these very symbols — perhaps even known their meaning.

He blinked and turned away, realising that Fathray was still looking at him.

"I'm sorry," he said, drawing a deep breath. "It's just that I don't know who I am any more — who my *mother* was... I mean, is."

Fathray smiled soberly, placing a hand on his shoulder. "Indeed you are a mystery, young man. You are the original — what do you people call them in the Other? Something quaint... yes: you are the original *jigsaw puzzle*."

Sylas did not smile or react, but his features slowly filled with a new resolve.

"Fathray, I need you to help me," he said, looking up at the old Scribe. "I know I'm supposed to go and see this Magruman person, but I need to find out what I can now." He dropped the Samarok on the table. "This has something to do with it, I know it does. I need you to teach me to read it."

Fathray hesitated. "But Sylas, these things are not..."

"Don't tell me it isn't possible," he said firmly. "After the last

228

few days I know nothing is impossible."

The two regarded each other for a moment, Fathray worried and hesitant, Sylas pale but determined.

"I have to know why I'm here," he insisted.

Fathray looked at Sylas and then at the Samarok. The gems in the cover sparkled more brightly than ever and the strange symbols glowed mysteriously. He ran his fingers over the beautiful cover, enjoying the feel of the leather, the stones, the long S-shaped groove.

"Such a marvellous thing, is it not?" he said. "The answer to so many mysteries."

He leaned forward and opened the book. It fell open at the page where Sylas had inserted Mr Zhi's piece of paper. Fathray first picked it up and scrutinised Mr Zhi's handwriting, then carefully set it down next to the Samarok. For some time he stared at the open pages with an expression of unfettered delight, his eyes flicking over the lines of Ravel Runes. He hummed his artless melody to himself, seeming entirely unaware of how ludicrous it sounded.

Finally he looked up at Sylas and winked.

"Come, young man, I have much to show you."

20

The Ravel Runes

"They are the very instruments of ideas, of thought and creation;
taking us wherever our winged mind may choose."

FATHRAY CLEARED HIS THROAT and pressed the Samarok flat on
the table.

"Let us begin with the basics," said the old Scribe, pulling
Sylas closer. "The Ravel Runes themselves. Look straight down
at the pages... what do you see?"

Sylas peered down at the runes, remembering not to expect
them to make sense. The characters shifted a little under his gaze
and, sure enough, he soon saw the strange shapes of the Ravel
Runes.

"I can see the runes," he said.

Fathray raised his eyes to Sylas's face for a moment, seeming
surprised.

"Good. Do they mean anything to you?"

Sylas moved his eyes along a long line of beautiful, intertwined
runes. "They look the same as always."

"That's fine. To be expected. You see, you won't be able to read
them until you have a reference, which — unless I'm mistaken —

is precisely what we have here..."

With a flourish, he took up the piece of paper bearing Mr Zhi's handwriting and pored over it for a moment. His eyes flicked along the lines, seeming to digest its contents in seconds.

"Yes, that's exactly what it is."

He put the piece of paper down on the table so that they could both see it and leaned across for the Samarok. He thumbed through the pages until he reached the opening lines of the book, then prodded it with his inky forefinger. "There! That's it!"

Sylas looked down at a page that looked like any other. "That's what?"

"Look harder!"

Sylas stared again at the page, then looked back at the piece of paper. Something caught his eye. He looked quickly backwards and forwards between the paper and the page. There, in the centre of the page, was a section of runes beginning and ending with a small space, as though arranged into a paragraph. It was about the same length as the paragraph written by Mr Zhi. He put his finger on the piece of paper and carefully counted the words. Eighty-one. Then he counted the words made up of runes. Eighty-one.

Fathray chuckled next to him. "Simple, isn't it? All Mr Zhi has done is translate the second paragraph of the book into English so that you have a reference, and I dare say that this particular paragraph contains all of the important letters of the alphabet. Now all you need to do is look at which symbol stands for which letter and you are on the way to understanding the Ravel Runes."

Sylas was already at work, his eyes moving rapidly between the piece of paper and the page. Sure enough, the first word of the paragraph in the Samarok contained four runes, and when he looked at the piece of paper, he saw that the word was 'They'. The same for the next word and the next word — all of them contained the same number of runes as there were letters in the English word. Where a letter was repeated in English, a rune was repeated in the Samarok. Each rune stood for a single letter.

"It *is* simple," he said, looking up at Fathray. "But surely that's too easy?"

Fathray laughed and patted Sylas's cheek. "Oh, Sylas! It's far from easy! Most people take years just to be able to *see* the runes! You are quite special! Quite special!"

Sylas frowned. "But I don't understand — it only took me..."

"Seconds! I know! Mr Zhi must have been astonished — I certainly was! Don't you see, Sylas? You may not be a Bringer by name, but you are one nevertheless!"

Sylas swallowed and looked back at the Samarok. A growing excitement began to course through him, partly because he felt closer to finding out why he was there, and partly because some strange, distant part of him was not in the least surprised. He felt the familiar feeling that he was on a path chosen for him, that he was discovering something that he was meant to know about himself.

Fathray was busily flicking through the Samarok. "Come, let us see if you can remember any of the runes. There," he tapped an open page, "try that."

"But I need to look at the first page," said Sylas. "I need to see which rune stands for which letter."

"Just see what you can remember."

"But I only worked out a couple of words..."

"Just try."

Sylas shrugged and looked down at the page. He scanned along the first line of runes, which was written in a beautiful, looping hand, but all he could see were the strange symbols. They travelled across the page in an incomprehensible web of interlocking shapes, broken only where one word ended and another began. He closed his eyes in frustration and looked away at the wall of symbols, staring at them for some moments, wondering how he was supposed to remember. But suddenly he had a thought. He had known some of the symbols on the wall before he had even heard of Mr Zhi or the Samarok, without even realising it. He thought back to when he had first tried to read the Samarok in his room and he remembered feeling that the runes were somehow familiar.

Perhaps there was part of him that knew the Ravel Runes as well.

He turned his eyes back to the page, tried to cut out all of the sounds of rustling papers and scurrying footsteps, and focused on one of the words in the first line. He allowed his mind to fall into the coils and curves of the Ravel Runes and he found himself enjoying their impossible shapes, savouring their complexity.

At that moment, without knowing why, he said: "Cold…"

His heart thumped with excitement and his eyes moved on to the next word. Inexplicably, without seeing any letters on the page, he knew what it was.

"Cold… creeps," he said in a shaking voice.

A smile formed on his lips and he glanced up at Fathray, who was visibly quivering with excitement. Sylas took a deep breath and looked down again, this time at the beginning of the line, moving his eyes with ever increasing speed between the words.

"As… we… leave… the… light… we… enter… darkness… as we… pass from… warmth the… cold creeps about us…"

He looked up at Fathray in utter bewilderment. "I understand them — all of them!"

"Yes!" cried Fathray, clapping his hands with excitement. "When you recognised the runes on the wall, I dared to think that you might know the Ravel Runes as well — you just needed to believe it! Oh, how marvellous!" He reached across and turned at random to another page.

"Here, try something else!" he cried, then rushed off, returning only moments later with a group of narrow-eyed Scribes.

"Watch!" he demanded. "Watch! It's a miracle! Right here — in our den!"

Sylas looked dubiously at the gathering, far from sure that he would be able to concentrate with such an audience, but he turned back to the page and tried to clear his mind. The runes were written in a jagged, untidy hand and were arranged into short lines, as though in verse. He fixed his eyes on the first word and began to read.

"*What… rule… is there… what law*
But… gnashing teeth… and… grasping claw…"

There were several gasps from those gathered round and they all leaned in, chattering excitedly among themselves.

"He's a Runereader!" gasped an old hook-nosed woman.

Fathray smiled broadly. "And all he needed to do was believe that he could! That's all this was for!" he said, waving the piece of paper in front of them. When they had all seen it, he drew it up to his beady eyes and pored over it with new-found respect.

Meanwhile Sylas was leafing excitedly through the Samarok, wishing that he could read it all at once. He finally settled on one of the last pages.

"*A path that… ends… ends not, but… leads back from… wh-whence it came*
And thus at this our… journey's end is another… just beginning."

A Scribe with yellowish-brown skin and dishevelled grey hair pushed forward. He was so extraordinarily stooped that he had to peer round someone's elbow.

"All very impressive," squawked the Scribe in an aged, dry voice. "But what I really want to know is, can you *un*ravel the runes?"

Sylas shrugged and shook his head. "No, I don't think so."

Fathray looked up from Mr Zhi's paper and smiled, pleased that his colleague had asked this question. "Listen well, Sylas," he whispered. "Galfinch here is our finest Scribe."

Galfinch was pushing at the others to let him through and he soon appeared next to Sylas, flicking his black eyes over the boy's features.

"You see, the most amazing thing about Ravel Runes," he barked, "is that they *un*ravel. Their coils and loops are so beautifully complex that they act like tiny nets, trapping the very meaning of a word. They hold it within their grasp until you allow them to let it loose. And when you do, when they release that meaning to the rest of the text, any other runes holding the same meaning themselves begin to unravel." He peered down at the Samarok with unbridled admiration. "Soon the whole text is reacting to that meaning, forging connections, one upon the other, to reveal an entirely new reading — a new way to see the same book…"

"Let him *try*, Galfinch," interjected Fathray. "It will make much more sense when he sees it for himself."

Galfinch huffed at being interrupted. He turned back to the book and rifled hurriedly through the pages, searching for something. Finally he stopped at a page that Sylas had already read and pointed his ink-stained finger at the same verse.

"There, this piece you read — what was it about?" he asked.

Sylas looked down at the words under his finger. "'Gnashing teeth and grasping claw'… Well, I suppose it's about the Ghor."

"Yes, yes — of course," said Galfinch. "But now focus your

mind on this section of the text, and open your mind to what it means. Think of the Ghor, picture them: how they move, their muzzles, their claws, the way they speak… their battle cry…"

Sylas turned his eyes to the page and looked carefully at the short piece of text, at the same time remembering the Ghor as they stalked past the Mutable Inn, prowling in formation along the street. As the picture in his mind became more and more vivid, so the runes started to change. At first it was almost imperceptible — one tiny line moving round another or a loop slowly coming undone — but moments later the runes slowly unravelled on the page, the curves straightening, their loops and turns uncoiling. Then, to gasps from the small crowd round him, the rest of the page started to change: all of the runes twisting and shifting until the whole text writhed under Sylas's gaze. They began to find a new shape: their lines slowly turning in upon themselves until they had settled into a new arrangement of words. Finally the page became still.

There was a long silence before anyone spoke.

"I've — I've never seen them work that quickly before," muttered Galfinch.

The others glanced from one to the other, apparently dumbfounded.

"He's not just any Runereader," whispered a balding man at the back of the gathering of Scribes, "he's *the* Runereader!"

Fathray put a trembling hand on Sylas's shoulder. "Read it, Sylas, from where you were before."

Sylas moved his eyes back to the same section of the page. Sure enough, the words had changed. He read aloud:

"*Of… beasts they spoke… of feral servants chained;*
Born to the… yoke of… man… yet sent forth… untamed."

And as he read, he understood. The Ravel Runes had changed

to take him to another passage about the Ghor.

Galfinch snorted and giggled with excitement.

"That's right! That's how the whole Samarok is knitted together – and it's huge! Immense! Imagine the amount that has been written by the Bringers over the centuries – it's all there! An entire library of it, there to be unravelled!" He leaned in so that Sylas had to look at him. "It's all about the *connections* – Essenfayle at its most glorious! Isn't it, Fathray?"

Fathray nodded. "And I believe we have found its greatest reader yet. Perhaps the reader for whom it was truly written."

There was a murmur of agreement from the assembled Scribes.

Fathray tapped the page in the Samarok.

"And *everything* is connected: just read the name at the bottom of that passage."

Sylas looked down the page to the very bottom, where three words had been penned in impossibly small letters. "Franz Jacob... *Veeglum*," he read. He looked up in astonishment.

Fathray nodded excitedly. "We all recognised his name when you said it at the Say-So!"

"Herr Veeglum? The undertaker? A *Bringer*?"

"Very much so!"

Sylas shook his head, struggling to believe it, but all the while his eyes were on the page. Something was nagging at him. He frowned at the signature. The barely legible jagged lines, the flamboyant V, the long, looped tail on the end of 'Veeglum': it looked familiar... He had no idea why, but he was sure he had seen it before.

And then something rushed into his mind. He reached into his bag and pulled out a crumpled piece of paper. The Order of Committal – the one that had sent his mother to hospital. His eyes travelled straight to the bottom of the sheet, to the signatures.

The first was his uncle's, the second...

He held the paper up against the Samarok.

The two scribbled signatures were the same. *Franz Jacob Veeglum.*

Herr Veeglum, Bringer of the Merisi.

"Why?" murmured Sylas, feeling sick. "If the Merisi are on our side, why would they have my mother taken away to a mental hospital?"

Fathray was still distracted by Mr Zhi's piece of paper, but he drew his eyes away from it and spread his palms. "Perhaps they knew that your mother needed their help. Do you know this Winterfern Hospital? Perhaps it is a place known to the Merisi."

Sylas shook his head. "Even if they have taken her somewhere good for her, why didn't they tell me? Why did they let me think she was dead?"

"I really don't know, Sylas." Fathray placed a hand on the boy's shoulder. "There are some things that books will not tell us. But now we know that your mother shares your connection to the Merisi and so to this world. And if that is the case, your journey to the Magruman and your journey to find your mother are one and the same."

Suddenly there was a commotion at the end of the hall. A large figure scrambled down the steps at a frantic run and Sylas immediately recognised Bowe's powerful build and glistening bald head, which dripped with perspiration as he reached the bottom of the staircase.

"They're coming!" he cried. "We have to go! *Now!*"

There were cries of despair from around the chamber. Fathray's face fell.

"Gather what you can!" he cried with a note of panic.

Instantly everyone was in motion, running for different parts of the room as they sought to gather up whatever documents and books they thought to be most important.

"Take what you can carry, but save yourselves! Use the tunnel!"

Fathray directed things from where he stood. He watched as his dear library was ransacked for what little it might yield in a few seconds: beloved volumes were pulled down from shelves, hurled hastily into sacks and swept from tabletops.

The first of the Scribes staggered with a mountain of paper to one of the shelves and pulled on a single volume, which released a concealed door in the wall at the end of the room. He disappeared into the darkness beyond, dropping parchments as he went. The sight of them being trodden into the dirt seemed too much for Fathray to bear and he turned away. For a moment he cast his eyes down, crestfallen, but then his gaze travelled once again to Mr Zhi's piece of paper. He took a long, deep breath as his eyes moved swiftly over the scrawl.

Suddenly he stopped. He stared at it with widening eyes, as though struggling to believe what he was seeing. Then he lifted his gaze from the paper and looked directly at Sylas.

His face was filled with wonder.

"What is it...?" asked Sylas.

Fathray turned away and grasped the Samarok. He leafed through to a particular page, then slid the piece of paper inside and closed it.

"Master Tate, you must take this," he said, his voice breaking. "Show the note and the page I've marked to the Magruman — it may explain..." he hesitated, struggling to find the words, "...it may explain everything!"

He passed Sylas the book and looked at him earnestly. "It has been a pleasure meeting you, Sylas Tate." He looked as though he wished to say more, but instead he pointed at the tunnel. "Into the tunnel! Scurry as fast as you can, like a good tunnel rat! They'll meet you at the other end. Run now, my boy! Save yourself!"

The old Scribe watched Sylas darting into the tunnel, then adjusted his glasses and allowed his gaze to drift slowly round his ransacked library, travelling over the remaining volumes and documents, the scattered papers and scrolls, rising slowly to the very top shelf. There, his eyes came to rest on the very same volumes that had drawn Sylas's interest when he had entered the den. Perched high above the hall, they had been overlooked by the other Scribes as they rushed to the tunnel, and their beautiful silver inscriptions still shone in a shaft of light:

The Glimmer Myth

Fathray turned and reached for a ladder.

"Who would have thought?" he muttered, the trace of a smile on his lips.

21

Burned, Scourged, Forgotten

"Homes burned, *gardens* scourged, *languages* forgotten; *and with them dies a blessed magic."*

THE TUNNEL WAS CLOAKED in a thick blackness that seemed to press in on all sides: the walls scuffed his shoulders as the passage twisted and turned, rose and fell without warning. But where others would have stumbled, Sylas sped on, well prepared by his years in the deranged corridors of Gabblety Row. He heard the yelps and curses of the Scribes, but he could not see them, not even when he almost collided with the man in front.

Suddenly he heard a shriek ahead of him followed by the sound of books and papers crashing to the floor. Before he had time to stop, the ground fell away beneath his feet and he felt himself sliding down a slope. He tried to slow himself by clawing at the passage wall, but it was no use — he was already moving too fast. He began to fear that he had fallen into some kind of trap, but then he saw a glimmer of light. Moments later his feet hit level ground and he was pitched forward through a curtain of twigs and leaves.

He landed heavily in mud and scattered parchments.

"Up! Off! Get *off* them!" came a bleating voice at his side. "You'll ruin them!"

It was Galfinch, scrambling on his hands and knees as he tried to gather up the scattered documents.

They were in a small clearing just a few paces from the water's edge. To their right, Sylas could see a swarm of people frantically loading a long line of rowing boats with documents, clothing and strange artefacts, all of them looking fearfully back towards the mill house and across to the other side of the river.

Galfinch pushed him to one side. "Every one of them is important now!" he blustered in a voice that seemed far too loud. "Quite priceless!"

All at once the bush behind him parted silently and a large powerful man raced into the clearing, kicking away parchments in his haste. He reached down to Galfinch and clamped his hand tightly over his mouth, then pulled him upright.

Galfinch looked at Sylas with terrified eyes and dropped his bundle of documents.

"Silence!" the man hissed in his ear. "Your squealing will kill us all!"

Sylas recognised the bear-like man as Bayleon: the huge bearded man who had spoken so strongly at the Say-So.

Galfinch nodded his head imploringly until Bayleon released him. He slipped down on to his knees and, stifling a sob, began gathering up his papers again.

"Leave them, you fool!" hissed Bayleon.

He took Galfinch by the arm, lifted him to his feet and started walking him towards the boats amid a torrent of sobs. As he passed Sylas, he lowered his eyes.

"Follow me," he said with a wink.

Something about that bold, conspiratorial wink made Sylas feel safer — that maybe things were not quite so desperate after all. He picked up the Samarok, wiped it on his tunic and set out after the two men, snatching up what parchments he could on the way.

The scene around them was one of feverish activity: some rushed backwards and forwards with the last bundles of belongings, others threw ropes across the piles of cargo and lashed them down, while the rest clambered fearfully into the boats and helped others into their seats. All of this took place without the utterance of a single word, as if it had been planned and rehearsed many times.

As he watched, all Sylas could think was that somehow this was his fault, that if he had not come, none of this would be happening. He felt ill as his eyes moved across the frantic scene, finally coming to rest on a small gathering of five or six people on the bank, with Filimaya at its centre. He recognised the small lithe figure of Ash and beside him Grayvel's anxious, bespectacled face; and as the crowd parted he saw Simia. She was speaking with her usual animation, her brow creased in a pleading expression, her hands clasped in front of her. Filimaya gave a final shake of her head and said something to the rest of the group. They all gave a slight bow, turned and hurriedly walked their separate ways towards the boats. Simia was motionless for a moment, but then flounced after Grayvel, muttering something under her breath.

Just before she reached the boats, she spotted Sylas. She said something to Grayvel, who tried to object, but she ignored him and ran over.

"They still won't let me come with you," she said as she ran up, her face flushed with emotion.

"Aren't we all going now?"

Simia shook her head. "Not to the same place."

Grayvel came up behind and put his arm round her shoulder. "Come on, everyone's waiting." He turned to Sylas. "It's been a privilege, young man. Good luck."

"Thank you," said Sylas. "And you."

The elderly man gave a brief nod and hurried Simia away. As they climbed into their boat, she looked over at him and mouthed a few words before being lost in the crowd: "I'll find a way!"

At that moment Bayleon strode up, having placed Galfinch securely in a boat where he was rummaging desperately through books and papers.

"I told you to follow me," he said gruffly. "Filimaya wants to see you."

They walked up to Filimaya as she was issuing final instructions to Bowe. Sylas was struck at once by her strange calmness — it was as though none of this surprised her, as though she had always known that this would happen. She made a few final points and then wished Bowe the best of luck. The Scryer made as though to leave, but then he hesitated and turned back to her.

"Why not go with Sylas? He needs you and... and it seems right that you and Paiscion..."

She reached over and placed a gentle hand on his arm. "I'm not the only one parted from the one I love," she said with a smile. "I know where I'm needed. I shall go with you and the others to the Valley of Outs. Go, my friend, and take good care of Fathray."

Bowe took her hand, clasped it tightly, then looked at Sylas. For a moment he fixed him with his large green eyes, then he turned and ran to the boats.

Filimaya looked down at Sylas. She frowned at his muddied clothes. "Are you hurt?" she asked.

"No — no, I'm fine," said Sylas. "What's happening?"

"They've found us," said Filimaya with a sigh. "It was bound to happen sooner or later."

"It's because of me, isn't it?"

Filimaya leaned over and fixed Sylas with her beautiful wise eyes. "Sylas, this struggle began long before you came to us," she said. "They were always going to find us one day. We're glad that you came, no matter what happens."

She smiled and wiped a little of the mud from his cheek, then took him by the shoulder and turned him to face the boats. She pointed to a small one in the centre that contained fewer belongings than the others. Ash was preparing it to leave.

"That will be yours," she said. "Bayleon and Ash will keep you safe and guide you to the Magruman."

"Aren't you coming?"

"Don't worry about the rest of us, Sylas, we'll be safe. Your path is far more—"

She was interrupted by a terrifying sound.

It was a swelling, mournful howl that began somewhere behind the mill, then swept along the garden wall and rose afresh on the other side of the river. It was not one, but hundreds of voices, each rising in pitch until Sylas had to put his hands over his ears. He looked at Filimaya, but she had turned away and was signalling to someone. In the next instant he felt himself caught up in Bayleon's powerful arms and hurled forward as they sprinted down the bank. He was dropped unceremoniously on to some canvas bags in the bottom of the boat and moments later the boat lurched forward.

The howls broke into a confusion of baying cries. They seemed louder and nearer than before, but when Sylas peered over the side of the boat, there were no Ghor in sight. Filimaya had taken her seat in one of the boats and they now all surged forward into the main current of the river. But as they gathered in the centre of

245

the waters, he saw that one had stayed behind — the one moored nearest to the tunnel. He knew both the occupants: Galfinch, standing in the stern, and Bowe, sitting at the oars. Galfinch suddenly pointed frantically towards the tunnel and Bowe raised himself to his full height, craning his neck back towards the Den of Scribes.

Then it began.

Fathray fell headlong through the mass of foliage in front of the tunnel, gathered himself and started limping towards the boat, clasping three large ancient books under his arms. Then something strange happened. The entire garden seemed to writhe and change. Sylas looked up to the treeline to see hundreds of pale, lizard-like creatures swarming over the garden wall, slithering between the trees and sliding down the waterways. It was scores of Slithen, half running, half snaking their way through the garden, moving towards the water with frightening speed.

"Run!" cried Sylas as he watched Fathray limp towards the boat. "They're coming!"

But Fathray was still only halfway there. He was moving too slowly, struggling with his burden of books.

Suddenly he stopped, looked up towards the wall, and one by one, let the books fall to the ground. He turned and waved frantically at the boat, shouting at Bowe to leave. Still the Scryer waited, pushing at the oars to stay close to the bank, hollering desperately at the old Scribe to leave his documents and run.

Then Fathray did the strangest thing. He sat down in the mud.

Galfinch gesticulated furiously, calling hopelessly to his friend. In the same moment Bowe looked from Fathray to the trees. He paused, perhaps for a moment considering a mad dash across the mud, but then he reversed the stroke of his oars.

Their boat moved away just as the Slithen emerged from the

foliage and squirmed down to the water's edge. They were almost entirely naked, wearing only a loincloth around their middle, their bodies glistening as though wet. Their limbs were long and thin and they moved on all fours, more like reptiles than men, their long torsos bent low, their jutting, angular faces just clear of the ground. Most slithered straight into the water, extending their long legs behind them to squirm free of the mud and propel them out into the river, heading directly for Bowe's boat, but those nearest to Fathray turned. Slowly, they gathered about him.

"No!" cried Sylas, leaning over the side of the boat, his voice straining. He turned to Bayleon who was still heaving at the oars. "Go back for him! We can't just leave him!"

Bayleon lowered his eyes and said nothing. Sylas felt a hand on his shoulder and turned to see Ash.

"This is what he'd want," he said, his voice full of emotion.

Sylas shook his head.

He looked back at the old man's distant figure. His face could no longer be seen, but he sat with his cloak gathered about him and his arms clasping his muddied books to his chest. There was something about his posture — the way he held his head — that was unafraid. Defiant.

Then, as two of the Slithen advanced towards him, the old Scribe turned to the fleeing boats and raised his hand.

Those who were watching quickly rose to their feet and raised their hands in response. Sylas and Ash too struggled to stand in their swaying boat and raised their hands as high as they could, straining to be seen. There they remained for some moments, hands held aloft.

"What will happen to him?" asked Sylas, not wanting to know the answer.

"That'll be up to Scarpia," said Ash grimly.

Fathray had disappeared amid the bodies of the Slithen and Sylas was about to avert his eyes when something caught his eye.

At first it looked like a trick of the light, but then it became more distinct: it was a wisp of smoke rising from the rear of the garden. It curled through the treetops and climbed high into the air, making a dark smudge on the horizon. The smudge quickly grew into a grey streak, then a vast black cloud. Soon he could see several black columns rising from the garden, feeding the ever more ominous pall above. Then a bright flicker of flames glimmered between the leaves.

"The den's on fire!" growled Bayleon solemnly as he pulled on the oars.

Sylas stared in horror at the leaping orange flames that now rose high above the canopy of the trees. It was a terrible sight: the beautiful Water Gardens belching thick black smoke through their leaves and, even worse, the library burning. He knew at once that he was seeing the smoke of thousands of volumes disappearing into the air. All those wonderful books, Fathray's books, all that history, all those years of painstaking work — lost forever.

"But why?" he cried, leaning out over the stern of the boat. "Why would they do that?"

Ash placed a hand on his arm. "It wasn't the Ghor, Sylas. It was Fathray."

Sylas whirled about. "Fathray? But he loves those books! He told me!"

"He had to do it, to save them from the Ghor," said Ash, squinting into the distance. "It's the originals that he's burning; we've brought most of the rest with us."

He pointed to one of the nearest boats. Sylas saw Simia sitting among piles of volumes and parchments, wiping her eyes with her sleeve.

"Why?" asked Sylas more calmly. "What would they do with them?"

"What they always do," said Ash, pulling his ragged hair away from his face and tying it into a ponytail. "They'd use them to find us: our hideouts, our meeting places – the few sanctuaries we have left. And then they'd find our friends, and those who've helped us."

Sylas stared at him in disbelief. "Why?"

Ash shrugged. "Because that's the will of Thoth," he said icily. "That's the Undoing."

Sylas heard a squeal to his right and turned to see Galfinch in the rear of his boat, jabbing at the water with a paddle while Bowe strained at the oars, heaving it through the river at an impossible speed. A short distance behind, a single grey form slid through the water, sometimes dipping out of view, sometimes rising to the surface and extending a single long arm towards the boat, grasping with slippery fingers. As Sylas watched, Galfinch brought the paddle down with a crack somewhere among the waves and the hand fell away, leaving the boat to surge onwards.

"Look sharp!" cried Bayleon. "They're gaining!"

Sylas looked up at the river and saw to his horror that the entire surface was boiling with snaking bodies. He could just make out the pale skin of the Slithen, their strange inhuman legs sweeping through the water, their long, narrow torsos twisting, turning, carving towards the fleeing boats. They seemed to be coming not only from Meander Mill, but also from the other side of the river. He glanced towards the bank and watched with revulsion as an endless stream of Slithen clawed and slid through the mud towards the water, joining an ever-swelling army of tangled bodies in the waves.

Something drew his eyes to the top of the bank where houses

lined the riverside and he felt a new chill pass over him. In the shadows, standing just a few paces in front of the houses, were the Ghor. There were hundreds of them, each standing an equal distance from the next, facing the river. None of them moved, but they leaned towards the river as though poised for action, their weird canine heads hanging low between their shoulders. He looked back at the mill and saw another long line of them, some standing sentinel on the garden wall, the rest lining the riverbank. They seemed to be waiting for something, their eyes fixed on a point further up the river.

Sylas followed their gaze, dreading what he would see. On a high promontory of rock stood a chariot of crimson, black and gold, its many ornate designs flashing bright in the sunlight, its giant barbed wheels rocking as if readying to charge. Straining at its harnesses were two gigantic Ghorhund rearing on their powerful haunches and gnashing at the air, their massive heads arching back to reveal thick collars of solid silver. But it was the occupant of the chariot that most caught Sylas's eye. Even at such a distance, Scarpia's elegant figure made a dramatic impression. She stood with poise and confidence at the reins, her proud head held high, a crimson train snapping behind her as the wind whipped from the river. Her perfect features were creased in a broad smile of triumph. She pulled sharply on the reins and almost at once both Ghorhund arched their spines and let out a chilling howl.

The assembled horde quickly gave their answer, their howls random and wild, building to a new crescendo. They showed their teeth and clawed at the ground; they thrashed their chains and snapped at the air; and, as they answered Scarpia's command, their deafening wail urged the Slithen on, telling them that they were near, that they would soon reach their quarry.

"Come on!" shouted Ash, snatching up a spare paddle with an anxious grin. "Let's give them a bloody nose!"

Sylas drew his eyes away from Scarpia, took the paddle and stood up. He looked out and saw that the massed Slithen were now only a few boat-lengths away. Those in the lead were breaking the surface, rising into the air and then arching dolphin-like back into the water, showing a ridge of small fin-like scales running along their spines. As they dived over the waves, he saw their eyes peering blackly out of the foam.

"They're sizing us up," shouted Ash, tightening his grip on the paddle and raising it above his head. "They'll come any minute! Look down — they'll come from below!"

Some of the leading Slithen disappeared from view, diving deep into the dark waters. There was a moment of eerie calm when only the sound of the oars and the baying Ghor could be heard, then the river erupted, exploding into a shower of foam and water. From the centre of the deluge two large grey figures flew high above the river, arching towards the stern of the boat, their three-fingered claws outstretched. Ash was looking the other way, distracted by another Slithen swimming alongside the boat.

Sylas was alone.

He just had time to raise his paddle. It caught the first of the Slithen under its chin, smashing its teeth together. It faltered in mid-air and pitched forward, dropping head first into the bottom of the boat. But even as it landed the other came on, leaving Sylas no time. He felt a stinging slap against his neck and suddenly he was falling backwards, flailing in the air.

He landed heavily in the bottom of the boat, hitting his head against something hard. For a moment he was stunned and disorientated, but then he felt something cold and wet tightening round his throat.

When he opened his eyes, he was looking straight into the hideous, disfigured face of a Slithen.

22

The Wave

"The Suhl are of Nature born, like the rising sun, or unfurling leaves, or a mounting ocean wave.*"*

THE GRUESOME SCALY FACE was drawn back in a snarl, baring a mass of tiny, sharp brown teeth. A strange clucking noise rose from the back of its throat as it panted over him, smothering him with a horrible stench of rotten fish. Its slimy hands tightened round his neck and its black, glassy eyes widened gleefully, its pink tongue running over its pale upper lip.

Sylas thrashed wildly, trying to push it away, but his hands slid off its slippery shoulders. It lowered its face towards his and tightened its grip still further.

"Die!" it hissed. "Die like the res-s-s-st of them."

Sylas flicked his head up, catching the Slithen on its snout and making it rear backwards. It held on to his neck.

He was starting to struggle for breath when a look of surprise came over the Slithen's face and suddenly its grip loosened. Without warning, it was wrenched away and Sylas looked up to see Bayleon grasping it by its ankles. With a quick rotation of his massive shoulders, he swung it high into the air and over the side of the boat. The creature squealed until it was silenced by a distant splash.

"That's for Fathray!" roared Bayleon after it, wiping his sticky hands on his trousers.

He turned to Sylas. "Anything broken?"

"No, I don't think so," said Sylas hoarsely.

He took Bayleon's hand and drew himself upright, glancing about to see what was happening.

Ash was busy beating another creature clear of the boat.

"Back, you haddock! Eel spawn! Sea slug!" he yelled, punctuating each insult with a fresh crack of the paddle.

Although his frame was small and lean, his gangly limbs were strong and he had soon fended off the latest assailant.

There now seemed to be more Slithen than ever, but there was something strange about the way they moved. They were still arching out of the water as they snatched glances at the boats, but they appeared to be struggling to break the surface as if something was holding them back. The river around them was rising and swelling into a great wave, lifting them higher and higher on a wall of granite-grey water until Sylas could no longer see the mill or the townhouses far behind. He shot a questioning look at Bayleon who was once again sitting at the oars.

"What's happening?" cried Sylas.

For the first time he saw Bayleon smile. His white teeth glimmered through his dark beard. He nodded towards the other boats.

Sylas looked across the line of vessels and there he saw Filimaya standing tall in the prow of her boat, one hand held out in front of her. At her bidding, the water ahead of the boats had fallen away leaving a great trough the full width of the river, and the water behind had risen to compensate, forming the towering wave. The boats were now tilted downwards and were surfing at increasing speed down the side of the wave. He felt the wind in his hair as their own boat gathered pace. Bayleon no longer rowed, but instead allowed the oars to scud over the surface of the foaming waters.

The bow was soon bouncing over the surface and sending spray high into the air and Sylas crouched down to keep his balance. Looking behind, he saw a large white crest forming on the wave, then tumbling down towards them. But it never quite reached them, for as fast as the wave moved, the boats surfed ahead of it.

The Slithen were not so fortunate. Sylas saw those that were closest drawn into the churning heart of the wave, until moments later they were catapulted out of its crest, their gangly limbs flipping over and over before they dropped out of sight behind the foam. His heart thumped in his chest and he turned and grinned at Bayleon, who was once again wielding the oars, breaking the surface of the water to steady and steer the boat.

"Sylas! Over here!" cried Ash, sitting on the stern, leaning forward to stop himself from falling. "We need to balance the boat, or we'll flip over!"

Sylas clambered backwards over the bags and boxes and carefully took a seat next to Ash. Instantly the bow lifted a little and it started to surf more lightly over the surface.

From here he could see the whole dramatic scene: the long line of boats careering down the great wave, the vast mountain of water and foam behind them and the expanse of river ahead.

But just as his spirits began to rise, he recoiled. Only a short distance ahead of them a huge stone bridge spanned the river, supported by five immense arches. Somehow the entire flotilla of boats would have to pass beneath it.

Ash nudged him and pointed to the water's edge. A column of

dark figures approached the bank, their bodies thrown forward in a full sprint, their powerful canine legs moving in perfect unison. They bounded with impossible ease, taking quick, loping strides that carried them swiftly over the uneven ground and, despite their speed, their angular heads remained entirely steady as they watched the boats and scented their prey. Snapping at their heels came the two giant Ghorhund, straining at their leashes, baying in their frenzy. Despite their wild movements, Scarpia steered the chariot with effortless skill, steadying herself as she clasped the reins with one hand and directed the chase with the other. Still she smiled her triumphant smile, relishing the thrill of the charge, sweeping her hand across the ranks of Ghor, driving them forward as one. The long train of her crimson dress flew out behind her, catching the afternoon light, snapping and cracking in the wind like a standard of war. As she saw the bridge, she let out a shrill, chilling cry, and at once her troops lowered their shoulders and lengthened their stride to run even faster.

The boats were now moving at an astonishing speed, but there seemed little doubt that the Ghor would reach the bridge first. Sylas glanced at the other bank and saw another troop tearing along the towpath, running further ahead of the wave.

Filimaya saw them too and raised herself even further in her boat. It was a marvel that she did not fall. The wave grew with her until it was a deafening maelstrom of foam, lifting the boats high above the river. They surfed at such an angle that Sylas had to lean back over the spray to keep his balance, and Bayleon too struggled to stay in his seat as he carved the water with his oars, keeping the boat on course. The other oarsmen were also fighting to keep control and he heard yelps of surprise and a clash of wood against wood as two vessels struck each other. To his dismay, he saw that Simia was in the rear of one, being hurled this way and that, clinging desperately to the side. Both boats leaned over so far that it seemed certain that they would flip over, but as they started to pitch their cargo into the river, the oarsmen plunged their oars deep into the water and managed to steady their path.

Simia clambered up and seated herself in the stern, peering ahead of the wave. For a moment she stared at the bridge, seeming to consider something, but suddenly she began shouting at the oarsman. Sylas could not make out her words, but then she started jabbing her finger towards the centre of the bridge. Suddenly he realised what she was saying.

"Simia's right!" he shouted to Ash. "We're all going to have to go through the middle arch —the Ghor will reach the others before us!"

Ash looked across to Simia and saw her wild gesticulations, then glanced at the banks, where the Ghor were already nearing the two entrances to the bridge. He nodded, waved to Bayleon and held his hand up in the direction of the arch. Bayleon lowered one of the oars so that it trailed through the water and immediately the boat changed direction, traversing the face of the wave towards the middle of the river. The hull rolled alarmingly as it ran against the flow of the water and Sylas and Ash braced themselves against the sides. They stayed as low as they could and watched as all of the boats started to converge ahead of the arch.

It looked impossible — the archway would barely fit ten boats abreast in low water, let alone when they were riding high on a wave and travelling at speed. But there was no other way.

Their boat crashed into the side of another, sending shards of wood into the air and almost snapping the oars trapped between, but somehow both stayed afloat, the occupants exchanging frightened looks as they sprang apart and then crashed into each other again.

"Hold them together!" cried Sylas, stretching a hand out towards the other boat.

The other passengers scrambled to the side of their boat and, as they came together again, they reached over, grasped Sylas's boat, and pulled it tightly against their own. He clamped his arm over the side and held on as best he could. The other boats were doing the same and, as they drew nearer and nearer to the archway, he could hear the loud crack of timber on timber and the cries of the passengers as they tried to take hold of each other's boats.

He dared not look around — his eyes were on the bridge, which the Ghor were already beginning to cross. Some leapt up on to the stone balustrades and started bounding along them at impossible speed, while others charged through the pedestrians in the middle, brushing them aside with the cruel sweep of a claw.

The precarious raft of boats spanned the middle of the river, twisting and buckling as it surged towards the archway. Somehow it held, bound by the straining limbs of its passengers. Yet, as they drew close, the archway seemed ever smaller and their own strange craft all too large. Sylas was thankful that he, Simia and Filimaya were in boats near the centre, but even there the archways seemed too low. Too close.

Suddenly a cry from somewhere on the raft caught his attention and he glanced across to a disturbance in one of the other boats. For a moment all he could make out was a struggle and raised voices, but then he saw a distinctive flash of red hair and a tiny figure in an oversized coat, scrambling from boat to boat, ducking under flailing arms and jumping over limbs and oars, staggering at one moment and leaping at the next. Already she had crossed two boats, then three, and suddenly she was in the neighbouring vessel. She sidestepped an attempt to pull her back and launched herself into the air. With the great folds of her coat fluttering about her, she landed lightly in the bottom of Sylas's boat.

"I told you I'd find a way!" shrieked Simia gleefully.

Sylas shook his head in disbelief, then grinned.

"Fool!" growled Bayleon.

She opened her mouth to reply, but suddenly her face fell. She looked past him to the bridge, and shrank back into the bottom of the boat. Sylas turned and instinctively did the same, falling back on his hands. The bridge reared above them, blocking out the sky, bearing down on them, seeming now like an impassable wall of stone. Suddenly they were there, plunging into shadow, the central arch passing just an arm's reach above their heads.

Their ears were hit by a deafening boom as the great wave hit the bridge, striking with such force that the entire structure seemed to shake and a terrifying blast of air rushed between the boats.

"Hold on!" Bayleon cried.

And then, as they were pummelled by a vortex of water and foam, Sylas felt the next boat being wrenched free. He was about to be dragged into the tempest as his hands flailed over the water, but he felt Bayleon's arm across his chest, drawing him back to safety. He saw the other boat disappear behind a dark wall of water, rising high into the air as it turned almost to the vertical. The bow of their own boat seemed to be dragged deep and the stern was whipped around, starting a vicious, gut-wrenching spin. He was thrown so hard against the hull that the wind was knocked out of him and he lay stunned against a discarded oar.

He looked up with wild eyes to see a shadowy wave looming over them, its foamy fingers turning inwards as though to drag them down, but just as it threatened to consume the boat, there was a loud crunch that echoed on the inside of the archway. The flimsy vessel shuddered as though it would break apart but, to his surprise, the timbers held firm. The spinning seemed to stop. A moment later they were thrown back out into the daylight.

Still gasping for breath, he glanced about him and saw that, miraculously, Bayleon, Ash and Simia were still inside the boat. They too had been thrown to the floor and were just starting to push themselves up on to their knees, reaching out for stray oars and paddles.

They were surrounded by mountainous waves, but Sylas could already see other boats, some unharmed, some splintered and damaged. Five, six, seven boats appeared from beneath the bridge. He did not have time to see who was safe and who was not, for he heard a shriek of rage and defiance above, and his eyes travelled up to the vast grey arches of stone, then the baying ranks of the Ghor glaring at them from the bridge, and then to Scarpia, rearing back in her chariot, heaving at the reins as she raised her hands to conjure some new horror.

But then she hesitated and looked up.

He followed her fearful gaze upwards to the skies.

He saw no sunlight and no pendulous clouds; instead he saw a mighty overhang of granite grey: a sheer face of water that towered over Scarpia, the Ghor, the bridge and the town.

With nowhere else to go, the great wave had launched itself upwards, rising to the height of many men before thundering back down towards the massed Ghor. It struck with seismic force, shattering stone and crushing all that lay in its path, knocking Scarpia from her chariot as it careered back towards the shore. Hundreds of black bodies were hurled into the air amid lashing foam and many more were swept into the raging waters below. Screeching howls pierced the roar and then were swallowed by the river, drawn down into its cold, suffocating depths. The surface frothed with flailing limbs and jaws as the Ghor struggled to stay afloat, some striking out towards the shore, others looking for something else to cling to.

Sylas saw three boats a little further from the bridge: two overturned and broken, a third taking on water, its occupants trying desperately to paddle clear of the writhing Ghor. A number of the Suhl were struggling in the tempest, surrounded by floating papers and parcels, straining to reach the upturned vessels. Salvo clung to a broken piece of timber and Galfinch was being pulled by someone towards a shattered hull, gathering his precious papers as he went. The rescuer's bald, tattooed head was clearly visible as he moved powerfully through the water. It was Bowe.

Around them the wave was rising again, fed by the deluge of water. It had lost its power, but it was sufficient to push those boats that were still afloat clear of the bridge. Sylas watched in horror as the desperate swimmers rose on the wave and rolled over the crest.

"Bowe!" he shouted helplessly, glancing round at the other boats, willing one of them to turn round, but knowing that they were too far and it was hopeless.

The Scryer had somehow managed to stand on an upturned hull, steadying himself as the waves cast him from side to side, and now he turned to the other survivors. His doleful face broke into a warm, comforting smile. This tiny gesture seemed so out of place, so extraordinary given all that was happening, that in itself it was an act of heroism. Still smiling, he began to speak, gently motioning for his friends to stay calm, to lock arms and draw closer, to make the three wrecks into one life-giving raft. They responded bravely, those who still had their strength helping those who did not, so that soon they formed an intimate gathering: a respite from the storm. And, as they met, they reached out for one another, drew close, held hands and whispered comforts.

Then they waited for the inevitable.

All around them the dark river churned with the writhing bodies of the Ghor. They no longer thrashed the surface, but moved silently, purposefully through the ragged waves and icy surf. Slowly, they converged upon the sinking boats.

Sylas was about to call out again when Simia took hold of his arm and he turned to find her face drained of all colour.

"Look!" she said, pointing to another part of the frothing river.

His heart fell. It was Filimaya. She too had been thrown from her vessel and was being cast about in the great tumult of dark water, her long silver hair floating over its surface, her pale face momentarily hidden from view as she struggled through the surf. She was not as far as the others, and was only now rolling over the failing wave, but she was still some way from the nearest boat. She was swimming strongly, more strongly than Sylas would have thought possible for someone of her age — gaining on the boat, but slowly, too slowly, for as Sylas cast his eyes back to the upturned boats, he saw a new, deliberate movement among the struggling bodies of survivors and the Ghor.

The surface of the river broke in long, advancing lines, as though something large and fast were passing just beneath, coursing through the waves torpedo-like, with absolute precision and purpose. And then the first of them broke the surface: an angular, reptilian brow carving with ease through the turbulence, the glassy black eyes blinking wide as it took in the ragged line of boats, the slitted nose scenting its prey. It regarded them for a moment and then, as it rolled its scaly back and disappeared, another rose, and another and another.

"So many..." said Ash.

Yet even as they came on, even as they closed in on poor Filimaya, the boats had almost slowed to a stop. The wave had died and now drifted out beneath the keels, leaving them stranded. This allowed Filimaya to gain more quickly on her boat, and its occupants were already leaning out, willing her on, offering their hands in readiness to heave her over the side. But if the boats did not start moving within the next few moments, they would all be overrun by the Slithen. A great chorus of cries had risen from the other boats, coaxing Filimaya on, trying to give her new strength, desperate for her to reach the boat. It seemed that no one else could summon the waters.

And, at that moment, Sylas suddenly felt peculiarly calm, because he knew that his friends were lost.

He looked from the great phalanx of advancing Slithen now churning the river white in their expectant frenzy, to Filimaya making her last desperate strokes towards the boat, and finally to his own companions: Bayleon, hunched over his oars, looking down as though he could not bear to watch; Ash yelling Filimaya's name with a faltering voice; and finally Simia, lowering herself to the floor of the boat, her hands rising to her face, tears welling in her eyes.

Perhaps it was that terrible image of Simia starting to lose hope that gave Sylas a new, inexplicable resolve; a quiet, calm determination. For, as he looked at these people who had been so good to him, who had brought devastation upon themselves to help him, he became sure that it all had to be for a reason. At that moment the chaotic sounds of the tumult fell away — the shouts and screams, the baying roar of the Ghor, the hissing surf of the boiling river — all of it faded, leaving his own thoughts.

They came relentlessly, one after the other. He thought of Mr Zhi's kindly face and of his fateful words; of the raging din of the Passing Bell and of his safe passage beneath it; of his hand passing over that shining face of the Aquium and the shoals dancing at his bidding; of his fingers stretched out over the stream, the silvery fish leaping as if to meet them. For a moment he dared to believe that perhaps, just perhaps, everything had led him to this moment; that he was meant to be there, witnessing the plight of his friends. And perhaps he had the power to help.

"... *You can see all that you are able to be,*" Mr Zhi had said.

Sylas grasped the side of the boat and pulled himself slowly to his feet, steadying himself as the vessel rocked and heaved on the churning waters. Bayleon leaned forward and tried to pull him back, but he stepped out of his reach, past Simia and Ash, into the stern.

"What are you *doing*?" cried Simia, pulling at his coat before she was herself thrown back into the boat by the slap of a wave on the hull.

Sylas was hardly aware of her. He was looking out over the river towards his friends swimming desperately for safety, towards the legions of Slithen gliding through the waters and the dark figures of the Ghor closing upon their prey. He was barely conscious of his hands rising in front of him, of his companions staring at him in confusion and amazement, of the triumphant surge of the Slithen as they leapt as one from the waves before diving deep, deep into the river for the final attack.

He looked into the waters, losing himself in their depths. His imagination pierced fathoms-deep, seeing the great swirling currents surging and shifting, ebbing and flowing, seeing the great shoals of fish gliding, darting, weaving. He sensed them not only in his mind but in his body, feeling their cool in his veins, flowing through his limbs, their watery chill consuming first his chest, then his legs, arms and fingers. He was not frightened but calm; he felt no panic, but instead sensed himself becoming something more, something deep in his beginnings, in his very essence.

And as his imagination became the river, the river became him. He opened his palms and somewhere deep in the belly of the river he felt the currents, the fish, the eels, the weeds gathering at his will, drawing themselves together, heaving themselves with common purpose up and up towards the straining limbs of the Slithen and the Ghor. He moved his hands wider and felt this calamitous torrent rising through the pit of his stomach, charging up through his gut and his chest, launching up, and up.

And so it was.

As a great tumult of all the river's life they came: swimming things and scuttling things, things from the mud and from the deep, things that grasped and clawed and snapped and sucked, things that coiled and tugged and blinded. And, as the Slithen and the Ghor eyed their quarry above, all this came from below.

Weeds coiled about their limbs, eels slithered about their necks, a maze of silver scales confused their path, sending them far from the surface, down and down into the belly of the river. There they were grasped by the residents of the darkness and the deep and the mud: the crabs and lobsters and catfish and the tangled weeds. And, as these things swarmed in upon the Slithen, Sylas felt them pressing at his ribcage, grasping his lungs; he felt the tangle of limbs, the grey bodies lost in the maelstrom of biting and clawing and sucking; he felt them flailing in the blackness, straining towards the light and the air, letting out drowned squeals of panic.

And then, just as this horror became too much, he felt his boat heave beneath his feet.

He became aware once again of the surface of the river, and saw that it was rising in a new wave, surging on, sending the boats of the Suhl dancing and skipping on its glistening face. He heard the elated cries of his companions and Simia's shriek of joy as Filimaya rose tall in the rear of her boat, her hands raised, commanding the waters once again.

But she was no longer lost in her magic — she was not even looking at the river — she was looking at him.

As their eyes met, he saw in her beautiful, pale face something between confusion and wonder. For some moments she simply gazed at him, as though seeing him for the first time.

Then she broke into a gentle, knowing smile.

23
To the Hills

"There is more to the hills *than meets the eye, for they hide in their inner folds a sanctuary that defies discovery, a place of improbable magic, a place called the Valley of Outs."*

FILIMAYA WAS ONCE AGAIN queen of the wave, standing tall and graceful in the rear of her boat while it leapt and pranced beneath her, her hand outstretched as her eyes scanned the river and shoreline ahead for any sign of the enemy. The great wall of water had subsided a little and it now rushed and tumbled at a less terrifying speed, conveying the seven remaining boats to safety.

Still there was no sign of the Ghor on the banks or in the river and Sylas noticed people gradually relaxing a little, no longer straining their eyes to check for dark figures moving stealthily along the riverbanks or for eel-like shapes gliding below the surface of the river. Instead they looked ahead, beyond the outlying buildings of the town, beyond the jetties and mills and cattleposts to the forested hills that now grew before them, offering the barely believable promise of sanctuary.

Sylas writhed from side to side trying to get comfortable in the back of the boat, fidgeting with the bags that he and Simia had propped behind them. In truth it was not the hard boards and the endless bucking of the vessel that made him restless, it was the adrenalin still coursing through his veins and the tension between him and his companions. No one had said a word since all that had happened at the bridge, and while Simia and Ash had caught Sylas's eye more than once, they had quickly looked away.

Sylas was full of doubts. Had he really made those things happen? Had he really just saved his friends? After all, no one had seen anything on the surface — the Slithen and the Ghor in the water had just seemed to disappear. But then why had Filimaya turned and looked at him like that?

He tried to clear his mind, to think of something else, but instantly it filled with the terrible scenes he had just witnessed. What would become of the Suhl now? What would they suffer because of him? They had helped him, laid down their lives for him and in return he had led the Ghor to them, destroyed their beautiful hideaway, their wonderful gardens, their precious books.

He lowered his head into his hands, staring fixedly at the bottom of the boat.

"It's not your fault, you know."

Sylas looked up at Ash.

"No more than it's our fault that we couldn't help. This is just what it's like. The Undoing."

Sylas was silent for some moments, but then he lifted his eyes.

"What *is* the Undoing?"

Ash looked up at the hills and narrowed his eyes. "Hatred. Loathing. All wrapped up in a name."

"That's about right," grunted Bayleon, lowering an oar to wipe his brow.

"It's Thoth's attempt to annihilate us," continued Ash. "Him and his servants, like Scarpia. To remove us from his world, to destroy us and everything about us: our writings, our homes, our magic, our history — everything."

Sylas frowned. "*Why?*"

Ash shrugged. "It's not as if he's ever explained himself."

Bayleon laughed despite himself.

"No one's sure why," said Ash more seriously. "Some say that he fears Essenfayle, but it's time we accepted that the Three Ways are far more powerful than our—"

"Essenfayle isn't finished yet," cautioned Bayleon sharply.

"Well, much good it's done us." Ash looked over the side of the boat at the passing banks. "Anyway, some say it's to do with Essenfayle, but most of us think it's more to do with the Other. In any case, it is as it is. To be honest, most of the Suhl have stopped thinking about why it's happening. It's been going on for generations. They've come to see it as a fact, like the changing of the seasons. They think it has no end and no meaning, it's just the way of the world."

"Is that what you think?"

Ash met his eyes. "No. It means everything."

Sylas lay back and considered this for a moment. "How do you mean it's gone on for generations?"

Ash looked at him questioningly.

"Well, you said it was all Thoth's doing, so how could it have been happening for generations?"

Ash exchanged glances with Bayleon. "Thoth has been around longer than anyone can remember. He was alive before my father, and before my father's father. He's as inevitable as the rise of day." He spat over the side of the boat. "And as the fall of night."

They soon passed the final scattered dwellings on the outskirts of town and the river swept them out into the open countryside: tilled fields waiting for the first sowing of spring; wild pastures, home to teeming herds of sheep and cattle; hedgerows and coppices hanging over the waters; verdant woods full of ancient trees.

Sylas looked across at the tiny flotilla of boats clinging to the wave. It seemed even smaller than it had in town. So few, he thought, so very few. The plight of the Suhl seemed so hopeless — their lives so precarious. He thought of Thoth and the Undoing and everything they had lost, and he wondered how they carried on — how none of them seemed cowed or broken by what had happened at the bridge. There was no sign of relief or joy on those sallow faces, but neither was there any evidence of defeat. Instead they talked in soft tones among themselves or sat quietly, thoughtfully, their eyes fixed resolutely on the grey horizon.

Soon the occupants of one boat began to sing, quietly at first but then louder so that the others heard and joined in. Bayleon struck up in a deep baritone and Simia and Ash followed him. Sylas did not recognise it at first, but then came a verse that he knew. It was the song Filimaya had sung at the mill.

And so we change as change we must,
When standards rot and sabres rust,
When the sun is set and night is come,
When all is lost, when naught is won.

When nations fall, when day is done,
When all is lost, when naught is won,
What nobler charge, what cause so great
As brother's plight and kindred's fate?

Sylas listened for a while and then joined them in their song, humming the haunting melody. And, as they all sang, that feeble company gathered its strength and became one: united and defiant. To his surprise, Sylas felt his eyes burning and he swallowed down a wave of emotion. How proud he was to be one of their number. One of these desperate, courageous few.

As the wave surged on, the mood in the surviving boats began to change. They knew that sanctuary was growing near and the singing gave way to a new, animated chatter. They spoke excitedly about the impending fork in the river, which would take them deep into the river's sleepy meanders, through the hills, far into the sprawling labyrinth of tributaries and byways, oxbows and rivulets that would keep them safe from discovery. And, from there, they would soon find their brethren, hidden deep in the forested hills of the Valley of Outs.

This was the topic of conversation in most of the boats, but not all. The travellers in Sylas's boat grew quiet in their anticipation. They knew that their fork in the river would take them somewhere else entirely, somewhere alien and dark, bleak and dangerous.

Sylas rested with his back against Simia's, looking out at the other boats gliding down the river, at Filimaya talking and smiling with the others, her hand still outstretched over the wave. He lifted his eyes and saw the great forested hills looming ahead, some covered with the skeletal shapes of winter-barren trees, others bearing a dark green blanket of evergreens. He watched as the ground started to rise around them and the banks became steep and rocky, climbing slowly towards the grey sky. Once again he was in the hills, and they seemed to be welcoming him back. But how much more he knew now, as he came to them again. About this world, about himself, about his mother.

His eyes shifted to his backpack. He reached down and drew the Samarok from it, holding the ancient book for the first time since the Den of Scribes. His fingers traced the hard-cut gems, the leaves of parchment, the soft leather, and he found his mind drifting back to Mr Zhi, to the day that now seemed so long ago when he had been given the mysterious Third Thing. How confused he had been, how lost he had felt.

"*You have much to learn about the world you live in, but most of all about… who you are,*" Mr Zhi had said, "*and where you are from.*"

How true that had proved to be.

For some moments he flicked through the pages of the Samarok, scanning the strange runes and countless entries, and his thoughts turned to his encounter with Fathray.

"*… your journey to the Magruman and your journey to find your mother are one and the same,*" the gentle Scribe had said.

Sylas's gaze rose from the Samarok to the river and the wave that drove them onwards towards the Barrens. His eyes travelled over the passing rocks, the towering forests that shrouded the hilltops; then still higher, up into the darkening sky, where a great grey blanket had dulled the encroaching sunset to a pallid glow. There, far above the green canopy, he saw the dark shapes of giant birds turning lightly on the breeze, tilting on invisible currents to form graceful, intersecting circles in the void. It was another familiar sight, like the birds he had watched from Gabblety Row, flying high over the distant hills, calling him on.

He was meant to be here. He knew that now. Just as Filimaya had said, this strange place *was* a mirror to his own world — not an alien world, but one that brought him closer to understanding his own. Already it had taught him about himself and about his past, about his mother and hers. And it held many more answers — he was sure of it. Perhaps, after all, this mysterious journey was his best chance of being with her again.

"*I'll try to understand,*" he had told Mr Zhi.

"*That is all that I can ask. And that is all your mother would ask,*" was the reply.

He looked downriver, towards the deep ravines in the hills and the glowering sky above the Barrens, and for the first time he felt ready for what lay ahead.

"I'm coming for you, Mum," he murmured. "I'm coming."

PART THREE

The Truth

24

Our Darkest Shame

"In these barren wastes our darkest shame
O'erhangs where once the greenest bowers grew…"

AT FIRST SYLAS WAS only dimly aware of it, for it was not the presence of something, but rather an absence. He walked on, the river far behind him now, hardly knowing that anything was wrong, but feeling a growing tightness in his stomach. Sweat pricked the back of his neck, as if his body was trying to tell him that something was amiss. And then, as they walked across a small clearing in the densely thicketed forest floor, he realised what it was.

Silence.

The birds had stopped singing. The insects no longer chirruped in the undergrowth. The great canopy of trees was silent and still, for even the hilltop breeze had died.

It had not happened suddenly but gradually, so that he could not know how long it had been, but now it was absolute and suffocating. He felt oddly disoriented, as though this thick, heavy silence was like a descending blanket of darkness.

Suddenly he heard a sharp crack somewhere ahead. The snap of a twig. He peered through the bushes and caught a glimpse of red hair, stark and bright against the thick undergrowth.

Simia. Just Simia.

He breathed deeply and picked up his pace, keen to catch up with the others. His boots crushed the leaves and twigs, rustles echoing from the trunks of nearby trees. He flinched and glanced about him, feeling that surely something out there was watching him, mocking him. He kept moving, pushing aside branches and bushes, forcing his way through the undergrowth until he drew near to Simia.

To his surprise, she seemed entirely unperturbed as she marched steadily through the forest, her great coat pulled tightly round her against the cold, humming a tune while coiling a strand of her hair round a finger.

She turned and raised an eyebrow, looking amused. "Something wrong?"

Sylas frowned and spread his arms wide. "What do you mean, '*something wrong*'? Can't you hear it?"

Simia paused, drew a long breath of dank forest air and listened to the silence.

"Nope," she said, moving on.

"But why's it gone so *quiet*?" demanded Sylas, falling in behind her.

"It's just the way of this place," she said, not turning, but the smile fading from her lips. "You'll see."

She picked her way onwards through the forest, her slight figure shifting nimbly this way and that despite the heavy folds of her coat, deftly dodging bushes, logs and low branches. Hardly reassured, Sylas glanced about him for his other two companions. He could just about make out the lithe shape of Ash somewhere far ahead, the faint, colourless light occasionally catching his great nest of wayward blond locks, but the bear-like form of Bayleon was nowhere to be seen, already lost among the silhouettes of mighty trunks and the dank overhang of leaves.

The quiet settled about Sylas once again, cold and heavy. He felt the chill biting at him through his tunic, pooling in his lungs. He tightened his belt and picked up his pace, glancing hopefully up at the canopy of leaves, yearning for a glimpse of brightness, a ray of sunshine. But there was nothing. The silence had brought with it a slow, gathering mist: a featureless fog that hung about the highest branches, robbing them of light, shape and colour. And that was when Sylas realised that it was not just the sounds of the forest that had deserted them, it was the colour too.

Gone were the livid greens and rich textures of the riverside trees where they had moored their boat; gone were the dappled pigments of moss and crisp dried leaves that had splashed the forest floor as they had made their way up that lush gorge; gone too were the greens, browns, oranges and yellows that had mottled their path. In their place, their poor cousin had taken hold, something less wholesome.

A creeping, doleful grey.

The shapes and features of the forest were still visible, but all had been infected by a contagion of grey, sucking from them all that made them distinct and beautiful. Leaves, branches, bushes, logs, even the very earth, were only distinguished by the drabbest shade of grey. Light and dark had themselves surrendered, giving way to the plague of drabness, becoming mere shades of that lifeless hue, so that there were no contrasts upon which to focus the eyes, no absolute forms, no respite.

"What *is* this place?" Sylas murmured to himself.

He reached out to a nearby bush and ran his fingers through the leaves, which left a cold slimy trail across his fingers. His instinct was to pull his hand away in disgust, but instead he pulled the slippery branch down towards him and peered at the leaves. In most respects they looked normal, with the delicate veins and elegant shapes entirely intact, but they were utterly devoid of colour. He reached up with his other hand, took hold of one of them between his thumb and forefinger and pulled. It separated like wet tissue paper and broke up on his fingertips, quickly becoming a grey sludge, like damp ash.

Out of the corner of his eye he saw Simia change direction. She walked towards a dense mass of foliage that seemed, if it was possible, even greyer than its surroundings, and there he spotted the waiting forms of Bayleon and Ash. They were deep in conversation, apparently discussing the route ahead. He was reassured by their easy manner, and by Bayleon's massive, imposing presence: his well-worn, weathered features gave him the look of one accustomed to such wild places.

Sylas wiped his hand on his coat and set out to join them.

"Unnerving, isn't it?" said Bayleon with a gentle smile as he walked up.

Sylas nodded. "What *is* this place?"

Ash puffed out his cheeks. "Nowhere. Nothing," he said. He nodded towards the tangled mass of colourless leaves. "It's what's through there that you ought to be worried about."

Sylas shot Simia a questioning glance.

"What he means to say," she said with a smile, "is that this is just the edge of it, the beginning."

"The beginning of *what*...?" pressed Sylas.

"Of the Barrens, Sylas," said Bayleon, placing an encouraging hand on his shoulder. "The Barrens of Salsimaine."

Sylas looked about him, a little confused. Somehow this was not how he expected the Barrens to be. He opened his mouth to say so, but saw Bayleon had already turned away and with his great arm was pushing at the veil of foliage. It buckled and snapped with surprising ease, pallid grey light showing between the branches.

"Welcome to the Barrens, Sylas."

Sylas found himself looking at a towering wall of featureless grey. But, as he looked more closely at the blank space, he squinted and blinked. He could see movement: great leaden clouds of grey drifting and billowing, granite shadows beneath and in their midst, tracing a path above, a trailing, ashen blanket. It was not a wall of grey at all, but a vista of staggering breadth and depth, stretching from his high viewpoint as far as the eye could see.

Sylas raised a hand to his mouth. "My God..."

It was a landscape of utter devastation, depicted entirely in shades of grey. He saw now that the horizon glowed slightly paler, but above and below, the grey became thicker and more sombre, advancing towards them in waves of dreariness. He could just make out the gentle undulations of open country leaving the base of the hill on which they stood and setting out into the grey void. It rolled aimlessly, despairingly into the vast colourless expanse, broken only occasionally by streaks of blackness, as though the sun had somehow penetrated the greyness to char the fog-chilled surface. A gentle breeze blew up from the plains, cold and harsh, bearing the scents of Nature's decay.

He shuddered. Such a place seemed so alien in this world of wonders, this world of Essenfayle and the Suhl. It was more like an old photograph he had seen in *Revelations* — the science book given to him by his mother — a picture of a landscape blasted by fire and raked by winds and cloaked in death: the aftermath of a nuclear bomb.

He turned to Bayleon, who was just stepping into the clearing. "What *did* this?"

281

"We did," he said.

"Well, Thoth played rather a large part..." objected Ash, following close behind.

The great Spoorrunner adjusted his leather breastplate and looked out over the dreary expanse of grey. "We were there too. This place shames us all."

For some time the small group stood staring out at the nothingness. They became so still, so silent, that it seemed to Sylas that the greyness was drawing their life from them. It was not only the cold, or the absence of light or sound, but a sense that something so terrible, so unthinkable had happened here that it had taken root, seeped into the earth and infused the air.

His thoughts went back to his conversation with Ash in the boat, about Thoth and his legions, about his war against the Suhl and all that they stood for, about his attack on their entire nation and way of life, their men, women and children.

"Is this where it happened?" he asked. "The Undoing?"

The Spoorrunner stared out across the Barrens.

"The Undoing doesn't end, Sylas: it is not confined to a single place or time. But you could say that this was the worst of its horrors." He drew a breath of the heavy air. "This is the place where our people made their last stand in a battle we called the Reckoning. This is where Merimaat fell and where we all despaired. The Barrens is a place of endings, Sylas. Nothing good happens here."

There was a short silence, then Ash ran his fingers through his tousled crop of hair.

"Not the most *cheery* way to begin our journey across the Barrens, is it?" he ventured.

Bayleon shot him a withering look.

"What? I'm just saying that we need to be a bit more..."

"I know what you're saying, Ash," sighed Bayleon. "Maybe you're right. Maybe this journey with Sylas will be the first good thing to come of this place, but for now, it fills me with nothing but dread."

Ash drew a long breath. "Lunch! Lunch is what we need! As my rather portly father used to say, 'Never despair on an empty stomach!'"

He walked to a nearby rock and laid down his pack. Sylas and Simia watched as he pulled open the drawstring and began unpacking some of his things.

Bayleon regarded his friend with the trace of a smile. He laid down his own pack and began emptying it, taking out a small axe and various objects that Sylas took to be the trail-finding tools of a Spoorrunner — something that looked like a compass, a glass orb, various measuring devices. Finally he produced a large chunk of cheese and a loaf of bread wrapped in a waxen cloth.

Soon they were all eagerly taking their share of bread, cheese, dried meats and a fruit that Sylas did not recognise. Ash made a show of taking out a small jar of a yellow substance and spreading it thinly on his piece of bread.

"Mustard!" he announced triumphantly. "The spice of life. Never cross a dismal wasteland without it!"

Simia wrinkled her sun-blotched nose.

They ate heartily and between mouthfuls found themselves discussing all that had happened on that fateful day.

"What exactly happened at the river, Sylas?" asked Ash. "When we were being attacked. Did *you* stop the Slithen? Or was that Filimaya?"

Sylas thought for a moment, then shrugged. "I'm not sure — I know I *couldn't* have, but it felt like I did. It was like the river was in the bottom of my stomach... the fish and the reeds... the crabs, the eels... everything... Like they were all... it sounds stupid, but—"

"Like they were all part of you," said Ash, grinning. "That's exactly what it's like!"

"Yes!" said Sylas excitedly.

"Well, I didn't see you do anything except stand up in a boat," said Simia grumpily.

The smile faded from Sylas's face. "Well, it felt like that... for a moment."

"Hang on, hang on," said Simia. "You're really saying that you stopped a whole legion of Slithen without anyone seeing anything?"

"I don't know, but—"

"You think you've mastered Essenfayle in... what? A *day*?"

"Simia, you're not listening," said Sylas irritably. "I don't know what happened, I'm just—"

"Well, it *sounded* like you were saying—"

"You didn't listen long enough to hear!" snapped Sylas.

There was a silence. Ash and Bayleon exchanged glances and raised their eyebrows, then deftly changed the subject.

They talked about their friends travelling to the Valley of Outs, about the fate of Fathray and Bowe, about the Barrens. Soon conversation turned to Paiscion, the man for whom they were making this long journey, the man in whom they had placed so much hope.

"Do you really think it's worth it?" asked Sylas, his eyes travelling across the great expanses of the Barrens, picturing the dangers he and his companions might face. "Crossing the Barrens just to see this one man?"

"Well, there isn't anything to go back for," said Ash. "There's nothing left. The mill, the work of the Scribes, the community

— it's all gone and what's left is hidden in the Valley of Outs. The only way is forward now. Your journey, wherever it leads us, might be our only hope."

Sylas looked at Ash's youthful face, set firm, brimming with vigour and determination, and he knew that he was right, that somehow his journey was now as much theirs as his, that his questions were their own.

Simia looped an arm through his. "Where's your sense of adventure?"

It was difficult to tell where it first came from. It began quietly like the solitary hoot of an owl, then gained volume, rose in pitch and hung ominously in the grey air until there was no doubt what it was.

A howl.

Even as it reached its crescendo, it was followed by another, this time almost certainly to their left, and then another behind. As more joined the devilish chorus, the entire forest seemed to resonate: the leaf-strewn ground, the dark trees, the hanging canopy, all of them seemed to moan and tremble. It was a savage, canine battle cry.

Sylas rose to his feet and glanced about the clearing, but all he saw was the forest.

"We have to run!" hissed Simia.

"Yes, but *where*?"

There was a slight movement ahead of them, at the edge of the clearing, and everyone froze. Their eyes searched the undergrowth until suddenly leaves parted and a broad black shape appeared, striding boldly from the shadows, directly towards Sylas.

Its predatory figure was thrown forward, its hood drawn low, its powerful shoulders swinging from side to side. As it reached the middle of the clearing, the shadows shifted, making the trees move darkly, and then more shapes emerged and began to advance in unison, silent and purposeful. As they prowled into the murky light, Sylas saw that they were larger and carried themselves lower to the ground, so low that their grisly canine jaws brushed the colourless grass, leaving trails of drool behind them. Their pale yellow eyes seemed to glow as they sighted their prey, and their manes of matted black fur rose menacingly on their shoulders, adding to their terrifying bulk.

Ghorhund. Scores of them.

He was vaguely aware of Bayleon and Ash stepping forward to stand at his shoulder, but his eyes were fixed on the lone figure, now just a few paces away. Still it came on, moving deliberately, steadily, like a hunter.

As it drew near, it reared up to its full height, raised a black hand from beneath its cloak and slowly drew back its hood.

The single barred window gave little comfort to the huddled captives, for the view that it offered was quite terrifying. It showed the sweating, bristling, arching backs of the Ghorhund as they bounded along the road, straining at their yokes, baying and snarling to clear the road ahead. So fast were they moving now that sometimes an unfortunate peasant or travelling tradesman was caught unawares, only to be snatched up in powerful jaws and tossed aside.

This was the scene the Suhl feared the most, because it drew them ever closer to the things of the Undoing: the city, the Dirgheon and Thoth. Nevertheless almost all of the pale faces in the carriage were turned to that window, for at least it offered a meagre shaft of grey light, and the world outside helped them to forget the dark, silent presence of the two Ghor crouching just a few paces away.

The only prisoner who took no interest in the window was a large powerfully built man who crouched at the rear of the carriage. He had a strange appearance, with a long, sad-looking face, rangy limbs and a glistening bald head, which bore strange markings and symbols. His doleful green eyes moved slowly around the shadows of the carriage, looking from face to face, taking in the expressions of fear and failing hope, then beyond, into thought and feeling. He saw the thick blacks and amorphous greys of hopelessness, the angular, purple sharpness of terror and the gaunt, thin blues of grief. In most he could still make out the dimmest glow of companionship, though even this was fading.

But one of his companions caused Bowe more concern than the others, for in him there was no glow, no purple sharpness, no greys or blues. Galfinch sat huddled in a corner, his knees drawn up to his chest, his eyes fixed ahead of him. He was chanting something to himself, rocking backwards and forwards in time with his murmurings. His voice was sing-song, almost carefree, though Bowe knew that to be far from the truth. The Scribe's voice became louder and as it did so the words became more distinct.

Bowe flinched.

"What rule is there, what law, but gnashing teeth and grasping claw—" muttered Galfinch— "what rule is there, what law..."

"Silence!"

The hoarse, almost-human bark made everyone start. One of the Ghor rose from its haunches to its full horrifying height. No one could see its face in the darkness, but they knew that its half-human eyes were fixed on Galfinch.

"... what law, but gnashing teeth and grasping claw," continued the Scribe. "What rule is there..."

"I said SILENCE!" roared the guard, travelling the length of the carriage in a single bound. It reached down, grasped Galfinch round the neck and heaved him up against the wall.

"Try this grasping claw, old man," snarled the guard. The prisoners recoiled as they heard him choking.

There was a struggle, then just coughs and spluttering, finally a gentle whimper.

Bowe could bear it no longer and started to push himself up, but just then a figure rose ahead of him. The face was shrouded in shadow and yet Bowe saw in him a remarkable light, a diffuse yellow glow that became brighter even as he watched. It was warm, gentle, compassionate.

"Guard, please don't hurt him. He is overwrought. He doesn't know what he's saying."

As he moved forward, the light from the window played across his kindly, wizened face, his white beard and his muddied clothes.

"What is it to you?" growled the guard. "Sit down!"

"He is a good man," said the old man firmly. "And he is my friend."

The guard turned towards him and a gurgling growl rose from its throat.

"Then perhaps you'd like to join him?" it barked.

Bowe saw distinct orange stabs of irritation flickering in the darkness. He rose to his feet, preparing himself for trouble.

The old man raised his hands. "Please, just let him go. I promise I'll keep him quiet."

Bowe's eyes moved quickly to the other end of the carriage, for there he saw fast, sharp stabs of rage. The second guard had already risen to its feet and was starting to move along the carriage, a low growl on its lips.

Bowe stepped forward. "Come, Fathray, let's not quarrel with them." The old Scribe turned. "But I must!" he insisted

"Galfinch is my friend..."

"And you are mine, my dear Fathray," said Bowe, placing an arm round his shoulders. He lowered his voice. "You've done all you can."

Fathray tried to protest again, but Bowe pressed him close and led him away.

"I'll not see two friends die today," he whispered.

The guards paused for a moment, then barked a scornful laugh and lost interest.

As Fathray and Bowe sat down, they heard Galfinch's last faint whimpers in the darkness, then the sound of his body slumping lifelessly to the floor.

25

The Chasm

"Into the dark chasm *of despair and plight*
Let these bright pages cast their learned light."

BAYLEON AND ASH LIFTED their hands and braced themselves, shouting at Sylas and Simia to get back. They strode out to meet the attacker, Bayleon seeming to swell beneath his leather armour while Ash moved lithe and catlike, his quick eyes taking in all around him. In response the dark figure raised itself up, drawing up its broad powerful shoulders and lifting its head until its face became visible for the first time. The features were blackened with mud and disfigured by a savage wound that ran from the forehead over the nose and cheek and ended somewhere far below the jaw. It was not a canine, but a human face; it was not monstrous, but one that had once been youthful and handsome. The hood fell away entirely to reveal tight-cropped black hair.

"Espen!" gasped Sylas.

Bayleon and Ash looked around in confusion.

"It's Espen! The one who saved me from the Ghorhund!"

He tried to take a step forward, but Ash held him back, looking frantically between the boy and the stranger.

Espen strode up to Bayleon and fixed him with a cool gaze. "Find a way out!" he commanded.

Bayleon eyed him carefully.

"Who are y—"

"There's no time!" growled Espen. "Just get the boy away!" He lowered his eyes, looked Sylas up and down for a moment and then turned with a sweep of his black cloak.

The Ghorhund were already clear of the trees and were advancing in a wide circle. Their baying had stopped and they now moved silently, stealthily through the undergrowth, barely disturbing the leaves beneath their claws. Their ragged, angular heads had fallen low to the ground, throwing their weight forward, preparing for a final charge. Trails of drool fell from their jaws and their black lips were drawn back, revealing glistening yellow teeth.

Espen was still in motion, striding back down the slope. As he reached the centre of the clearing, he raised his arms towards the prowling figures. They seemed to hesitate, glancing at one another uncertainly, and then there was a sudden groan from somewhere in the deathly forest, followed by a creak of straining wood and a sound like bark scraping against bark. The trees were swaying, as though caught up in a gust of wind. It was a strange and unnatural motion, as the air around him was entirely still. As Espen brought his hands to his chest, the entire forest seemed to let out a wail of protest, which grew into a chorus of screeching limbs and creaking boughs so loud that Sylas and Simia had to cover their ears.

Then it moved. Its great grey branches fell from the sky, arching as one down into the clearing. Thick boughs bent at impossible angles, branches twisted as though straining under a great wind and twigs reached out like fine fingers, clutching and clawing at the air. The trees became vast gnarled hands feeling blindly for whatever they could find.

The Ghorhund wheeled about and saw the approach of the tangled limbs. With vicious snarls, they lashed out at them with their claws, sending twigs and shards of wood flying across the clearing, tearing through bark and mauling all that drew near. But still the trees came on, sliding their sinews round legs, haunches and necks. The beasts flailed about them, wrenching at writhing branches, biting at twigs and kicking at boughs.

But it was too late. Soon their limbs were bound, their movements confined to vain thrashings. For a few seconds they stayed pinned down like snared animals until, all at once, Espen raised his hands and they flew up into the air, carried aloft by the great confusion of branches: entangled like black flies in a web. As they ascended, they let out snarls so savage that Sylas and Simia found themselves shrinking away, but then they heard another chorus of growls behind them. They whirled around to see more of the beasts being wrenched up into the air just a few paces from where they were standing.

Bayleon ran to Sylas and Simia.

"Come! Now!" he cried, reaching out and pulling them towards the edge of the clearing.

As they ran into the gloom of the forest, Sylas felt the sting of falling twigs and splinters on his face and looked up to see the struggling forms of the Ghorhund suspended in the canopy above, ripping at the limbs that held them. As he scrambled beneath, he thought he saw one wrench itself free and ease its great weight down to a lower branch, but thankfully he lost sight of it as he sped on.

They careered down the hill, running for their lives, struggling to keep up with Bayleon's giant figure as he bounded with surprising ease over the treacherous forest floor: between trunks, over branches, across ditches and drops.

The forest became darker and more sombre and the familiar grey mist hung ever more thickly about its canopy. The trees thinned and the smothering greyness of the Barrens opened up in front of Sylas: grey cloud in the sky, grey earth below, grey air and mist ahead; nothing but a desperate continuum of grey.

Finally they charged between the last remaining stumps of the forest, past the final few clumps of grass and gatherings of moss, out into the sombre plains.

Clear of the trees, Sylas saw Bayleon slow to a stop. He drew up to him and slid to a halt, his chest heaving. Simia arrived moments later.

As he caught his breath, he became aware of the silence. It was even deeper than before: no birdsong, no rustling of leaves, no hiss of wind through grass — nothing. He raised his head and looked about him. He was standing on a flat expanse of cracked grey earth, the surface crazed with fissures, parched of water and devoid of life. The Barrens were just as they had seemed from afar: a deathly, empty, hollow place without the slightest hint of life or trace of colour.

Bayleon adjusted the bag on his back. "Get ready to move!"

"I'm not sure... I'll ever move again," murmured Simia, still gasping for breath.

They heard another set of footsteps and turned to see Espen thundering towards them with Ash's limp body slung over his shoulder. The younger man's face was drained of all colour.

"What happened?" asked Bayleon, leaning down to examine his friend.

"One of the Ghorhund took him," said Espen as he adjusted Ash's body over his shoulder. "I managed to get him back, but he fell from some height."

Bayleon moved Ash's hair aside, revealing a gaping wound

on his temple. "He's bleeding," he said with alarm. "We need to bandage him — let me…"

"No," said Espen firmly. "Not now. They're already free of the trees — we must go."

"But where will we hide?" protested Simia, desperately casting her eyes across the wide plain. "There's nothing for miles."

Espen seemed to notice her for the first time. He raised a scarred eyebrow and ran his dark eyes quickly over her ruddy face, dishevelled hair and dripping, oversized coat.

"Then you had better run fast, little one," he murmured gruffly, and strode out past her into the nothingness of the Barrens.

"But there's nothing there!" cried Simia, beginning to run nevertheless. "I *know* the Barrens!"

Despite the weight of Ash over his shoulder, Espen's movements were so fluid and effortless that Sylas could see how they had thought him one of the Ghor. He sprang lightly from his toes, sending up a cloud of grey dust as he sped away from the forest.

At the rear of the group Bayleon too carried his bulk with surprising ease, seeming within his element: his great limbs spanned huge distances with each stride. His Spoorrunner's light armour left his arms to swing freely at his sides, giving him even greater balance and poise. His eyes were in constant motion, searching for tracks or signs of danger, shifting quickly from the treeline behind them to the horizon ahead; from the shadows of the weird landscape to the dry earth beneath their feet.

Sylas found that the crust of dry soil gave way under his feet, making it hard to keep his balance and wrenching at his calves, but his strong legs carried him forward more swiftly than Simia, who struggled to regain the ground she had lost.

"I see you run… faster… when you know… what's chasing you!" she panted from behind.

Sylas slowed to run at her side. "Do you think Ash is all right?"

"Think so," she wheezed. "I think... Bayleon's got some of Filimaya's balm. They can use it once the bleeding has stopped."

They glanced ahead at Ash's lifeless body, hanging all too limply over Espen's shoulder.

Still they ran, spurred on by the thought of how much faster his hunters were.

The landscape changed little as they fled further and further from the hills. Sometimes it rose a little, sometimes it fell, but any change was so slight that it might have been a trick of the feeble light. The greyness neither brightened nor dimmed, but lay close about them, making them feel peculiarly claustrophobic, even in such a vast expanse.

Finally, after some minutes of scrambling across the featureless terrain, they came across something that broke that monotony. A dried riverbed. The plain was fractured by low banks that fell away to an ancient sandy bed, the markings of water long since disappeared.

Espen slowed as he reached the near bank, looked quickly both ways along its length, then jumped down, took three long strides and leapt up on the far side. Sylas and Simia followed at a rather slower pace, having to clamber carefully down the crumbling bank and help each other to climb up a few paces on.

Espen had stopped only a short distance ahead and lowered Ash to the ground. They slowed to regain their breath and Bayleon quickly overtook them. He ran up to Espen and they began an animated conversation, which the two children heard as they approached.

"Why?" asked Bayleon. "Before you seemed to think we had a better chance if we kept running!"

Espen did not raise his eyes, still tending to Ash. "They move much faster than us. The girl's right, there's nowhere to hide. Our best chance is to make a stand right here."

Bayleon shook his head and threw out his arms. "But then why did we run? Why didn't we stay where we were?"

Espen turned away and looked back towards the hills. "You'll see," he said quietly.

Bayleon stared blankly at him for a moment, but then his face started to flush with colour.

"What do you mean, 'you'll see'?" he growled, trying to control his temper. "This is our lives! If you have a plan, tell us what it is."

Espen gave no reply, but busied himself unfolding a blanket from his pack.

"You're not even one of us!" continued Bayleon, stepping closer. "You want us to trust you, but we don't even know who you are!"

His voice had become threatening, but Espen remained silent and calm. He placed the blanket gently under Ash's head, and then looked up at the Spoorrunner.

"You know me well enough."

Bayleon was exasperated. "What's that supposed to mean?" he growled. "I've never seen you before in my—"

"You know me." Espen's voice was firm, insistent.

Bayleon began to bluster: "Well, if you mean what you did for Sylas then..."

Suddenly his voice trailed away and a frown of puzzlement came over his face. His eyes traced Espen's features: the thick-set jaw; the scarred, slightly hollow cheeks; the ebony skin and black eyes.

He took a step back and his face paled. "You..." he whispered.

Their eyes met and Espen gave him a slight smile before turning away to face the horizon.

"But we… we thought you were…"

"Dead. I know," said Espen, standing and looking out across the plain. "Not yet… but I'm working on it."

He squinted and leaned forward, peering into the distance. Everyone followed his eyes.

About halfway between where they stood and the sombre hills, shimmering in the haze of the Barrens, was a long black line. It looked almost still, but not quite: it rippled as they watched, undulating as it followed the contours of the plain. Then, very gradually, it broke into parts. The parts took the form of a snaking line of distant black figures, equally spaced, moving in a chillingly precise formation. The silhouettes took shape: some broad, bounding on all fours, swinging their low-slung heads; others higher with fluttering black robes, moving lithely, swiftly.

For every one of the Ghorhund there was now one of the Ghor, spread out across the advancing line, swelling the already terrifying numbers. And, as the fugitives saw their hunters, so the hunters saw them. A single howl rose from their ranks, hanging eerily in the air. It was quickly joined by more until a horrifying battle cry filled the thick, still air.

Simia looked at Espen. "What now?"

"We wait," he said, his eyes still fixed on the approaching Ghor.

He crossed his arms in front of him and bit his bottom lip, seeming to be taken by a sudden thought, then he glanced down at Sylas.

"You may be able to help," he said.

Sylas raised his eyebrows doubtfully. "*Me?* How?"

Espen took his hand and led him a few paces away. They looked out across the plain, watching the black figures grow larger and larger, their devilish forms becoming more distinct. There were even more than Sylas had first realised.

"Do you remember the Shop of Things?" asked Espen.

"Yes, of course," said Sylas, startled by the mention of the shop, which now seemed so far away.

"And the Flight of Fancy?"

Sylas looked up at Espen with a frown. "No — I..."

"The mobile. Do you remember the mobile?"

"Oh... yes."

"And Mr Zhi told you how it works?"

Sylas struggled to think back, all the while watching the approaching Ghor with a thumping heart. "Yes... yes, he said I did it with my imagination."

"Good." Espen fell silent for a few seconds and then said: "Sylas, they will not pass the dried river."

"Why?"

"Because we shall imagine it so."

Sylas looked at him. "Imagine... *what*?"

"When I tell you, you must imagine that the entire riverbed has fallen away — that it has crumbled into nothingness — that all that remains is a chasm."

Sylas peered incredulously at the huge solid banks of the ravine. "I can't do that."

Espen squatted down and brought his scarred face close to Sylas's. "Did any of this seem possible before you met Mr Zhi?"

"No."

"Then don't tell me what can't be done."

Espen stood up and turned to face their enemy.

Sylas took a deep breath and tried to clear his mind. He thought of all the life of the river rising up and seizing the Slithen. Then at least his imaginings *had* seemed to come true. But he couldn't be *sure*, could he? Just as Simia said, he hadn't seen it — no one had seen it.

He looked over at the riverbed, trying to picture the sandy bed collapsing and falling away, leaving behind only a dark, gaping chasm. He found his eyes drifting back to the bared teeth and tearing claws of the approaching Ghorhund and the unnatural, bestial movement of the Ghor. Already they were so near that all he could hear was the thunder of their charge and all he felt was the ground trembling beneath his feet.

"Raise your hands!" cried Espen, more urgently now, lifting his arms in front of him. "They'll focus your mind!"

Sylas hesitated, terrified by the approaching legion.

"Do it!"

He brought his hands up until they were in line with the riverbed, framing the scene. He realised that this was just what he had seen the others doing when they had conjured their magic: Espen in the town, Simia in the hills, Filimaya on the river.

"Now you take that part of the river!" cried Espen, raising his voice above the baying of the Ghorhund. "I'll take this!"

Sylas moved his hands until one was directly in front of him and the other was held far out to his left, wide of the last of the advancing beasts. He saw the river between his fingers, held in his grasp.

Still they came on, the Ghorhund tossing their heads and gnashing at the air, the Ghor seeming to glide effortlessly in their midst. Then, as the ground started to shake beneath the stampede of claws, they fell silent. They ceased their baying and howling and drew together, closing the line until all that could be seen was a wall of blackness, broken only by yellow eyes and the dull glint of teeth. And in that moment, as the hunters smelt their prize and prepared to strike, Sylas's heart failed. His hands wavered in the air and he shot a frightened glance up at Espen.

He found impenetrable eyes already looking down.

"Imagine it so, Sylas," said Espen. He raised his head and looked away.

Sylas bit his lip, steadied his hands and focused his mind on the impossible. They were just paces away now and already some of the Ghorhund had launched themselves into the air, heaving their massive shoulders over the riverbed.

And, in that instant, he imagined oblivion.

He imagined the hard-packed earth of the riverbed cracking; the ancient sands belching upwards into the air; the tumbling banks turning in upon themselves. And, as he pictured those things in his mind, so they happened. The great sweep of the river flowed once more, not with water, but with gravel, earth and dust. And, as the cracks widened into gaping ravines, so this weird torrent drained into them, pouring vast floods of dirt into the nothingness below. He pictured waves of sand hurled into the air and, as he saw them in his mind, so they rose, catching the flailing claws of the Ghorhund, enclosing them in their clinging mass, snatching them out of the air, pulling them down. He pictured the banks widen and break away, collapsing into gaping darkness, and so they fell, ensnaring black limbs in the deluge of earth. He pictured a black abyss, a mighty void opening in front of him, swallowing all that lay in its path.

And so it was.

Scores of creatures fell from sight, snarling, wailing and baying as they were consumed by the earth; grasping claws flailed at crumbling banks and gnashing teeth rolled back into the darkness.

As the last of the Ghor let out a wailing howl, Sylas was consumed by his vision. He imagined the chasm falling in upon itself, closing up over the heads of the falling beasts. In that moment the ground shuddered beneath their feet and, with a calamitous boom, the towering walls of the chasm crashed into one another, sending up a great rush of wind and, with it, a curtain of sand that rose hundreds of feet into the air.

The vast cloud of dust and sand slowly sank towards the ground, settling about the fugitives as they stood in silence, staring at the turmoil of earth where the river had once been.

One by one Simia, Bayleon and Espen turned to look at Sylas, their eyes wide with fear and wonder.

26
Tales Untold

"You ask about the host of tales untold*?*
Read on, let the Ravel Runes unfold."

THE GLOAMING LIGHT FADED slowly to a dull smudge on the horizon. Pale greys darkened into charcoals and blacks that gradually closed in upon the three figures in the open plain: two working feverishly amid heaps of earth, the other lying motionless to one side.

"Yes, but how did you *do* it?" pressed Simia, wiping her brow.

"Like I say, I just thought about it," said Sylas, plunging his small wooden shovel into the dust. "Imagined it. And whatever I thought about just… happened."

Simia shook her head and turned back to the pit.

"Well," she said, picking at the sides with her shovel, "I've never seen anything like it. I mean, OK, that's how Essenfayle works — using your imagination and everything — but not like *that*. Not unless you're a Magruman or something."

Sylas carried on working in silence, scooping up dirt from the bottom of the pit and throwing it on to the growing pile at his side. It was as much a mystery to him as it was to anyone else. Even thinking about it made his stomach turn over: the screams of the falling beasts haunted him even now. He tried to avoid Simia's eyes, hoping that she would stop questioning him or even better change the subject.

But, as usual, Simia had different ideas.

"So were you scared?" she asked, dropping her shovel and wiping her hands on her tunic.

He sighed and thought for a moment. "No, I don't think I was. I mean, I was terrified before it started and I'm pretty scared thinking about it now, but while it was happening — I don't know — I guess it just felt... right."

Simia frowned. "Right?"

He nodded.

She rested her hands on her hips. "So let me get this straight. You split the earth open, you threw a whole company of Ghor into it and you turned the world upside down, and you felt... right?"

He shrugged. "Right."

"Right." She stared at him quizzically for a moment. "You're quite scary, you know that?"

He smiled and turned back to his work.

Simia picked up a shovel and drove it into the side of the pit. Just moments later she stopped, holding the spade in mid-air.

"So hold on a minute, why are we breaking our backs digging a fire pit when you could do it with... I don't know... a nod of your head or... or a sneeze or something?"

He sighed. "Because Espen told us to use a spade?" he suggested.

She grunted.

"Besides, I have a feeling I can't do that kind of thing just... whenever I want."

"Why not? You haven't tried."

"No," he said flatly, "and I don't want to."

The thought of any more magic made him decidedly uneasy. It was one thing to try this kind of thing when he was told to — with Espen standing next to him — but it was quite another to do it just because he could.

"I won't tell," she whispered, glancing at their unconscious companion. "Ash won't either."

"Look," Sylas snapped irritably, "I've done enough magic for one day — I'd rather just use a spade, if it's OK with you."

She looked piqued. "Fine," she said, jabbing savagely at a clod of earth.

They worked in silence for some minutes, Simia making swift progress as she vented her annoyance on the hard-packed earth, Sylas moving rather more slowly, his mind wandering from the task. He felt guilty for having snapped and he tried to think of another topic of conversation.

"So why do we need to build the fire in a pit anyway?"

"So it can't be seen, of course," mumbled Simia, flinging a shovelful of earth on to a heap. "If we made a normal fire, it'd be seen miles away. Obviously." She looked over at him. "That's deep enough. Now we use the dirt to make a bank around it — you know, to block the light."

She started to shape one of the piles of loose earth so that it formed a neat ring around the pit, several paces back from its edge. Sylas climbed out and began to help.

"How do you know this stuff?" he asked.

She was silent for a few moments. "Because I used to live here."

He stopped digging. "You *lived* here?"

She kept working, but nodded.

"Why would you live *here*?" he asked incredulously.

She shot him a sharp look. "Well, not because I wanted to, stupid."

Sylas watched her for a moment as she jabbed irritably at the earth with her shovel, then decided that it was best not to ask any more and turned away.

They continued to dig and shape the heaps of dirt, Sylas moving one way round the circle and Simia the other, neither talking. As the ring took shape, he saw just how effective it would be at hiding the flames, but not only that, it would act as a windbreak and a support as they rested around the fire. She really did know what she was doing.

Soon it was nearly finished. As they shaped the final pile, they gradually closed the circle and found themselves working near one another. Simia glanced at him a couple of times, then finally broke the silence.

"I'm not *from* here. My parents just brought me here," she said. "We came during the war."

Sylas nodded, but carried on working, sensing that it was best just to listen.

"Just about all of us were on the move then — running away, or trying to fight. My father thought it was best to do what most people were doing, and most were coming here."

She patted the final load of soil into place, then laid down the shovel and sat on top of the pile of earth.

"Took us months to get here. I don't remember much about the journey now, but I know it wasn't easy. My parents were really determined. They said that this was a special place — beautiful. They said that all the Suhl would be here and we'd be safe." She laughed emptily. "And, for a while, we were. In fact, it was great: open grasslands where we could farm our crops; forests we could play in; cool rivers…"

She glanced over to where the dried riverbed had been, now just a sea of sand dunes and dust.

"There used to be hundreds of those, all over the place. And we were all together — thousands of us — tens of thousands. Even Merimaat was here."

Sylas looked up. "Who exactly was Merimaat?"

"She was our leader — the leader of all the Suhl," said Simia. "A really great leader — as powerful as Thoth; more powerful, even…" She lifted her chin a little. "I met her once, a few miles from here…"

"You *met* her?"

"I did," she said, raising her eyebrows and looking away, as if talking of something incidental. "In fact, in a funny kind of way, she saved my life."

Simia paused for dramatic effect. Sylas sat down on the pile of earth and looked at her expectantly.

"Well, we were both crossing a river," continued Simia, "maybe even this one for all I know. There were some stepping stones. I was small and scared of the water and I was even more petrified when I realised she was behind me. I kept slipping off one stone and tripping over the next. I was drenched, and I was only part of the way across. Anyway, she caught up with me, put a hand on my shoulder and whispered something in my ear. She said: 'They aren't trying to trip you, they're trying to help you.'"

She paused, smiling to herself.

"I know it sounds silly when I say it, but when she did, it just sounded clear, simple… like real, absolute truth. Then we walked across, hand in hand at first, but then on my own. And I didn't slip once. Didn't even wobble." She laughed to herself. "By the time I reached the other side I was almost skipping over the stones."

She fell silent, enjoying her memory.

Sylas frowned. "And what happened then?"

"That was that — she went one way and I went the other, and I never saw her again."

"So how did she save your life?"

"Oh, it was only later that she saved me — when the war started. It was what she said to me... about the stones trying to help me. I came to see that she wasn't just talking about the stones and the river, she was talking about much more than that: not just me, but all people; not just the river, but all of nature. Everything."

Sylas thought for a moment, then shook his head. "Nope. I still don't get it."

"Well, what I mean is, she changed the way I look at things. I started to see that it wasn't only the stones in the river that were trying to help me, it was everything in Nature: the sun and the rain, the rivers and the plains, the trees and the grass..."

She got up and started to pace round the fire pit.

"They always talked about the connections between things at school, but for the first time I started to see what they meant — that even *I* was part of those connections — that Nature was there to help *me*." She gave him a steady look. "It sounds stupid, I know, but it's true. It really is. And when I looked — when I really opened my eyes and my ears and my mind and... and breathed it in — when I *lived* it... I knew that it was true. It was all around me."

"And... that's what saved your life?"

She nodded, gathering the folds of her huge coat around her shoulders.

"We'd only been here for a few months when Thoth and his Magrumen came. The Reckoning, they called it. Their army was huge: the Ghor, the Gherothians, the Basetians and the Sur — legions of them. Tens of thousands of them." The wistfulness left her face and was replaced by contempt. "Overnight this place became a battleground: the Suhl on one side and everyone else on the other. Essenfayle against all the Three Ways — Kimiyya, Druindil and Urgolvane. Everyone fought — my parents, my teachers, even the kids…"

Her voice trailed off and she fell silent for a moment, remembering something that made her wince.

"Even I fought."

Sylas looked about him into the blackish grey of the Barrens. "That's how all this happened… the magic?"

She nodded. "Not Essenfayle, but the rest. The problem with the others is that they change Nature, twist it. They do awful things… things that shouldn't be possible…" She shuddered and looked away. "We started to lose and that was when it got really bad. Every kind of hell you can imagine: firestorms, boiling water, seas of mud, lightning falling like rain, howling Ghor, winds that stripped the trees and carried people away. The ground was scarred, forests were burned, rivers were poisoned. They didn't just stop at killing people, they destroyed everything: our homes, our farms — even the land we lived on." She kicked at the charred earth with her heel. "Everything."

Sylas sat in silence, trying to imagine what she had seen and, at the same time, almost frightened to. Simia seemed even smaller, her face paler in the cold, empty light of the evening. But what shocked him were her tears. Her eyes were turned away, but he could see that she was crying. He knew at once that she had rarely spoken of these things. He wanted to say something — that he was sorry or that he wished it hadn't happened or that he wished he could have helped or… something, but all those things sounded trite and meaningless.

In the end he said simply: "But they didn't get you, Simsi."

Simia smiled with some effort. "No, they didn't."

"So how did you stay alive?"

"Skills. Cunning. Guile," she said, grinning, brushing her sleeve across her eyes. He smiled with her.

She brought her shoulders up and rubbed her arms to warm herself against the growing cold, then tucked her hands beneath the sleeves of the coat.

"It was what Merimaat told me that helped more than anything. During the peaceful time, in the six months or a year before Thoth came, I got to know this place so well that it felt like part of me. I knew the sounds in the trees, the way the wind moved, how the rivers flowed. I started to see them as I had seen the stepping stones that morning — that they weren't things *outside* of me, moving *around* me, doing things *to* me — they were part of my world... part of me almost." She turned and looked at him. "That if I was open to them, they would help me, just like the stones. And when it all got bad, that's just how it was. I trusted that the world around me would help me, and it did. Somehow I knew when and how to keep myself hidden — behind banks, in ditches, holes, riverbeds. When water was poisoned, somehow I managed to find streams that no one knew about. I knew how to keep myself downwind of the Ghor so they wouldn't smell me, how to move through the grass so I couldn't be seen, where to run at night without any moon. I wasn't the only one — anyone who knows Essenfayle can do that kind of thing. But I was good..." She turned to him with an earnestness in her eyes. "*Really* good."

He looked at her with admiration: suddenly she seemed a little older, and for a moment she almost seemed to fill the many folds of her father's coat.

"Will you teach me?" he asked.

She shrugged. "Sure. If you teach me about those birds you talked about."

He looked at her quizzically.

"You know, the ones made of paper and string."

Sylas suddenly remembered telling her about his kites when they were in the Mutable Inn. "Oh yes, sure I…"

Suddenly they heard something behind them.

"As I remember you in those days, Simsi, you were quiet as a mouse…" Ash pushed himself up on one elbow, fingering the bandage around his head. "How things change."

Simia rushed over and helped him to sit up, but was waved off. Ash looked about him a little unsteadily.

"Well, I've either died and gone to hell, or I've lived and… gone to hell."

Simia giggled. "Ash, you sound as good as new. How are you feeling?"

"Never better," said Ash witheringly. He cast his eyes around the makeshift camp. "So what kind of mess are we in now?"

They told him everything that had happened. When Simia described the earth cracking in two and the deafening thunder as the chasm closed up, even Ash seemed impressed. He looked Sylas up and down.

"I knew there was something about you," he said.

Sylas smiled, dropping his eyes.

At that moment they heard muffled voices somewhere out in the blackness. They all fell silent, instinctively lowering themselves to the ground. They soon made out two male voices talking rather loudly a short distance away in the direction of the river.

"Espen and Bayleon," Sylas said, relieved.

They heard Espen's words first: "… And so I followed the boy to the mill, and then here."

"Yes, I understand," replied Bayleon. "But why didn't you just come and tell us when you reached the mill?"

"You know I can't show myself in public, Bayleon. It's not time for that. There are spies everywhere – even in the mill."

"Not in the mill," grunted Bayleon. "I'd stake my life on it."

"Well, after all I have seen in the past few years I wouldn't stake mine. It was a risk I couldn't take."

"So instead you risk our lives by having a Slithen spy on us!"

"I couldn't have known it would betray me," protested Espen. "I had worked with it before without problems and I was paying it well. Anyway, I had to be able to protect the boy while keeping myself a secret. Surely you understand that?"

"No. I don't understand at all," Bayleon replied gruffly.

Both men fell silent and all Sylas could hear was the thud of footsteps in the dirt. Finally the two huge black silhouettes emerged through the gloom, striding directly towards the camp. They clambered into the circle, dropped their loads of firewood and looked about them.

"That's a very fine fire pit," said Espen, his voice betraying his surprise. He looked at Simia. "You've done this before."

She grinned, her white teeth glowing in the darkness. "Told you," she said, patting the earthen bank. "I know my way around this place."

A fire was laid and before long they were all gathered around, sitting back against the bank, the trace of an orange flicker playing across their faces. Bayleon had prepared a pot of meat and potatoes and laid it among the embers, and the first warming aromas were rising in trails of steam. Everything was silent except for an occasional crackle or hiss from the fire and all were lost in their thoughts, staring into the fire, watching the dancing flames as they licked the sides of the pit and occasionally leapt into the blackness.

Simia was sitting next to Espen and was trying to draw him into conversation. She searched his face with such interest and attentiveness that it was as if they were engaged in the most fascinating debate, but in truth Espen seemed hardly aware of her: his eyes darting around the group, his expression solemn and distracted. Occasionally his lips seemed to move as though murmuring something under his breath, playing out his own secret conversation in the confines of his mind.

Bayleon sat silent and alone on one side of the fire, his face dark and serious, only occasionally raising his eyes to glance at Sylas or Espen. He had not spoken to anyone since his return.

Ash looked bored. He tapped a spoon on his knee absent-mindedly and looked about for some kind of amusement. His eyes moved from Bayleon's face and then to Espen's, but they didn't acknowledge him. He tugged at his great mop of hair in frustration, then placed his spoon at his side. Quietly, he rested his hands on his knees and straightened his fingers. They danced lightly as though he was playing on a piano, shifting from side to side, up and down according to some strange and inaudible rhythm. Above him, the many sparks that rose from the fire began to perform a silent ballet in the darkness, leaving a trail of incandescence in their wake. The pinpricks of fire swayed and whirled, leapt and fell, tracing impossible pathways through the air. His display soon drew the eyes of the group and they watched in amusement as the sparks began to form patterns in the night sky, gliding between, above and below one another until they seemed to settle in one place.

"There you are," said Ash triumphantly. "What need of the night sky when we can make our very own!"

Simia looked at the sparks more closely and then frowned. She cocked her head on one side.

"It is!" she gasped, pointing up at the glowing lights. "It's the stars! That's the Southern Star! And there — look! That's the Panhandle!"

She reached into her bag, pulled out her notebook and flicked to a page towards the back. "Yes! I thought so! And that's the Bear!" she cried, jabbing her finger at a collection of sparks and then pointing at the page in her notebook. "And there — there's the Ewe!"

Bayleon and Espen tilted their heads and shifted to get a better look.

"Clever," grunted Bayleon with a smile, returning his eyes to the fire. "Just don't be long about it — the whole point of a fire pit is to avoid being seen..."

"I agree," murmured Espen, breaking his silence for the first time. He gave Ash a nod of appreciation. "But you *are* good. You control them well."

Ash shrugged. "Nothing exciting," he said, watching as the patterns slowly rose into the night and faded away, "just Essenfayle."

Espen raised an eyebrow and a look of amusement passed over his face.

"*Just* Essenfayle indeed," he murmured. "When you have Essenfayle, what need of anything else?"

Ash gave no answer, but he shook his head and smiled to himself.

Sylas sat alone on the far side of the fire. He had been only distantly aware of the astonishing lights above his head: his body was tired and his mind was full. He was aware that he ought to be amazed by this new wonder, that he ought to be excited about all that had happened in that impossible, magical, overwhelming day, but above all else, he wanted to clear his head and sleep. He wanted quiet, a brief solace from all these marvels — some time to rest, that was all.

He shifted position, trying to get comfortable, hoping that the flames would soothe him and the darkness would ease him into slumber. But, as the little camp fell silent and the fire offered its lullaby of crackles and hisses, the world of miracles rushed back in. His mind filled with the astonishing sights and sounds of his journey.

So many things to be understood. So many questions.

He puffed out his cheeks and turned over. There was no way he was going to sleep. He looked over at Espen as he lay back with his cloak arranged about him, occasionally nodding or shaking his head as Simia spoke. Surely, if anyone could answer his questions, it was Espen. He had been there at the beginning, in Gabblety Row; he had helped him to reach the Passing Bell; and now he had suddenly reappeared out of nowhere, to save them all.

Sylas pushed himself up on one elbow and opened his mouth to speak, but before he made a sound, Espen lifted his eyes.

"It would seem a good time to talk, Sylas, would it not?" he asked.

Sylas drew breath. How did he—?

"No vicious beasts snapping at your heels, no mystic bells ringing in your ears... We must take what few opportunities we have, don't you think?" An enigmatic smile traced his lips.

Sylas smiled. "I was... I was just thinking the same thing. I wanted to ask you—"

"There are three pressing questions," interrupted Espen, raising his hand by way of apology. He pushed himself up into a sitting position and rested his elbows on his knees. "The first is who I am. The second is why I am here. The third — and I must say that this is far more interesting — is who the devil are you?"

There was a gruff bark, the slap of a bolt and suddenly the large timber door fell away. A cool blue-grey light flooded the interior of the carriage. The prisoners shielded their eyes and retreated to the furthest corners, drawing closer to one another in fear.

One of the Ghor guards vaulted down on to the riverbank and heaved a crude wooden ladder into place while the other bounded back into the crowd of prisoners and began hauling them to their feet.

"Get up, vermin!" it growled, pushing them towards the ladder. "Time for a boat ride!"

The terrified captives filed down the ladder, squinting to see what new torment awaited them. They found themselves on a riverbank, in the dank remains of a wooded glade. The trees had lost all of their leaves, which had long since rotted away, and the silver trunks were hung about with decaying bark, which gave them a ragged, unnatural appearance. Large pendulous clouds rolled above them, cutting out the sunlight and cloaking the scene in a cool grey. Most of the Suhl lowered their eyes, knowing all too well what place this was, not wishing to see any more of it than they had to. To them, the borderlands of the Barrens were a reminder of their defeat, of the abominations of the Reckoning, and worse, a promise of what lay at the end of their journey.

But while most trudged despairingly between the armoured Ghor guards, trailing towards the barge, two of their number were different. Fellfith and Hinksaff had slowed to the rear of the group, their eyes casting about anxiously, their gait certain and purposeful, their faces lively and focused. They counted the guards in the glade, spied the Slithen harnessed to the barge, peered into the deathly woods beyond, looking for signs of others.

It was this energy that had drawn the attention of the Scryer.

Bowe had also slowed to the rear of the column so he could watch them more closely, and he became anxious at what he saw. He looked past the world of sight and sound, past the steely visages of the two men, past the muddle of the crowd. He saw instead a rich tapestry of colour and form: the piercing blues of hope, the swirling steely greys of courage, the sharp, stabbing reds of rage. He knew the meaning of these things and it filled him with dread.

He drew alongside them, fell into step and took them both by the arm.

"Don't!" he whispered urgently.

"Silence!"

One of the guards leapt forward and swiped at Bowe's chest. Despite his size, Bowe was lifted bodily into the air and hurled backwards, landing some distance from the other prisoners. He slithered down the riverbank and came to rest just inches from the foul grey waters.

"Bowe!" cried Fathray, straining against one of the other guards.

Bowe groaned and looked up. He saw all too well what was about to happen. Fellfith and Hinksaff were already in motion, using the disturbance as a distraction to step clear of the column of prisoners, gather their thoughts and begin.

Hinksaff turned his freckled, youthful face to the skies, casting his arms up into the air as if praying to some god. And he seemed to receive an answer, for instantly the clouds began to boil and swirl, heave and shift. Some began to fall from the skies, others twisted and turned, while others still folded in upon themselves, exposing the blue sky above. Shafts of sunlight pierced the gloom, sending welcome beams on to the riverbank, over the watching crowd, into the eyes of the Ghor. They darted and wove, flashed and subsided, disappearing here only to reappear somewhere else, brighter and more intense. The effect was utter confusion, a bewildering muddle of light and dark, motion and form: an effect that was only compounded when the falling clouds swooped over the river, descended over the barge, the Slithen, the unsuspecting Ghor.

But that was not all: Fellfith was at his friend's side, his arms extended towards the river, sweeping in wide arcs over its surface. As if answering his call, the waters began to swell and churn, the surface boiling and frothing as though heated by the sun's rays. But it was not the sun that made the sickly waters bubble: it was what lay within. Suddenly a great surge of life erupted from the deep: great shoals of leaping, grey-flanked fish; writhing hordes of eels; troops of scampering crabs; armies of wriggling worms; and scurrying legions of insects all closed in upon the bank, filling the barge, clambering over the Slithen, scuttling between foot, fin and claw.

The Ghor were in utter confusion, looking for their commander, who was lost somewhere in the crowd, fogs and sunbeams, battling with great swarms of creatures that assailed it from all sides.

"Run!" cried Fellfith to his brethren as he marshalled the slithering hordes, backing towards the edge of the glade.

"Make for the trees!" bellowed Hinksaff as he wove clouds and sunbeams, retreating at his friend's side.

Already they were entering the gloom of the woods, sensing that soon they would have some cover, hope of escape. They called again to the others, and some began to break from the crowd, running for the edge of the clearing.

Suddenly Bowe rose to his feet and waved his arms in the air. "No!" he cried. "No! No!" But it was too late.

The chariot crashed through rotting trunks, snapping them like twigs, its golden wheels shattering the timber and pressing it deep into the mud. A single figure stood tall behind the reins, her crimson gown billowing around her elegant form, her beautiful face set firm as she reared the Ghorhund to a halt. The two beasts clawed the filthy mud, baying and howling as they brought the great weight of the glittering chariot to a shuddering halt in the centre of the glade. Scarpia's eyes flashed with rage as she took in the scene: the great swarm of beasts and insects, the muddled sunbeams, the shifting fogs, the confusion of her guards.

She let out an almighty shriek, a hideous scream of fury that rose to a shrill battle cry. She cast down the reins and threw her arms wide, her small hands grasping at thin air, clawing into fists. In the same moment there were screams from the crowd of prisoners as great sections of the riverbank buckled and broke, folding in upon themselves, trapping fish, eels and insects, uprooting trees, wrong-footing the Ghor commander until it too fell into the muddy morass. Then, as Thoth's Magruman raised her fists and swept them towards the fleeing Suhl, the great writhing piles of mud and beasts were hoisted towards the heavens, arching across the glade, colliding with a thunderous boom, sending down a shower of filth and debris.

Slowly, calmly, she opened her fists and dropped her hands.

Bowe sank to his knees and tears fell down his cheeks. He watched the massive weight of trees, mud and beasts fall from the sky, crushing what remained of the wood at the edge of the glade, engulfing Fellfith, Hinksaff and two other fleeing prisoners as they ran.

The fogs dispersed, rising back to the darkening sky. The remaining creatures writhed and squirmed their way back to the river or flapped and gasped on a muddy grave.

As the surviving prisoners wept, the sunbeams faltered and died.

27

The Glimmer Myth

"Reach for the silvered glimmer *on the lake…"*

ASH STIRRED, DRAWING HIS knees up and leaning forward so that he could hear a little better. Bayleon continued to stare into the fire, but his shifting eyes betrayed his interest. Simia shuffled so far forward that she was rather too close to the flames, but in her excitement she seemed entirely unaware of them. Her eyes sparkled expectantly.

"Let's begin with the easier of the questions," said Espen, patting his chest. "As Bayleon will tell you, I have not always gone by the name Espen. Like many of our kind, I have had to change my name since the war." His eyes moved from face to face. "I was once called Espasian."

Ash sat bolt upright and glanced over at Bayleon, who nodded without raising his eyes from the fire.

Simia's jaw fell open and for a moment even she seemed lost for words. "Espasian? The *Magruman*?" she blurted.

Espen nodded.

"But… you were killed," blurted Ash, squinting a little as he scrutinised the stranger's face more closely. "I mean… we thought

319

you died at the Reckoning."

"As did I," said Espen, arching a scarred eyebrow. "And I should have died. But this brings me to the question of why I am here, and for this you must allow me to tell a little of my story."

He settled back against the bank and the others leaned in even further.

"After the battle I woke half buried in earth with my shoulder torn open. I lay there, amid the fire and devastation, wondering if this was some terrible perversion of an afterlife, some punishment for Merimaat's death — for all that we had allowed to happen." His eyes flicked briefly to Bayleon's face. "But I should have known better: such abominations are things of this world and not of that. The Ghor soon appeared, picking through the dying and dead, their voices oiled with pride at their victory. And to heap shame upon shame, they found me. Drooling at the glory of it, they gathered me up and hurled me into a cart with a few other unfortunate souls."

Ash's eyes narrowed eagerly. "Did you recognise any of them?"

Espen shook his head. "I didn't see them — we were kept apart."

Bayleon grunted and poked the fire violently, which sent a shower of sparks crackling and hissing into the air.

"What I do remember is that the Ghor carried Thoth's standard, so they were almost certainly taking us to the Dirgheon. But I, for one, never reached it. On the second night I escaped from their camp and took to the Barrens."

"And the others?" asked Ash.

Espen dropped his eyes to the fire. "I don't know. I only just managed to get myself out before..."

"You're a *Magruman*!" interrupted Bayleon, heaving his bulky frame forward so that the flames lit his broad features. "How

320

could you leave your own people in the hands of those animals?"

Espen was silent for some moments, then picked up a dry, rotten stick and tossed it into the fire.

"I was injured and exhausted, Bayleon," he said. "But it wasn't just that. It was defeat. The legions, the Spoorrunners, the Scryers, the Casters, the Sea People, the Magrumen, Merimaat herself — all of us — we had all seen the end, watched everything fall. It was all I could do to keep *myself* alive let alone others. You remember what it was like — we had nothing left. Nothing."

Bayleon's brow furrowed and he clenched his hands into fists. He eased himself back into the shadows to rest on the bank. "But *we're* not Magrumen," he growled quietly, sliding his hands behind his head.

Sylas listened to all this in some bewilderment. He had thought Espen to be someone of the Other, of his own world — one of the Merisi perhaps. Now that he knew that the stranger was as much a part of this peculiar place as the rest of his companions, he felt even more alone.

"So why were you in Gabblety Row?" he asked.

Espen was still preoccupied with Bayleon's remark and took some time to respond.

"When I escaped, I was unsure what to do next," he said with a resigned sigh. "There was nowhere to run: all of our settlements were gone, most of our hideouts had been destroyed, there was no real resistance to speak of and I couldn't be sure who, if anyone, had survived. We were starting again — starting with nothing. I couldn't risk going into towns or happening across any patrols and it was pointless trying to cross borders, so for some days I just stayed here, on the Barrens, trying to regain some strength, to come up with some kind of plan—" he smiled sadly — "trying to imagine what Merimaat would have done. The more I thought about it, the more it seemed obvious that I had to make contact with the Merisi. I knew that they wouldn't have been caught up in the Reckoning and I hoped that they might be able to help."

"But how did you get into the Other?" asked Ash, bringing his face closer to the fire. "Hadn't all the circles been destroyed?"

Espen shook his head. "Not Salsimaine, though they'd made every attempt."

"Circles?" said Sylas. "What are they?"

"Stone circles," said Espen.

Sylas looked at him blankly.

"Our ancestors used circles of stone for worshipping the sun by day and its opposite, the moon, by night. Then they found that somehow, because those rings harness both opposites, they have a special power to forge other connections — connections between opposite things. That's how they finally opened a way into the Other."

"*That* kind of stone circle!" said Sylas, his eyes widening. "Like the ones we have in my world?"

"Not *like* them — identical to them," said Espen, smiling. "Doorways between the worlds. Salsimaine is one of the biggest."

Sylas sat back in wonderment. He had visited a huge stone circle with his mother. He remembered the gigantic square-cut stones arranged in perfect arcs for reasons no one really understood, by a people no one really knew. His mother had been fascinated by them.

"On the fourth day," continued Espen, clearly determined to finish his story, "I managed to make my way to Salsimaine. I found it deserted but for a few sentries who were easily overcome, and I used what little power I was able to muster to make the Passing — to enter the Other. Then I made contact with the Merisi in the usual way."

"What's that?" asked Simia, her eyes bright with excitement. "What's the *usual way*?"

"If you don't mind, Simia, I think we'd better leave such details for another time," replied Espen dismissively.

Simia's face fell.

"The Merisi were horrified to hear of the Reckoning. They called a vast gathering of their order, something that they have only done a few times in their long history. It was the grandest Say-So I have ever seen, attended by hundreds of Merisi, young and old, many from faraway lands, wearing strange clothing and speaking tongues I had never heard. All the Bringers of recent years were there: Mutumba and Xiang, Fitz and Veeglum.

"Long discussions followed, some of which I was allowed to hear, some of which were held in secret. Finally they concluded that I should be given sanctuary as long as was needed, but that nothing further could be done without Mr Zhi himself."

Bayleon drew himself forward out of the shadows to hoist the pot of stew from the fire, a bitter smile across his face.

"Go on, Espasian, tell them," he said. "Tell them *why* you were sent to see Mr Zhi. Tell them what took you so far away from our troubles."

Espen regarded him wearily and dropped his head between his shoulders.

"I am not ashamed of the truth, Bayleon."

"Clearly not!" retorted Bayleon defiantly. "Tell them!"

Espen's gaze hardened for a moment, obviously unaccustomed to such a tone.

His response was firm: "I went because of the Glimmer Myth."

Ash stared at him in disbelief. His face creased into an uncertain smile and then he laughed hesitantly, as though waiting for the Magruman to say that he was jesting.

"*The Glimmer Myth?*" he cried. "You're joking! Surely you're joking?"

There was no humour in Espen's face. The younger man saw his expression and his smile dropped.

"You're… you're *not* joking. No, I can see that now."

"What's the Glimmer Myth?" asked Simia, searching their faces.

Espen regarded Simia distractedly for a few moments, then turned to Sylas. "I had hoped to explain this a little differently, but now it does seem best that we begin with the myth. Where's the Samarok? We're going to need it."

Sylas turned and rummaged in his bag. He felt its reassuring weight in his hand and pulled it out until it was illuminated by the fire. As he did so, Simia darted round the pit and took a seat next to him.

He gave her a questioning look.

"What?" she said defensively. "I missed this at the mill — *that's* not going to happen again."

"Now," Espen began, eyeing Simia with something between irritation and amusement, "how well can you read the runes?"

Sylas shrugged. "OK, I think. Fathray explained them to me and Galfinch taught me to unravel them."

Ash and Bayleon exchanged an astonished glance.

"Good. Then I need you to look at two things. The first is at the beginning of the book. Turn to the very first page — the first with writing on it."

Sylas lifted the front cover and saw that the opening page was blank. He turned it over. The second page contained just three lines of writing, about a third of the way from the top. He remembered looking at these before, when he was alone in his room. He lifted and turned the Samarok so that the page caught the glow from the flames and, as he did so, Simia suddenly lunged across him, throwing herself towards the fire.

He snatched the Samarok out of the way. "What are you doing?" he cried.

"Saving this!" she said indignantly, holding up a small piece of paper.

It was Mr Zhi's message — the note that he had given Sylas to help him decode the runes. Fathray had inserted it at this very page. This was the one he was *supposed* to read.

He muttered his thanks to Simia and turned back to the page. He looked hard at the runes in the dancing light, clearing his mind until they started to shift and change. Then, slowly, he began to read:

> *"Reach for the... silvered... glimmer on the lake*
> *Turn to the... sun-streaked shadow in your... wake*
> *Now, rise: fear not where none have gone..."*

He read it over again in silence, but even then it made little sense. He looked up at Espen who was smiling quietly.

"That," he said, "is the source of the Glimmer Myth."

Sylas looked back at the runes, reading them over and over as Espen continued.

"That's where it gets its name: from the '*silvered glimmer*'," he said in a low voice. "The myth is ancient. Most believe that it is older than the Merisi or even the Suhl. This is the only surviving fragment of a poem about the myth, a poem written by none less than Merisu, the great father of the Merisi."

"So they say..." grumbled Bayleon.

Espen ignored him. "As you hear, many of my brethren consider it to be preposterous or dangerous—"

"Or both," muttered Bayleon.

"... so it is only spoken about quietly," continued Espen, "in hushed tones, among friends."

"Good, creepy campfire talk," interjected Ash, with a grin.

"Quite," said Espen. "But the Merisi have always seen it quite differently. As you have found, it is very prominent in the Samarok and many Bringers considered it far from mythical. Some even say that the Merisi were founded in order to bring it to light."

Bayleon shook his head slowly as he stirred the pot of stew, a smile playing on his lips.

"But what *is* it?" cried Simia impatiently, unable to contain herself any longer.

"You're right, Simia," replied Espen, "we're straying from the point."

Simia smiled proudly.

"Sylas — read the first line again," instructed Espen.

Sylas read it out loud: "*Reach for the silvered glimmer on the lake...*"

The Magruman nodded. "What do you think that refers to — the *silvered glimmer*?"

"I'm not sure," he said with a shrug. "A reflection?"

"Precisely," said Espen. "Now read the next line."

"*Turn to the sun-streaked shadow in your wake...*" Sylas thought for a moment. "It's talking about your shadow — you know, your shadow in the sunlight."

"Exactly. The poem is telling us all to turn to our own reflection, to our own shadow." He leaned forward so that his face was lit brightly by the flames. "To another part of ourselves."

Bayleon dropped the spoon and threw his arms in the air. "Oh, this really is too—"

"The myth poses us a question," continued Espen, speaking

326

over him. "What if each of us has another side? What if there is a part of ourselves that we can turn to — a 'Glimmer' of our own being — one that we can reach out and touch?"

Sylas and Simia looked at each other in puzzlement.

"I don't understand," said Sylas.

Espen held his gaze. "We all know that our two worlds are connected in some way." His voice was still quiet but excited. "They have the same hills and mountains, the same rivers and seas, even the same sun and moon. The very seasons are the same, but in reverse — when it is winter here, it is summer in the Other — as though they are the *reflection* of one another. Just as you see your own image in a mirror or on the surface of a lake: the same, but reversed. Do you see?"

Sylas nodded uncertainly, starting to wonder where this was leading.

"Well, the poem is telling us something even stranger. It tells us that it is not only our two worlds that are twinned — not just the fabric, the things, the places. It tells us something far more profound, something that runs to the very heart of us." He looked into every face in the circle. "It tells us that *we* are twinned too. Each of us. All of us."

Sylas's eyes searched Espen's face long after he had finished speaking. Was he *serious*? Each of us with a person just like ourselves, but different — changed in some strange, unnatural way. Surely it was impossible.

Simia clamped a hand on either side of her head as though to contain the great torrent of thoughts. "But this is all so... so—"

"Ludicrous? Insane?" interjected Bayleon with a bitter smile. "I quite agree. Espasian, you know as well as I that this goes against our whole philosophy! The entire basis of Essenfayle! We believe in connections and togetherness — the bonds that bind all things. How are we to believe that two parts of our own being could be divided and separate? There are good reasons why such ideas have been spoken about in hushed tones: they're a child's fantasy! Worse than that, they're an affront to Essenfayle and all it stands for!"

"And yet we accept that the world itself is divided," Espen reasoned, his tone conciliatory. "And we accept the divisions between night and day, earth and the air, men and women. The myth simply completes the picture: it is the final piece in the puzzle."

"No, Espasian, it is fanciful! And dangerous! And wrong!" snapped Bayleon.

He turned away and, as though to signal the end of the conversation, began ladling a portion of stew on to a plate.

Espen looked at him steadily. "But Bayleon, some of the most important people in our two worlds have believed this fancy."

"People like you, you mean?" scoffed the Spoorrunner.

"Yes, like me." He paused while Bayleon scoffed again. "And like Merimaat."

The Spoorrunner froze with the ladle halfway to a plate.

"People like Filimaya and Mr Zhi."

The camp was suddenly entirely still. Espen turned and looked earnestly at Sylas.

"People like Sylas's mother."

28
Deceit

"... and so these men, these Priests of Souls, drank deep of their ill-gotten power, clothed themselves in deceit*, and set out into the world."*

Sylas felt the breath rush from his lungs. He stared at Espen.

"Did you say *my mother*?"

"I did," said Espen.

"You *know* her?" He pressed his palms into the dry, packed earth.

"Yes, Sylas, I know her," said Espen softly. "Though the Merisi know her far better than I." He paused as if unsure whether or not to continue. "Your mother and Mr Zhi have known each other for years."

Sylas's lungs burned and his heart pounded in his chest. Fathray had been right: she and the Merisi *were* connected.

"Why?" he asked, looking up at Espen.

"Your mother is special, Sylas. Almost as special as you."

Bayleon was no longer smiling. He had lowered the ladle into the stewpot and his eyes were fixed on Espen.

"It was to do with her dreams," said Espen.

Simia frowned. "Her *dreams?*"

Sylas was silent.

"They helped to convince her — and Mr Zhi — that the Glimmer Myth is true."

Sylas dug his nails into the dust. He thought of her illness, her nights sobbing in his bed. He felt a shiver run down his spine.

"Her dreams..." he whispered. Images of her long nights of suffering rushed through his mind, of her talking to herself, of her pleading and sobbing, of her quiet chatter when no one was there.

And then, almost despite himself, he said: "She spoke... she talked as though someone was in the room... like... like it was a..."

"A *conversation*," said Espen.

Sylas's eyes flicked to the Magruman. Espen looked at him with uncharacteristic tenderness, and nodded.

"I don't think your mother was ill at all," he said quietly. "I think she shares your gift. She shares your connection with this world. But hers is with her Glimmer."

Sylas covered his face with his hands, trying to take it in.

"It seems that for whatever reason," continued Espen, "your mother was aware of her own twin in this world. The Merisi weren't sure how, but Mr Zhi, who spent a great deal of time with her over the years, said there was little doubt."

Sylas raised his head from his hands. "Her *twin*," he said under his breath.

There was another long, awkward silence. Simia placed a tentative hand on his knee.

Ash gave a low whistle. "This is for real, isn't it?" he said to nobody in particular.

"It was Mr Zhi who had her taken to Winterfern?" asked Sylas, rubbing his temple. "To the hospital?"

Espen nodded.

"And he visited her?"

"He did. Often. And even before that, at your home."

Tears suddenly welled in Sylas's eyes and he looked away to the fire. Bayleon stirred, straightening his back.

"Leave the boy alone," he said firmly. "He's heard enough for now."

"No!" snapped Sylas. "I want to know why they made me believe she was dead. How could they *do* that? How could *she* do that?"

Espen's eyes searched the boy's face for a moment. "I know very little, Sylas, but of this I am certain: the Merisi believed that her gift came with great dangers, both to herself and to those she loved. They did it because they truly believed they had no other option."

"But how could they let me suffer like that?"

"They did all they could to ease your—"

Sylas felt a swelling rage in his chest. He scrambled to his feet and glared down at Espen.

"Did all they could?" he cried, tears burning his eyes. "What did they ever do for me, except send me to this godforsaken place?"

Espen was silent for a moment. "They had you brought to Gabblety Row, Sylas. They gave your uncle rooms and made sure he had a business. They had Veeglum watch over you."

Sylas took a step backwards and stumbled slightly on the pile of earth. He turned from Espen to the faces around the fire. He tried to find words, but finally he whirled about, clambered unsteadily over the heap of soil and walked off into the night.

Espen stood and took a step to follow, but stopped himself. "Don't go far!"

Simia leapt to her feet and pulled her coat about her shoulders.

She jumped over the earthen barrier and darted off into the blackness.

"He can't go alone. I'll stay with him!" she shouted over her shoulder.

Sylas walked blindly, taking deep breaths of the chill night air. He had no idea where he was going or why. All he knew was that he needed to get away, to think. He stumbled until the dim glow of the fire had faded into nothingness and all that was left was silence and blackness.

He stopped and turned slowly about, blinking at the emptiness, soaking up the smooth closeness of night on the Barrens. He lifted his hand before his face and saw nothing; he looked to the sky and saw the same oily void as everywhere else. In some part of him he knew that this should terrify him, that such darkness was his worst fear, but now, just as everything seemed meaningless, chaotic, undone, he surrendered to it. He sat down in the black dust, drew his knees up to his chest and rocked gently backwards and forwards.

He thought of the last time he had seen his mother, her pretty face looking down at him in their kitchen, smiling at him, drinking in the sight of him. He remembered only a few fragments of conversations about school, his painting, the kites. Why hadn't she said anything? How could she have kept all this a secret? He replayed her gestures, her expressions, her slow words, but he saw no trace of mystery, no hint of a world of magic and shadows and Glimmers. She had kept all that to herself. Alone.

He felt tears burning in the corners of his eyes and brushed them away. "Why…?" he whispered to himself.

"Because you didn't need to know."

It was Simia's voice, just a few paces away. He looked about, but saw only blackness.

"How did you find me?"

"I told you — I know this place," she said, sitting down somewhere to his right.

They were quiet for some time, listening to the silence, staring into nothingness, and Sylas was surprised to find that he did not mind her being there. He wanted to be quiet and she seemed to know that without asking. It was comforting somehow — just knowing that she was there, somewhere out there in the night.

Finally he broke the silence.

"Why did you say that? *'Because I didn't need to know.'*"

He heard Simia shift on the hard earth. "It's something my dad used to say," she said. "I used to ask him stuff all the time, you know, why's this happening, what's that for, who did such and such and how'd they do it. And most of the time he'd tell me, even if he made a joke out of it or missed out the interesting bits. But sometimes, just sometimes, when I was asking about the worst stuff, the things even adults didn't like to talk about — Thoth or the Dirgheon or the Undoing — he'd go quiet. He'd think about it, and then he'd say: 'Simsi, you don't need to know.'"

"Wasn't that just annoying? Especially for you."

"Yep," said Simia, a smile in her voice, "and I used to kick up a real stink, but I always stopped after a while. It was something about the way he said it — a kind of knowing and softness at the same time — I knew that he was doing what was best for me." She drew a sharp breath. "Of course, now, after everything, I understand exactly what he was doing."

"What?"

"He was letting me be a kid. For as long as he possibly could."

They fell silent again. Sylas stared into the night, the image of his mother in his mind, her voice sounding in his ears, and he knew that Simia was probably right. Perhaps she *had* protected him, kept him safe, kept him away from whatever all this was about — the Glimmer Myth, the Undoing, who she was, who *he* was. Perhaps she'd done it to let him be himself — to be young while he could.

He felt tears start to roll down his cheeks. He did not wipe them from his face. He just sat quietly and wept. And Simia let him.

The darkness closed in about them and both were lost in their thoughts. Sylas thought back over the years, of his relationship with his mother, the good times, the happy times, and then the despair, the grief and the loneliness, when all he had of her was her faded picture, and the few gifts she had given him. His mind turned to the book of science, with its inscription:

"*Learn all that you are, my dear Sylas, learn all that you are able to be.*"

He knew then that she had not wanted to keep anything from him, she had just wanted him to find out at the right time. Find out for himself.

They sat in silence for a while longer and then he said: "We have to work all this out."

Simia was quiet for a moment. "What?"

"Who I am, who brought me here, this Glimmer Myth, the Undoing — all that stuff. It's all connected."

"Well, that's why we're going to see Paiscion, isn't it?"

"I know, but before I was just doing it because everyone seemed to think I should — because everything was leading me there. But now... now I really *want* to go. I want to go there and wherever I have to go next. I mean, if everything Espen said is right, if the Glimmer Myth is true and my mum and I have some part in it, this could be the most important thing I ever do."

Simia thought for a moment. "I suppose it could be the most important thing *any* of us ever do."

§

It could hardly be called a dawn. There were no rays of light, no traces of sunshine, no promises of warmth, just endless expanses of white mist glowing ever more sombrely as the day struggled into being. Neither was there any sound, for the Slithen rarely broke the surface of the river and, when they did, their oily flanks caused barely a ripple.

The prisoners huddled at the rear of the ancient, slimy boat, pressing in against the cold, straining their senses for any sign of the world around them, any sign of life. For the most part they had to settle for the occasional looming darkness of a riverbank or withered tree, and perhaps the hunched silhouette of a heron searching for fish in the putrid waters. When there was nothing else, they would look ahead to the tangle of chains that stretched in front of the crude vessel and disappeared into the depths, where the Slithen strained at their harnesses.

So the boat sped on, like a ghost ship, carried forward without sails or breath of wind, cloaked in a deathly silence.

If there was solace to be found on that awful vessel, it was in the form of Bowe. He met frightened glances with a compassionate smile or a nod of the head, in a manner that left his companions in no doubt that their worst fears had been understood and shared. He placed a firm hand on trembling limbs and more than once gathered the frail into his giant frame to give them warmth. Fathray too sat close at hand, gaining some strength from his friend as he cast his eyes out into the nothingness and stroked his long moustache in quiet reflection, humming his strange, tuneless melody. Thus, as shadows became the dismal glow of day, Bowe somehow gave the hapless prisoners a brief, uneasy calm.

It was shattered in an instant.

"No…" moaned one of the women suddenly, "no… no… no…"

Her eyes were wide with terror and fixed somewhere high above the thinning mists. Others followed her gaze and saw what she had seen: a vast pyramid of shadow towering into the miserable sky, looming over the river ahead.

The Dirgheon.

They took up the woman's lament and Bowe exchanged a knowing look with Fathray. Now, as he looked at his companions, he saw something that filled him with a new fear, for his Scryer's eyes saw nothing but the coiling, smothering blackness of despair. It gathered about his brethren like the dark wings of a predator, taking from them any last vestiges of hope. He saw tears in the eyes of grown men, and felt the woman at his side become listless beneath his arm.

Great torrents of horror emanated from the prison ahead, from the thousands of broken hearts, lost hopes, vanquished dreams. He searched his mind for light, for stillness, for relief, but all he saw was the thick, oily blacks of despair; the harsh, thin blues of grief and loss; the sharp, cutting reds of hate and anger; all these endlessly swelling and receding within an ocean of feeling.

And then, suddenly, something changed.

The dark rolled back to the edges of his mind. In its place something slow and still emerged. Something light. Warm. Hopeful. It rose like a dawn from the dark horizon, banishing the grim hues of the Dirgheon and, in their stead, offering hope, solace… *love.*

Bowe opened his eyes and saw a vision of beauty and joy.

He extended his fingers, as though this apparition could be touched, and his large green eyes glazed with tears.

She was there. He could feel her.

His beautiful daughter.

"Naeo." He spoke the name tenderly, under his breath. He looked up at the dark pyramid and, for the first time in a long while, he allowed himself to think of his little girl. He thought of her in a boat similar to this, perhaps seeing this very same sight. He pictured her arriving there. Being taken inside.

He turned to his companions. "We go to those we love," he said.

29

Of Myth and Legend

"What myth *is there that does not here find substance?*
What legend *that does not here draw breath, or walk in the*
light of the sun, or crawl in the shadow of the night?"

It was a picture of sun-spangled beauty framed by the delicate, white-edged fingers of evergreens. The sun beamed from its bright blue throne, its rays glancing from the frosted fingertips, scattering through prisms of ice so that they sparkled and danced in the icy breeze. Sylas gazed up at this glorious vision, the sun playing warmly on his face, only distantly aware of the creeping cold that inched through his limbs, working its way sleepily, lazily to his heart. His eyelids began to feel heavy, blissfully heavy, drooping like the snow-laden branches above.

"Wake up. Your journey is not done."

The voice was gentle but close, as if at his ear. He blinked and drew a sharp, icy breath. The biting chill chased away the encroaching sleep and, as it did, he heard the muffled crumple and creak of footsteps in the snow. He raised his head and looked about him, across the glistening, lustrous blanket of snow, between the stark shadows of trunks and branches, and in the dappled light he saw them: a perfect trail of footprints, leading off between the trees.

He summoned an almost-lost reserve of energy and brought his stiffened limbs painfully to task, heaving himself from his too-soft bed of snow. His breath clouded about him with the effort, obscuring his path, but as it cleared, he saw the trail, straight and true. He staggered at first, wrong-footed by the clinging powder at his feet, but soon he had fallen into her tracks, matching her steps, her easy gait. Like her, he descended a bank and pushed through a pleasant veil of frosted green, feeling the cold-tipped tendrils grazing his face.

His heart suddenly leapt, and a new, unexpected warmth flooded his veins. He wanted to cry out for joy, cry out to her, but he had no voice. She sat with her back to him, only her cheek visible beneath the hood, which glowed radiantly by the light of a crackling campfire. Her head inclined towards him and she extended a delicate hand, motioning for him to join her by the heat of the flames.

He sat down, his heart full, tears in his eyes, and he turned to look into her lovely face.

She turned away, and her soft voice sounded somewhere in his mind. "Know me, and you will find me."

SYLAS WOKE TO A fearsome, crippling cold. It cracked his bones, thickened the air in his lungs, slowed the blood in his veins. He yearned to return to his sleep, to his dream, to his mother. There had been no time, no chance to reach for her hand, to look into her eyes, to see the face he loved so much.

"Know me, and you will find me," she had said. Perhaps, he thought, he was only now coming to know her. Know all of her mysteries, her torments. Only now, in this terrible place, so far from her.

He drew a gasp of icy air and slowly, painfully, forced himself awake. After some moments he mustered the energy to push himself up on to his elbow.

The camp was entirely still beneath a shroud of thick, dark grey cloud and a low mist, which drifted over the figures of three sleepers huddled beneath their blankets. The fire had burned down and now glowed a deep red at his feet, though he felt no warmth, heard no hiss or crackle. The sombre blackish-grey of the Barrens lay about them like a deathly blanket. There were no birds heralding a new day, no scent of dew, no glint in the sky; only the reluctant light of a day that would rather be night.

"Let's bring this fire up," came a low voice from somewhere behind. "You'll feel twice the cold this morning."

Espen's broad figure loomed into view, carrying fresh firewood under his arm. He stepped over the bank of earth and laid it down quietly so as not to wake the others, then took up a handful of twigs and threw them on to the fire.

He sat down next to Sylas, leaning forward to warm his hands.

"How do you feel?" he asked, without turning.

Sylas thought for a moment. "Cold."

Espen smiled.

Bayleon stirred on the other side of the camp. He stretched his thick arms above his head and yawned noisily, which woke the other two.

They were all soon sitting up and eating a breakfast of porridge and dried fruit. Simia was white from the cold, but she ate heartily and it was not long before she had regained some of her colour and cheer. Ash too looked much recovered and to Sylas's astonishment, when he removed his bandages, they revealed no sign of the cut on his temple: healed by Filimaya's strange balm.

The conversation soon became lively, though it was Simia and Ash who did most of the talking. Espen sat quietly watching the others, while Bayleon seemed altogether detached, gloomy and preoccupied. Sylas was still too busy thinking about all he had been told the previous evening to take much interest in the discussion, but as the warming, sweet porridge had its effect, he too found himself smiling at Simia's wild stories of life on the Barrens.

After a while there was a lull in the conversation and he decided to ask something that had been on his mind.

"Espen?"

"Yes?"

"If we all have one of these twins — these Glimmers — and they are a mirror of us, doesn't that mean we would have to be born at the same time?"

Espen nodded. "That's what we think."

"But doesn't that mean we'd have to have the same parents?" he asked. He screwed up his face and rubbed his temples. "Or is our Glimmer born to the Glimmer of our parents?"

Espen smiled. "Now you see why many think it to be a myth," he said. "The truth is that nobody knows."

"But do we live and die at the same time as our Glimmer? I mean, how does *that* work?"

"Yes and why don't we *feel* like half a person?" added Simia. "I mean, surely we should feel weak or... something?"

Espen opened his palms and shrugged. "Again, I'm afraid that—"

"He doesn't know..." mumbled Bayleon. "What a surprise!"

Sylas looked from Bayleon to Espen. He so wanted to ask more, but he stopped himself: talk of the Glimmer Myth had done little to improve the tension between the two men. He decided to change the subject.

"I've been thinking... Now that you're here, Espen, do we really need to see Paiscion?" he asked. "I mean, you're a

Magruman: don't you know just about as much as he does?"

Bayleon scoffed and jabbed at the fire. "You'd think so..." he muttered.

Espen levelled his gaze at the Spoorrunner for a moment, then turned back to Sylas. "But you still don't know who you really are, do you?" he asked. "You still don't know how or why you were summoned here. Neither do I. I know part of your story, Sylas, but by no means all of it. Nobody does, because it's still unfolding. Of course you're right to be seeking Paiscion, because if anyone can help you to discover more of those final truths, he can."

"But what's so special about Paiscion?"

The Magruman smiled. "Oh, there's much that is special about Paiscion. He was always the most powerful of the three of us, and certainly he has the greatest powers of seeing and communing, which in your case could be very useful. He is the one that the Scryers and the Scribes always looked to, and he certainly has the best understanding of the Samarok. You must meet with him." He paused and kicked the embers of the fire. "Where exactly are you hoping to find him?"

"Don't answer that," instructed Bayleon gruffly.

There was an awkward silence. Espen regarded him with a perplexed expression.

"Bayleon, you really don't need to keep secrets from—"

"We'd better get moving," said the Spoorrunner, getting to his feet and beginning to stuff his bag with pots, blankets and utensils. "We must reach the circle before sundown."

Espen raised an eyebrow. "Bayleon, we were—"

"Let's just get one thing clear," snapped Bayleon, turning towards him. "None of us answer to you — not any more. And I for one don't trust you. Filimaya told us to make sure that Sylas reaches Paiscion by tomorrow and that's exactly what we'll do."

Espen regarded him calmly for a moment, then shrugged his broad shoulders and bowed his head. "As you wish," he said.

Ash looked nervously from one to the other, then clapped his hands.

"What finer day for a stroll in a wasteland?" he chirped.

Nobody smiled.

Sylas and Simia heaved their aching, heavy legs over the earthen bank and set out on to the Barrens. The thought of leaving the fire behind was almost too much to bear, but deep down both wanted to press on and reach the city. They took a wary look at the dark, glowering horizon and shuffled on.

Bayleon strode out far ahead of them to scout their route, quickly becoming a smudge of grey, almost invisible against the relentless murk of the plain. Espen stayed back, watching the open plains at their rear, leaving Sylas, Simia and Ash to walk together.

"What *is* it with those two?" said Simia, keen to take her mind off her legs and stomach. "Bayleon's been at Espen's throat ever since he turned up."

"I know," said Ash. "Old scores, I think. Bayleon hasn't forgiven him."

"What for?"

"The Reckoning."

Simia frowned. "But why's Espen to blame? Surely that was all Thoth's doing."

"When you lose your wife and your children, you need more than one person to blame," said Ash soberly, looking ahead to Bayleon's solitary figure on the plain. "Espasian — Espen — ordered the Spoorrunners to find a way out for the others. It's because of Espen that Bayleon wasn't there... at the end."

"But that means it's because of Espen that he's still *alive*," said Simia.

"Precisely," said Ash.

There was a pause. "Oh," said Simia.

"We all have a sorry tale to tell, don't we?" said Ash, with a weak smile.

They fell silent for some moments as they trudged over the parched, dusty surface of the plain, lost in their own melancholy thoughts. But, with the passage of time, the sombre light and deathly emptiness of the Barrens had a way of turning melancholy to sadness and sadness to despair. Sylas was keen to revive the conversation, no matter what the topic.

"Tell me about it," he said. "The Reckoning."

There was a long hesitation.

"We don't often talk about it..." began Ash.

Sylas saw the look on his face — a mixture of awkwardness and distaste — and immediately regretted raising it. "It's fine, don't worry about it."

"No, you should know. It's important," said Ash, drawing a long breath.

"People call it a battle, but in truth it wasn't a battle at all. It was hopeless from the start, wasn't it, Simsi?"

Simia lowered her eyes and kept walking. Clearly she liked this subject even less than Ash.

"But we had no choice," continued Ash. "We had to fight to the end. Even once Thoth was joined by the other two Priests of Souls, and we knew that the war was all but lost. Not only was Merimaat fighting three of her own strength, so were each of her Magrumen. Thoth's army of Gherothians and the Ghor, who had been weakened by months of fighting, were reinforced by the Sur and the Basetians. What had been a fairly balanced fight turned into a rout — worse than that, a massacre. They outnumbered us and they used magic the like of which we'd never seen: strange mutations of living things — probably some kind of Druindil; devastating Urgolvane forces that tore into our ranks and charred the very earth beneath our feet; and all manner of awful devilish creations — no doubt the work of Kimiyya, Thoth's own magic. Within weeks, our settlements had been utterly destroyed and the tide of the war had turned. We were in retreat, and we needed to find a way out.

"It was Espen's idea to go south. These plains were once riddled with rivers, all of them flowing towards the sea no great distance away. The Suhl Magrumen — Espen, Paiscion and Blissil — were to use the dry riverbeds to take the weak and the sick out by night, while what remained of our fighting army and Merimaat stayed behind. Once the fugitives reached the sea they were supposed to be met by the Ghalaks — a sea-faring people working for hire — hardly allies, but they were outside Thoth's influence and were reliable enough if you paid them well."

Simia had fallen behind, not wanting to hear any more, and was trying to strike up a conversation with Espen. Ash looked sombre as he paused to take a swig from his water bottle.

"We don't know how," he continued, "but Thoth found out about the plan. While the other Priests of Souls stayed to fight Merimaat and the army, Thoth and Scarpia, the most powerful of his Magrumen, followed our people to the sea. There they found them gathered on the sand flats, looking out at an empty bay, crying out in despair. The Ghalaks hadn't come. That's when Thoth and Scarpia attacked. They summoned downpours of acid rain, torrents of molten rock and flames that belched from the sea. It was like the end of the world, and in an enclosed bay like that, there was no escape. Blissil was killed in the first attack and Espen and Paiscion were too busy fending off the onslaught to have any hope of helping. In despair they sent the Spoorrunners to search for a safe way out.

"While they were away, Thoth walked alone out on to the headland, cloaked all in black and silver, wearing his dread mask of cloth. He looked down on the Suhl and raised a terrifying magic: the earth began to tremble and quake as though it was about to break in two; the sands beneath the waves churned and boiled, mixing with the water, seething like they too were part of the sea. Soon they were little more than a liquid morass, heaving, swirling, eddying. Slowly at first, then all too quickly, they engulfed the people, swallowing them into the earth, pulling them beneath the waves of sand and water."

Ash paused, checking that Simia was still far behind, then he added in a low voice: "Within minutes, everyone was gone, lost beneath the sand flats of Salsimaine."

Sylas shook his head. "Everyone?"

"Everyone. Except a few, including Espen, it seems. And Paiscion — he was still fighting on the headland."

"And Simia's family?" whispered Sylas, glancing behind him.

"No, not there," was the hushed reply.

"But she seems so…"

"The Reckoning touched us all in its own way," replied Ash with a glance behind.

His face was drained. Once again Sylas felt overwhelmed by the scale and horror of it all. It was an unthinkable, hideous thing, an evil that he could not even begin to comprehend.

"I'm sorry," he said. The words sounded feeble.

Ash offered no reply.

They walked on in silence. The terrible images of people sinking into the sands grew in Sylas's mind, for Ash had painted a vivid picture, and thoughts of such horrors formed all too easily here on the Barrens. He was relieved when Simia finally tired of trying to engage Espen in some kind of conversation and caught up.

They had long since lost sight of their meagre camp somewhere in the grey behind them. The view was exactly the same in every direction: flat, empty plains whose only features were occasional slopes, undulations and dried riverbeds. It was a wonder that Bayleon knew where to go without landmarks or the sun, and Sylas marvelled as he watched him walking confidently on, stooping every now and again to examine the ground underfoot, then setting out again with renewed energy. Sylas thought back to Ash's account of the Reckoning, to the huge responsibility that had rested on Bayleon and these other Spoorrunners.

"You've never told me about the Spoorrunners," he said as the three of them clambered up a riverbank. "What do they do exactly?"

Ash glanced in Bayleon's direction and smiled with admiration. "They're a dying breed," he said. "And Bayleon is one of the last. They do two things: they guide and they hunt. Guide, because they can find their way just about anywhere; hunt, because they can find anybody or anything just by following their tracks — not the kind of tracks that you or I can see, but ones we don't even know are there."

"Like what?"

"They spot the tiniest things, like scuffed dirt or a bent leaf or a blade of grass out of place. But what's really weird is that they even *feel* changes in the wind and vibrations in the earth — there's no getting away from them."

"Too true," said Simia with a sigh.

Ash laughed. "Simia's tried more often than most!"

Simia grinned proudly. "Bayleon's always finding me up in the hills or in the tunnels under the temple or in the fish market. I don't know how he does it."

"And the things in his bag? Are they for tracking?"

"Some of them," said Ash. "But they use most of them for showing others the way — they normally don't need such things themselves. It comes naturally to them: passed from father to son, mother to daughter. Bayleon himself is from the Spoor family — the family that gave Spoorrunners their name — and his great-great-grandfather was the most famous Spoorrunner of them all."

Then he cleared his throat. "He's also a bit of a know-all of course..."

Sylas smiled. "Of course."

They walked on in silence, all of them looking ahead to Bayleon's impressive figure, his assured strides consuming the empty miles of the Barrens. It was a great comfort to have him there.

The hours passed slowly. At one stage they reached a point that was a little higher than the rest of the plain and Sylas hoped that they might see something — anything — that broke the tedium of grey, but they looked ahead on to yet more of the cold, desperate expanse, punctuated only by scores of the black, inky stains where the earth had been scorched. They picked their way onwards between ravines and riverbeds towards the distant horizon, which was now darkening ever further as the sun retired. The cold and stiffness had finally left Sylas's limbs, but the endless trudge was sapping and he found himself desperate to know how much further they had to go.

"Are we nearly there?"

"When we're nearly there," said Ash cheerlessly, "you won't need to ask."

By the time that moment came, the dwindling light had become little more than a grubby mark on the horizon. Sylas had started to wonder if they would reach their destination after all, but as they climbed a low rise, something caught his eye. It was a curious, jagged break in the long, featureless line between the earth and the sky. He made out several shapes like crooked teeth rising from the earth, silhouetted in the gloomy grey light. He squinted, trying to see more, but they soon lost sight of them. They walked for some time without seeing anything, but as they climbed another slope and rounded its top, he saw it, directly ahead of him.

It was a massive structure, hewn from giant blocks of stone as tall as a house. Some stood proud from the ground, rising at haphazard angles high into the air; others lay across their tops, bridging one stone to the next. Although they at first seemed to be arranged at random, a pattern soon became clear: it was a vast circle with majestic, sweeping arcs, spanning the length of a football field, with other smaller rings inside. The result was at once a collection of mighty stones, each astonishing and splendid in its own right, and a single vast monument in which every part played a role, forming a complete pattern, a closed circle.

But there was something wrong. Many of the stones were not whole, but had corners missing, deep cracks and fissures running across their surface, sections broken away. Many were blackened and charred. Others seemed to have symbols chiselled crudely into their surface. Some leaned over at impossible angles, the earth at their base ripped up into great mounds, and many had been toppled entirely and now lay next to the deep holes in which they had once stood.

Espen strode up behind them.

"Welcome to the Circle of Salsimaine," he said. "Or what's left of it."

30

Betrayed

"Even as they had deceived their kin, so the
Priests of Souls betrayed *themselves."*

FOR SOME MOMENTS SYLAS and his companions were still, looking silently down at the great monument of Salsimaine, marvelling that it was the creation of men. They could hardly believe their eyes: here, in the midst of so much devastation, such absolute oblivion, something so immense and so beautiful had survived. It was as though it would not be subdued, would not be destroyed.

"Come," said Espen, patting Sylas on the shoulder and striding out in front, "I want to show you something."

They walked down a gentle slope towards the ancient ruin, stepping between splinters of rock and walking over large tracts of blistered, scorched earth. Some terrible battle had been waged here, its violence leaving nothing untouched: the ground cracked underfoot as though it could bear no more; the air smelt so strongly that at times it seemed that they were breathing smoke; and their path was strewn with piles of earth and boulders.

As they reached the bottom, they encountered one boulder so large that it was clear that it had been placed there deliberately, like the stones in the circle. It had been broken by an unimaginable force, snapped at a sharp angle across its centre. Gouged into the face of the exposed rock was a hideous graffiti symbol: a bird with high shoulders and a long, cruelly arched beak.

"This," said Espen, running his hand over the cold surface, "is the most important of all the stones. The Scrying Rock."

Everyone gathered round except Bayleon, who walked on without pausing and made his way towards the centre of the circle.

"This is the point from which the circle is meant to be seen," continued Espen, directing their attention back towards the ruin. "From here, its true significance becomes clear."

Sylas turned and looked back, then took a sharp breath. The great circle looked like a solid wall. It was not complete, as many of the stones to the right had fallen away or were missing large sections, but everywhere else the stones entirely shut out the faint light from the horizon. Where there were spaces between the stones of the outer circle, they were blocked by stones inside, and where there were spaces between those of the inner circles, stones at the far side filled them in. The result was an almost perfect black wall of stone, which seemed to stand as an impenetrable barrier not only to all who would pass, but to the very light of the sun. Only in two places could any light be seen. In the very centre, the criss-cross of vertical and horizontal stones seemed to have been designed to frame, not to block, the light. They formed two perfectly shaped windows, one precisely above the other, near the top of the exact centre of the wall.

"Those windows are the Scrying Holes," said Espen, following Sylas's gaze. "They are the only place in the wall of rock where—"

"Scrying?" blurted Simia, pushing past Ash to get a better look. "What — scrying like Scryers do?"

Espen looked a little irritated. "Well, I was just coming to that,

Simia. As their name suggests, they are for scrying, but this form of scrying is far older than anything done by the Scryers. It's not about the connections between people, it's about the connections between the sun and the moon."

Simia looked excited. "I know about this! I learned it at school! It's something to do with sunrise and… and priests… and the sun and the moon…"

Her voice tailed off.

"I think we had established that the sun and the moon were involved, Simia," said Ash sarcastically.

She frowned at him reproachfully. "Well, I *do* know. Just… not right now."

Ash looked at Espen. "I think you should put her out of her misery."

The trace of a smile passed over Espen's lips. He leaned back against the Scrying Rock.

"Once every eighteen years, at the summer solstice — the longest day in the year — the sun and the moon come together right here on this spot, showing for all to see that, although one rules the kingdom of night and the other of day, they are connected: two parts of a whole. For a whole month surrounding the solstice, the moon rises so that it passes through that tiny window at the top of the great Circle of Salsimaine. It happens every night, and people came from all around to stand here, at the Scrying Rock, to witness it. But the most important moment happens every eighteen years exactly. In those years, on the summer solstice, the sun shines through the lower window just before it sets and then, just minutes later, while the crowds would still be muttering their amazement, the moon would rise. It would climb behind the wall so that no one could see it and then, in a moment of seeming magic, its sacred white light would beam through the other window."

Simia rolled her eyes. "That's right, *now* I remember," she said triumphantly. "Isn't there something about the stars as well?"

Espen raised an eyebrow. "The constellations? Yes, there is. The Circle of Salsimaine connects the sun, the moon, the stars, the seasons, the months of the year — every part of the cosmos. Its full significance has been lost over the years."

"No wonder it was this that finally took us to the Other," whispered Ash, staring reverently at the black stones.

Espen nodded his agreement.

"And this is the same as the circles *we* have?" asked Sylas. "There's one called Stonehenge not far from where I live."

"Exactly the same," said Espen, smiling. "Two sides of the same coin, like the rest of our two worlds. And the one that you mention, Stonehenge, is in exactly the same place as this one, though of course it's in your world, not ours."

Sylas stared at the stones with new wonder. This stone circle... in the very same spot as Stonehenge? It hardly seemed possible.

"And you used these to pass between the worlds?" he asked.

"This is one way, yes."

Sylas felt a growing excitement. "So I could get back to my world right now? I could go back and look for my mum?"

Espen stiffened. "In theory, yes."

"What does that mean, '*in theory*'?"

"It means that yes, you could go back, but perhaps that isn't what she would want. Not yet."

"Don't tell me what my mum wants!" snapped Sylas with a sudden surge of emotion. "I'm sick of everyone thinking they know her!"

Espen's face darkened for a moment and he looked away, as if to consider how to react. He laid a hand on Sylas's shoulder. "Of course you know her better than anyone. I just meant that she *knew* about this world and about the Glimmer Myth. In a way she and the Merisi led you here: to this world, to these discoveries, to the Suhl. Do you really want to turn away from that now?"

Sylas lowered his eyes, the familiar confusion clouding his thoughts. He knew that what Espen said made sense, but he yearned to see her with all his heart. How could he do nothing, knowing that this place might take him to her? But then he too believed that this journey was somehow what she wanted. That the answers lay here, not back where he started. He kicked out at the dry earth, sending up a cloud of dust.

"No," he said.

"Come on, it's late," said Espen, drawing himself up. "Let's set up camp."

He headed off towards the Circle of Salsimaine. Ash patted Sylas on the shoulder and set out after the Magruman, but Simia stayed behind.

"He might be right," she said quietly, "but that doesn't make it any easier."

She linked arms with Sylas and together they set out after their companions.

They made their way between some of the fallen stones, clambering over the rubble that had once been part of the great monument. Soon they were walking among the vast uprights, some jutting straight up into the darkening sky, others topped with stones just as mighty as themselves, forming an eerie arch that seemed like a doorway into the unknown. There was so little light that they cast almost no shadow, but they seemed to Sylas to draw in what dying rays there were, deepening the gloom of the Barrens. He reached out and touched one of the smooth sides, running his fingers over the cool surface until they fell into a deep crack. He felt the cold, damp interior and snatched his hand away.

They moved past the outer circle, which swept off to their left and right, and stepped beneath the arches of the first inner arc, which seemed in better condition. Finally they entered the smallest of the circles. Here the stones were whole and, although some were cracked or crudely engraved with the glaring face of Thoth, they were still well formed. This was the inner sanctum. After hours of staring into wide open spaces and endless horizons the giant perfectly crafted enclosure was breathtaking. Sylas could sense the presence of the creators in the looming stones, as though their souls were even now bound up in the dark rock. It was at once frightening and comforting; ominous and exhilarating.

A vast stone table lay in the centre of the circle, supported at its two ends by great plinths of rock upon which some ancient carvings were still visible. Bayleon had already unpacked his bag on to the table and was now busy digging the ash out of an old fire pit.

"Good of you to come," he said gruffly, between strokes of the shovel.

Within an hour, the fire had been lit, the remains of the stew were bubbling on the fire and the travellers were gathered round the warming flames. Simia and Ash were quietly trying to outdo one another's knowledge of the Circle of Salsimaine: a battle that Simia seemed quite certain she would win even though she knew far less than Ash. Espen was half listening, seeming amused but distracted. By far the hungriest of the group, Bayleon had occupied himself with the stewpot, leaning over it as if hoping that the aroma alone might fill his stomach.

Sylas lay back and watched the firelight dancing across the nearest of the dark stones. He could hardly believe that these slabs of rock had the power to take him back — back to everything he knew: Gabblety Row, his uncle, even his mother.

He felt a pang of hurt and guilt. It felt so wrong not to be returning to her, especially now that he knew a way. But try as he might, he found Espen's logic hard to deny. Everything he had discovered told him that this journey and the journey to his mother were one and the same. And yet here in this strange place, somewhere in the confounding blackness of the Barrens, he seemed further away from her than ever.

He tried to control his thoughts, to think back over the past few days, to make some kind of sense of them. For some time he stared into the flickering flames, lost in his thoughts.

Suddenly he remembered his final conversation with Fathray... the Scribe's final words about the Samarok:

"*It may explain everything.*"

Why hadn't he thought of it before?

He rolled on to his front, searched through his bag and brought out the Samarok. He opened it to the page that was still marked by the piece of paper, which he tucked under his thumb. He focused his eyes on Merisu's poem and slowly the Ravel Runes wound about each other, forming shapes that he recognised. He began to read.

"Reach for the silvered glimmer on the lake..."

He mouthed the words to himself, savouring each one, trying to draw out its meaning.

"Turn to the sun-streaked shadow..."

As he reached the end of the second line, he had to shift Mr Zhi's piece of paper out of the way and suddenly his eyes flicked to it. There was something about it — something that he was supposed to remember. Fathray... in the Den of Scribes, at Meander Mill — he had said that it was important — that Paiscion had to see it. He cast his eyes over Mr Zhi's smudged handwriting, whispering the words under his breath. He came to the end of the passage, frowned and started again. Still it made no sense — nothing seemed relevant. He read it three times, laid his head back and turned the words over in his mind.

Bayleon came over and handed him a bowl of stew, which was quite enough to distract him. He laid the Samarok at his side and ate ravenously, taking up big chunks of meat with the broth. They all feasted greedily, restoring their faded energy, gradually feeling new warmth flowing to their tired limbs.

When they had finished, they lay back against the earthen ring, basking in the heat from the flames. Prompted by Sylas's interest in the Samarok, Simia produced her treasured notebook from her bag and began scribbling down her experiences of the journey so far, then reading them to the group as though they were the memoirs of some great and esteemed adventurer, or the writings of a seasoned journalist. This amused them all for some time, but soon her muse left her and they again fell silent.

"I think we could all do with something warming to carry us through the night," said Espen suddenly, producing a large leather bottle from his bag. "I have some Plume if anyone would like some."

Simia looked up excitedly. "What kind?"

"Cider fudge."

She screwed up her nose. "No, thanks," she said. "I don't like apples and I don't like cider and I don't like fudge."

Sylas smiled. "I'll try," he said, leaning over to take the bottle.

He raised it to his lips and took a swig. Instantly his mouth was filled with a deliciously fudgy, tangy flavour that drifted smokily down his throat and into his chest. The taste of tart, just-ripe apples mixed with a sweet creaminess that was quite intoxicating.

"Wow," he said, breathing out a yellowy-green cloud.

He savoured this brief moment of colour in the midst of so

much greyness. He handed the bottle to Ash who took a long swig and then lay back, blowing yellowy-green smoke rings into the air. As he raised a single finger, every other one broke to form long, snaking lines of smoke, which writhed through the darkness, coiling and twisting until they passed through the remaining rings. Soon he had formed another of his wonderful displays: at once playful and beautiful.

Sylas watched for a while and then turned back to the piece of paper and the Samarok. This time he turned to the first full page, then laid the piece of paper next to the second paragraph as Fathray had instructed. He turned his eyes from one to the other, checking that they matched, and sure enough, each and every word of the paragraph appeared to be the same. He frowned. That told him nothing except how to read the Ravel Runes. He thought for a moment, then let his eyes drift up the page to the very top, settled back and started to read.

"Here are recorded the chronicles of the Merisi, begun by our hand in this year of Our Lord one thousand two hundred and twenty-nine. Know that we, followers of Merisu, Master of the Sacred Arts, do set down this History willingly, in good faith and without evil disposition. In His name, we hereby give witness of the nature of these two worlds, of the history of our peoples, and our account of the evil and cruel infamy of the Priests of Souls, who have brought suffering and misery to the people of all the world such that they are, forever more, the enemy of Mankind

"They came from the cool of the sand-scented temples: from the long dark of the coiling passages and the oily flicker of many-columned halls..."

He paused. So that was the meaning of the paragraph on Mr

Zhi's piece of paper: it was about the Priests of Souls... Thoth, and others.

He glanced around the fire. Bayleon and Ash had already settled down to sleep and Simia was sitting with Espen as he told her more about the Circle of Salsimaine. She sat enthralled at his feet, her arms thrown round her knees, and her face bearing an expression that Sylas had not seen before: engaged, almost admiring.

Yawning and rubbing his eyes, he continued from where he had left off.

"In the beginning there were twelve: one from each of the great Kemetian temples, devout priests, worthy priests, each and all. So they were until one day summoned by their king to a valley between the cataracts, to a secret place, not known to common men, but hidden deep within the rock..."

His chin fell on to his chest and the Samarok fell closed. With the taste of apples on his lips, Sylas fell into unconsciousness.

When Simia woke, the fire had already burned down to a dull red glow. Even in that faint light, she saw the large dark figure striding silently away from the camp. Bayleon. She looked quickly to where the others lay and saw Sylas and Ash sleeping close to the fire, breathing loudly over the deathly silence of the Barrens. But there was something wrong. There was a space next to them, and one of the packs was missing.

Espen had gone.

Simia pushed back her blanket, gathered her father's coat close about her and set off after Bayleon.

As soon as she was clear of the camp, she began to run: she

knew that Bayleon would move quickly and that her only hope of following in this darkness was to keep him in sight. By some stroke of luck the cloud seemed thinner tonight and there was just enough moonlight to show the way. She slipped quickly between the massive stones, brushing them with her shoulders as she darted from side to side, trying to catch her first glimpse of Bayleon somewhere ahead. Her head was clear now and questions flew through her mind. Where was Espen? Why had he and Bayleon left the camp in the middle of the night? And was she *really* trying to chase a Spoorrunner?

She ducked beneath a slanting stone, turned sharply round another and suddenly she was out on the open plain. A chilling breeze caressed her face, drifting out of the vast black void. She stumbled on some loose rubble and as she steadied herself she saw a movement somewhere out on the flats. It was Bayleon, stooping low to the ground and then starting forward again into the darkness.

Dropping her head and shoulders, she sprinted, determined to keep up. Her heavy coat made it difficult to run, but it enclosed her in its folds and protected her from the penetrating chill of the open plains. She heard the crunch of charred earth beneath her feet and almost by instinct caught up some of the blackened dirt and rubbed it over her face and hands. The perfect camouflage for a night on the Barrens.

She sped on, keeping Bayleon just in sight as he loped on through the darkness. At one point he suddenly stopped and lowered himself to the ground. She did the same, pressing herself into the dust. She scoured the darkness for whatever he had seen or heard or felt, but whatever it was eluded her. Moments later they were off again, Bayleon jogging at a careful, measured pace, Simia at a full run.

They went on like this until her chest was heaving. Finally Bayleon slowed and she glanced about her, trying to guess what he had sensed, unnerved by the thought of what might be out there, unseen, watching. When she looked back, she froze: Bayleon had stopped. She threw herself on to the ground, struggling not to splutter as she breathed in a cloud of acrid dust.

He too lowered himself on to all fours and then on to his stomach. For a moment he was still. The silence settled around them: a complete absence of sound that made Simia all too aware of the pounding of her heart and the rushing of blood in her ears. They were still for what seemed like minutes until finally he began clawing forward, hand over fist, dragging himself over the cracked earth.

Hardly daring to breathe, Simia inched her way forward, pushing with the tips of her toes. Every turn of a stone, every scrape, every movement seemed enough to give her away, but she kept moving. She could still see him not far ahead of her, his great bulk pressed so close to the earth that he looked almost like a shadow.

She stopped. Just a few paces ahead of her was a dark gash — a deep riverbed that swept round her and continued ahead until it passed near to Bayleon. Holding her breath, she began to move towards it: slowly, carefully, trying to peer over the edge. She halted. A flicker of firelight played across the far bank of the river and at the same moment she heard voices. Deep, growling, guttural voices: voices that hacked at the night air and rumbled in the sand.

They were not human sounds, but the sounds of the Ghor.

Fear closed her throat and drew the air from her lungs. They were only paces away. She pressed her face down into the dirt, too terrified to move, her mind racing. She tried to slow her breathing, to calm herself, to gather her thoughts. At this distance they would surely smell her at any moment. She would have no chance — Bayleon would have no chance — there was nowhere to hide.

But then she was struck by a thought. Surely Bayleon would not just stumble into a camp of the Ghor as she had — he must have known what he was doing. She slowly lifted her face and, as she did so, she felt the gentle breeze on her forehead. It was blowing directly towards her, across the dried river. Of course, they were downwind. If she was quiet, they might not know that she was there.

She dared to lift her knee and slowly, painfully, she eased herself forward, her chin grazing the dirt as she edged towards the bank. Her heart thumped against her ribs, seeming too loud, and she found herself holding her breath as if to slow it down.

The final push seemed to take an age, but finally Simia was there: the ground dropped away in front of her and she found herself squinting into bright firelight. She felt the same heave of panic that she had felt just moments before.

There, gathered in circles round three large campfires, was an entire regiment of Ghor.

Most were leaning in towards the fire, concealed beneath cloaks as defence against the cold, but some had drawn back their hoods. The red light from the fire gave their grisly features an even more hideous complexion, highlighting the patches of skin on their dark, hairy snouts and making their almost-human eyes gleam lividly as they flicked around the circle. Their tattered, pale ears shifted beneath their thick manes as they exchanged harsh growls and barked out words, and occasionally one would raise its fearsome jaws and a hoarse, snarling cackle would issue from deep in its throat. One of them tore raw meat from an unrecognisable carcass and handed scraps to those around the nearest circle. In a motion almost too quick to be seen, they devoured it with a single gnash of their cruel teeth.

Only one small group seemed disinterested in the meal: three tall figures that stood to one side, not far from where Simia now lay. She focused on them, pulling herself forward just a little more to try to get a better look. One was of immense build, with shoulders far broader and more muscular than any of its brethren, and it was wearing a cloak of finer material, hemmed at the bottom with crimson thread and embossed at one side with the symbol of Thoth. It was nodding and speaking animatedly to its two hooded companions, who were leaner but taller in build. Perhaps to emphasise its point, the mighty Ghor shifted to one side and raised a burly arm into the air and, as it did so, the light from the fires fell upon the furthest of the group.

Her heart missed a beat.

It was Espen.

He was speaking now, grim-faced, pointing back towards the Circle of Salsimaine, directing their attention towards his sleeping friends.

And then, just briefly, he smiled. He raised his hand, placed it on the shoulder of the Ghor commander and smiled.

Simia covered her mouth. She felt sick to the pit of her stomach. How could he *smile*? The world seemed to have turned upside down. She clamped her hand over her mouth in an attempt to stop herself from crying out, or from being sick. Unable to watch any longer she rolled on to her back, staring up at the empty black sky. Espen? How could it be? Their own *Magruman*!

She tried to calm herself, to control her breathing, to clear her mind. Perhaps she was wrong. Perhaps he had been captured and he was negotiating, or misleading them, or… something. She had to know what he was saying. She had to get closer.

Turning on to her front, she pulled herself as slowly as she could along the edge of the bank, bringing herself a little nearer the group. She longed to reach a point where she could hear him, find out that she was wrong — that all this was a misunderstanding. A few moments later she was crawling out of the part of the bank that was nearest to Espen.

She heard his voice: serious, insistent.

"That wasn't the deal. *I'll* bring the boy. That's what we arranged."

A chill ran down her spine.

"The *deal*?" It was a woman's voice: a silky, feminine, playful voice. "My dear Espasian, the *deal* was struck before you annihilated an entire company of Ghor."

"There was no alternative," said Espen coolly. "And anyway, that was the boy. I had no idea he had that kind of power."

"All the more reason to take him in hand now," purred the woman menacingly. "While we still can."

Breathless, Simia raised her head over the bank and looked down.

The woman was clearly visible now. She was almost as tall as Espen, though her figure was slighter and more elegant. The feminine lines of her body were visible even beneath the folds of her long black gown. Her dark complexion made her face barely visible in the shadow of her hood, but her features seemed delicate, even feline, and the whites of her large narrow eyes glowed brightly in the flames.

"Scarpia," whispered Simia contemptuously.

Espen leaned towards Scarpia threateningly. "You know that would be a mistake. We can't control him out here. He knows now. He knows what he can do."

"Just how much does he know?" asked Scarpia calmly. "Has

he used a Glimmer Glass?"

Suddenly Simia stopped breathing.

She could feel something on her ankle. Something was creeping up her calf, grasping her leg.

She whipped her head round in terror and saw a white hand clasped round her ankle. She felt a cry of horror rising in her chest, but somehow she kept it in, pressing her lips together.

Then she saw Bayleon's face in the darkness. His finger was at his lips and a frown creased his sweating brow.

He did not speak, but mouthed his words silently: "Quiet! Come, now!"

Simia felt a great wave of relief. Relief to see Bayleon's face, and also because, had he not found her just then, she really had no idea what she would have done next. The world seemed to be coming to an end. Espen had betrayed them. It all seemed so wrong, so unreal.

She dipped below the edge of the bank and began shifting backwards, away from the light. Her mind was still a flurry of thoughts as she slithered over the dry earth and when she felt a resistance against her shoulder she pushed without thinking.

Suddenly a seam tore open, threads gave way.

She froze, holding her breath, daring to hope that the wind might have carried the sound away. But as she listened her heart fell. The noisy chatter had stopped. Everything was still.

She looked desperately towards Bayleon and he met her eyes.

In that moment his face showed an agony of fear, self-reproach and then despair. In the next his features were set and he seemed resolved.

"Take this!" he hissed, wrenching something from his bag. "It'll show you the way. Now run, Simsi! Run like you've never run before! Get Sylas to Paiscion!"

And then, as if to pre-empt her reply, he swung his feet beneath him, gave her a brief, bold smile and stood up.

Simia cried out despite herself. What was he doing?

But her voice was drowned by a hideous chorus of howls that erupted from below. As Bayleon stepped forward into the light, they became wild, rising to a fever pitch.

With an expression of scorn and defiance, the great Spoorrunner climbed down the bank. His shoulders were back, his head was held high and his eyes were fixed on Espen's face.

31

What Cause So Great?

"When nations fall, when day is done,
When all is lost, when naught is won,
What nobler charge, what cause so great
As brother's plight and kindred's fate?"

IT WAS AS THOUGH she was aflame. Her lungs burned in her chest, her muscles screamed and hot tears scorched her cheeks. She fled on to the open plains, away from the horrifying baying of the Ghor, out into the night.

For some time she stumbled and ran, unsure where she was headed, just desperate to get away, to keep moving, to stop thinking. She gasped and sobbed in equal measure, struggling to breathe. But, as the noise faded behind her, as the night wrapped her in its cool blanket, her mind began to clear. She thought of Bayleon's last words.

She reached into her pocket and felt the smooth, cold ball of glass that he had given her. Without slowing, she brought it out and held it in front of her, straining to see it in her hand. It caught the dim moonlight and, for a moment, she saw a gleam of silver somewhere in its heart. Then blackness. She shook it, her steps starting to falter, but still there was nothing.

Then Simia saw something in the corner of her eye. A trace of silver light on the plain, so faint that she almost doubted that it was there.

She changed direction, heading towards it, her eyes scouring the darkness. She saw it again: a thin, shimmering line of silver on the ground, somewhere to her left.

As she drew nearer, it seemed to grow brighter and more distinct. She looked at the black orb and closed her hand about it. The line disappeared. She opened her hand wide and it glowed once more, just a few paces away. She saw that it was not so much a line, but a muddle of silver markings in the dust.

She slowed to a stop, gasping for air, and stooped down over them. They were large silver footprints heading back towards the dry riverbed. Between them, she saw a collection of smaller ones: less regular than the others, one foot turned slightly inwards.

She gathered her coat about her, sucked in a lungful of air and set out along the silver tracks.

He watched her as she walked silently down the verdant bank, her long train of fair hair feathered by the wind, her gown billowing and her elfin frame moving effortlessly towards the lake. He let his eyes pass over her thick glossy hair, her narrow shoulders, her small fragile figure. He caught a glimpse of her rosy cheek, her smooth skin. Something stirred in him: an impossible mix of despair and hope.

"Wait for me!" he cried.

She whirled about, her hair flying up in the breeze, partly shrouding her lively features.

There, looking back at him, was a face that he knew. She was shouting now, her face panicked, afraid. There was no sound, but suddenly he heard her in his head.

"Wake up! They're coming!"

"They're coming!"

Simia's face was contorted with fear, her eyes bleary and bloodshot.

"They're coming!" she screamed again.

Sylas felt a surge of adrenalin as he was wrenched from sleep.

She had her hands on his shoulders and was shaking him violently.

"Espen's betrayed us!" she sobbed.

He rubbed his eyes, still confused from a deep sleep. "What do you mean?"

"He was leading us into a trap! He was taking you in... taking you to Thoth!"

"Espen?" repeated Ash, sitting bolt upright. "That doesn't make any sense..."

Simia closed her eyes and let out a slow sigh. "I *know* it doesn't add up, I *know* it doesn't make any sense! I just saw him with a whole company of Ghor and... and I saw Scarpia too."

"*Scarpia?*"

"Yes. They've got Bayleon — he gave himself up to save me. I only just got away."

Sylas felt a surge of panic, but he could see that Simia was far worse: her face was pale and streaked with tears and her hands trembled as she tucked them under the arms of her coat. She seemed haunted, staring wide-eyed at the last red glow of the fire, rocking slightly backwards and forwards.

"He did it because of me. It was my fault..."

"Come on," he said, taking her arm. "Let's get out of here."

He helped her to stand up. He and Ash quickly gathered their things and stuffed them into their bags. They hesitated over Bayleon's and Espen's belongings, but quickly decided to leave everything where it lay. Ash kicked over what remained of the fire and they were plunged into a blue-black darkness.

"Which way should we go?" asked Sylas, pulling his bag over his shoulder.

"Follow me," said Simia. "I know the way."

She set out towards the far side of the circle of stones and Sylas turned to follow.

Ash took a few steps, then hesitated and stopped. "Wait," he said.

The others turned and looked at him questioningly.

"I'm going to stay. They'll probably guess that you're heading to the city. If we all run, they'll find us before sun-up. If I stay behind, I can buy you some time."

"No," said Sylas flatly. "We can't just leave you — we've already lost Bayleon."

Simia stepped back into the circle. "Ash is right," she said reluctantly. "We've got almost no chance on the Barrens unless one of us stays behind."

Ash nodded. "Good then."

"I'll do it," said Simia.

"You will *not*!" cried Ash. "What we need is confusion, mayhem, chaos! This is my kind of job!" He grinned broadly, though his eyes betrayed his anxiety. "Besides, you know your way across the Barrens far better than I do."

Simia hesitated: there was no doubting that Ash's magic would be the perfect foil for the Ghor or that she knew the Barrens far better than he.

"Let me do something," said Sylas suddenly. "Something like

370

I did before — at the river..."

"This time you're not only facing the Ghor," said Ash, putting a hand on his shoulder. "There are probably two Magrumen out there as well." He drew himself up. "I'm staying and that's final. Don't worry, I'll catch up with you in the city — at Paiscion's place."

Sylas hesitated, looking first at Ash, then at Simia, certain that this was wrong. Too many people were risking themselves for him, for this strange, unfathomable journey he was on.

"I can't let you do this... not for me."

"Listen," said Ash firmly. "I'm not doing this for you — I'm doing it for Bayleon, for Fathray — for all of them. You once asked why I couldn't help them on the river. Well, I couldn't without doing more harm than good. But I *can* do this — I really can — and this may just help everyone. Go," he said imploringly. "If you hang about much longer, it won't matter which of us stays behind!"

Ash held out his hand. Sylas looked at it for a moment, then extended his own.

"Thank you, Ash," he said earnestly.

Ash winked. "I'll be right behind you."

"We'll be waiting for you, Ash," said Simia. She held his gaze for a moment, then turned her back.

They walked quickly to the other side of the circle, between the standing stones and out into the night.

Ash stood in silence at the centre of the clearing and watched them go.

"Good luck, young man," he muttered under his breath. He sucked air through his teeth.

"Now, what *am* I doing?"

He swallowed hard, turned on his heel and started to survey

the camp. His eyes moved slowly from the fire pit to Espen's blanket, to Bayleon's bag, to the great stone table, then back to the fire pit. He stared at it for a moment and smiled.

He walked over to Bayleon's bag and rummaged through it, discarding ropes and strange objects until he found the shovel, which he pulled out and examined closely. Then he took a small jar from his own bag and stuffed it in his pocket. He gazed round the circle of stones and then walked decisively across the clearing towards a large arch. He stepped up to the stone on the left, which had been sheared from its top corner, leaving a ragged, sloping surface. His eyes traced a path up the rough, broken stone to the flat platform at its top.

He patted the rock. "Good," he said, and set off into the darkness, swinging the shovel at his side.

The Circle of Salsimaine still loomed some distance behind them when Simia finally slowed her pace. She turned to check that Sylas was with her and found him right at her shoulder.

"How could Espen *do* this?" she panted, shaking her head.

"I don't know," he replied. "He seemed to be helping, right from the start."

"But did he, really? Or was he just pretending?"

"He *did* help me. He saved me from the Ghorhund — that's how he got the scar on his face."

"I know…" said Simia thoughtfully. "But when he spoke to Scarpia, he made it sound like he'd only done what he had to — you know — to make us trust him."

Sylas searched his mind. Could he really have been pretending all along?

"No. I don't believe it," he said firmly. "Even Mr Zhi trusted him."

"So Espen *told* you," said Simia doubtfully. "You never actually saw them together. Maybe nothing he said is true. Maybe he's been working with Thoth all along."

Sylas lowered his head and felt the sick, empty feeling returning to his stomach.

"I don't know. Maybe."

Simia scuffed the ground with her heel and drew a deep breath. "Well, if anyone will know what's going on, it's Paiscion," she said. "He knows Espen better than anyone alive. Come on — we have to keep moving."

Sylas sighed. "How far is it?"

"Five hours… I'd probably do it in three if I ran most of the way."

"So let's run."

Simia looked at him doubtfully. "It's not that easy — even for me. It's dark and there are ravines and fall-aways and…"

"Go as fast as you like — I'll keep up," said Sylas, remembering the dingy passages of Gabblety Row.

She raised her eyebrows, smiled briefly and then set off at a jog, quickly disappearing into the night.

It was less Simia's speed that made her difficult to follow than her curious sixth sense for spotting uneven ground, cracks in the earth, rises and drops. Even in the darkness she seemed to know where to turn, where to slow down and where it was safe to accelerate to a sprint. While she would dart nimbly to one side to avoid a ditch, rock or mound, Sylas would see the obstacle a moment too late and stumble into it, fall over it or drop into it. It was all he could do to keep her in sight and stay on his feet.

But soon he learned to follow her steps exactly, settling into a more manageable rhythm. They ran and ran, their feet thumping the dust until sweat poured from their brows, and their legs and chests burned.

Finally, to his very great relief, Simia slowed to a jog and suddenly came to a complete stop.

"Sun... will be up... soon," she panted, resting her hands on her knees. "Best to get... out of sight."

"How?"

Simia made no reply, but took a step forward and jumped into the darkness. He heard her coat flutter around her and her shoes scuff the earth and, in an instant, she was gone.

He peered into the darkness. "Simia?"

"Down here."

He looked down and saw the pale glow of Simia's face some distance below him, then the gleam of her broad grin.

He was standing on the very edge of another deep bank, so deep that Simia's head was level with his feet. He looked around and saw the faint, dark outline of a narrow channel snaking off into the blackness. It was an old dried-up creek, so narrow that he had not even seen it. He blew out a long breath — if he had taken another step forward, he would have fallen headlong into it.

"Come on," said Simia. "They won't see us down here."

He slithered down the bank, causing a small landslide of soil and dust.

"Nicely done," she said sarcastically.

"Thanks," muttered Sylas, dusting himself down.

"Now it's going to be difficult to follow me down here..."

"Difficult *down here*?" retorted Sylas.

"Yes, well, it's worse down here," she said emphatically. "You're going to have to do what I do. You need to *feel* your way a bit more."

"Well, I felt that ditch I fell into back there," he said ironically.

"You mean like that?"

"Absolutely not like that. You're only falling into things because you don't feel them *before* you reach them. If you feel something with your hands, it's too late. Feel with your mind."

"My *mind*?"

"Remember the story I told you about Merimaat and the stepping stones — how she told me that they weren't trying to trip me, that they—"

"... want to help."

"Well, it's just like that. You need to remember that everything's connected — that you're linked to everything: the air, the Barrens, the earth in these riverbanks. You need to *feel* them — know where they are just as they know where you are. See?"

Sylas reached out to the dark bank at his side. "You mean, even when I can't see them?"

"Exactly," said Simia. She squeezed his arm. "This is Essenfayle — *real* Essenfayle — much purer than what you did with the Ghor. You'll have to concentrate. Come on — let's give it a go."

She turned and set out into the darkness. Sylas stood for some seconds pondering her words, then sprinted after her.

He struggled to make out her figure as she turned quickly left and then right. He threw his weight one way and then the other and, to his surprise, he brushed smoothly past two great banks of earth. He corrected his balance and looked ahead to see a shadow darting to one side, disappearing behind a wall of earth. He shortened his pace, heaved his weight to one side and ran headlong into the bank.

The commander slowed to a halt in mid-stride, its massive shoulders heaving slowly from the exertion of the sprint. It lifted its snout and took a long, deep breath of the night air. Its faded yellow eyes blinked and it drew its broad glistening brow into a frown. It was silent for a moment, then it released a growl from deep in its throat, which summoned two of the company to its side.

When it spoke, it was with a deep, inhuman voice: a collection of hacking and rasping sounds that hissed through its teeth. "Two tracks," it said. "You — take that one; and you..."

It stopped.

A pinprick of light had broken the darkness somewhere on the horizon. It flickered and flared, then burst into life.

"Fools," it rasped. "We'll have them before dawn."

It lurched forward, taking long, athletic strides towards the light, lowering its great upper body as it ran. The others fell in behind, mimicking its step, moving perfectly in time. As they gathered speed, there was hardly a sound: only the wind about their cloaks and the deep, almost inaudible *thump, thump, thump* of their clawed feet in the dust.

Before they had travelled any distance, they suddenly reared up behind their leader.

Another pinprick of light had flared out of the darkness, far off to their right.

The commander let out a low growl, turned and called gutturally to the nearest of its lieutenants, then barked a series of orders. The lieutenant sped off, leading a small group of Ghor in the direction of the new fire, while the rest of the company continued on their original path.

No sooner had they settled into a pace than another fire erupted out of the blackness, this time off to their left. Then another flared in the distance. Once again the commander paused, sniffing the air, trying to pick up a scent. After a long pause it snarled in frustration and motioned for the company to divide again. Soon there were four groups prowling silently through the darkness, nearing the four sources of light.

The commander lowered itself still further, its foul tufted jaws sweeping just a few inches from the ground, its cloak brushing the surface of the plain. The fire cast a halo of bright light that was difficult to look at after the blackness of the Barrens, and it drew its hood low over its eyes.

As they took their final agile steps, its black, drooling gums twisted upwards and back, baring its long yellow teeth, still bloody from the earlier feast. Raising its great head, it issued a wild howl from deep in its chest, rolled back on its haunches and threw itself forward as the death cries of its brethren pierced the night. The other groups were also attacking.

The commander bore down on the fire, crashing into the light with a vicious gnash of its jaws, searching for its prey. It roared at the light, snapped at the air and raged at the dust.

There was no one there.

The other Ghor loped about the fringe of the light, searching for any sign of life, but they found nothing.

"It's a trick!" the commander roared, turning its fierce eyes towards the fire. "This is no camp!"

It turned its mighty frame towards the flames and jabbed at them with one of its claws. The fire went out in an instant, as though it had been smothered. It snarled contemptuously, lowered its snout to the small pile of sand that was left behind and sniffed. It retreated, its ears pressed back against its head, then it sniffed again.

It tilted its head to one side.

"Mustard..." it growled.

Sylas's heart hammered in his chest as he sped through the low riverbed, a grin of excitement growing across his face. He charged into the darkness, sometimes sprinting ahead, sometimes darting inexplicably to one side. He could *feel* them: he could sense the walls of the riverbed around him, feel their approach as he slid between them. He could smell the dry earth in his nostrils, feel its weight pressing on his chest, see it through the gloom: black upon black, grey upon grey. Occasionally a wall of the creek grazed his shoulder as he took a turn too sharply, but otherwise he ran, ran as though he had passed this way countless times before, as though he knew these twists and turns as he knew those of Gabblety Row.

But it was more than that: he felt as though he belonged there, like the water that had once boiled and churned and flowed between its walls. He felt part of it, connected to it, as though it was welcoming him, opening itself to him and showing him the way. In his mind's eye he could see the creek zigzagging across the plain, imagine its contours and its deep, dark banks, as though his imagination had taken the place of sight. And the further he ran, the surer he became that this was not a new feeling. He had felt this before — not often, but sometimes: in the deranged corridors of Gabblety Row, in the darkened streets of the town, in the forested hills. He had felt what he had not even known. It was within him — natural to him.

He accelerated, kicking up dust with his heels as he hurled himself forward, feeling a strange urge to laugh and to cry out. He heard Simia's steps and then saw her, lunging left and right in the gully ahead. Soon he was right behind her, bearing down on her and then, as the gully widened a little, he surged past her, letting out a whoop of triumph as his shoulder scuffed the wall and he bounced back in front of her.

"How..." panted Simia, "how... did you... do that?"

"I don't know!" shouted Sylas. "I think I've always been able to!"

He banked left and then right and sprinted down a long, straight furrow, with the sound of Simia's footsteps fading behind him. It was exhilarating, liberating. He raced on, hardly thinking about what he was doing, feeling his path unfolding ahead of him.

He laughed out loud. "It's like... like a new kind of seeing!"

He heard Simia's footsteps somewhere off to his left.

"You're going the wrong way!" she bellowed.

The smile fell from his face.

Espen ran so silently that even the Ghor did not hear him pass. He stooped low, seeming to glide over the grey surface, little more than another shade of night. He watched them raging at the dust, snatching up great clumps of earth between their jaws and casting them high into the air, clawing wildly at the pile of earth that just moments before had been aflame. His scarred face contorted with contempt.

He sped on, adjusting his long, loping strides to take him wide of the first group of Ghor and towards the second. There too he saw them in disarray, prowling about for some sign of their tormentor, snarling and snapping at the pile of earth. But, just as he was about to move on, they suddenly froze and lowered themselves on to their haunches, peering out on to the plain.

Espen dropped to the ground and followed their gaze. Through the blackish grey of early dawn, he saw a movement. It was no more than a fleeting shadow, but there was no doubting that it was there. It turned sharply, dropped low to the ground and then disappeared from sight as though it had slithered into some ditch or gully.

The Ghor had already started in its direction. Espen paused, his eyes narrowing. He turned back towards the other group and saw that they too were giving chase to a shadow that prowled swiftly across the plain and suddenly dropped out of view. He watched for a moment more, seeing the shadow rise a little ahead of them and then fall again, as though goading them, drawing them on.

A smile formed on his lips.

He ran on through the murky greys and muddy black, on over the dry, cracked earth of the Barrens. He did not pause, or slow, or seem to draw breath.

It was not long before the vast skeletal structure of the Circle of Salsimaine rose bleakly from the nothingness, picked out in drab shades and deathly shadows. Espen stood to his full height and slipped silently between the great stones, moving deftly from shadow to shadow until he was sure that he could not be seen.

Drawing himself down behind a fallen stone, he peered back out on to the plain, towards the meagre trace of dawn that now clung to the horizon. He saw another movement: another strange translucent shape rising briefly from the ground, then falling out of sight. No sooner had it disappeared than three or perhaps four hooded shapes rose out of the same ditch and pursued it down into the next, pressing in upon each other to be the first to grasp it in their jaws. But instantly another shape rose some distance away, shimmering above the horizon for a few seconds before moving at speed into another gully. A third emerged, and a fourth, each of them leading some of the Ghor behind it, drawing them between and among the deep furrows in the earth.

And then he saw something else. The very dust of the Barrens began to dissolve, breathing forth a silky white vapour that rose in growing clouds and lingered unnaturally in the cold, grey air. As he watched, it thickened until a great shroud of mist lay about the plain, pouring into the creeks and crevices, frustrating the dark pursuers in its midst.

Espen cocked his head a little to one side and considered the chaotic scene for a moment, then raised an upturned hand. Very slowly, he lifted his forefinger. Almost instantly one of the strange shapes emerged from the nearest of the gullies.

It was not a solid thing, but a fluid, shifting apparition. It did not have lines or form, but instead was a blur that shifted and morphed as he watched, clawing up the sand and mist and spinning it in a wild vortex until it had shape and colour. At its base its tail lashed and whipped the ground viciously, tearing at its surface, while above its spiralling, gyrating body widened and widened until at its top it spat out a flurry of dust and vapour.

A whirlwind. A man-sized desert twister.

A grim smile passed over Espen's face.

"He has them chasing the wind," he muttered admiringly.

He dropped his hand and heard the baying of the Ghor as the whirlwind descended among them.

Turning away, he slid onwards, moving silently between the stones.

In just a few moments he was at the innermost circle. He pressed himself against a jagged, broken rock and his eyes passed quickly over the scene: the lifeless fire pit, the abandoned blankets, the glass orb discarded in the dust. With a quick glance in both directions, he moved again, still in a crouch, his eyes searching the dust, scrutinising the tracks to and from the empty camp. He paused by the fire to pick up his pack, then stooped down and touched a pair of smaller tracks, his eyes darting between them and the far side of the circle. He drew a long breath and shook his head.

"That meddlesome girl," he muttered.

He considered the tracks for some moments, but — for now at least — he did not follow them. Instead he turned back towards the camp, looking for something more.

It did not take long.

In seconds he was poring over a patch of dust, touching it lightly with his finger, tracing the line of a larger footprint. Slowly his eyes followed the tracks to the opposite end of the circle, then to one of the standing stones, a stone that had been sheered from the very top to the bottom. His gaze traced its ragged edge, up to the great stone platform that lay across its top, up still further to the slight figure standing high above, feet apart, hands and arms working like a conductor of some silent symphony.

Even in this pale light he could make out the wild nest of blond hair, the quick hands, the youthful fingers in a blur, summoning whirlwinds from the dust and weaving madness in the gullies below.

Ash turned and looked at the Magruman. The blood had left his cheeks, but if his heart had failed, it did not show: a defiant smile played on his lips.

32

The Centre of Everything

"One emerges above them all, one of cunning and ruthless guile, one at the centre of everything."

BLACK TURNED TO CHARCOAL grey, which surrendered reluctantly to the ashen blues of morning. It was too long since they had stopped to rest and drink water, but they kept up their pace, determined to go a little longer, a little further. They had slowed to an exhausted, haphazard jog and, although they could now see, their weary legs often carried them into the dusty walls.

Sylas's euphoria had long since faded. He had given up asking where they were or when they would reach their destination. They had not spoken for over an hour. He hurt all over – his legs, his arms, his parched throat – and as time went by he started to feel a new pain: a hollow ache in his wrist, around the Merisi Band. He had almost forgotten that it was there – so smooth and well crafted was its surface and so perfect its fit – but now it felt as though it was pressing on a nerve. He rubbed it as he ran, trying to improve the flow of blood.

Just when he was beginning to wonder if the monotony of sandbanks and earthen walls would ever end, there was a change. It was only slight at first, so slight that it took them some time to notice, but soon the crack of light above their heads began to broaden out, the ground beneath their feet became harder and stonier and, as it did so, the creek bed began lifting them up towards the light. The sky too seemed different. It was still a dull, depressing grey, but it was less monotonous: pale streaks started to show among the curling clouds and soon definite patches of light began to appear.

They turned a sharp bend in the creek and suddenly it widened. The path ahead was strewn with rocks and boulders, resembling the bottom of a mountain stream. Simia slowed, staggering slightly to one side as her feet slapped the ground, her shoulders hunching over from exhaustion. She wandered over to the nearest boulder and sat down. Sylas was quick to follow.

It took some time for them to catch their breath and take in some water. Finally Sylas wiped his mouth and looked across at her.

"Tell me we're nearly there," he said.

Simia sucked the last drop of water from her bottle and shrugged. "We're nearly there," she said in a husky voice.

He looked at her steadily. "*Are* we?"

She seemed far more interested in the nozzle of the bottle, into which she frowned, demanding that it yield more water, but finally she nodded.

He stood painfully and handed her his own.

"Well, I can't see anything."

"That's because we're in a ditch," she said witheringly. She drank down the contents of the bottle in one gulp and belched rather more loudly than seemed possible for such a small person.

Then she pointed to one side of the gully.

"Try standing on a boulder. You'll see."

Sylas walked over to the nearest one and, with a wince, hoisted himself up on to its top.

He felt a bracing breeze on his face, but it was not that that made him draw breath.

The ground rose in a long, gentle slope and there, at its top, was the city.

It erupted from the earth in defiance of the great desert of the Barrens: vast, dark and powerful. There were buildings of all conceivable shapes: long blockish ones; narrow upright ones; buildings that sagged in the middle and buildings that rose to a point; some that leaned a little to one side; others that had tilted over so far that he wondered how the roofs stayed on. Still others — those huddling at the very fringe of the city — appeared to be made of little more than scraps of wood and canvas, sewn together in a vast shabby patchwork of miserable colours. But at least they were colours, he thought.

This was the vision to his left and to his right: a seemingly endless mass of low roofs muddling the horizon. Beyond, another jumbled horizon rose in a paler shade of brownish grey and beyond that another, until the great sea of buildings disappeared into a distant murk. It was a wonder that he could see this far, for myriad chimneys disgorged an endless stream of yellowish white smoke into the sky, which drifted slowly upwards and collected in a brooding cloud high above. This in turn seemed to be on the move, rolling sluggishly over the city, but it did not drift in one direction, rather it appeared to be surging inwards, as though drawn by some inexplicable force towards a single point.

At first Sylas could not see where it was headed — all he could make out was a place at which the smoke seemed to congregate and begin a new motion: a swirling, spiralling, twisting flow that rose still higher into the air.

His eyes lingered on the smoke — searching for something at its centre — but then he looked up above the churning plumes.

The hairs prickled on his neck.

Looming through the shades of grey was a shape so vast that it took him a moment for his eyes to find its edges. It was a colossal pyramid of shadow, soaring out of the heart of the city towards the heavens, looming over the maze of houses and streets, the maelstrom of cloud and smoke, even the Barrens themselves. Its great mass seemed to block out the light across a giant portion of the sky, casting a sharp, angular shadow over the cloud. As he watched, some of it cleared, revealing a triangular wall of jet-black stone, which seemed to draw in the light. It had no features, no breaks in its surface: nothing but a dark, solid expanse of stone sloping up towards the point of the pyramid.

"The Dirgheon," murmured Simia, who had climbed up next to him.

Sylas turned to her. She too was staring up at the monstrous building. He saw at once that it had a strange effect on her; her ruddy cheeks had paled.

"What is it?" he asked breathlessly.

"Thoth's citadel. The centre of everything."

He swallowed. "That doesn't sound good."

"It isn't," she said, drawing her eyes away as if she could not bear to look at it any longer.

"What's inside?"

"Bad things. Very bad things. Thoth and his Magrumen; the birthing chambers of the Ghor; plenty of things that you just don't want to know about, and you don't want to meet. And then—" her eyes moved back to the giant pyramid — "there are those they've captured but haven't yet killed."

Sylas followed her eyes to the pyramid's base. "It's a *prison?*"

"Like you wouldn't believe."

She drew a lungful of the chill morning air, then jumped down from the rock. "Come on, we have to keep moving — they may not be far behind. And believe me, we won't hear them when they come."

Sylas took a last lingering look at the Dirgheon. His eyes traced one sloping wall to the other, trying to imagine how many thousands of rooms and halls lay within, how many squalid cells and endless, twisting passageways. He thought of Bayleon and Fathray and Bowe and wondered if they would be taken there — if they were there even now — to languish in some forgotten room at the end of some lost, lightless corridor.

"Come on!" snapped Simia impatiently.

"OK, OK," he said, his eyes lingering on the pyramid for a moment longer.

He leapt down from the rock and followed Simia to the wall of the gully.

"We'll have to risk it from here," she said. "The sooner we're in the city the better."

She clambered up the bank using what few footholds she could and, glancing warily in all directions, pushed herself over the top. Sylas scrambled up behind her and heaved himself on to the flat ground beyond.

They lay still for some seconds, searching the low, flat horizon behind them for any sign of their pursuers, but saw nothing. The Barrens were shrouded in a mist that boiled and churned ominously in the breeze.

Slowly they stood up.

Immediately Sylas heard the sounds of the city. It gave off a low rumble, as though its walls and streets were growling spitefully at the new day. The noise was unnerving after the silence of the Barrens, but as he listened, he realised that it was no more than a chorus of sounds, each lending resonance to the city's guttural voice: cartwheels on stone, yells from the market, hammers on anvils, whining from sawmills, hooves in the mud — these and a thousand other sounds of life came together as a single thunderous growl. He felt his heart quicken at the sound of people living their lives and he felt the Barrens' deathly blanket start to recede, as if his blood was flowing more freely.

"We'll have to go in through the slums," said Simia with distaste. "They might be looking for us on the roads. Just stay close behind me and don't say a word to anyone or anything — no matter what."

They moved quickly, no longer running but walking briskly, trying not to look conspicuous.

The nearest shacks were only a short distance away and it was not long before they started to see people: a man labouring under water buckets, a woman hanging out grubby washing and a child running down one of the alleyways. Simia kept walking, her arms swinging confidently at her sides, humming a tune under her breath.

Sylas's stomach tightened as he noticed a waver in her voice.

In another minute they were there, walking up to the first makeshift hovel: walls made of mud and scrap wood and a roof of some kind of canvas. As he walked past it and into an alleyway, he noticed a strong smell: the unmistakable stench of sewage. It seemed to issue from every dark corner, every putrid ditch and tumbledown shelter, and it only became stronger the further they walked into the slum.

He tried to keep his eyes down and straight ahead as they

wandered from one alleyway into another, but he caught occasional glimpses of withered men and women sitting in dark doorways smoking a pipe or cooking at a fire, filthy children playing in the dust, old people sleeping in hammocks or on the hard earth. And while the sounds of the city were louder than ever, Sylas realised that none of them were coming from the slum: this was a silent, depressing place; a place of sickly murmurs and shuffling feet; of wheezing and coughing and disease.

He turned a corner and nearly walked headlong into a thick wooden pole driven into the earth. He heard a flutter overhead and looked up to see a huge red flag flapping against the grey sky. A skeletal white face glowered down from among the folds, shifting with each curl of the flag so that it almost seemed alive: frowning, glaring. It was Thoth's standard, presiding over these poor people as if he himself was there, peering down at them, mocking them in their defeat. Sylas hurried on, staying close behind Simia.

They entered a warren of tiny passageways pressed in so tightly that there was little light to see by. She moved confidently, turning this way and that without hesitation.

"You know this place, don't you?" he whispered.

She nodded.

"How?"

"I lived here. After the war," she whispered, turning to press her finger to her lips. She walked on.

Sylas looked again at the squalor around him. She had lived *here* — in this? He found it hard to imagine her — someone with so much life and energy — living in such a horrible, deathly place, a place where people seemed broken and without hope.

As he followed her, he looked about him with new interest, trying to picture her in the dingy backstreets and squalid homes. The more he allowed himself to see, the more he believed that it might be true. The people were not so different from Simia after all: beneath their matted hair and grimy skin they had faces like any other, some with bright, lively eyes and others whose expressions betrayed intelligence and humour. He saw children playing with a ball made of rags, laughing gleefully as one of them swept at it with her bare foot and missed completely, falling unceremoniously on her back. Some of the old people lying in doorways returned his gaze, occasionally showing interest as they passed. One of them turned his head to watch him go, craning his shrivelled neck, seemingly unable to move his tired old limbs.

And then Sylas saw something familiar. They had just crossed a low bridge made of pieces of wood and hard-packed earth, blocking their noses against the stagnant drain below, when he saw a symbol scratched crudely into a broken wall.

A feather.

For a moment he was unsure, but as he drew nearer, he became more and more certain that he knew it.

He turned to Simia, who had paused further up the lane, and pointed at the symbol.

"*Filimaya* was wearing this," he whispered. "It was on her gown."

"Shhhh!" hissed Simia, rushing back and taking him by the arm. "Don't use her name here! There are spies everywhere!"

"But what is it?" he pressed, pulling his arm away. "What does it mean?"

"It's the mark of the Suhl," murmured Simia, looking about her warily as they walked.

"*Here?*"

She looked a little surprised. "We're everywhere," she whispered, "but *especially* here. These are some of the unlucky ones — those who didn't get away after the war. You'll find the

Suhl in every slum of the world. Slums are safe — no order, no guards, nobody checking your papers or collecting your taxes. This whole place is one giant sanctuary. Problem is, it's almost as bad as what they're hiding from."

"So the others at the mill — they were the lucky ones?"

She nodded. "The stronger ones — the ones who still had some fight in them, some hope. There are a few places like the mill, but not many. The rest are in places like this, or out there—" she gestured towards the Barrens — "in the wilderness."

They rounded a corner and entered a broader street in which there were a few sparse stalls selling a few limp vegetables and cheap offcuts of meat. Sylas paid them scant attention, for above them loomed the gigantic silhouette of the Dirgheon, now clearly visible between the clouds and smoke.

He saw for the first time that its vast sloping sides were made up of thousands of blocks of stone placed together in perfectly straight rows, like a giant staircase rising on all sides towards a distant point high above the clouds. He saw too that they were not entirely black, for a vast red banner had been hung from the very centre of each. They trailed over the black steps like rivers of blood, widening as they descended. In their very centre was depicted the now familiar image of a giant skeletal face: the face of Thoth glowering down over his city as though watching everything, scrutinising everyone. Beneath his imposing visage were three symbols: the hunched bird; two circles, one within the other; and a scroll. The effect of the banners was just as his creator had intended: a show of absolute, terrifying power.

As they moved further down the lane, Sylas saw that it was not the only vast structure in the city. Just to their right and a little nearer, a great stone tower loomed over the shambolic skyline. Unlike the dark, brooding form of the Dirgheon this was an elegant building, constructed entirely of exquisite white stone. Its smooth sides bowed inwards until they almost met in the middle, before they broadened at the top like the branches of a vast tree to support two gigantic circular platforms, one above the other, with a series of arches between. Around these archways was carved a breathtaking collection of human figures in poses that Sylas could not quite make out, gathered round myriad symbols and shapes.

Sylas's eyes moved between this and the Dirgheon. It was hard to imagine two more contrasting buildings.

"The Temple of Isia," whispered Simia at his side, breaking into a run. "Come on, and *stop staring*!"

They jogged down lane after lane, street after street, passage after passage. The character of the buildings began to change, becoming far more substantial than any they had seen in the slums, made out of wattle and daub or even stone, some constructed over two storeys. They were clearly entering the heart of things, the centre of Thoth's great city. The lanes became narrower and darker, the light blocked out by the towering structures that leaned in above them, using up every last bit of space.

Then they turned a corner to see the lane opening out, the final buildings giving way to an entirely new scene. They walked out of the alleyway and into the light.

A broad view of the river opened up in front of them. Like at the mill the vast body of water swept in a wide arc, turning almost back upon itself in a perfect meander. But that was the extent of the resemblance. Instead of the cool, blue-grey waters at the mill, these were brown and opaque; instead of the lively current was a rolling, sluggish churn that swallowed and regurgitated an endless flow of sewage and detritus. The sloping banks heaved with litter and filth and even the ravenous birds that circled above seemed to peer down with distaste. When they dared to descend, they swooped and snatched up their mouldy prize without touching down.

Sylas covered his nose and mouth. "It's disgusting," he mumbled.

Simia said nothing. She was not cringing but smiling. She was not looking at him but staring out across the river.

He followed her eyes. "What are you looking at?"

"Paiscion's home," she said.

S

The snap of the lock woke Bowe in an instant. He recoiled as the great iron door of his cell flew open and a giant figure appeared in the doorway.

It was like no Ghor he had ever seen: taller, broader, its head less stooped, its posture more human. The feeble light from the corridor illuminated the beast's great mane of hair, the gold collar around its neck and the fine armour covering its muscular chest, arms and thighs. At the centre of the breastplate a single symbol was picked out in gold: a skeletal face, devoid of all expression, empty and dark. It was the livery of Thoth's personal guard.

Before Bowe could react, the guard took two athletic bounds, reached down and grasped his neck in a vice-like grip, then slammed him up against the wall. It leaned forward, bringing its short, half-human muzzle and canine teeth within inches of his face.

It growled a deep, slow and murderous growl. The stench of its breath made him turn his face away. The grip tightened instantly, and the growl became fierce. He turned back to look the guard in its pale, human eyes.

"Listen to me, Scryer," it said contemptuously, its voice clear and man-like. "I am to take you to the Master. Few things please the Master, but many things displease him. I never, *never* displease the Master." It pushed Bowe further up the wall, his feet now far off the ground. "So we will do this quickly. We will do it silently. We will enter his presence with reverence. Do you understand?"

Bowe managed a half-nod.

He was dropped to the ground, coughing and spluttering, gasping for breath. Before he could even reach for his throat, the guard's claw grasped the back of his neck and he was thrust forward, out of the cell and into the flickering light of the passageway. Despite the Scryer's considerable size, he was propelled forward with such force that his feet barely touched the ground. They moved down the corridor at speed, passing door after door set deep into the stone walls.

Bowe tried to struggle, kicking out at the walls to try to set the guard off balance. The grip around his neck tightened again. This time he felt as though he might black out.

"Don't make me repeat myself, Scryer," growled the guard at his ear.

It lashed out with its teeth, gashing his cheek and shredding part of his ear. Bowe cried out in pain. Instantly the guard threw him with huge force against the damp, cold wall. His head struck with shattering force and he reeled backwards, already feeling the blood pouring from his temple.

"Quick. Silent. Reverent," growled the guard, its claw closing round his neck. "Obey."

Bowe felt himself slip gratefully into unconsciousness.

33

The Sound of
the Moon

"How is it that music captures what cannot be caught: the sound *of night and shooting stars, of darkness and the rising* moon*?"*

"WELL, I HAVEN'T ACTUALLY *seen* it before, no," said Simia defensively.

Sylas frowned. "But you brought us here," he muttered. "I thought you knew where you were going."

"I do know where I'm going!" she snapped, putting her hands on her hips and glaring up at him. "It's exactly where Filimaya said it would be. I'm telling you — this is it!"

Sylas looked doubtfully over her shoulder towards the river. "Well, it doesn't exactly look like the home of a—" he lowered his voice to a whisper — "of a Magruman, does it?"

"Well, no. It *is* a bit disappointing."

"*Disappointing...*" murmured Sylas.

He gazed despairingly ahead of him, feeling his body give in to a crushing weariness. He had *so* wanted this to be an end to his journey — an answer to all his questions. He thought back to the fall of the mill and the terror of the chase, to the cold, bleak days on the Barrens, to Bayleon's capture and their desperate, exhausting flight from the Circle of Salsimaine. All of that — for *this*?

His eyes passed slowly over shattered decks, a broken mast that leaned precariously against another; tattered, forlorn-looking sails that hung by threads from the frayed, tangled rigging. The hull of the ship carried the colourful insignia and intricate carvings of grander days, but now the paint was faded and peeling, the proud designs around the fittings were almost unrecognisable and the lovingly chiselled wood was rotting and falling away. Indeed the only ornament that remained almost intact was a faded, lopsided nameplate, whose forlorn letters spelled: the *Windrush*.

But what was least impressive about this decrepit ship was its positively muddled attitude towards holes. There were no holes where there should have been, for the portholes had been blocked with crudely nailed planks and the entrances on the decks were covered with piles of broken timber and discarded canvas. And yet, most alarmingly, there were very many holes where holes ought *not* to be, giving the sad vessel the appearance of a capsized Swiss cheese.

There were holes in the deck timbers and holes in the sails, there were holes in the forecastle and there were holes in the hull. Indeed this utterly wrong-headed approach to holes made the ship something of a miracle, as despite the water lapping round its many dark cavities, it remained above the waves. The entire hulk leaned threateningly towards the bank, but nevertheless it rocked and rolled with the gentle motion of the putrid river. It was quite implausibly, but quite undeniably, afloat.

Sylas's musings were suddenly brought to an abrupt end. With a loud clatter of chains, a section of the hull fell open and landed with a thump on the muddy bank.

They both slithered several paces backwards. They stared fearfully at the wooden ramp, leading to a dark, square doorway.

"It's a door," whispered Sylas.

"No kidding," muttered Simia, glancing at him with narrow eyes.

They stared at it for some moments, waiting for someone to emerge from the shadows within, but no one came.

Sylas took a few steps forward, looking with interest at the ramp. "Do you think we should go in?"

"Maybe. You first."

Simia stayed well back, poised to run, but Sylas continued to creep forward, still staring at the ramp. His eyes were trained on something carved into the surface — gouged out of the rough, damp wood. The nearer he came to it, the more certain he was that it was a symbol: a collection of strange lines and dashes that shifted a little even as he looked at it.

A Ravel Rune.

He stared at it for some moments until it began to change before his eyes, its many lines turning and contorting until they formed a perfect letter P.

"P!" said Sylas excitedly. "P for Paiscion!"

Simia scowled, peering with some interest over his shoulder. "Where?"

Before he could reply, the symbol had started to change again, its strokes curling about themselves until something new started to form, something different but just as familiar. Somehow the many markings in the timber of the ramp had morphed before his very eyes until they formed a perfect, delicate shape.

"A feather!" exclaimed Sylas, taking another few steps down the stinking, slippery bank and feeling new hope stirring inside him.

Simia joined him. She peered over his shoulder at the ramp.

"A feather? Where?"

"There!" said Sylas, pointing at the symbol.

"That's not a feather! It's just a load of scratches!"

"It's not! You've got to look at it right — it's a Ravel—"

Are you coming inside, or not?

Sylas stopped, startled.

"Did you hear that?"

"Hear what?" said Simia irritably. "Stop being so weird."

He turned to look at her. How could she not have heard it?

You're wasting time. My time. Come inside, or go away.

"There! There it was again!"

Simia stared at him, suddenly looking a little frightened.

"Stop it!" she said reproachfully. "Now you're scaring me."

He turned and peered into the dark doorway of the vessel. The more he thought about it, the more certain he became that *he* had not *heard* the voice either — it had been inside his head, just like Mr Zhi's voice had been when Sylas was standing outside the Shop of Things.

"Come on," he said firmly. "He wants us to go inside."

"Oh, really, and he just *told* you that?" mocked Simia.

Sylas slithered the last few steps down the bank and she realised that he was serious. Her face straightened.

"How... How do you know?"

He stepped on to the ramp and turned to face her, giving her an encouraging smile. "I just do. I've seen this magic before. With Mr Zhi."

Simia looked at him doubtfully, twirling a strand of her red hair round a finger. Reluctantly, she followed him down.

As they stepped into the shadows, the first thing to strike them was the astonishing smell. The foul stench of sewage gave way to the incongruous fragrance of grass and fresh flowers lightly flavoured with woodsmoke. It was as though they had suddenly been transported out of the ship and away from the city to some distant mountain meadow. Almost straight away they started to feel calmed and refreshed. Sylas took a deep breath and felt sweet, wholesome air fill his lungs. He heard Simia step up the ramp behind him and she too gasped as she crossed the threshold.

Watch your backs!

Sylas jumped. The voice was louder and clearer than ever: a sharp, male voice that had the tone of someone who was used to being obeyed.

Without warning, the chains rattled above their heads and the ramp was drawn closed behind them. There was a loud clank as a latch was drawn into place and suddenly they were plunged into pitch-blackness.

"Sylas?" hissed Simia. "Are you there?"

"Yes."

"This was your idea."

"I know…"

Down the steps, please.

A torch suddenly burst into flame above their heads and then another ahead of them, followed by more beyond. They cast an orange, flickering light on a narrow passageway that led to a staircase just a few paces in front of them.

"Come on," said Sylas, turning to Simia's wide eyes. "He wants us to go down."

She arched her eyebrows in the half-light. "Oh. Right. Good then."

He stepped forward and, feeling for the broken banister, started to lower himself down.

They descended towards a roughly hewn door at the bottom

of the steps, the fresh fragrance becoming even stronger as they went. But they hardly noticed the scent any more; instead they were entranced by the faint sound of music. It seemed to be coming from beyond the door.

As they clambered down the final uneven steps, the beautiful sound became louder and louder, echoing between the faded wooden panels of the walls and reverberating within the timber of the door.

"What *is* that?" whispered Simia at his ear. "It's beautiful…"

"I think it's a piano," he said.

She frowned. "Never heard of it. But it sounds *amazing*…"

He hesitated for a moment with his hand on the door handle and his face pressed against the wood, listening to the doleful, haunting notes of the piano.

It *was* beautiful, and yet also unutterably sad. A deep, resonant note chimed every few beats like a call to mourning while above, a triplet of notes repeated over and over, sometimes rising and falling, but always in time with the irregular, heartbreaking chime, like the sound of loss or regret. A simple lilting melody laced the music, but while it was at times light and always gentle upon the ear, it carried tidings of sadness.

The music was washing over Sylas when, to his horror, he heard the creak of the hinges. The door swung open under the gentle pressure of his cheek, and he found himself staring into the open space beyond.

He blinked at the shaft of dusty light that bisected the gloomy room, zigzagging between a number of mirrors about its edge, illuminating a bare, featureless, cold chamber. On the opposite wall, below the single porthole, a series of crooked bookshelves offered the room's only decoration: a vast collection of papers and books. The sole covering on the rough floorboards was a threadbare rug at one end of the chamber, upon which rested a wooden rocking chair and a low table. The table bore three objects: a tall, fluted glass of wine; a pair of spectacles; and a large wooden box from which rose a graceful, curving brass tube that opened wide at its mouth like the bell of a horn.

"Is that the piano?" whispered Simia, her eyes wide with excitement.

"No, it's a gramophone," whispered Sylas.

"I thought you said it was a piano."

"It is, but—"

"What he means to say is that it is both, and neither," said a sharp voice that resonated around the room.

A figure moved out of the shadows. The beams muddled around him, making it difficult to see him properly, but as he reached the centre of the room, a bluish light fell directly upon him.

He was not a large man, but the way he carried himself made him seem bigger than he was. He stood perfectly straight with one arm behind him and his shoulders pulled back. His chin was high and the little light that played across his face revealed strong, taut features with a heavy brow and striking high cheekbones. His eyes glinted as they passed swiftly over the two children, tracing their weary faces, their tired limbs, their dishevelled clothes. They lingered a while on Sylas's wrist.

Sylas glanced down and saw that the Merisi Band was showing and instinctively covered it with his sleeve. A flicker of interest passed over the man's face, but he quickly looked away.

"This," he continued in his precise, clipped voice, "is the sound of a piano, which you are hearing through that machine, which is a gramophone. But these are the least interesting things about what you can hear, for in truth this—" he waved his finger in

the air, as if pointing at the notes as they drifted across the room—
"is the sound of moonlight. It is moonlight curling on a misty
lake, sloping through a ruined church, caressing the dew-specked
spider's web. It is moonlight on barren hilltops and ragged cliffs;
moonlight in sunken wrecks and forgotten graves. Moonlight
captured in a sonata. And the captor, the great genius who thus
captured the moon, was a man. He was Ludwig van Beethoven."

He fell silent, as though to allow the full significance of these
words to be discerned and understood.

They listened to the music for some moments, Sylas slowly
realising for the first time that this was music of his own world;
Simia struggling to understand how something called a piano
could be heard through something called a gramophone and what
that had to do with the moon.

"Beautiful, is it not?" said the man.

Sylas nodded. "Yes, yes, it is."

"Of course it is!" snapped the man, as though Sylas was
foolish for thinking he needed to answer. "Music is the language
of the heavens, the voice of Nature herself! She speaks through
such sonatas, such concertos and nocturnes." He gazed dreamily
towards the gramophone. "And in symphonies... well, in
symphonies, She sings."

He let out a long sigh as he listened to the final bars of
Beethoven's 'Moonlight Sonata'.

The triplet of notes changed into a melody and in its place
the low, sad chime took up a new triple beat, ending the piece
in a mood of overwhelming melancholy. The final notes tumbled
towards their conclusion and, when the gramophone fell silent,
the arm of the needle trailed to the centre of the record, clicked,
whirred and swung back on to its rest.

There was a brief silence. Suddenly the man turned and

clapped his hands together, making them flinch.

"So! I take it that you know who I am; why else would you come to such a godforsaken place? What is far *less* clear is who — by the sun and the moon — are *you*?"

He took two quick steps to the rocking chair and flung himself into it, rubbing his hands together as though relishing the mystery. He reached over to the table at his side, picked up the wire-rimmed spectacles and placed them on his nose. The lenses were so thick that they contorted his features, making his quick eyes seem unnervingly large. He flicked them over the two children, squinting a little as though struggling to see. He bore an interested, quizzical expression, as though he was regarding a word that was misspelled or a sum that would not add up.

Both Sylas and Simia were about to answer, but to their surprise the Magruman began to answer his own question.

"You have not known each other for long — that much is quite obvious — and yet... you have experienced a good deal together... interesting, very interesting. I am certain that it is you, young man, who is responsible for the adventures you have undertaken together, for you are quite certainly in the wrong world and by the way you wear the Merisi Band I can see that life as a Bringer does not suit you well—" his eyes narrowed to slits— "if, indeed, you are a *Bringer* at all..."

Sylas shifted uncomfortably, wondering if he was really that transparent. He felt he should say something, but Paiscion's magnified eyes had already shifted to Simia and were scrutinising her with interest.

"You have been a good companion, I think... yes, I can see that in you: lively, pugnacious, plenty of spirit... but there's more than that..." He adjusted his tie, which Sylas noticed for the first time was faded and heavily worn. "Yes... you share something,

something important. A loss perhaps… Yes! You have both lost a loved one… a parent… Of course. And that is your father's coat, for why else would it fit… so… poorly…"

His voice trailed off as he leaned forward to peer at Simia's coat more closely. She retreated a little into the doorway, bewildered by Paiscion's forensic scrutiny and by the startling accuracy of his pronouncements.

Suddenly his face softened a little and his lips parted.

"Daughter of Roskoroy, you are most welcome here."

Simia gasped and stared at him, her mouth wide.

"Your father was a good man… a *very* good man."

Simia seemed undone by the mention of her father, but then, slowly, her face brightened and she stepped further into the room.

"He was," she said, beginning to smile. "I'm… I'm Simia."

Paiscion sat back in his chair with a look of satisfaction, crossing his legs and gathering his threadbare smoking jacket about him.

"So, Simia Roskoroy, who is your friend?"

Simia placed a hand on Sylas's shoulder.

"This is Sylas. Sylas Tate. Filimaya said that he should come to see—"

The Magruman uncrossed his legs and sat forward again.

"*Filimaya* sent you?"

"Yes — it was agreed at a Say-So. She said that—"

"She's still at the mill?" asked the Magruman eagerly.

Simia hesitated, curling her hair round her finger. "No… we all had to leave. The Ghor came and we had to get out quickly."

"Everyone?"

"Yes."

"And Filimaya?" he demanded, a little anxiously. "The Valley of Outs?"

She nodded. There was a short silence. Paiscion reached for his glass of wine and swallowed the contents in one draught, seeming distracted.

"You were telling me who this young man is," he said, settling back into the chair.

Simia stared at him blankly: "Well... what I was going to say was... I mean, that's why we're here. You see... we don't really know."

Paiscion frowned and leaned forward, resting his elbows on his knees. He looked from Simia to Sylas. "Well, that is no way to make an introduction! You are aware, no doubt, how strange that sounds?"

Sylas looked sympathetically at Simia and cleared his throat.

"We are," he said. "Until a few days ago I thought I knew exactly who I was, where I was... but then I met Mr Zhi and everything changed."

"*Mr Zhi*, you say?" said Paiscion, his interest piqued still further. He started rocking his chair slowly backwards and forwards and a smile passed over his gaunt features. "My! Haven't you been keeping good company? Here's a *real* mystery!"

He thought for a moment and then gestured to two crates next to the weathered rug. "Take a seat, Sylas of Questionable Descent," he said with a gracious sweep of the hand, his magnified eyes glittering in the feeble light. "Tell me your story. Tell me from the very moment you met Mr Zhi. Tell me everything."

Sylas and Simia looked at each other uncertainly and then sat down. They were now close enough to see the Magruman properly: his meticulously combed dark hair greying at the sides and thick eyebrows flecked with white; his sallow, colourless cheeks and the black smudges under his glistening black eyes; the deep lines that criss-crossed his forehead and gathered around his eyes and mouth. It was a weary face, a face of care and worry. His clothes were on the one hand immaculate, with a white collar, a tie, tight-buttoned waistcoat and a smoking jacket, but they were all past their best: the collar had been re-sewn along one edge; the waistcoat had lost two of its brass buttons and the tie and jacket were faded. Thus, despite his proud, precise demeanour and his quick, lively features, he gave the impression of a man who had fallen from greatness; who was — if only a little — broken. He sat back in his seat, pushed on the worn heels of his scuffed shoes, and began to rock slowly backwards and forwards.

Sylas started to tell his story. Paiscion listened to this with some interest, and as he told it, the Magruman resumed his rocking, his thick eyebrows knitted tightly in concentration.

In a few moments Sylas had reached his first encounter with Espen. As soon as he started to explain that he was in fact Espasian, Paiscion exclaimed.

"Espasian? *Alive?* These are good tidings indeed! Continue! Please!"

Sylas lowered his eyes, wondering whether or not to mention Espen's betrayal, but decided he could only tell the story just as it had happened.

Paiscion slowed his rocking as he heard of Fathray's capture at the mill, and the fate of many in the boats. Some of the excitement drained from his face and a little of the weariness returned. He waved for Sylas to continue.

The story had reached their escape from the Ghor and Slithen at the bridge and Sylas mentioned his own part in calling upon the life of the river.

"And *you* did this?" asked Paiscion, with new excitement.

Sylas nodded, feeling a little proud. "It happened just as I imagined it."

"Indeed!" muttered Paiscion, fingering his tie. "How

illuminating! More! Tell me more!"

As Sylas reached the moment when he, Simia, Bayleon and Ash had parted from the others, Paiscion made a slight motion with one hand and suddenly there was a loud, startling rattle above their heads.

Sylas stopped mid-sentence.

Paiscion seemed a little irritated. "Go on!" he cried. "I must hear it all! For better or worse!"

So insistent was he that Sylas continued even as more curious things started to happen: first there was more clanking of chains on the deck and the distant screeches of rusted winches somewhere in the rigging, then the great old framework of the ship began to creak and moan. Finally the whole room heaved and tilted, making everyone reach for something to steady themselves. Sylas found it impossible to continue.

"What's going on?" he asked, clinging on to the crate as the room lurched again.

Paiscion frowned. "We're setting sail, of course!" he cried over the sound of a wave buffeting the side of the boat. "You seem to trail trouble wherever you go, and it would seem prudent to stay a little ahead of it. The Ghor will not be far away."

Sylas looked up at the porthole and, sure enough, he saw the opposite bank of the river tilting out of view, then rising again a few moments later: they were on the move. He glanced up at the ceiling as there was another thump from above.

"Who's up there?"

Paiscion gave an amused smile and lowered his spectacles on his nose.

"What need of rum-swilling swabbers, young man, when you have a ship as gallant and loyal as the *Windrush*!" he cried, patting one of the timbers at his side. "Now the rest of the story, if you please!"

Sylas gazed out of the porthole in wonder, then gathered himself and continued with the story, telling of Espen's reappearance and the chase out on to the Barrens. Paiscion's face became bright and animated at the mention of his fellow Magruman, and he clapped his hands and made a low whistle as he heard about the fate of the company of Ghor.

"You? Again?"

Sylas shrugged and nodded. The ship was rocking gently backwards and forwards now and he could hear the occasional thump of a wave striking the bow.

As he reached the part of the tale where Espen had betrayed them, Paiscion stopped his rocking altogether and stared at them. His cheeks were drained of colour.

"Is this true?" he asked quietly.

Simia shrugged her shoulders and nodded. "And… Scarpia was there too," she said. "Espasian was *talking* to her."

Paiscion walked to the chair and sank into it, clasping his hands in front of him, his eyes closed. He let out a long sigh. For a while they were all silent, listening to the heaving and creaking of the boat.

Finally Paiscion looked up. "That is hard to believe," he said. "Espasian is a Magruman of the Suhl and a man of honour. A maverick, but a great man nevertheless."

"I *heard* him," retorted Simia. "I saw him with Scarpia!"

"Indeed you did," said Paiscion. For some moments he closed his eyes, seeming to retreat into his thoughts.

Suddenly he drew a sharp breath, stood up and walked across the room to the porthole.

"Sylas, bring me the Samarok, if you please. And Mr Zhi's note."

Sylas reached into his bag for the Samarok. As he extended

his arm, he felt a sharp, shooting pain in his wrist. He gasped and pulled it out, massaging around the Merisi Band.

Paiscion's gaze shot to the bracelet. "The Merisi Band hurts?"

Sylas nodded. "It's been hurting on and off since last night. Why, what does it mean?"

Paiscion simply held out his hand. "If you please," he said.

Sylas reached into his bag with his other hand and felt for the rich leather of the Samarok. He pulled it out, brushed away a thick coating of grey dust and handed it to Paiscion. The Magruman looked at it with quiet admiration before taking it in his small pale hands.

"And the note?"

"Inside. At the page Fathray marked."

Paiscion let the book fall open in his palm. There was a flurry of pages and it settled on the correct page. The piece of paper still lay tucked into the binding. His quick eyes scanned the lines of runes and a flicker of pleasure passed over his face. It was with some reluctance that he finally looked away at the piece of paper. He perused it for a moment and then nodded, as if to acknowledge that this was indeed the hand of Mr Zhi. His expert eyes moved briskly over the writing, then he frowned and started again at the beginning. He read it through again and looked searchingly at Sylas.

"*This* is the paper? The one that so interested Fathray?"

Sylas nodded. Paiscion turned his attention back to the tiny creased note and ran his eyes over it again, his face taut with concentration. As he reached a point about halfway down, he stopped and suddenly his eyes moved quickly over the text, dancing about the paragraph. He returned to the top of the scrawl and moved his eyes carefully over the lettering.

Suddenly he met Sylas's eyes with a long, searching gaze.

"What is it?" whispered Simia excitedly.

The Magruman blinked. "A message from the Merisi."

"What? What does it say?"

He looked from the paper to Sylas and back to the paper, as though struggling to believe what he had read. Then he drew in a long breath and said: "Sylas, you say you have read Merisu's poem?"

Sylas thought back to the poem that Espen had showed him when they were on the Barrens. He nodded.

Paiscion handed him the Samarok. "Read it again for me."

Sylas's throat was dry and he swallowed nervously before turning his eyes to the page.

> "*Reach for the silvered glimmer on the lake,*
> *Turn to the sun-streaked shadow in your wake,*
> *Now, rise: fear not where none have gone...*"

Paiscion nodded. "Good. And do you know why there is no rhyme in the final line?"

Sylas thought for a moment. "Espen said it was a fragment... that some of it was missing."

"Quite right!" cried Paiscion, almost speaking over him in his excitement. "For many years the ending was disputed and so it has never been recorded in the Samarok, but the Merisi believe that it should read:

> "*For then, at last, we may be one.*"

Sylas looked blankly at Paiscion for a moment, but then tried to think back to the meaning of the rest of the poem. He turned it over and over in his mind: *Reach for the silvered glimmer... what* had Espen said that meant? "Turn to our own reflection... to another part of ourselves." *Fear not where none have gone...* Slowly, hardly believing his own thoughts, he started to understand.

He opened his mouth to speak, but then hesitated.

"Go on," said the Magruman.

"Does it... does it mean that the two worlds... that they can *come together?*"

A new smile creased Paiscion's face. "That is what the Merisi believe: that the worlds are two parts of a whole; two parts that perhaps, just perhaps, were never meant to be apart." He leaned down and added in a whisper: "They believe that this is the natural conclusion of the Glimmer Myth. The conclusion that will one day prove that it was never myth at all, but an astounding, terrifying truth. Someday, somehow, the worlds will be brought together."

There was a long silence. Simia frowned and shook her head.

"What's this got to do with Sylas?"

He turned to her and smiled. "It seems, daughter of Roskoroy, that this has *everything* to do with Sylas," said the Magruman, turning his eyes slowly to the piece of paper.

Sylas and Simia followed his gaze.

"Mr Zhi's note..." muttered Sylas under his breath.

"Take it," said Paiscion, handing it to Sylas. He leaned down and peered over his shoulder. "Now do you see how the paper is smudged? How some letters are faded?"

Sylas looked again at the scrawl, his hands trembling. Sure enough, every now and again, a letter was blurred or discoloured.

He shook his head and looked up. "It got wet in the rain," he said. "It's just blotchy."

"No, Sylas," insisted Paiscion. "*Read* them. Read only the fainter letters."

He turned back to the paper and tried to see it with new eyes. He read slowly, moving carefully from one faded letter to the next.

They came from the cool of the sand-scented temples: from the long dark of the coiling passages and the oily flicker of many-columned halls. They rose as leaders of men in that ancient land, men of words and vision whose mystery brought hope to the squalor-born... But while the people lifted their eyes upon the gentle countenance of these blessed men, they saw not the cool and dark of their hearts, nor the oily flicker behind their eyes.

He felt the hairs rise on his neck. The more he read, the surer he became: they formed words. Letter by letter, word by word, they started to make sense. In a wavering voice, he began to say them aloud:

"So... at... last... we... may... be... one."

34
Here or There?

"Are the answers here *in this world or* there *in that?*
Are they here, *in the face that I know, or* there, *in the face*
that I do not?"

PAISCION'S JACKET FLEW UP around him as a gust of wind buffeted the dingy corridor. The only light came from several large gaps in the planking above, which gave way to large tracts of open sky and a lattice of loose rigging.

"Come!" he shouted over the noise of wind and waves. "To the Bow Room!"

"So you think that... that the poem's about *Sylas*?" shouted Simia incredulously, chasing along behind him while trying to read Mr Zhi's note.

"That is what the Merisi seem to believe and I have no reason to doubt them!" cried the Magruman, bursting through a door into another passageway.

Simia wrestled with the door and caught him up again. "And you think he can — I don't know — bring the *worlds* together?"

"That's not quite what Merisu's poem says."

Simia frowned. "Then I don't get it."

"It says that Sylas must 'reach for the silvered glimmer'," said Paiscion, pulling at another door.

She thought for a moment, then her eyes widened. "You mean he has to... *find* his Glimmer?"

Paiscion made no reply as his shoulder crashed into another door.

Sylas ran along behind them in silence. He had not spoken a word since he had read Mr Zhi's message. He was lost somewhere between disbelief and resignation: disbelief that the message could possibly be for him and yet an odd kind of resignation that it may very well be so. After all, nothing made sense any more: nothing could be taken for granted. Not now. He had seen the whole world change around him. He had witnessed magic beyond his wildest dreams. He could not even trust his memories of his mother any more. In the midst of this storm of questions the message from Mr Zhi seemed almost plausible.

The Magruman led them down some steps and the evening light faded to blackness, but only for a moment, for in the next instant he threw open a door and they were bathed in a pale blue light. Beyond the threshold was a very peculiar room indeed. It was not square or oblong as a room should be; indeed it had no straight lines or right angles whatsoever. Its two side walls swept towards one another in long arcs until they met at a point opposite the door, making the room triangular in shape. Even more confusing, its ceiling was far larger than the floor, its curving walls leaned outwards towards their top and every timber, beam and fixing was crooked or warped. The only semblance of order or design was provided by a procession of large rusted portholes mounted along both sides, which were quite uncharacteristically intact and gave an exhilarating view of the world outside. As Sylas entered, he saw the grey light of the sky through the bleary glass, but in the next instant, as the ship plunged forward, the portholes were submerged in a greyish-brown soup, giving the briefest glimpse of the murky depths of the river before they climbed on another wave.

"Mind your step!" cried Paiscion, glancing over his shoulder. "We're coming into the estuary now — it's going to get rough!"

He started to make his way across the room towards the bow and, as he did so, Sylas saw that much of the floor was taken up with a mass of strange objects. At his feet was a tub of greenish sand that shimmered in the light. Next to it was a large glass cylinder containing a blue fluid with what looked like a long, twisted root suspended inside. Just to one side there was a large ornate contraption that looked something like a metronome — the device his mother had used to keep time as she played the piano. In front of him was a large leather chair inscribed across its back with countless golden symbols and on its cushion an embroidered white feather. Everywhere he looked was something curious and magical. He glanced at Simia and she too was staring excitedly around the room.

"Look at that!" she whispered.

Sylas followed her gaze and frowned. It was a dark grey typewriter. Not a modern but a steel one, with the keys suspended at the ends of scores of little metal arms. It seemed utterly out of place. It was the kind of thing he had seen many times in antique shops and markets, but never expected to see here.

But then he started to see other strange reminders of his own world: an old pedal-powered sewing machine; a pair of binoculars in a worn leather case; a small wooden box of tiny tools and measuring devices, like the ones that he had seen his mother using when she was drawing; an old box camera, complete with wooden tripod. The whole room was filled with such bric-a-brac, nestled among countless things of magic and mystery. It was like a museum, a private collection of treasured things: things of both worlds that had somehow escaped the ravages of the Undoing. It reminded Sylas of the Shop of Things. The only difference was that here there were no crates or parcels: instead everything was laid out for anyone to see. Everything, that is, but a large pile of objects that had been crammed thoughtlessly into one corner, one piled upon the other. To his surprise, he saw that they were things all too familiar to him: a lamp with a light bulb, a gleaming toaster, a kettle, a television, their electric leads tangled pointlessly around them or trailing down to the deck below.

"Please don't touch that!" snapped Paiscion as Simia reached for a clockwork train. "The Things you see here are perhaps the last of their kind!"

She snatched her hand away and looked up with practised innocence.

"Don't worry," murmured Sylas when Paiscion had turned away. "There are *plenty* of those left."

Paiscion shot a stern look over his shoulder. "In your world, certainly, but not here! The Bringers took great risks to give us these Things, and others have suffered even greater peril to keep them safe."

They made their way along the crooked, narrow pathway between the piles of strange objects until they were very near the thick, vertical beam that formed the bow. Drawing alongside Paiscion, they saw that the final triangular patch of decking was entirely clear except for a single chair that faced directly into the bow. Sylas thought this strange until he looked up and saw two large mirrors mounted on the walls, one with a white frame, one black. They had been positioned so that from the back of the chair they could see themselves in both.

"They're like the mirrors that Mr Zhi showed me!"

"Yes, yes, they are. This is a Glimmer Glass," said Paiscion, stepping forward to dust the mirrors down. "Of course, this particular one is larger and much, much older than the one you would have seen in Mr Zhi's shop, but they do the same thing. At least they used to... it's been a very, very long time since..."

"*Glimmer* Glass?" repeated Sylas, a look of realisation passing over his face. "Mr Zhi said that the mirrors would let me see all I am able to be. Did he... did he mean my *Glimmer*?"

A smile grew across Paiscion's pale face. "Naturally," he said. He patted the back of the seat. "And now that is exactly what you must do."

Sylas's stomach turned over. "*Why?*"

"Because that is what Merisu is *telling* you to do," said Paiscion. He lowered his face so that he could look into Sylas's eyes. "That ancient poem is all about you and your Glimmer, Sylas. Merisu's writings, the work of the Merisi, the Samarok, the Passing Bell — somehow all of it is about you." He turned and looked at the mirrors. "You and whoever is on the other side of that glass!"

Sylas looked at the mirrors and saw his own pale face staring back. Finally things were starting to make sense — perhaps this was it — *this* was how everything was going to become clear... about his journey... his mother even... in these strange mirrors. Perhaps now he was nearing the end. But the longer his eyes traced the lines of his face, the more apprehensive he became. It all seemed so strange, so impossible. Who was he about to see? And then he had another thought:

"Are you... are you sure this is *right*? I mean... *natural*?"

"I am quite sure," said Paiscion with a smile of encouragement. He placed a hand on Sylas's shoulder and drew him forward. "This is what the Glimmer Glass was made for. This is what Mr

Zhi wanted to show you!"

Sylas thought back to the dark aisles of the Shop of Things, to Mr Zhi's excitement as he had taken the mirrors from the packaging. *That* was what Mr Zhi had intended — to prove that Sylas was able to summon his Glimmer — that this was *meant* to happen!

"*You can see all that you are able to be,*" he had said.

Sylas stepped forward, around the side of the chair and sat down, hearing it creak under his weight. He was breathless and frightened, but as before, he was carried forward by a feeling that this was where he was supposed to be. This is where his journey had led him. This is where his mother had led him.

"That's right," said Paiscion. "Now move the chair until you can see yourself in both mirrors. Good — that's it. So do you know how this works?"

Sylas shook his head.

"Look into one mirror, not into both. You must try to see what is in the other without turning your eyes. Like with the Ravel Runes, see what is *there*, not what you expect to see."

Sylas took a deep breath and nodded. "I'll try," he said, glancing nervously at Simia.

She grinned at him, her eyes darting excitedly between his face and the mirrors until, to her evident annoyance, Paiscion drew her a few paces back, so that Sylas alone could see his reflections.

He turned his eyes to the one with the white frame. The border was engraved with symbols made up of beautiful curving lines and, as he looked more closely, he recognised them as Ravel Runes. He let his eyes rest on them and, as he cleared his mind, they began to change. They twisted and turned and curled and untangled until letters began to form.

"*Reach for the silvered glimmer,*" he whispered, a shiver tracing his spine.

"What?" demanded Simia, lunging forward. Paiscion pulled her back by the shoulder and frowned sternly.

"The words on the frame," said Sylas. "They're the ones from Merisu's poem."

"Indeed so," smiled the Magruman, and then, under his breath: "And so it all comes together."

Sylas turned his eyes from the white frame to the mirror itself and again saw his pale face staring back. He tried to let the world around him fade, to focus on what was in the mirrors. It was difficult, for the ship was rising and falling, yawing and pitching, and the sound of the waves striking the bow was deafening. He closed his eyes, slowed his breathing and opened them again. He stared at his face and at the same time turned his attention to the other mirror, trying to make out the blurred reflection in the corner of his eye. He tilted his head slightly.

The image shifted, just as he would expect.

He moved in his chair and rubbed his sweaty palms together. Still his eyes were fixed on the white mirror and still he focused his mind on the other indistinct image. A wave caught the side of the hull and the room lurched to the left, making everyone sway to one side.

Sylas frowned. He had moved, but the image in the black mirror had not.

Gripping the arms of the chair, he tried to focus on the other reflection, to see its shape, its lines, its features. Suddenly it moved, as if his own head had turned. But he had been still.

"I think I can see someone," he whispered excitedly.

"Good!" cried Paiscion. "Describe them to me!"

Sylas strained his eyes. "I can't... I can't quite..."

He winced as a pulse of pain shot through his wrist — beneath the Merisi Band. As he reached for it with the other hand, he lost concentration and, without intending to, he shifted his eyes to the black mirror. He saw only his own face. The other reflection had gone. But in the same instant the image in the white mirror changed, its lines altering, becoming finer, narrower. The effect was dizzying and in his confusion he let his eyes drift back to the white mirror. Instantly the face in the black mirror changed. The two images had swapped again.

"It's there! But I can't see the face!" he cried.

"You must!" bellowed Paiscion over the boom of a wave striking the hull. "We must know who it is!"

Sylas groaned a little as the pain surged again through his wrist. He pulled it up to his chest, massaging it with his other hand.

"The band is telling you that your Glimmer is near!" cried the Magruman. "The pain will go! The face! You must see the face!"

"I'm trying!" snapped Sylas.

He rubbed his eyes. It was hopeless: all he could see was a blur and every time he shifted his eyes across to the other mirror it had moved to the other before his eyes reached it.

He closed his eyes and tried to think. There must be a way. He thought again of his conversation with Mr Zhi. "*You can see all that you are able to be,*" he had said. Now those words made more sense than ever. Mr Zhi had meant that he was able to see his whole self — *both parts* of himself... So why was it so difficult? There was something else. Sylas tried to remember the rest of the conversation about the Things and the mobile and the mirrors.

Then it dawned on him. They had been talking about his *imagination*... about how his *imagination* made these things possible.

He raised his eyes to the mirror and again drew a long breath. He could see the other reflection moving within the frame almost as though it was trying to attract his attention, but he ignored it and focused on his own image, shutting out the sounds of the ship creaking and the chains clanking and the surf crashing against the timbers. Then, apprehensively, he began to imagine. He imagined his face changing, the lines blurring and morphing into the face in the other mirror; he imagined their two faces becoming one, his own face slowly fading and that of his Glimmer taking its place.

And, as he imagined, everything in the room became distant.

He stared at his own reflection, his own dark brown eyes, dark hair, anxious face. He was so intent on his own image that he hardly noticed when the other reflection started to fade. Only when it entirely disappeared did he realise that something was happening.

The images were drawing together, in a single mirror.

At first Sylas thought it was simply the shifting light catching his hair, but as the moments passed, he saw that its very colour was morphing. It was becoming lighter. At the same time he became sure that it was changing shape: his untidy curls twisting and unfolding until they crept down around his face. It was a mass of blond hair. His face, too, started to change, becoming smaller, thinner. His eyes altered in shape and they too changed colour — changing from brown to green to blue; his very skin seemed to change in tone, becoming lighter and finer.

He was staring in astonishment at a face that he knew.

"I can see her," he muttered through his teeth, frightened to move his face.

"*Her?*" repeated Simia, looking confused.

"Of course!" cried Paiscion excitedly.

"It *is*... it's a girl!" repeated Sylas, still struggling to believe what he was seeing. "And I've seen her before..."

Simia wrestled free of Paiscion and stepped forward.

"Where?" she demanded.

"In my dreams..." he murmured. *The silvered glimmer on the lake... the sun-streaked shadow...* his thoughts flew to his hazy, indistinct memories of his dreams. Dreams of the figure walking through the forest and beside the lake... the face peering back at him... the face he knew.

Not his mother, but this girl – his Glimmer!

Paiscion clapped his hands and cried out triumphantly: "Oh, but of course!"

Sylas barely heard him. He was staring into the girl's eyes and he had the strangest sense that she was staring straight back.

He found her face magnetic: her blue eyes radiant and warm; her fine, narrow features somehow familiar and safe. And although she was a girl, although she was quite clearly different, he saw *himself* in her. He saw it in the way she tilted her head, in the curl of her mouth and in the rise of her cheek; but most of all he saw it in her expression of fear and wonder. He leaned forward a little in his seat and, in the same instant, so did she. He stopped and frowned and so did she. He drew a sharp breath and her lips parted.

He leaned in still further and, as he expected, she moved nearer. But while he smiled, her expression was different. Suddenly he felt a terrible pain in his arm and in the same instant panic passed over her face. He opened his mouth to speak to her, but suddenly she turned sharply and peered over her shoulder into the darkness.

Then she was gone.

§

Bowe's passage from unconsciousness was slow and torturous. His mind was lost in a great darkness, a constant, throbbing pain that gathered about him like great black clouds. He was aware of trying to reach the surface, striving for the light, but he felt heavy, as though his limbs were being dragged down, sinking down, down, into the deep.

And so, when the light did come, it was a surprise, a relief. It appeared to him like sun breaking through the pendulous clouds, like an end to a long and silent storm. But what emerged from behind the clouds were not the dazzling rays for which he so yearned, but a dull and flickering glow. And, as the clouds rolled back, he saw not an open sky, but a vast horizon, a landscape of sand and scrub. Near at hand, a great stone circle rose majestically from the dust, high and proud, casting dark shadows at its feet. At its centre was another circle, but not of stone: it was twelve figures in long robes, their hands joined, their hooded heads cast to the heavens.

His eyes flicked open and he blinked.

The image of the circle of priests remained, suspended in front of him. He raised his throbbing head, biting his lip as a pain shot through his bleeding temple. He saw at once that he was lying on a great stone table, his hands and feet held tightly in manacles and chains. He lowered his head gently on to the cold surface and the scene appeared once again. It was not in front of him, but suspended high above. It was a huge intricate mural, painted on the ceiling of this great chamber, bordered on all sides by an ornate golden frame. Beyond, he could make out more paintings, each depicting historical scenes of magic and wonder.

But he took little interest, for as he became more wakeful, the pain raged through his body: in his ankles and wrists where the manacles cut into his skin; in his shoulders and arms, which had been wrenched high above his head; in his skull, which ached with the blow he had received in the passageway. He tried to move, to ease the pain.

One of the chains slipped. It rattled noisily on to the stone.

Bowe held his breath as the sound echoed around the chamber.

A bolt was drawn back somewhere behind him, across the chamber, and a gentle breeze flowed through the room. The air was not fresh but sweet and putrid. It only took him a moment to place: it was the scent he had come to know on the field of battle, a scent that made him retch. It was death. The unmistakable aroma of rotting flesh.

But he was aware of it for only a moment, for suddenly his Scryer's mind was assailed by a devastating calamity of colour, form and motion: torrents of black and grey, mountainous waves of purple and blue, great fires of red and orange, all surging through his consciousness with unstoppable force, ripping through his thoughts, overthrowing his senses.

He strained against his chains and screamed and screamed and screamed.

A voice seared through his brain and burned in his chest. It sounded not like one, but a legion of voices: male, female, young, old, deep and shrill, all speaking together, forming one overwhelming sound.

"And *this*, the father of greatness?"

35
The Name of Truth

"Despite all perils we must find the Lost Chronicle.
In the name of truth, *we must find it."*

THEIR EYES WERE FIXED on Paiscion, who in turn stared at Sylas with wide eyes. They filled the lenses of his spectacles, moving slowly, painstakingly over Sylas's face, tracing every line and shape, every curve and feature. His expression was stern and solemn, but his eyes gleamed brightly in the Bow Room's faint, shifting light.

"I should have seen it," he said quietly. "I should have seen it before — as soon as I met you. *Blue* eyes, you say?"

Sylas was still rubbing his aching wrist. He nodded. "Yes, but there's something about her that... well... looks like me."

Paiscion continued to gaze at him wistfully. "I know," he said, deep in thought. Suddenly he sucked a breath through his teeth: "Sylas, I believe I know who she is."

Outwardly Sylas paled, but inwardly he felt a new surge of adrenalin and his heart quickened.

Simia started to bounce up and down on her toes and finally she was unable to contain herself any longer.

"*Who?*"

Paiscion leaned down to meet Sylas's eyes, addressing his answer solely to him.

"Her name is Naeo."

Instantly Sylas felt a sharp pain shoot through his wrist. He winced.

"You *know* her?" he asked, turning the Merisi Band in an attempt to ease the discomfort.

"We all do," replied Paiscion. "All of the Magrumen, though I know her family rather better than the others. I fought with her father during the war — an extraordinary man — a Scryer of exceptional talent." He smiled reflectively. "He gave himself utterly to the practice of his art. He even resurrected the ancient tradition of his forbears, shaving his head and tattooing each of the mystical symbols of Scrying into his scalp—"

"Bowe?!" exclaimed Sylas and Simia in unison.

Paiscion blinked through his spectacles. "You know him?"

"Yes, of course," said Simia, glancing at Sylas. "He's a friend. He was at the mill!"

The Magruman's face brightened. "Well, how extraordinary! What a relief to know that he is alive and well! But then if anyone was sure to survive all that has happened—"

"He was taken," interjected Simia reluctantly. "When we were leaving the mill — he and Fathray were together."

Some of the familiar weariness returned to Paiscion's face.

"Ah," he said. He was silent for some moments, then he murmured: 'I've never seen such a gift for Scrying. Not before, and not since. He had such insight, such *feeling*... he would tell me not only where the enemy legions were, but who led them, where they would attack, whether they were resolute or undecided, whether the men were loyal or rebellious. Envoys and scouts arrived to find that Bowe had given me their message hours

426

before. And traitors and liars… well, they gained no quarter when Bowe was at hand…"

"That sounds like him," said Simia, smiling sadly.

Paiscion nodded. "And now it seems that he is again lost to us. In truth I thought we had lost him at the Reckoning, like so many thousands of others."

He drew a deep breath and glanced over at the mirrors.

"That was the day that his daughter, Naeo, came of age."

"How do you mean?"

"At the battle…" said Paiscion rather absently as his mind drifted back. "She… she was magnificent."

"Naeo was there? At the battle?"

"More than that," said Paiscion solemnly, "she very nearly changed the course of it. The battle and perhaps even the history of our people."

He moved past Sylas and sat down in the chair, then stared at each of the mirrors in turn as if trying to catch a last glimpse of the young girl.

"After the fall of the Circle of Salsimaine she and Bowe travelled by night to join those of us who sought escape upon the sand flats. Of course, Bowe was much needed and he joined our ranks, but Naeo must have been told to wait, because she found herself a little spot high on the rocks, overlooking the bay. And there she watched. She looked on as Thoth appeared upon the headland and our army began to panic; she watched as the sky was filled with fire and the beach became a boiling morass. She saw the caves give way and she watched her people sinking beneath the sands. Finally she looked on as mighty waves rose from the depths of the sea, their foaming peaks clawing at the sky before tumbling towards the shore, bearing away all who remained."

"And where was Bowe?" asked Sylas.

"Until now I thought he was among those who were lost," said Paiscion. "And I'm certain that Naeo thought the same."

Simia put her hands to her face. "How could she bear it...?"

"She couldn't," said Paiscion. "At that most horrifying moment, she found something in the very darkest, the most hidden parts of her soul. For, even as the first of the waves threatened to bear her father away, she was seen standing fearlessly, high upon some rocks. She held her arms aloft, stretched out across the bay, and she glared defiantly at the passing waves.

"At first her gestures seemed futile: the seas continued on their devastating path, pounding the cliffs and hurling legions of men to their deaths. But then an onlooker called out, and soon there was an entire chorus of hopeful cries. Espasian and I turned to see an astonishing, glorious sight. The waves were turning. Instead of crashing into the few survivors they slewed to one side, collapsing under their own weight, falling on one edge and rising to impossible heights on the other, banking sharply away from our brethren. They began to travel across the bay, away from the rocks on which she stood. Every new wave that Thoth sent to crush the survivors instead fed a mounting surge of water that careered directly towards the headland. Before he was able to rally, a monstrous mountain of water was bearing down on him, threatening to sweep him from the clifftop. For some moments — some blessed seconds — we all dared to believe that this tiny girl — this great natural force of Essenfayle — might just succeed, that she might strike him down. But alas, the crest of the wave was not quite high enough. It struck the cliff face on the headland with a thunderous clap and sent a sheet of water high into the sky. When it fell, Thoth remained."

He took a long breath. "It was an act of greatness," he added, "for few have come so close to harming the last of the Priests of Souls. And the fact remains that, in those few moments, Naeo

428

saved many lives."

He turned his tired eyes to Sylas. "And she is your Glimmer."

Sylas had listened with growing awe. This girl seemed more strange and distant than ever, and yet he felt curiously proud, as though her triumph was in part his own.

"How did she do it?" he asked.

Paiscion shrugged. "How did you open a chasm in the riverbed? It seems that there is something special about you both, something that makes you gifted in the arts of Essenfayle. And why should it *not* come to you naturally? After all, Essenfayle draws upon the most natural of all powers — the energy that flows through us and between us; an energy that is everywhere, in everything. All it needs to show itself is someone who understands it, senses it, *feels* it. Like a great composer feels the song of the flute, the yearning of the horn, the thunder of the drums, and from those things creates a symphony."

Sylas looked at him blankly. "But I really don't feel *any* of those things," he protested.

"It is in you, Sylas, just as it is in Naeo," said Paiscion, with a resolve that left the matter beyond doubt. "You felt it when you summoned the life in the river at the bridge and when you defeated the Ghor on the Barrens; you felt it when you ran at night through the dried streams of Salsimaine and when Naeo spoke to you in your dreams. You felt it when she summoned you with the Passing Bell."

Simia had been scrutinising Mr Zhi's piece of paper, absent-mindedly twirling a lock of her hair round a finger, but she now blinked and looked up. "I thought only Merimaat and the elders knew how to use the bell?"

"That's what we thought," said Paiscion with a shrug. "But Naeo has surprised us before — why should she not do so again? Sylas knew nothing of Essenfayle three days ago, and yet the very next day he defeated a company of the Ghor!" He leaned forward and lowered his voice. "What if Sylas and Naeo have a power the like of which no one has ever known? What if they — together — are all that Essenfayle promises to be? Two parts of a magnificent whole!"

Sylas shook his head and looked appealingly at Simia, but she had turned back to Mr Zhi's message, holding it reverently between her hands.

He wanted to change the topic. "What happened after the Reckoning?" he asked. "What happened to Naeo?"

Paiscion lowered his eyes to the creaking deck. "Ah well, there lies the problem," he said. "I'm afraid Naeo had made herself far too conspicuous and Thoth had no intention of letting her get away. He sent a legion of Ghor to find her and — despite Espasian's efforts to protect her — they were both eventually taken. I was far across the bay by then, trying to help the few survivors to escape, but I heard reports that they fought even as they were carried away. When he was finally captured, Espasian was limp and lifeless — we assumed that he was dead."

"If only," mumbled Simia without raising her eyes from Mr Zhi's note. She reached into her jacket, pulled out her notepad and began scribbling.

"So where do you think she is now?" asked Sylas, feeling once again that he already knew the answer.

Paiscion dropped his head. "There is only one place she can be," he said reluctantly. "The Dirgheon."

"Of course," muttered Sylas, shaking his head. "How do we get to her in *there*?"

The Magruman sat up straight and looked surprised. "My dear Sylas," he exclaimed, "I think the real question is how is Thoth going to keep you apart?"

Sylas looked unconvinced.

"You are clearly *destined* to come together!" exclaimed Paiscion, getting to his feet. "Can't you see that? Now is the time! Now, when the people of Essenfayle are defeated, when our nation — Naeo's nation — lies in ruins, when Thoth threatens to consume us all! This is Nature's balance! Nature's hand reaching out to set things straight. She is working through Naeo, through you both!"

Sylas shook his head, struggling to comprehend.

"Hey!" shouted Simia, staring wide-eyed at her notebook.

"You must have faith in the gifts you have been given!" said Paiscion, placing a hand on Sylas's shoulder. "You have to see beyond…"

"I said, *hey*!" cried Simia, raising her head. "I've found something!"

"What?" snapped Paiscion irritably.

"Something… really, really strange."

"What is it?"

Simia looked back at the piece of paper. "I was just reading this," she said breathlessly, "the secret message… you know… 'So at last we may be one'…"

"Yes, yes, we've talked about that!"

"I know *you* have," snapped Simia, glaring up at Paiscion. "But you missed something. Something really important."

Paiscion's eyes suddenly dropped to the paper on Simia's lap and a look of interest passed over his face.

"It seemed strange to me that the message wasn't quite the same as the poem," she said excitedly, holding up her notebook. "You see? It says '*So* at last' instead of '*For then* at last'. Well, you wouldn't expect Mr Zhi to make a mistake, so I started thinking that maybe there was a reason. Maybe the letters themselves are important. I started playing around with them — you know —

mixing them up, reading them out of order, as if they were Ravel Runes or something…"

"Yes, yes," said Paiscion impatiently. "What did you find?"

Simia crossed her arms and looked at him steadily. "I found the word *Naeo*," she said, "and her father's name, *Bowe*. As in Naeo, daughter of Bowe."

Paiscion looked unimpressed. "I don't see how that—"

"You will in a minute," continued Simia defiantly. "When you take those letters away, only a few are left… an S… a Y… an L… an A…" She grinned as she saw a look of astonishment pass over their faces. With a flourish, she turned her notebook around so they could see her workings.

Sylas's eyes moved rapidly over Simia's scrawled letters.

Impossible.

"Our names…" he muttered.

"You see!" cried Simia. "The letters in '*So at last we may be one*'… they spell 'Naeo Bowe' and 'Sylas Tate'!"

Sylas glanced from Simia to Paiscion.

"So your very names are a message!" exclaimed Paiscion excitedly, rushing over to grasp the piece of paper. His quick eyes flew across Mr Zhi's message and he mouthed the names under his breath. "Yes! Yes, of course!" he exclaimed, the corners of his mouth twitching with excitement.

"Oh," muttered Simia, poring over her notebook. "I think I made a mistake…"

The smile fell from Paiscion's face. "Why?"

"Because there's an 'M' left over. The 'M' in 'may'."

Paiscion thought for a moment and then slowly the smile returned. "Oh, this really is TOO perfect!" he exclaimed, looking reverently at Mr Zhi's message. "Yes, that's it! You see, over the years the Merisi have sent the Suhl many messages, some in the

Samarok, some in letters, some in codes parchments or encrypted texts. There have been many authors too: Mr Zhi, the Bringers, other elders of the Merisi. But one thing always remains the same..."

"What?" probed Simia impatiently.

"They sign their messages with a single letter... 'M'!"

Simia frowned, but slowly her face filled with wonder.

Sylas grew pale. "So you're saying that my name is just part of a message?"

"Not just your name, and not just any message," said the Magruman, his voice quivering with excitement. "You yourself are part of the ultimate message! The message we have all been waiting for since Merisu wrote his poem! The ancients — at least the ancients of our world — believed that the soul had five parts: the shadow, the essence, the spirit, the soul and, very importantly, the *name*, the Ren as they called it. They believed that the name was more than just a label, much more. It defines you. It makes you who you are."

"But hold on a minute..." muttered Sylas, rubbing his temple. "That's... that's the name my *mum* gave me," he said.

"Well indeed, and there's only one explanation!" cried Paiscion. "She must have *known* about all this, all along."

"She *couldn't* have..."

"Why shouldn't she have known?" said Simia, her cheeks now flushed with excitement. "We already know that she knew the Merisi — her Glimmer even! She might have known them since before you were born! And if she did, she'd definitely know Merisu's poem!"

Sylas shook his head and stared at the deck. "But *why*? Why would she?" he exclaimed. "It's my *name*!"

"To *speak* to us, Sylas," said Paiscion, with a solemn expression. "To tell us beyond any doubt that you and Naeo are those foretold by Merisu and our whispered myths. That you are meant to be here, that you are meant to find Naeo. That together you will do the unthinkable."

Sylas raised his eyes and stared out of the nearest porthole, trying to gather his thoughts. A grey wave crashed against the glass and fell away to reveal a wild, churning expanse of water stretching as far as he could see. How could any of this be true? Just days ago he had been forgotten and alone in a dusty corner of Gabblety Row, and now he was supposed to believe that he had some kind of special destiny? It was ridiculous.

Aware that the room had fallen silent he glanced at Simia. "I just can't make sense of it," he said, for once hoping that his strong-minded companion had something to say.

Simia leaned forward. "It's *your* name, Sylas," she said. "Maybe it's also your mother's message to you. She'd have known that you wouldn't believe any of this — how could you? And what better way to tell you that she knew who you really are? That this is what she knew you had to do."

Sylas looked through the porthole on to the ceaseless motion of the waves and tried to think. Maybe this was what she had intended. But even if it was, how would it bring him any closer to finding her? And yet surely she wouldn't knowingly do anything to keep them apart?

"If it *is* a message for me, what do I do with it?"

"Start by believing it," said Paiscion, patting him on the shoulder as he strode across the room. When he reached the door, he whirled about. "Come! To the deck!"

"What for?"

"To compose a symphony!" cried the Magruman.

S

"The name!" raged the mercurial voice, possessing Bowe's mind, ravaging his thoughts. "The name of her mother!"

Tears poured down Bowe's cheeks as he strained against his bonds, his glistening body twisting on the stone table, his teeth drawing blood from his lips. His mind had almost given up its battle, overwhelmed by the forces that assailed it. He was lost in a vast unending torrent of emotion and thought. Now more than ever he cursed his gift, cursed all that made him the Scryer that he was, for here, in the presence of Thoth, he felt as though all the hate, love, joy, despair, anger, all the gathered feelings of mankind, were flowing through him, possessing him, forcing from him all sense of himself. He felt flayed, empty, exhausted.

And yet, still, he refused to speak. He shook his bleeding head.

A roar of unimaginable horrors sounded in his ears, a chorus of raucous screams and soulless wails, smashing his head against the stone, tearing through his mind. He felt his ears begin to bleed.

"No!" he cried. "Kill me if you will! I WILL NOT tell you."

He felt a terrible chill pass over his whole body. Something icy and damp crept around his skull. The stench of rotting flesh filled his nostrils with new intensity. He felt his head grasped by cold, deathly fingers, then turned sharply to one side.

"Do you see her?"

He gasped and strained against his bonds. Bound to a chair on the other side of the chamber was a girl. Her face was white and drawn, her frightened eyes streaming with tears.

An overwhelming sob rose in his chest.

"Naeo!" he cried, reaching out to her with a manacled hand.

Once again the chilling, resonant voices of many filled the chamber.

"I will not kill you, I will kill her."

36

Nature's Song

"What exquisite song *must* Nature *sing?"*

THE SKY WAS DARK and the low-hanging clouds seemed almost to brush the tops of the shattered rigging. The dank grey estuary extended as far as the eye could see, its vast expanse making the broken carcass of the *Windrush* seem even more hapless and frail. Everything was in motion: the great tempest of waves that buffeted the creaking timbers; the low fog that muddled the horizon; the drapery of frayed ropes and torn sails that flapped and fluttered in the wind. A powerful scent of salt and seaweed filled the thick sea air, which resonated with the low rumble of waves crashing against a distant shore.

Sylas and Simia sat hunched against the elements on a pile of damp wood and canvas, sipping from large glasses of water, staring out at the great tumult of surf and cloud. Neither knew quite what to say.

"Where do you think he's gone?" asked Simia after a long silence.

Sylas shrugged. "Don't know."

They watched a flock of seagulls approaching the ship, flying low over the surface of the water, rising and falling with the crests and troughs of the waves. A bird turned in a wide arc around the stern of the ship and, making a loud yelping cry, came to rest on the trapdoor through which the Magruman had disappeared.

"How are you doing?" asked Simia hesitantly.

He took another sip of water. "I don't know. It's all too much to take in." He paused and turned towards her. "But... something about it feels... this is going to sound weird... something about it feels *right*."

Simia gathered her oversized coat about her and leaned forward on her elbows. "We've talked about this before," she said with a grin. "What do you mean by 'right'?"

"I'm not sure," said Sylas, scratching his salty hair. "I suppose what I'm trying to say is that there was nothing particularly *right* about what I left behind. You know, my mum in hospital, my uncle bossing me around... and I've never even known who my dad was. Ever since I can remember all I really had was my room and my kites and the things I made up in my head. But since Mr Zhi came — since all this started to happen — it's been... it's like I've had a purpose. Like I've been heading somewhere... somewhere everyone seems to think I'm meant to be, even my mum. And that's something... isn't it?"

Simia stared out at the foggy horizon and took a deep breath of sea air. "I think so," she said. "And this certainly beats sitting around at the mill talking about the past."

Sylas pulled his knees up to shield him from the cold wind. "And there's something else — something about Naeo. *She* feels right too. I can't really say why, but I feel like I know her. More than that even — when I saw her in the mirrors, it was like seeing myself, but from behind, or from the side or through a thick piece of glass or something. It felt like I was seeing myself... properly..."

He caught himself and looked over at Simia with an apologetic smile. "Weird, right?"

"I'm getting used to it," she said, and drank down the rest of her water.

Suddenly there was a loud bang and they looked along the deck to see the trapdoor clattering against the timbers and the seagull squawking and fluttering in the air. Paiscion's head emerged from the dark hatch and he climbed up the steps, cradling his gramophone in his arms. He moved with great care, taking each step very slowly so as not to knock his treasured machine against the sides.

"Sorry for the wait," he said brightly, stepping on to the deck. "It took me some time to find just the right piece."

"Was it broken?" asked Simia, pushing herself to her feet.

Paiscion sighed as he laid the gramophone down on a crate. "Piece of *music*, Simia. We are going to create a symphony, and to do that we need a little help from a master."

Sylas walked up to the gramophone. "Beethoven?" he asked, trying his luck with the only composer he knew.

"No, but good try," said Paiscion. "Dvořák. Another master. And this—" he pointed at the record and turned to smile at Sylas — "this is his masterpiece. He called it his 'New World Symphony'. Suited to the occasion, I think."

His eyes sparkled as he leaned down and took hold of the winding arm of the gramophone. He turned it several times, then lifted the needle and drew it across to the third track on the record. There was a brief crackle and then a long, quiet hiss.

"Now, Sylas," said the Magruman, straightening himself and smoothing the creases out of his jacket. "Observe, for what you are about to witness is true Essenfayle."

He closed his eyes, bowed his head and relaxed his arms at his sides.

Simia drew Sylas to one side and leaned into his ear. "This'll be good," she whispered.

"You've seen this before?"

Simia frowned. "Are you kidding? From a *Magruman*?"

Suddenly their eyes flew to the brass horn of the gramophone as a chorus of violins erupted from the darkness at its centre, issuing a series of pulses, then quick-fire, staccato notes. When they looked back at Paiscion, his arms were raised above his head, poised in readiness.

And then he began.

First came the quick melody of a single flute and, as its opening note sounded, so the Magruman's left hand moved, darting to one side. In the same instant a single white seagull feather leapt from the deck and launched itself into the air, fluttering this way and that as though carried on the wind.

But it did not drift away or fall back to the deck. Instead, as the sound of a horn joined the flute, it began to dance in time with the minute movements of Paiscion's hand. Then, as the violins took up the melody, it rose in the air, twisting and twirling until it quivered directly before Sylas's eyes. The horns sounded and in that moment the feather pirouetted on its point like a quill, as though showing off. As the kettle drums rumbled and the music swelled, it began leaping and dancing around Sylas, as if carried by the rhythm of the music. He watched with wide eyes, turning with the feather, flinching as it brushed his face. He was about to reach for it when, as quickly as it had risen, the music suddenly subsided. The final notes died away and the feather floated across the deck to hang in the air in front of Paiscion.

Then the cycle of music began again, but this time, as a single flute sounded, it was Paiscion's other hand that was in motion, sweeping in a wide arc over the side of the ship. Sylas peered all about him and saw nothing.

Simia suddenly squeezed his arm. "The mist! Look at it!"

He glanced to the horizon and saw that the great white plumes of fog seemed to be shifting, drifting over the waves, away from the *Windrush*. They moved ever more swiftly, rolling into the distance, churning and billowing like fire smoke and then, as the drums sounded and the music swelled, Sylas saw that it was not only the fog that was drifting, it was the clouds too. It was a strange movement, as though the wind was blowing from all directions at once. The music rose to another crescendo as it did so, a shaft of sunlight slanted between them, followed moments later by another and another. Soon an endless forest of sunbeams had pierced the greyness and the whole estuary was dappled in pools of gold.

"Isn't it *amazing*?" cried Simia, jumping up and down next to him.

Sylas nodded, but dared not take his eyes away. The music resolved to the gentle melody of a single clarinet and Paiscion began weaving his hand through the air as though he was passing a thread between the clouds. In that instant the wide fan of sunbeams began to dance: gliding between and around each other in a fluid, rhythmical motion, seeming to keep pace with the music; waltzing over the waves like ballerinas on a stage, moving swiftly, elegantly, in perfect unison.

Then Paiscion's left hand was again in motion. The feather danced in response, leaping, twisting and looping in time with the sunbeams, rising slowly towards the mottled sky. As it climbed, it wove an impossible path through the great tangle of ropes and beams, dallying to flit and flutter around braces and yards before continuing its ascent. And then, as the violins once again took up the melody and the horns sounded, Sylas nearly cried out, for he looked to the sky and saw two great flocks of seagulls, one approaching from the bow and one from the stern, gliding and swooping towards them. With the pounding of kettle drums, the symphony rose to a new pitch and, as the single feather fluttered and danced like a standard above the mast, three beams of glorious sunlight converged on the ship, bathing all in gold: the bright canvas flapping in the wind, Simia's flame-red hair as she laughed and jumped, Paiscion with his arms held wide. The seagulls darted above the decks and through the criss-cross of rigging before sweeping high into the air and spreading their shimmering wings to turn sharply into a perfect circle around the mast.

Simia shrieked with delight and clung on to Sylas's arm. "Isn't it the most beautiful thing you've ever seen?"

Sylas was silent. It was, and there was nothing more to be said. He stared at the circling birds, and the dancing feather lit bright in the sunbeams, and he hoped that it would never end. He listened to the music reach its crescendo and slowly die away to a single cello. Then a new, playful melody emerged in its place.

"Look! Look!" cried Simia, pointing wildly out to the estuary.

He dropped his eyes to the waves. As far as he could see in all directions, fish were leaping: large ones that rose amid showers of sunlit water, flapping their mighty tails in the air; small ones that skipped and skidded on the surface; entire shoals jumping in broad arcs over the tumultuous waves. But what made the sight truly magnificent, what sent a shiver down Sylas's spine, was that they appeared to be rising and falling in time with the music, playing merrily among its harmonies, splashing and flapping to its rhythm. It seemed to Sylas that Nature had become Her own symphony, Her own glorious harmony of sound and sight. And somehow, standing here on the ship in the middle of it all, they were part of it, and it was part of them.

Suddenly Paiscion whirled about, his hands a blur in the air. "Nature *is* a symphony, Sylas!" he cried as though reading his thoughts.

Sylas looked up at him and saw, to his surprise, that his face showed no strain, no effort.

"Everything in Nature is connected, everything is in harmony! Essenfayle simply changes the melody!"

He lowered his left hand and suddenly the wide circle of seagulls let out a chorus of yelling calls and broke formation. Moments later they re-formed, now wheeling in the other direction.

"Do you see?" he cried.

Sylas began to nod, his eyes filling with tears.

"Come and stand here," said the Magruman, taking a backwards step to make space for him.

Sylas stepped forward so that he stood directly in front of Paiscion. He could see the Magruman's hands leaping and sweeping above him and, in response, the birds, fish, clouds and sunbeams dancing and turning, their breathtaking display keeping perfect time with the melody of the music.

Then, without warning, Paiscion dropped his arms, bent down and whispered in his ear.

"Your turn."

Sylas froze.

"Me? But I..."

"You are a more worthy conductor than I, Sylas!" yelled Paiscion, seizing him by the shoulders. "You have shown it more than once. Think of the Shop of Things, the Den of Scribes, the river, the Barrens, the Glimmer Glass! Think of the Passing Bell! This is *your* magic, Sylas. Essenfayle is *yours*!"

Suddenly a shadow passed over the deck and Sylas glanced up to see the clouds coming together, extinguishing the shafts of light. In the same moment he saw the formation of seagulls falter and the feather, no longer shining in the sunlight, beginning to fall, rocking from side to side. He looked down to the waves and saw no fish leaping. Fog was rising on the horizon.

"It's stopping!" cried Simia. "Sylas! *Do something!*"

"What? Do *what*?"

"Imagine it, Sylas!" hissed the Magruman at his ear. "Imagine it so!"

Sylas recognised Espen's words. *Imagine it so!* He mumbled the words under his breath. He raised his hands and closed his eyes. He tried to imagine the fishes leaping, the clouds parting, the fog rolling away, but in his excited state he found it impossible to hold the images in his mind. He opened his eyes and frowned, then tried to gesture at the clouds with his hand. Nothing happened.

"Let the music help you!" whispered Paiscion. "Feel its harmony, its song!"

Sylas drew a long breath and tried to calm himself. He turned his mind from the gathering clouds and the seagulls yelling above and instead he listened. He allowed the music to wash over him, to enter him, to seize him. For some moments he stood with his eyes closed, listening to the oboes, flutes and horns, and then he heard the violins answering them, echoing their tune, adding to it, developing it. And slowly he started to see the estuary in his mind. He saw the clouds shifting and swirling until a single beam broke through. He saw the seagulls give answer, rising on the wind and looping back towards the mast, and he saw the fish leaping again as if in reply. Suddenly he felt as if the music was inside him, part of him, guiding the beautiful images in his mind. He breathed in time with it, felt it coursing through his veins, warming him, holding him.

"That's it, Sylas!" cried Paiscion. "That's it!"

He opened his eyes and saw that his arms were raised in front of him and his hands were moving in time with the music. He looked past them and gasped.

The rays of sunlight had returned and were moving across the water in a great ballet. The fish were leaping once more, rising with watery trains that caught and scattered the golden light. Above, the great wheel of seagulls had formed and now turned faster than ever.

"*Now* do you see?" cried Paiscion, seizing his shoulders. "They are part of you, Sylas, and you are part of them!"

A thrill travelled through Sylas's body as he realised that *he* was doing this — that all of these beautiful things were connected through him. He shifted his hand, imagining the clouds parting and the rays of sunshine converging on the ship, and in the same instant it was so. He looked up and saw that the feather had fallen among the rigging and he imagined it borne upwards on a gentle breeze, dancing to the melody, darting in and out of the rope-work, and then he realised that he was watching it happen.

All of this without thought or effort: it was like drawing breath.

Suddenly he heard the return of the single flute and in that moment he turned to look out on to the estuary. For the first time he thought it within his reach, an extension of himself, all of it: the blue-grey waters; the hazy air; even the leaping, dancing fish. And then, without thinking, he raised his hand to the sky and drew it down towards the waves. He heard shrill cries somewhere high above and then, as the violins joined the flute and the music gathered pace, two columns of seagulls dived down in front of him until they reached the surf, then — almost seeming to touch the crests of the waves — set out across the waters. As the melody surged and waned, so the flocks banked and turned, responding to the tiny movements of his hands. The music approached another crescendo and the two lines of gulls became four, weaving among the flying fish: some sweeping left and right over the surface, others darting beneath arcs of silvery scales.

Simia clapped and cried out in excitement, but Sylas could not hear her. He felt consumed, as though he was among the gulls and sunbeams, skipping over the waves. Still the music surged — gaining pace and volume — and all the while his hands were aloft, directing some new performance somewhere out on the estuary.

Simia glanced about her, trying to see what new wonder he had conjured, and as he raised his arms still further, she saw something: a disturbance on the distant grey horizon, a fleck of white, a shifting of lines. The violins rose through a scale and, as they ascended in pitch, so the furthest waters also seemed to rise, as though the river and open sea were by some miracle reaching for the sky. Sunbeams scattered as they caught the surface as if it was no longer flat, and then they fell upon a long white line on the horizon that leapt and rippled in the light. Still the waters rose, and as the horns soared towards a crescendo, Simia realised that she was watching a gigantic wave, a wave that had appeared on every horizon and even now was building, growing and surging towards the *Windrush*. She turned wide-eyed to Sylas and saw him drawing his hands inwards, towards his chest, as though calling the wave on. The violins, flutes, oboes and clarinets seemed to obey, rising in volume, tempo and pitch, resolving to a single melody, reaching their climax. As they did, the mountainous wave roared and thundered as it clawed at the sky and hurled surf and spray high into the air.

She took a step backwards. "Sylas, what... what are you doing?"

Sylas met her eyes without dropping his hands. His face glowed in the sunlight, his eyes glistened.

"I believe now," he said, the trace of a smile on his lips.

The loud report of a horn led a glorious harmony of violins, drums, flutes and clarinets that seemed to join the thunder of the wave to form a towering, almighty voice: the cry of Nature Herself. In that moment the great circular wave closed in upon itself, meeting at its centre, at the *Windrush*. A deep, resonant boom shuddered through its timbers as the entire ship was propelled upwards on water and foam, up and up towards the broken clouds until, as the gramophone played the final strains of the symphony, Sylas, Simia and Paiscion looked down on the sun-spotted estuary, the seagulls carving the surf and the silvery fish leaping in their midst.

As the *Windrush* descended slowly on a great cradle of water, Sylas reached out and plucked the feather from the air.

37

Council at Dawn

"Our council with our souls must end.
Done is the pleasant dreaming of night.
Now is dawn, and the long day awaits."

IT WAS A DREAM to cling to; a dream of light and music and hope. It was warm and bright like summer meadows, awash with beautiful sounds like babbling brooks and a mother's song and birds at the birth of day. It made him feel alive, invigorated, expectant. When the world tried to pull him from his sleep, he strained against it. He pressed his eyes closed, pulled up his blanket and tucked his knees into his chest. He knew the sounds that threatened to wake him: the slap of waves near his head, the creak of ancient joists, the *pat, pat, pat* of oars, but he tried to fend them off with light and music and hope.

Pat, pat, pat.

Sylas groaned and forced his eyes open. A shaft of orange light bisected the Bow Room from the single porthole to the door, which swung lazily on its hinges. The quality of the light shifted and changed with every second, rippling against the timber, shimmering on the Glimmer Glass. Otherwise nothing moved: all was as it should be. He turned his mind back to summer meadows, letting his eyes close.

PAT, PAT, PAT.

He pushed himself up on his elbow and listened. The sound was getting closer, and now he could also hear the clunk and creak of rowlocks.

He turned to where Simia had been sleeping among Paiscion's many Things, but her bedding was rolled back and she was gone. Gathering his blanket round his shoulders, Sylas pushed himself to his feet, staggered a little as the *Windrush* swayed to one side, then started to make his way between the bric-a-brac to the door.

As he passed the Glimmer Glass, something made him stop. He looked back at the two silvered panes. He was sure he had seen a movement: a blur in the corner of his eye.

He edged a little closer.

As his pale face moved into view in the white mirror, the black one sprang into life. He made an effort to keep his eyes fixed on his own image and as he did so he saw a shape forming at the edge of his vision. A familiar shape.

The girl's face.

He had so struggled to see the previous day, but it was now clear and true. Something had changed: it was more distinct, more urgent. She no longer glimmered serenely in the glass, but glared across the void.

Her features were taut with fear.

Sylas felt the hairs rise on his neck. He fought the urge to look directly into the mirror. She was speaking. No, she was shouting.

He saw the words plainly on her lips:

"Find me, or we will die."

Sylas clattered through the hatch into the reds and oranges of a chilly dawn. He spotted Simia and Paiscion silhouetted against the morning sun, both peering over the side of the ship.

"I just saw her again!" he shouted, running up to them. They both swung about, startled.

Paiscion gathered himself first. "You saw Naeo? In the Glimmer Glass?"

"Yes, she spoke to me! She was scared! *Really* scared!"

"What did she say?"

"It was clear, almost as though I could hear it. She said: 'Find me, or we will die.'"

Paiscion's face darkened, his eyes betraying his alarm.

Simia sucked her teeth. "That doesn't sound good."

Sylas raised his eyebrows. "No kidding."

"This certainly changes things," said the Magruman thoughtfully. "I had hoped that we would have more time to prepare, but it seems that we must now move more quickly."

"How soon could we go?" asked Sylas.

"Tomorrow, perhaps even—"

There was a clunk against the side of the ship and then somebody cursed loudly. It was a young male voice.

"No, no, don't worry, I'm fine!" came the voice again. "Don't let me interrupt!"

The rope ladder over the side of the ship went taut, then a mass of unruly blond hair came into view, followed by a slight, pale face.

It was Ash.

He looked up and beamed at the gathering. "Aren't you just a little bit glad to see me?" he asked sarcastically, hoisting his bag on to the deck. "Or were you hiding from me too?"

"Ash!" cried Sylas and Simia in unison, extending their hands to help him up.

Ash stared at the two hands and guffawed. "*Now* you want to be friends!"

They all laughed and helped him up, exchanging greetings. Simia took his bag from him and Paiscion ushered him over to a collection of crates, where they all took a seat and began exchanging stories.

After some moments Paiscion disappeared below and reappeared with a steaming pot of tea, which he poured while Simia asked Ash all manner of questions about what had happened since they parted. Ash, however, was in a playful mood and took to answering every question with a question, such that before long he knew all of what had happened to Sylas and Simia, while nothing was known of him.

Finally, however, Paiscion politely but firmly insisted that Ash tell his story.

"Yes, and start at the Circle of Salsimaine," Simia demanded. "Like I *asked*."

"Right, yes," said Ash, pushing back his unruly hair and rocking back on his crate.

He told how, shortly after Sylas and Simia left, he had had the idea of using the dried rivers to confuse and divide the Ghor using an old trick that he learned from the Muddlemorphs. He described the moment when the Ghor had first appeared out of the darkness and, with some pride, he told how he had distracted them with fires formed of mustard and dust.

Paiscion's face darkened. "You used *Kimiyya*?"

Ash tugged at a lock of his hair. "Yes," he said defensively. "It's so useful for—"

"Nonsense! It has no use whatsoever, especially not in the hands of the Suhl! Such sorcery has robbed Nature of the things She holds most dear!"

450

Ash lowered his eyes and shrugged. "Well, I didn't think a few little fires—"

"The Barrens were *forged* in such fires!" snapped the Magruman. His gaunt, pale face had become flushed as he glared through his thick glasses. "You know better than this, Ash!"

Ash was a little bewildered to find himself under attack – he had been quite prepared to be heralded as a hero. "Well, I did what I thought I had to," he grumbled. "I couldn't face them with just Essenfayle."

"'*Just* Essenfayle' he says," murmured the Magruman. He took a breath. "I know you mean well, young man, but you must remember that Kimiyya is the plaything of Thoth. *Nothing* good can come of it. Surely we have learned that from the Undoing?"

Ash cleared his throat. "I wanted to give them the best chance."

Paiscion leaned back on his crate. "Of course you did," he said wearily. "But the Undoing will only end when Nature is healed; it will only end with *Essenfayle*. You *do* see that?"

Ash nodded. "Yes, but—"

"Then carry on," said Paiscion, closing his eyes and waving at him impatiently. "You have a story to tell and are too long about it."

Ash drew a long breath and widened his eyes at Sylas and Simia, then continued.

He told of the Ghor moving like silent shadows across the Barrens; of the fires that drew them to the dried rivers and the whirlwinds that they mistook for human shapes. He described how he had stood on top of the Circle of Salsimaine and watched as they chased the air, how he led them further and further from the stones and the scent of their quarry, how he had made them stumble across each other and in the darkness. And then he told of the moment when something had caught his eye, something slow and silent and near: a human shape, standing just paces away, in the shadows. He related how he had felt the hairs rise on his neck and how he had turned to see a familiar figure in the circle below.

"Espen!" exclaimed Sylas.

Ash nodded. "The very same."

"He *found* you?" gasped Simia, horrified. "How did you get away?"

"I didn't have to," said Ash. "He let me go."

Simia frowned, then glanced at Sylas and Paiscion.

"But... he *betrayed* us. Why would he—"

"He let me go, Simia," interjected Ash. "He told me that there is hope, that we must be swift, and then he let me go."

There was a long silence. Everyone stared at Ash.

"Well? What does *that* mean?" blustered Simia.

"I don't know," he said with a shrug. "It was all pretty quick — there were plenty of Ghor closing in, remember. He said his piece, then he just disappeared into the darkness. I couldn't have followed him even if I'd wanted to."

Paiscion stood and paced round the circle of crates, rubbing his sallow cheeks with his palms. "It means that we were wrong to doubt him," he said.

"Just because he *says* so?" exclaimed Simia incredulously.

"Paiscion's right," said Ash. "I think we can trust him."

"But why *should* we?" cried Simia, throwing her hands out in exasperation. "We trusted him before and he—"

"Because he let me go," said Ash. "And he let you go."

"What do you mean he let *us* go? We got away! We ran the whole way in the dark..."

"He was right behind you, Simia!"

She put her hands on her hips and seemed about to argue, but Sylas laid a hand on her shoulder.

"Simia, they're right," he said, remembering Espen's strength and pace as he had run across town and the Barrens. "If he was that close behind us, we'd never have outrun him if he hadn't let it happen."

She clamped her mouth shut and then turned to stare out to sea.

"Well, I still don't trust him," she mumbled. "You're forgetting that I *saw* him with Scarpia."

Paiscion watched her for a moment and then lowered himself back into his seat. "Well, whatever we think about Espasian, we know that his message is true — we must be swift. Naeo needs our help."

"Yes," said Sylas, glad to be returning to the topic of Naeo. "There was something so *desperate* about her — as if something terrible was going to happen. Maybe it was already happening. And I didn't dream about her last night — that's the first time since all this started."

"You're sure she's in the Dirgheon?" asked Ash.

Paiscion nodded. "She was taken by Thoth's own guard."

Ash let out a low whistle. "Well, this isn't going to be easy."

Simia was suddenly struck with a thought. "What do you expect to happen exactly? If Sylas and Naeo meet, I mean?"

Paiscion looked at her steadily. "No one can know that."

"So how do you know it's *right*? Talking to her in the mirrors is one thing, but two parts of the same person *meeting*?" She shook her head. "Isn't that... weird? Unnatural?"

The trace of a smile showed on Paiscion's thin lips. "A fair point, Simia," he said. "But we must not confuse the unknowable with the unnatural. Essenfayle teaches us that togetherness, *connectedness*, is the natural state. How can it be right that a person should be kept from their Glimmer? What if *we* are the unnatural ones? Those of us who know nothing of their own Glimmer."

Simia frowned. "That makes no sense. How can we all be unnatural?"

"Sylas's world and our world may be different," said the Magruman, "but they have far too much in common to be two separate places. The Merisi have long believed that they are two parts of a whole, divided by some force and for some reason we do not yet understand. And how *could* we understand, for we ourselves are divided. Each and every one of us has a Glimmer: a part of ourselves we do not know, that we cannot see, hear or touch." He turned his eyes to Sylas. "But there *is* something different about Sylas and Naeo. We've all seen it — Essenfayle of such purity and power that they wield it like Merimaat herself. Essenfayle so natural and true that the divisions break down, the Passing Bell rises from the earth and rings again. They meet each other in their dreams; they are even able to look one another in the face." He looked back at Simia. "No, Simia, this is not unnatural. Far from it. In Sylas and Naeo, the two worlds come together."

Simia looked doubtfully at Sylas.

He shrugged. "I don't know. Everything that's happened to me, to us, leads to Naeo. And..." he hesitated, "I do believe now that this is what my mum wanted. I have to trust that. This may even be the only way for me to find her too."

She sighed. "Well, I don't know." She looked back at Paiscion. "If it's so natural, why did the bracelet hurt him when he was using the mirrors?"

"Because that's what it's meant to do," said the Magruman.

"*Meant* to do?"

"Yes, it's a warning."

"A warning that something bad's going to happen?"

"You need to remember that the Merisi Band was made

for Bringers, not for Sylas. It was there to protect them from accidentally coming face to face with their Glimmer..."

"Protect them! They need *protecting* from their Glimmers?"

Ash rocked forward on his crate. "She's got a point, Paiscion," he said. "Why were Bringers so afraid of their Glimmers?"

The Magruman let out a long sigh. "Because it's happened before." He lowered his eyes.

"And? What happened?"

"They died."

"Died?" cried Simia.

Paiscion raised his eyes to Simia and then looked over at Sylas, whose face had paled. "They thought it was the shock," he said, "but that was a long time ago and it was different. Sylas and Naeo are—"

"Well, that's it as far as I'm concerned!" Simia exclaimed, turning to Sylas. "I think you'd be mad to go — at least until we know more. It's just too—"

"Simia!" snapped Paiscion. "I've told you, Sylas and Naeo are *different*. Everything has conspired to bring them together, not to keep them apart. You speak of the Merisi Band, well, remember it is the Merisi who began this journey — it all started with Mr Zhi. For Sylas the band was just another way to prove that Naeo is his Glimmer!"

"Yes, but no one can be *sure!*" she shouted, throwing her hands wide. She looked to Sylas for support.

He sat in silence for some moments, then he put his hand on her shoulder. "Thanks, Simia. Really," he said. "But I think Paiscion's right."

Simia gasped. "How can you—"

"Because I think I'm *supposed* to be doing this. Because I think Naeo needs our help."

"Yes, but—"

"And we're forgetting something," he said. "Something in Merisu's poem."

"What?"

"The third line. It says, *'fear not where none have gone'*." He shrugged. "Don't you see? It's like Merisu wrote that poem about this very moment. He *knew* that I'd be frightened, he *knew* that we'd have doubts, and he said go on, you have nothing to fear. Do it, because then *at last we may be one*."

Simia looked long and hard into his eyes, then slumped back in her seat.

"You're impossible," she said, blowing out a lungful of air.

Ash suddenly clapped his hands together. "Well, this is too fine! Breakfast and a spirited debate! What better way to start the day!" He reached over and patted both Sylas and Simia on the shoulders. "I've missed you two!"

They both gave him a weary look.

As a sallow sun climbed in the morning sky, the *Windrush* drifted far out in the estuary, rising and falling on the waves from the open sea. An occasional wind gathered in the half-set sails making them flap and tug at their ropes, as if the old ship was straining at its leash.

"It's not going to be easy," sighed Ash, shaking his head. "The Dirgheon is impregnable. Its defences have never been breached... entire *armies* have fallen at its walls. The Ghor legions that patrol them are the finest under Thoth's command. Even if we find a way inside, it's vast. No one knows how many rooms there are, how many corridors and forgotten passages. And, if by some miracle we found her, how would we get her out?"

There was a long silence.

Paiscion had been looking out on to the estuary, lost in thought, but suddenly he sat forward.

"Most would say it is impossible," he said, picking up a glass of water from the table. "But there may just be a way."

He stood and motioned for them all to follow.

He led them just a few paces to a part of the deck that still lay in shadow, shrouded by one of the *Windrush*'s torn sails. They looked at one another expectantly. Paiscion held out the glass until it caught one of the passing beams of light and instantly it glowed with the sun's reds and oranges. It scattered the light, casting it on to the deck at their feet so that it danced over the timbers as the water lapped in the glass. He flicked the side of the glass with his finger, making it ring with a long, resonant note that seemed to hang in the air. Inside, the surface of the water also began to vibrate and, as it did so, strange patterns formed over its surface: tiny ripples like the whorls and curves of a fingerprint.

"Behold the Dirgheon," said the Magruman, pointing out over the shaded deck.

They turned and gasped, for there, depicted in the bronze light of dawn, was a perfect image of the Dirgheon, its harsh angles and jagged lines blazing out in the darkness. Around it there were streets and buildings, pathways and squares, even the river – all of them marked out in shimmering light: their outlines rippling and undulating as though made of liquid fire. The scene was viewed from somewhere high above such that the great mass of the Dirgheon looked almost square, with each of its four triangular sides clearly visible, dominating the huddling rows of buildings at its base. As the light from the glass moved, they saw the jagged rows of stone from which it was constructed and, towards the peak, the few dark openings: ominous windows, like dark eyes presiding over the cowering city below.

Paiscion turned the glass slightly and in the same instant the entire scene turned as though they were flying in a wide arc over the city. The vivid lines of the map warped and contorted as the water undulated in the glass, but then settled and once again became distinct.

"How do you *do* that?" whispered Ash, full of wonder.

Paiscion smiled. "Just Essenfayle," he said crisply.

Ash looked down and made a face.

"Now, all of you, look carefully," commanded Paiscion. "Look there, where the river passes closest to the Dirgheon — an inlet — do you see?"

Sure enough, they saw a place where the river met a stream or perhaps a canal, its narrow sides straight and regular. It passed between a series of low buildings, then seemed to disappear beneath one of them.

"It's a canal," continued the Magruman, "a waterway that passes deep below the city and into the heart of the Dirgheon itself."

Simia leaned in to get a better look. "What's it for?"

"It serves two purposes. It forms a private route between the Dirgheon and the Temple of Isia, and it is also a gateway — a concealed entrance to the Dirgheon for those whom Thoth wishes to keep out of sight."

"Like who?"

"Like us," said Ash under his breath.

Paiscion nodded. "That tiny canal was the last many of our sisters and brothers saw of the world."

Sylas shifted uneasily. "And *that's* the way I have to go in?"

"As Ash said, the main entrance is watched over day and night by Thoth's personal guard. I'm afraid this is the only option."

"But surely there are still guards there?" said Simia, far from convinced.

"There are, but a much smaller garrison. Its reputation is such that they hardly expect anyone to try to enter it."

"Ending's Gate..." murmured Ash.

"Indeed," said Paiscion reluctantly, "some do call it that. But, as I say, the garrison that guards it is small. Small enough to be distracted, I would have thought. That will be my task."

"And if we get through this... this Ending's Gate...?" asked Sylas with increasing scepticism. "How will we find her?"

"*You* will find her, Sylas. Espasian has seen to that, whether he intended to or not."

Sylas looked confused. "How do you mean?"

Paiscion's eyes travelled to the bracelet on his wrist.

Sylas gasped. "Of course! The Merisi Band!" he said, turning it in his fingers. "It'll *tell me* when I'm near Naeo!"

He gazed down at the perfectly smooth band of silver and gold: it too was there for a reason.

Ash peered at it over Sylas's shoulder. "This could just work..."

"Yes, it might," said Paiscion soberly. "But the last challenge remains. Getting out... Anything I do to distract the guard will only raise the alarm — they're likely to double or treble their number by the time you're finding your way out. That needs some more thought..."

"And there's no way out other than the main entrance?" asked Ash.

Paiscion shook his head. "Two ways in, two ways out."

"What about those?" Sylas pointed to the dark windows near the top of the Dirgheon.

"Well, yes, they're openings, but they're no use. Once you're out on the terraces you can be seen for miles around; you'd never reach the bottom. No, that part of the plan is a problem."

He drew a long breath and once again flicked the side of the glass. The lines of the map blurred and began to move and then, slowly, new shapes began to form on the deck. It was a new map, showing corridors instead of streets, rooms in place of buildings. "Now not very much is known about the inside of the Dirgheon, but from what we have been told—"

"I know!" exclaimed Sylas suddenly. He was not watching this new display; he was staring straight past it and along the length of the *Windrush*.

The Magruman searched his face. "You know... *what?*"

"I know how to get out of the Dirgheon."

§

The sentry stood in the darkened hallway, guarding the ornate doors into the Apex Chamber. It had been bred for precisely this purpose, trained for it from birth. It held its gigantic frame perfectly still and to attention, even though there was no one to see it. Even its wolfish eyes were fixed and steady, staring down the long flight of stairs that led to the chamber, alert to the slightest movement. The only motion came from its ears, which turned slightly on the sides of its mongrel head, catching the faintest sounds from the chamber, listening, attentive.

Even for its Master, this had been a long and vicious interrogation. For hours it had heard the sobbing and pleading of the human child, the cries of pain from her father, the torment, the refusals. More than once its Master had lost his temper, filling the Apex Chamber with a terrifying roar of anger, or a scream of rage that rattled the doors on their hinges.

But now, and for some time, all had fallen quiet. Even the child had ceased her whimpering.

"Guard!"

Thoth's pervasive voice pierced the silence. Instantly the

guard turned and pulled the doors wide, squinting as it entered the relative light of the Apex Chamber. It stood proudly to attention, knowing that it made a splendid sight, its burnished armour glistening in the torchlight.

"Take her to Scarpia. I have what I need."

The voices of many echoed round the walls, whispering into the corners.

The guard strode forward and untied Naeo's bonds. It lifted her tiny limp body from the chair and carried her to the doors. It turned and bowed deeply, then stepped backwards.

In another moment, it was gone.

Bowe lay on the slab, watching the door close. He blinked away a tear of sweat and blood.

She was gone.

38

Magruman of the Suhl

"A Magruman of the Suhl commands the very skies; the ocean laps at their feet and the earth rumbles their name."

THE WATER WAS BLACK and flawless, smooth and heavy, like oil. It stretched around them like a vast mirror to the night sky, reflecting its dark, empty face. There were no waves, no ripples, just lazy undulations that licked the putrid banks. The surface never broke as it slid past the sides of the boat and rose in a silent wave behind the stern; instead it heaved and rolled reluctantly, making no sound.

Paiscion's black silhouette appeared briefly as they passed flickering lamps high on the shore and dimly lit windows in the eaves of buildings, but in moments it was gone, swallowed back into the night. The little boat glided unseen and unheard, borne forward on the silent wave.

"Where are we?" asked Sylas, turning to Simia's blackened face.

"Don't know," she whispered, "but it can't be far now."

"Unless he's missed it and we're on our way back to the mill," mumbled Ash somewhere in the darkness. "Wouldn't that be nice?"

As he spoke, a pair of lamps came into view. They swung on the icy breeze high above the river, illuminating Paiscion's figure in the prow of the boat. Gone was his neat, worn shirt and threadbare smoking jacket and in their place he wore a long, flowing black robe that fell to his ankles. The change suited him. This was his rightful dress, the clothing of a Magruman. He carried himself differently, seeming larger, more substantial.

He lowered himself to a crouch and turned towards them.

"Quiet," he murmured. "We're there."

The boat changed direction slightly and started to head in towards the shore a little beyond the lights. As they drew nearer and the lamplight faded behind them, they saw a low arch rising from the water. The stone was grimy, coated in filth, moss and lichen, giving the opening the appearance of a sewer. The stench of rank, stagnant water poured from the gaping blackness at its centre and the illusion would have been complete were it not for an overgrown carving in the keystone of the arch: two staring, empty eyes, framed by a skeletal face. The symbol of Thoth.

"Ending's Gate," whispered Ash, his pale face glowing in the darkness.

The boat surged on, towards the arch and the narrow inlet beyond. As they entered, a shudder ran down Sylas's spine, partly from the cold, partly the hateful smell, and in part because he knew that this — this place of decay and filth and darkness — was the last so many of the Suhl had seen of the outside world. The last thing that Naeo had seen. He felt her creeping horror as he saw the rotten stones passing overhead; her despair as the walls of the canal closed in. He became aware of Simia shivering next to him and slipped his hand into hers. She held on.

Paiscion guided the boat with such skill that it moved along the narrow channel without once striking the walls, making their passage almost silent. Soon the buildings of the city loomed around them and they looked nervously at the warren of brick, stone and timber for any sign of movement, but they quickly realised that there were no openings: no windows, no doors, no way for the occupants to witness what travelled on that narrow canal. It had been built to pass the city by.

They heard a clatter in one of the upstairs rooms and a chilling howl somewhere far away, but then all was quiet. The world was sleeping, unaware of their passing.

Paiscion turned. "Here," he breathed.

Ash reached out and caught hold of one of the grimy stones, drawing the boat into the side. It came to rest silently against a patch of moss. Paiscion picked his way carefully towards the stern.

"This is it," he whispered, tying the boat to a tangled root. "Here we must part. Simia, Ash — you must go there, between those two buildings." He pointed over the top of the canal wall to a narrow passageway leading off into the city. "Get ready. Sylas, we'll use the towpath."

Simia and Ash were already in motion, gathering large bundles from the bottom of the boat and heaving them up on to their shoulders. One by one they pulled themselves on to the towpath.

For a moment the four companions hesitated, looking from one to the other, wondering what to say, but finally Ash leaned forward, shook Paiscion by the hand and wished him good luck.

Sylas looked steadily at Simia, then pulled at one lapel of her oversized coat. "See you later," he said.

They embraced awkwardly. "Good luck," said Simia, her white teeth showing in an uneven grin.

"Not far now, my friend," said Ash, grasping Sylas's shoulder.

Sylas gave him a brave smile. When he turned back to Simia, she had already set out towards the passageway, her huge bundle swaying on her back. Ash set out after her, stooping forward under the weight of his pack.

Sylas watched them go, his hand sliding down to his belt where he had tucked his white feather. He slid his fingers over the silky fibres, drawing comfort from the sensation, from his memory of it. He looked up at Paiscion.

"OK," he said, in a voice that sounded stronger than he felt. "Let's go."

They walked swiftly down the towpath, Paiscion ahead, his black robe billowing about him. They reached the point where the canal narrowed and they had to press themselves close to the wall, their shoulders trailing through undergrowth and scraping the rotten stone beneath. Rounding a slight bend, Sylas cast an anxious eye along the canal, but still it extended far into the night. There was no sign of the entrance and, looking up, neither was there any sign of the Dirgheon itself, for all was shrouded in blackness. Nevertheless he could sense it now, looming above them.

Something made him look to his left, across to the buildings on the other side of the waterway and then up, over their roofs, to the sky above. It took him a moment for his eyes to adjust, but then he saw a towering white pillar; a massive structure that soared towards the heavens, so huge that they had been beneath it for some time without seeing it. The Temple of Isia. He steadied himself against the wall and gazed up at the smooth, tapering sides, his eyes following them until they disappeared into the darkness. But something else captured his attention. It was a feeling, a presence, the proximity of something.

"Sylas, come," hissed Paiscion. He had stopped some way ahead and was beckoning.

Sylas set out again, trailing his hand over the slimy wall to keep his balance, straining his eyes to see the narrowing ledge that was now all that remained of the towpath.

They hurried along it, struggling to keep their balance as they leapt over decayed, broken stones and forced their way through the succession of creeping vines and sprawling bushes that grew from every crack and fissure.

Suddenly Paiscion slowed his pace and pointed ahead.

There, not far ahead of them in the gloom, was a new pitch of blackness, a dark oblong of night that seemed deeper, emptier than all around it. It was an opening. A building rose above it giving the impression of a dead end, but there was no doubting the dark emptiness beneath its foundations. It led the canal underneath the sleeping city to the Dirgheon, which was now so near that Sylas could sense its colossal mass towering above him. He looked up and saw it at once: a vast pyramid, blacker than the deepest darkness of night, brooding over the sleeping city.

Paiscion drew him into a small alcove formed by two crooked, intersecting walls. "We must be careful. There's no telling what is in the shadows."

Sylas ventured a look round the corner, over the smooth, reflective surface of the waterway to the thick darkness of the opening. He wondered if, even now, something lurked within, watching them, waiting for them. He saw only blackness, but he felt a stirring of fear in the pit of his stomach.

Paiscion leaned down. "Don't be frightened," he said. He drew Sylas's chin up with his other hand so that their eyes met.

"You are far more prepared for them than they are for you."

Sylas nodded.

"Good," said the Magruman, his eyes sparkling in the darkness. "So you're ready?"

Sylas pushed back his shoulders. "As I'll ever be."

"Of course you're ready," said Paiscion, smiling broadly and holding out his hand.

Sylas reached out and shook it, holding his gaze. The Magruman's black eyes twinkled with excitement. "Now let us have a reckoning of our own."

With that, he stepped forward on to the towpath and raised his arms, opening his palms to the heavens. Sylas looked up at him from behind, his eyes tracing the powerful shoulders, the graceful stance, the long black robe, and he sensed Paiscion becoming one with everything around him: the water in the canal, the still air, the stones, the blackness. He seemed to become larger and yet at the same time less distinct, as though he was somehow folding into the night. His robe became more like a shadow, his outstretched arms like a trick of the half-light. Everything about them grew quieter, as if the night had become more intense.

Sylas looked about him, felt the change and knew that he was about to witness something miraculous.

Paiscion twisted his hands, then very slowly drew them together. At the same moment there was something like the rumble of distant thunder high above them, followed by a low, almost inaudible howl. Then, as his palms met, there was the briefest silence, before he drew a deep lungful of air and brought his arms swiftly down towards the ground.

There was a great explosion in the skies, like a clap of thunder, but louder, deeper. It made walls tremble, slates fall from roofs, timbers shift and creak. Even the stagnant waters danced and slapped the sides of the canal, as though trying to escape the deafening boom.

But it was too late, for no sooner had the explosion died away than a new, more terrifying sound pierced the night: a raging, devilish howl that seemed to descend from the bosom of the sky. A cry of doom. It echoed through every street, square and lane, rattling windows, flinging shutters wide, rousing the bleary-eyed occupants, chilling them to the bone. And as they staggered in nightgowns to their windows, as they peered fearfully into the night, half expecting to see some beast of legend devouring their city, they saw the unthinkable.

The skies were in motion towards a single point, the dark clouds rolling and churning as they converged. Their destination was a vast column of light and darkness that lay over the temple, shrouding it in a great downdraught of cloud, wind, rain, hail and lightning. It was as if the skies were draining away: being consumed by a gaping chasm in the earth, a breach in the world.

Sylas pressed his hands to his ears and watched in awe as clouds blasted from every passage and lane, borne on a vicious, freezing wind. Moments later they were engulfed and he was thrown against one wall of the alcove, drenched and battered by rain and hail. He looked past the Magruman to the vast pillar of cloud twisting and swirling above him. It was wild but at the same time beautiful, glowing with a lattice of lightning and explosions, its shifting surface reflecting the silver light of the moon, which had now been unveiled in some other part of the turbulent sky.

"Look!" bellowed Paiscion, turning and pointing along the canal. "There!"

Sylas peered round the corner at the dark opening. At first it seemed still, but then there was a movement in the shadows.

A figure became visible, one blacker than the night. It stepped forward until it was almost in the moonlight, then turned its head slowly upwards towards the pillar of cloud and light. Another figure appeared behind it on the narrow towpath, and another, barely visible in the darkness.

It had worked: the Ghor guards were on the move. The two at the rear were bent low, straining to see past the leader and up above the rooftops, but after only a few moments their curiosity seemed to get the better of them, for they stepped out of the opening, striding in unison along the towpath. Sylas recoiled as he watched their smooth, easy movements: their bodies carried low, their malformed, powerful legs bending the wrong way, ready to launch themselves forward, to pounce. They paused, exchanged looks and perhaps some unheard words, then in one motion they leapt their own height on to the canal wall. There they stood and watched for some moments, appearing to hesitate, but suddenly one of them broke from the group and disappeared down one of the dark, wind-blasted lanes. The others watched for a moment and then followed.

Paiscion leaned down and hissed in Sylas's ear. "Now! Go! And don't look back!"

Sylas looked up at the Magruman's face lit by flashes of lightning and the shifting light of the moon and for the first time he saw none of the gauntness, the weariness of before; instead he saw eyes burning with vigour and hope.

He took a gasp of the freezing air and sprinted down the towpath.

The lone Ghor ignored the distant rumble of thunder, continuing its endless patrol along the base of the Dirgheon, treading the same path that it had trodden thousands of times before. The stone plaza had been worn away by the incessant fall and scrape of generations of claws, forming a long, perfectly straight groove beside the bottom step of the pyramid. It moved silently over this familiar smoothness, its lithe limbs hardly straining as they paced out another empty night. Its head swung low between its shoulders, lulled by the pleasant sound of claws against stone and the swaying motion of its massive limbs, only occasionally turning to cast a look out across the deserted plaza.

When the great howl erupted from the sky, it reacted in an instant. Its body tensed and it crouched on its haunches, the tufts of matted hair bristling on its powerful neck and a low growl rising in the back of its throat. Its quick yellow eyes surveyed the plaza and then flicked skyward as the first lightning forked through the blackness. It saw the convergence of cloud, the great swirling vortex. Its ears pressed back against its head and a snarl curled its lips. Its eyes narrowed as it took first one step, then two out on to the plaza, leaving the well-worn pathway behind. Then, as an immense thunderclap shook the stone beneath its claws, it swung itself forward and began loping towards the pillar of cloud and fire.

Simia and Ash pressed themselves into the shadows and exchanged a triumphant look.

"Now!" whispered Simia.

Instantly both were in motion, sprinting for all they were worth across the exposed plaza, bent low beneath their huge packs. They dared not look behind them or to the side; instead they just fixed their eyes on the black stones, strained every muscle and ran for their lives. The packs were heavy — too heavy — making them stagger and sometimes stumble, but by some miracle they stayed on their feet. After what seemed far too long they neared the Dirgheon. With burning lungs, they looked up to see the first row of large black stones glistening in the moonlight. Above was another and another and another, rising steeply like a giant staircase into the night.

They came to a halt next to the bottom step, which rose above Simia's waist. They lowered their packs from their shoulders and craned their necks to peer into the darkness.

"There has to be an easier way," muttered Simia.

"New worlds don't come easy," said Ash with a grin. "Come on, I'll race you to the top."

39

Through Ending's Gate

"O what evil plight, what hellish fate
Attends those who pass through Ending's Gate?
What torments foul, what curse untold
Do those awful, deathly arms enfold?"

THE PORTCULLIS GATE CLANGED ominously as it swayed in the moaning wind. It spanned the top half of the passage ahead, its jagged teeth silhouetted against the orange, smoky torchlight. The canal disappeared into the darkness and Sylas paused, covering his nose against the foul stench and glancing anxiously about him. Nothing, just blackness. But, as he set out again, something crunched underfoot.

His heart quickened and he looked down.

The ground was strewn with something white, something that glowed dimly in the firelight. It was a carpet of bones, hundreds of them, piled one upon the other: some old, brittle and grinding to dust, others with flesh still clinging to them. For a brief, horrifying moment he thought he had stumbled upon the scene of a massacre, but then he saw that the bones were small and fine — the remains of chickens, pigs and sheep — all that was left of countless meals cast carelessly aside by the guards of Ending's Gate.

He drew his eyes away and looked up at the massive hulk of iron swinging lazily from the ceiling. This was the point of no return. He set his teeth, ducked his head beneath its arrowhead points and stepped inside.

"I knew you'd come."

The voice was deep and resonant, but it cut through the sound of the wind. The words echoed along the passageway making it impossible to tell where they had come from.

Sylas stopped breathing. His muscles tensed.

He looked frantically about him, trying to see any sign of movement, any shape in the shadows. Then he saw something. A tall, dark, human shape stepping from the shadows just a few paces ahead.

The figure reached up to its hood. When it fell away, it revealed a dark, chiselled, once youthful face marked by a terrible wound.

Espen.

Sylas froze, his instincts divided: to stay or to run.

His eyes passed quickly over Espen's face, taking in the piercing eyes, the creased, weathered skin, the livid gash. The Magruman bore an expression that was hard to discern, his brow furrowed, his eyes focused and urgent.

But Sylas thought he saw something else. A warmth that looked like relief.

"I know you don't trust me, but I can explain everything," said Espen, taking a step forward. "We must go somewhere safe."

"Here will have to do," said Sylas firmly, his voice shaking a little despite himself.

Espen was silent for a moment. He glanced back down the passageway.

"Very well," he said. "But the Ghor will soon find Paiscion in the eye of his storm, and then they will return. We must move on as soon as you're ready. Agreed?"

Sylas shifted nervously, unnerved that Espen knew about Paiscion. He nodded.

"Good," said the Magruman. "I am sorry you had to find out my lies. I wanted to tell you myself. The problem with discovering a lie is that you do not know where it ends — it infects everything, corrupts everything you know of a person." He fixed him with an earnest look. "Whatever you may think, Sylas, I have not betrayed you."

"How can you *say* that?" demanded Sylas, a little louder than he intended. "What about Bayleon?"

Espen frowned. "That was regrettable, but he is safe enough."

"*Regrettable?* How can you—"

"Sylas, you *must* let me explain myself — explain my lies. Then you can decide whether or not to trust me. Is that fair?"

Sylas looked at him with narrow eyes. He shrugged.

"I told you that I was captured by the Ghor after the Reckoning, but that I escaped on to the Barrens. Do you remember?"

He nodded.

"That was a lie. I was unconscious when they finally took me from the battlefield, and when I woke, I was here, in the Dirgheon. I lied too when I told you that I went to the Other in the hope that there might be some truth in the Glimmer Myth. I *knew* that the Glimmer Myth was true and I *knew* that our salvation depended on it."

He fell silent, as if waiting for Sylas to respond, but the boy looked at him blankly.

"It was Naeo, Sylas... Your Glimmer. You should have seen her at the Reckoning! Such a natural mastery of Essenfayle... There *had* to be something special about her. As soon as I saw her, I thought of Merisu's poem, of the Glimmer Myth. She had to be the one!"

Sylas eyed him carefully. "So you've known since the Reckoning?"

Espen nodded. "But so has Thoth. He had no idea what her power might mean, but he understood that it was extraordinary and dangerous. I knew that she wouldn't be safe for long. On the one hand she was enticing to Thoth, for he might be able to learn from her, but on the other she was a threat." He drew a deep breath. "So, I decided I had to tell Thoth something that would make her more enticing than threatening; too valuable to be killed."

Sylas's eyes widened. "You told him about the myth?"

Espen nodded. "I told him about the myth and I told him that if Naeo was capable of fulfilling all that it foretold, then her Glimmer was the key. I told him that you must exist, and that if anyone would know who you were, it would be the Merisi."

"But why tell him so much?" asked Sylas, confused. "Why not just tell him that Naeo was — I don't know — a great magician, and leave it at that?"

"Because he already knew better, Sylas. This was no girl who had mastered Essenfayle — she was something altogether different. And also because this way I thought I might just get him to *help* me — to help us all."

"How?"

"By allowing me to bring you together."

Sylas frowned. "But why would he do that?"

"For your power. Either to use it, or if it proved impossible to harness, to put it beyond our reach. I told him that when Naeo grew a little older I would teach her how to raise the Passing Bell so that you could be summoned. I told him that, if he let me travel between the worlds over that time, I would find the Merisi and then you, and ensure that you were prepared for the journey. Then, when you were both ready, Naeo would summon you and I would guide you to the Dirgheon to deliver you into his hands. I told him that I would do all this if he would let all three of us live."

"And he fell for that?"

"Not quite. As I suspected, the thought of having both Naeo and you was too much for him to resist. But he had two problems: first, he knew that I was not to be trusted, and second, he knew that whatever this power was, it was likely to be dangerous. He considered my proposal for several days and finally he summoned me…"

He shot an anxious glance past Sylas to the distant opening of the tunnel. Sylas turned and squinted, finding it hard to see anything through the murk. There was a flash of lightning, followed by another. In that momentary light he saw a slight movement, a dark shape shifting next to the canal wall.

Then he saw two and then three stooping figures.

"They're coming back," he said, turning to Espen.

Espen looked at him anxiously. "Will you follow me?" he asked urgently.

Sylas hesitated, scrutinising Espen's open face. "I will. But I want to hear more."

Espen grasped his shoulder. "As we run!"

He whirled about and took three or four paces along the towpath, paused to make sure that Sylas was following, then darted into an opening in the wall. Sylas hesitated for a moment, and then followed.

Inside, the darkness was even more complete than in the tunnel: there was no glow from the moon, no lightning, no torches but one that flickered in the distance, somewhere high above them.

"There's a staircase ahead of us," hissed Espen. "It'll take us to the first level."

They began climbing a steep flight of stone steps, bracing themselves against the dank walls.

"They were coming back to lower the portcullis," said Espen when they were at a safe distance. "You won't be able to get out through Ending's Gate. We'll have to think of another way."

"We've taken care of it."

Espen glanced over his shoulder. "You have? How do—"

"I'll tell you when I'm ready," interrupted Sylas. "Tell me about your meeting with Thoth."

The Magruman smiled, as if proud of Sylas's new confidence, then continued to climb.

"Thoth is known to enjoy his games," he whispered as he went, "and the crueller and more merciless they are, the more amusing he finds them. Scarpia, one of his Magrumen, came up with a scheme that seemed to fulfil his every wish: it would allow me the freedom to help him, but keep me under his control; it would allow you to reach Naeo if that was your destiny, but if not, it would ensure that you could be no threat to him; and, best of all, it would become a pleasant diversion for him — a game of cat and mouse."

"And let me guess... I'm supposed to be the mouse?"

Espen turned and smiled. "You're *supposed* to be, yes, though it hasn't worked out that way."

He continued to climb and, as they were drawing near the torchlight at the top, Espen lowered his voice to a whisper.

"He told me that I could do as I proposed, but that there were two conditions. The first was that I would tell no one the truth about what I was doing; if I did, it would cost Naeo her life. That was fine, as I had no intention of leading the Ghor to any of my brethren, and in any case, I wasn't sure that anyone would believe me."

He reached the top step and raised his finger to his lips. He braced himself, then peered round the corner. The long, dark corridor extended both ways as far as the eye could see, lit only by an occasional flame. There was no sign of movement, no sound but the occasional spit of wax and drip of water.

"Paiscion is doing a fine job," he whispered. "The guards must have been summoned to the defences. Come — and keep an eye out behind us."

They stepped out into the corridor. A stale wind blew along its length, making Espen's cloak fly up behind him. It carried a new, appalling smell: the scent of unwashed bodies, open sewers, disease. Sylas put his hand over his mouth and nose and ran to keep up with Espen.

"What was his other condition?" he murmured.

"One that I didn't expect," said Espen ruefully. "He told me that from the moment I told him of your identity — which had to be before the ringing of the bell — you would be treated by him and his forces as a threat; we would both be tracked and hunted as his enemy, and if we were found, we would be killed. He would send his Ghor and his Ghorhund, his Magrumen and his Slithen — anything he chose. It was a great novelty for him: he would test the foulest of his fiends against us and be sure of the outcome. If I kept you safe, you would be delivered to him; if I failed, we would be killed, and he would have no more to fear from you, me or the Glimmer Myth. What's more, he was placing me in an impossible position: if I refused, Naeo and I would be executed anyway; if I agreed, I would have no quarter to raise a plot against him, for I would only expose Naeo and anyone we met to terrible danger."

Sylas felt a creeping realisation. "Like everyone at Meander Mill..." he murmured.

Espen turned and met his eyes. "I had no way of knowing, Sylas," he said. "I was right behind you, but I couldn't have known that Filimaya would hear the bell, or that Simia would guide you so skilfully and fearlessly across town. And, once you were inside the mill, I was lost: I had to know what was to become of you, but I didn't dare enter the mill or meet with any of the Suhl. No, I realised that I had to find a way to spy on you, which was a problem: only a Slithen could scale the walls of the mill, and of all the foul beasts in Thoth's legions, the Slithen are the last to trust. So I paid one I knew, one I thought too stupid to know your value, to think of betraying me. But I was unlucky: he overheard your plans, which he knew would be valuable information to the right people. And, to make matters worse, he saw the Merisi Band around your wrist. He thought there would be a bounty on your head — a bounty far greater than I was able to pay."

As they walked along the corridor, Sylas thought through everything Espen had told him — it was labyrinthine and hard to grasp, but it did seem to make some kind of sense.

Then something occurred to him.

"You've been going through to the Other — working on this — *for years?*"

Espen nodded without looking back.

"So... when did you first go?"

Espen slowed to a stop, then turned. "Just after the Reckoning... and just before your mother was taken to hospital."

"So did you have something to do with—"

"It was the only way to keep her safe, Sylas," said Espen softly. "We knew the dangers of the pact with Thoth — dangers not only to you and Naeo, but to those you love. Given your mother's condition — given her connection to this world — she too would have been—"

"...a threat," murmured Sylas.

Espen reached out and squeezed his shoulder. "So now you see."

Sylas nodded slowly, still trying to take it all in.

Espen turned and stepped out down the corridor. "Come on, we have little time."

Sylas took a lungful of the stale air and followed.

They had begun to pass a series of large openings set far back into the stone walls, each closed off by stout iron doors riddled with strengthening rivets and held firmly in place by a giant bolt and padlock. A great overhang of dusty cobwebs spanned the doorways, which gave the impression that they had not been disturbed for quite some time. At first Sylas had passed them by with little interest, far too intrigued by what Espen was telling him, but the more of them he saw, the more interested he became. Then, as the last of Espen's words faded away, he heard something. It sounded just like the scrape of stone against stone. A whispered voice.

It was coming from behind one of the doors.

He stopped. "What *are* these?"

Espen turned and followed Sylas's gaze. "Cells," he said.

"Who's inside?"

The Magruman drew in a long breath. "Our brethren."

Sylas's eyes moved from the long procession of doors to the crack beneath the one at his side. He saw a slight movement inside.

"The *Suhl*," whispered Sylas.

"And anyone who helped us — if they survived the Undoing, that is. Thousands of them. No one knows how many."

A chill passed over Sylas. This was where the smell had been coming from: from people — hordes of silent, despairing people — locked in tiny filthy cells. He thought of the Suhl as Simia and Filimaya had described them: a gentle, peaceful people. That they had been brought to this seemed unthinkable. An overwhelming sadness seemed to seep from the walls and haunt the passageway.

"We have to get them out," said Sylas firmly.

"I know. But not now, Sylas," reasoned Espen. "Your priority has to be Naeo — everything depends on you and her."

Again Sylas saw movement underneath the door.

"But what if—"

"Sylas," interjected Espen sadly, "it can't be done. Just look."

He pointed along the passageway ahead of them. The procession of flickering torches disappeared into the distance and between them countless doors punctuated the damp walls.

"And there are at least a hundred corridors just like this!"

Sylas stared hopelessly, shaking his head. He turned back to the crack beneath the door and saw that the shadow had gone.

"There must be a way…" he said.

"There is," said Espen, taking him by the shoulders and looking earnestly into his eyes. "Find Naeo. *That's* our only hope."

Sylas held his gaze for a moment and then, reluctantly, he nodded.

"Come," said the Magruman, guiding Sylas in front of him.

They continued down the corridor, soon leaving the door and its occupants far behind them. They walked in silence, their eyes lowered, trying not to focus on the doorways that they passed, or the occasional movements beneath them. Sometimes Sylas thought he heard a cough or a shuffle or a whisper, but otherwise the silence was oppressive — somehow far more horrifying than groans or cries for help. It was the sound of defeat, of lost hope.

They walked for what seemed an age, passing an endless

parade of grim, grey-faced doors. Every once in a while a dark passageway or staircase led off to one side, some climbing towards distant lamplight, others descending into the deeper, darker bowels of the building, hinting of more misery and despair beyond. A continual flow of stale air emerged from these depths and flowed along the corridor, carrying upon it the smell of sweat and sewage and decay.

Suddenly Sylas stopped. He winced and clasped his wrist and the Merisi Band.

"It's hurting," he whispered.

"So it works..." said Espen, seeming pleased. He pointed ahead of them to an opening off the passageway that was broader and darker than the doors. "That's the staircase. Her cell is directly above us, one flight up."

Moments later they turned into the opening, Sylas first. He looked up to see a towering flight of steps, lit by a single distant torch at its very top. He could just make out two large wooden doors next to it, glistening with brass fittings. Rubbing his wrist in an attempt to ease the pain, he began to climb.

He knew that the end of his journey was drawing near and he began to feel stirrings of excitement and apprehension, but with every step, he also felt a gathering fear at the prospect of meeting Naeo: at the thought that there, beyond those doors, was his Glimmer. Was it really possible that there, just a few paces ahead, he would find... what...? His other self?

His heart quickened and he felt sweat running from his brow. He tried to concentrate, to focus on what had brought him here: everything that Mr Zhi and Fathray had revealed to him. He thought about the passages he had read in the Samarok, about the meaning of his name, about all that Espen had now explained. But for some reason he still felt uneasy, as though he had not yet heard the whole truth. As they mounted the last few steps, his nerves were on edge — still, something seemed wrong.

They were now nearing the doors and, as he looked up, Sylas saw that they were ornately carved with shapes and patterns, most of which were inset with bronze. They seemed oddly out of place after the squalor of the dungeons.

"Espen?" he whispered.

"Yes?"

"You never explained why you're here." Sylas slowed and turned. "Why *are* you here? At the Dirgheon?"

Espen muttered something under his breath, stepped past him and turned one of the large bronze handles. There was a loud clunk as the bolt slid across and then it swung open.

What lay beyond was not a dark, dingy corridor or a procession of grey cell doors; it was a vast hall, lit brightly by hundreds of oil lamps mounted high on the walls, held in glistening gold brackets. The doors they had entered were at one end of the chamber, so they could see its full splendour: its towering, vaulted ceiling; its polished marble floor; and covering the expanse of grey stone walls, long lines of bookshelves crammed with tens of thousands of books. Above them enormous dramatic oil paintings spanned huge sections of the hall, each the height of several men. Every one depicted a sprawling scene: vast armies battling on verdant plains, deserts and mountainsides; fleets of galleons on calamitous seas beneath whirlwinds and lightning and evil skies; pyramids like those of the ancients — just like those of the empires of Egypt — amid oceans of dust and fire.

But one of them drew Sylas's eye: the one nearest to them, at the very end of the hall. It was a vivid, heroic picture of a single figure on a headland, a bay spread out below him and on the sands, thousands of tiny figures beset on all sides by mounting waves, downpours of rock and streams of fire. Despite all these horrors, none of them were in flight, for these wretched people were sinking, consumed by the sand, some bound by their ankles, others already gripped to their waists or their chests.

Sylas covered his mouth and drew his eyes away. "The Reckoning..." he murmured.

Suddenly a searing pain sliced through his wrist making him cry out.

The double doors at the far end of the hall swung open. Three dark, cloaked figures stepped out of the shadows, dragging with them flailing, struggling prisoners.

Sylas recognised two of the captives straight away.

Simia and Ash.

He felt an overwhelming, crushing panic. His throat closed. The air was squeezed from his lungs.

Slowly he turned to Espen. His lips parted but he could not speak.

Espen looked down at him. There was no surprise on his face. No dismay. He glanced at the other end of the hall, but made no attempt to run.

Sylas began to back away towards the door. "No!" he cried.

Suddenly Espen knelt, reached out and grasped him tightly by the shoulders.

"It was the only way to keep Naeo alive!"

Sylas's eyes began to fill with tears: tears of rage and despair.

"You led me to them!" he muttered between clenched teeth. "You *knew* about Simia and Ash!"

The Magruman shook him. "No one else matters now," he said in a voice charged with emotion. "No one but you and Naeo."

With that, he took Sylas roughly by the collar and began dragging him down the hall.

40

Where None
Have Gone

"Now, rise: fear not where none have gone,
For then, at last, we may be one."

IT FELT LIKE THE world was ending. Simia had been right all along. He tried to fight back, but it was hopeless: Espen was far too strong. Sylas looked back at his friends and saw that they too were trying to pull away from their captors, but their attempts were just as futile. As he watched, a long line of Ghor entered from behind them and now stood guarding their only exit.

"No others?"

The surprisingly soft, feminine voice came from beneath the hood of one of the three black figures, the one holding Simia.

"None," replied Espen, his voice suddenly gruff and harsh.

"Was there trouble?"

"He suspected nothing," said Espen.

"Traitor!" shrieked Simia, pulling even harder to free herself. Her face was pale with fury. "I knew you were a traitor!"

"Quiet, child," purred the hooded Magruman. "You didn't

seriously expect to succeed, did you? One puny boy and those flimsy contraptions?" She cackled, sneering at Ash. "Pitiful! You're all pitiful."

She reached up and pulled back her hood, revealing her beautiful feline face, proud arching eyebrows and smooth, dark complexion. It was Scarpia.

The other Magrumen immediately did the same: one a narrow-faced woman, with unnervingly pale skin and hair, and eyebrows that were so blonde that she could have been albino; the other a man, older than the others, with curls of greying hair and taut, angular features.

But Sylas took little interest in the Magrumen, for his eyes were now fixed on the third of the captives. The closer they drew to one another, the more the pain raged in his wrist, the more certain he became.

It was Naeo.

She did not speak or make a sound, but there was something about the way she moved, the shape of her face, the way she fought with her tormentor as he fought with his. But it was more than that: something deeper and more primal. It was a sense he had that this was not a person at all — not in the way he knew people to be. As he drew closer and saw that she too was looking at him, he knew that she was thinking the same thoughts.

As he squinted to take in her features, she squinted to take in his.

As he drew in a gasp of air, so did she.

And there was something more powerful than all of this: when their eyes met, he felt his fear leaving him. In place of the confusion and doubt he had felt for days — perhaps longer — he felt a new certainty, and with it, a strange stirring of joy. Joy like he had felt in the forest, standing in the path of the Passing Bell.

Suddenly Espen stopped just a few paces short of Scarpia. She extended a long, elegant arm from beneath her cloak, her fingers reaching for Sylas's collar. He was just out of reach.

There was a silence: a long, unexpected silence.

Scarpia shifted nervously and tilted her head questioningly to one side.

Sylas raised his eyes to Espen's face. The Magruman looked down and for a moment he smiled an open, unguarded smile.

"Go to Naeo!" he cried. "Now!"

In one motion he released Sylas's collar and threw his arms in the air. Instantly a roar rose from somewhere deep in the Dirgheon, somewhere in the tunnels and passageways far below. As he threw his hands forward, his features contorted with the effort. Scarpia raised a hand as though to defend herself, but it was too late. A grating, vicious scream erupted from the staircase behind him and, with a thunderous bang, the doors flew wide, splintering against the walls.

The entire hall shook as a great wind surged along its length, ripping books from the shelves and hurling them high into the air, striking the Magrumen and the Ghor with devastating force. In seconds it filled the room with the foul stink of the bowels of the Dirgheon, the filth and squalor of a thousand forgotten souls, the rot of years of neglect. It was as though the imprisoned masses had suddenly broken their silence and exhaled a cry of rage.

The prisoners were ripped free of their captors and sent sprawling towards the far end of the hall. The Ghor were lifted bodily into the air and hurled against the walls to the sound of cracking skulls and breaking bones.

Only the three Magrumen remained standing, their black cloaks flying around them as the pestilent wind struggled in vain to gather them up. Even as it struck, their arms were rising in unison, their faces set, their eyes focused on Espen.

To Sylas, this was all a distant blur, for his eyes were fixed on Naeo.

He could see her, there, just beyond the billowing cloaks of the Magrumen. She was halfway to her feet now, drawing herself away from the twisted limbs of one of the guards, her eyes on Sylas; like him, throwing herself forward, half leaping, half sliding towards him.

In the midst of the wild fury of the wind and the cries and the screams, Sylas felt an astonishing stillness: a stillness born of certainty — certainty that they would meet, that they were meant to meet, that it had always been intended. His eyes passed over her blonde hair, her intense blue eyes, the features he now remembered from his dreams, the features he saw to be so similar to his own.

He was her. She was him.

They were the same.

The pain in his wrist had become unbearable: no longer an ache or a stabbing pang, but a constant, searing fire that consumed his wrist, his hand, his arm. And when he looked down, he saw that the Merisi Band was aflame, its shining surface glowing with a bright light of its own, its shape now indistinct, in motion. But it was not the flickering motion of fire, it was the shimmer and ripple of molten metal.

He sensed that Naeo was now close and despite his pain he looked up and saw her just an arm's reach away. Instinctively he held out his burning hand, his fingers searching for hers. In the same instant she reached out for him, her face straining, her body stretched to its limit.

Their hands met. Their fingers curled. And they held on.

Despite the desperate scene, despite the significance of the act, it felt natural — almost ordinary — like clasping his own hands or touching his own face. Yet there was something beyond the physical touch, something in his heart and his mind. It was like a great surge of energy, not the kind that moves limbs or courses through veins, but a feeling, a knowledge of completeness. Of strength.

Something strange started to happen to the Merisi Band. From the liquid metal rose a silvery vapour: barely visible trails that twirled and twisted in the air, forming an ethereal mist. It was entirely unmolested by the wind: instead it first rose, then turned in the air and drifted down to Naeo's wrist. She and Sylas watched entranced as the vapour slid beneath her arm, then around, meeting itself to form a perfect ring — a band of its own. Even as they watched, it became more distinct and solid. The trace of silver became opaque and began to reflect the light; a true silver band began to form. And when Sylas looked to his wrist, the Merisi Band had changed, no longer broad but fine and narrow; no longer silver and gold but gold alone.

A calamitous crash made them lift their eyes. There they saw a scene of desperate battle: thousands of books flying from the shelves on both sides of the hall and slamming together in mid-air; Espen, standing alone in their midst, directing the winds, somehow managing to stop the great storm of books from striking him; staggering now, beginning to fall; Simia and Ash running towards him hand in hand, bending low, but assailed by the flying books; Simia clasping her shoulder, looking directly at Sylas, screaming something.

He was already in motion, rising and launching himself towards his friends. He did not turn to look for Naeo; he knew that she was at his side. He felt her there. As soon as they were on their feet, they were met by a hail of books that hurtled towards them from the shelves, scything, spinning, slicing through the air.

Sylas threw his hands up to protect himself and closed his eyes.

To his surprise, he felt nothing. None of the books found their mark. He looked about him and saw that they were falling out of the air as if they had met an invisible barrier. He lowered his hand a little and the books flew on. He raised it again, and abruptly they faltered and crashed to the floor.

Could it be that he was doing this? *They* were doing this?

Ash and Simia drew close to them and they moved forward as one, somehow protected amid the torrent of books. Moments later they were gathering around Espen. He was no longer on his feet, but on one knee, his bloodied hands still raised in an attempt to control the winds. He seemed near defeat: his tunic had been torn to reveal an open wound in his chest; his scarred face was streaked with sweat and blood, drawn with agony. Sylas instinctively moved to help him, leaning down to lift him by the shoulder.

Simia shouted again.

He saw her panicked face and followed her eyes to the three Magrumen. To his horror they were walking swiftly towards them, their hands sweeping before them as they hurled new missiles through the air: massive, tumbling, black shapes. It was the broken bodies of the Ghor, tossed aloft by some horrifying force, spinning and twisting as they flew; some still conscious, snarling wildly and gnashing their fearsome teeth.

Sylas let go of Espen's shoulder and stood to his full height, aware of Naeo at his shoulder. They did not flinch or hesitate: they raised their arms towards the wretched bodies of the Ghor and opened their palms. For a moment there was a complete silence. The wind ceased howling and the books and the guards hung in the air as though time itself had stopped.

Simia and Ash glanced at one another; the Magrumen shifted nervously; Espen turned his bloodied face up to Sylas and Naeo, and the trace of a smile creased his lips.

Then, as they dropped their arms, everything tumbled to the floor: the books, the Ghor, the debris, all landed with an ear-splitting crash on the marble.

Another moment of stillness followed. The last pieces of torn parchment fluttered to the ground and Scarpia and the Magrumen glanced at one another uncertainly; Simia raised her hand to her mouth; Espen rose slowly to his feet.

Then two things happened at once. The Magrumen moved in perfect unison, extending their hands outwards over the marble floor, and Sylas and Naeo lifted their arms high above their heads.

Simia looked down at the patchwork of marble beneath her feet, wondering what new horror to expect. She caught her breath. The joins between the stone tiles had begun to blur and merge, the white ones starting to seep into the black. They were becoming fluid: melting into one another. The entire floor around them seemed to be in motion, becoming something it should not be – could not be. She felt the grip of panic as her feet became unsteady and she saw white and black ooze over her shoes.

"Sylas! Do something!" she cried.

"They *are* doing something!" shouted Ash. "Look!"

She looked up to the vaulted ceiling and recoiled.

The entire edifice was alive with fire.

Long, snaking tendrils of flame grew from the oil lamps on both sides of the hall, worming and twisting around one another, forming a breathtaking, living mesh of fire. They looped and spiralled beneath and over each other, forming an impossible knot of golden, flickering flame. This blistering weave of heat and light began falling slowly towards the Magrumen – drifting relentlessly towards the end of the hall. As it passed the oil paintings, fingers of flame reached out and touched the canvases, setting them instantly alight, forming pools of fire that rippled outwards towards the frames, feeding the inferno. The rumble became a roar. One of the Magrumen — the old man — changed his stance and raised his arms towards the approaching hellfire, seeking to fend it off. Instantly Naeo reacted, pointing a finger in his direction and, at the same moment, tendrils of fire wound round each other and launched at him, striking him roundly in the chest.

His face bore a look of surprise and horror. His cloak burst into flames, engulfing him in a searing ball of fire. A chilling scream echoed through the hall and suddenly they saw his burning figure falling through the open doors at the rear.

Scarpia and the other Magruman looked around, surprised, even frightened. They glanced up to the great web of fire now just above their heads, hesitated, then turned to Sylas and Naeo. They seemed unsure where to direct their attentions. They began to back away towards the doors, keeping their hands raised to protect themselves.

Their retreat came too late.

A furious wind rose from behind Sylas and Naeo, howling through the splintered doors, screaming into the void. It blasted along the hall, gathering pace as it went, tearing at the walls, clawing at the ceiling. It lifted the burning paintings and hurled them forward, flipping them end over end towards the Magrumen, spinning like murderous Catherine wheels, spitting a shower of sparks, smoke and flame.

Scarpia's eyes widened. She raised her arms, but as she did so, the wind breathed into the lattice of fire, giving it new, terrifying energy. It flared as bright as a sun and bellowed a thunderous battle cry, then surged forward with horrifying force, closing in

492

upon its prey. Scarpia's sleeves burst into flames and with a shriek of pain she gathered her arms to her chest, charging towards the doors that were all too far away. The other Magruman threw herself to the floor, clawing hand over fist to the opening, but before she reached it the fiery web suddenly opened wide like a grasping claw, then collapsed into a fist of fire, engulfing them both. There were desperate screams and a calamitous crash as the burning paintings whipped into the heart of the flames, smashing into the floor and wall beyond.

The blast of heat subsided; the final traces of the lattice thinned and disappeared into smoke. All that remained was a wall of leaping flames and the crackle and roar of the settling fire.

Sylas and Naeo suddenly seemed smaller, almost frail. Children once again.

Their arms wavered in the air and fell slowly to their sides; their feet shifted uncertainly in the ooze and then, as if not knowing what else to do, they turned to each other.

They gazed at one another for a moment and then, silhouetted against the mounting flames, they clasped hands.

41

From the Darkness

"From the darkness the sun will rise,
and lay before it a carpet of light."

FOR A MOMENT EVERYONE stared at the raging fire, trying to take
in what had just happened. Their eyes passed over the splintered
remains of bookshelves, the scattered books and pictures, the
orange flames licking up the walls and the great plumes of black
smoke climbing rapidly towards the vaulted ceiling.

Finally Sylas turned his pale face to his friends. "Are you all
right?" he asked in a husky voice.

Espen raised his bloodied face and answered with a broad
smile. Simia and Ash looked at Sylas with a mixture of wonder
and fear.

"We're... fine," said Simia hesitantly. "You?"

"Yes, I think I'm OK," he said, surprised. The trace of a smile
creased his lips. "Did you finish? Before they took you?"

"Just about," she said.

She shifted her gaze to take a proper look at Naeo. It was
bewildering: the face she knew so well, Sylas's face, yet changed,
different, somehow more feminine and delicate, her expressions

quicker and sharper. Naeo met her eyes for a moment and then, looking unsure of herself, she glanced away, moving a little closer to Sylas. The two of them stood easily together, shoulder to shoulder, relaxed with each other. Neither looked at nor spoke to the other, but somehow they responded, seeming to know one another's mind.

"We need to get to the Apex Chamber," said Simia. "To the opening on the south side."

"Well... I hope you have a plan," panted Espen doubtfully. "There's no way down from—"

"We do," she interjected, rather more harshly than she intended.

Espen raised an eyebrow and thought for a moment. "I know how to reach it. This is the Medial Chamber – it leads to all parts of the Dirgheon. There are staircases behind the shelves – one of them should take us there, though I'm not sure which..."

"Scarpia took me that way once."

It was Naeo's voice. She spoke more softly than Sylas and she had a different accent, but her voice was uncannily similar: the tone, the cadence, the way she formed the words – all were the same.

"You've *been* there?" asked Simia.

"I've just come from there," said Naeo. She glanced at Sylas. "I left my father—"

"*Bowe?*" exclaimed Ash, feeling a surge of renewed hope for their friend.

Naeo nodded. "He was..." Her voice faltered. "He was barely alive."

"Then show us the way," said Ash with new urgency.

She pointed to the large bookcases now bearing just a meagre scattering of books. They made their way across the hall through the strange black and white ooze, shaking and stamping the peculiar liquid stone from their shoes. When they reached the bookshelves, Espen and Naeo moved along them, investigating each one, searching for the one that formed a concealed entrance. But, despite pulling and heaving and shifting books, the shelves seemed to hold firm. They looked at each other anxiously and walked back to the end of the hall, trying each in turn.

Sylas tried some as well, but had no more luck. He began pulling out some of the books, wondering if they concealed a secret latch or lever of some kind. None seemed to hide anything, but soon he became distracted by the volumes themselves, which looked very different from the leather-bound books he had seen in the Den of Scribes or on the *Windrush*. The covers were shiny and colourful and the text seemed neat and regular: printed rather than written. He tilted his head and looked at some of the titles: *The Age of Industry* read one; *Man and Machine* read another. He felt the hairs begin to rise on his neck.

These were books of his own world.

His eyes came to rest on a small group of books that still lay undisturbed on the shelf. He read the titles under his breath:

"*The Encyclopaedia of Weaponry... Technology of Warfare... Science and Supremacy...*"

He gathered one of them off the shelf and looked through it, turning to page after page of photographs and diagrams depicting engines, factories, cars, guns, planes, missiles... He raised his eyes and looked about him... to the other shelves. He saw legions of books about technology, industry, weapons and war. This was not a hall, but a library — a collection of knowledge taken from his own world. The wrong kind of knowledge.

"They're all about science and war..." he murmured. "They're *learning* from us..."

He felt a new dread. He knew instinctively that these books had no place here; that however they had been brought here, whatever their purpose, they were not to be used for good. Gathering his strength, he did something he would never have dreamt of doing before — he hurled the pile of books into the fire.

Behind him Naeo pushed against one of the bookshelves. There was a loud click. Instantly it sprang back and swung open, a rush of cool air entering the hall. They all gathered around to peer into the dark passageway beyond.

Espen leaned cautiously into the blackness. "This is it," he said. "Let's go."

He led the way into the shadows, taking just a few paces before beginning to climb a steep, spiralling stone staircase. Simia and Ash set out after him, followed by Sylas and Naeo, who kept an eye out behind.

The cool of the stone stairwell was pleasant after the hall's searing heat, but once they had left the doorway behind, the darkness was almost absolute. They found themselves searching the shadows for signs of movement, their eyes lingering on every dark shape, every misshapen step and uneven wall. Several times Sylas and Naeo thought they heard footsteps below them and they both stopped, holding their breath, straining to listen. Each time they paused for a few seconds until they were sure that it was nothing and then, without saying anything to the other, continued the climb. Sylas had the strange sense that Naeo was thinking the same thing at the same instant, that as he resolved to continue, she would be at his side. It was peculiar, but at the same time comforting.

The staircase was behaving like a giant chimney, drawing smoke from the inferno below up into the cooler air above. It was thick and acrid and it quickly started to sting their eyes and fill their lungs, making them cough and splutter. Espen continued to lead, climbing with remarkable speed, but his breathing was heavy and laboured and Simia saw him wince a number of times, as if racked with pain.

A dim glow appeared above them and moments later they saw the top step. A large dark hallway extended beyond, flanked by two faceless statues, their arms clasped to their chests. They stepped into the open space and saw the source of the light: a long, vertical crack at the far end of the hallway — a gap between two doors.

They all paused for a moment, bending low to take in gasps of clean air, and then Espen walked up to the doors. Crouching low, he pressed his hands to the wood, listening for a moment before putting his eye to the light.

The others stayed at the top of the steps, trying not to cough, getting their breath back.

For some moments the Magruman peered silently into the room beyond. Finally he rose to his full height and glanced over his shoulder.

"We seem to be in luck," he whispered. "There's no one here."

Naeo stepped forward. "No one?"

"I don't think so." He drew a wheezing breath and pushed on the doors.

They squinted into the light. As their eyes became accustomed, they saw a vast square chamber — several times larger than the hall. It was lit by huge flickering flames that rose from four giant urns of oil, one in each corner. There was an opening in the centre of each wall, which provided enticing views of the night sky beyond — a promise of escape. But their eyes were drawn to the strange splendour of the room: floors decked with red carpets and animal skins, strewn with seats and pillows of glittering gold fabric; in the centre a broad circular pool of still black fluid, accessed by white marble steps; walls covered with tapestries depicting scenes of magic and battle.

The towering ceiling was painted with a host of murals, each telling its own story: peoples trekking across deserts and mountains; feasts and banquets attended by strange, unnatural beasts; priests chanting incantations in a magic circle; maps of castles and great cities; yet more battles; yet more magic.

But one of these pictures, the one in the very centre of the ceiling, dominated all others. A vast, empty, skeletal face depicted in bland silvers and greys. The terrifying visage of Thoth glowered down at the entire chamber, giving the fugitives the sense that he was watching them even as they hesitated in the threshold, mocking their futile attempt at escape, daring them to pass.

"Follow me," said Espen firmly.

He led them over the soft carpets and skins. They glanced in all directions, checking every opening, every corner, every hanging. All was eerily still except for thin, delicate drapes gathered at the sides of the openings, flowing and fluttering on a gentle breeze. They felt fresh, clean air blowing across the room, offering a tantalising taste of the open night beyond.

Yet escape still seemed far away, for between them and the world outside lay the trappings of luxury, privilege and power: thick incense on the air; couches of velvet and gold; pitchers and goblets studded with jewels; silver-clad volumes stacked neatly on shelves; ancient maps laid open on tables of polished wood; a beautiful, ornate cello laid on a golden stand... a stone table, decorated with intricate red engravings, golden chains and manacles...

"That's where my father was!" hissed Naeo, instinctively moving towards it.

Espen took hold of her shoulders. "It could be a trap!"

"But I have to find him!" protested Naeo. "We can't leave without him!"

"You *must* leave without him. We don't know where he is, and soon this place will be swarming with guards."

She struggled against him.

"Naeo! His only hope is that you escape! *Think!* He wouldn't want you to be captured again. You can't risk that! Not now that you've finally found Sylas!"

She hesitated, tears welling in her eyes. The Magruman drew her away as gently as he could, pulling her close, tenderly, caringly. His manner revealed a deep affection.

He began leading her across the chamber. The others followed, looking with horror at the place of Bowe's torture, noticing traces of blood and signs of a long struggle.

They moved quickly, without pausing, trying to keep their eyes to the shadows and openings. As they skirted the pool, Sylas chanced a look down. The haunting face of Thoth glared up at him, mirrored on the smooth, glassy surface. He knew it was only the image on the ceiling, but he found it hard to look away. The large hollow eyes seemed darker and emptier than ever before and yet, at the same time, he felt that they were seeing into him, gathering his thoughts, mocking him. To his surprise, the primal face showed not an absence of humanity, but an abundance of it: an endless transition between amusement, anger, despair, hatred and malice.

He shuddered and turned his eyes away.

Where was Thoth? Surely he was somewhere nearby?

Onwards they rushed, half walking and half running, the dark window rising in front of them, the air becoming crisp and cool.

Naeo moved onward in a daze, trying not to think of her poor father, sobs rising in her chest. At last they were at the drapes, feeling the first traces of hope, lifting their heads, gathering pace. The carpets gave way to stone and suddenly they were taking the last ten paces... five... then out on to the threshold, into the open air, jumping down on to the first of the huge stone steps.

They gulped deep draughts of the chill night air.

Below them the city looked almost beautiful. It was a broad shimmering carpet of pinprick lights, its tangled, twisting streets occasionally picked out by the last flickers of lightning. There was no sign of Paiscion's storm. The clouds had risen to expose broad horizons: the greyish shimmer of the winding river and the open sea; the endless blackness of the Barrens.

Suddenly a ghastly, appalling sound rose from the base of the Dirgheon.

A howl pierced the night and hung in the air. Far below them the base of the pyramid seemed to be moving, shifting, rippling in the dim moonlight. It was as though it was being consumed by some thick bubbling blackness, some foul surging growth rising up the sloping wall, moving ever more quickly towards them. And, as they watched, its smooth darkness began to gain shape and form. It took the appearance of a great swarm of dark bodies: an army of leaping, thrashing beasts.

"Ghorhund!" cried Ash.

Naeo put her hand to her mouth. "There are thousands..." she murmured, watching with horror as beasts crawled over beasts, hurling each other down the steep sides of the pyramid in the blind fury of their charge.

She turned to Espen. "What do we do?"

He too was peering down the side of the vast Dirgheon, shaking his head. But then something caught his eye. He looked past her and out across the side of the pyramid.

The trace of a smile formed on his lips. "It seems our friends are one step ahead."

She followed his gaze and saw Sylas, Simia and Ash running along the terrace, then leaping down to the next and the next. She looked ahead of them and gasped. There, lying across the stone terraces, were two gigantic structures of wood and canvas.

Their beautiful, broad wings caught the moonlight.

She stepped towards them, her mouth falling open. "Birds..." she said.

"Not birds," said the Magruman, with a fascinated smile. "They are something from the Other."

Espen turned, lowered his broad face to hers and smiled warmly. "You have much to learn from Sylas," he said, brushing the hair from her face, "and he from you."

Naeo turned away and her eyes found Sylas. He was beckoning them frantically, calling for them to follow. She watched him for a moment. She felt a strange kind of completeness, a peculiar certainty that her future lay with him.

"I know," she said.

Espen and Naeo ran out along the terrace and began leaping down to where Sylas, Simia and Ash were hoisting the first of the two great birds off the stones. Sylas was explaining how each of the parts worked, pointing beneath to a single horizontal bar for steering and a broad sling of canvas.

"... So this is where you hold on, and this is where you rest once you're in the..."

Simia put her hands on her hips. "We *know*, Sylas."

"And you pull back to..."

"Sylas, if we don't get moving, it won't matter which bit we pull where," said Ash, eyeing the throng of Ghorhund below.

"OK... yes," said Sylas. "So it makes sense that Espen goes

with you to keep it balanced..."

Espen reached over and placed a hand on Sylas's shoulder. "We are the Suhl, Sylas. The winds are with us."

Sylas looked at him doubtfully and drew a long breath. "Right. Yes. Of course..." He glanced from Espen to Ash and finally to Simia. "It's just that I've never made these before... they're much more complicated than kites.... *please* be careful."

Simia reached over and squeezed his arm. "Don't worry, Sylas," she said with a grin. "Birds of paper and string, remember...? It's what you *do*."

His eyes met hers and he smiled.

Suddenly a chorus of chilling howls erupted from the Ghorhund as they caught the scent of their prey. They charged up the final steps with a renewed bloodlust.

A single harrowing scream sounded from the opening behind them.

They all looked from the Ghorhund to the opening and saw, standing just outside the threshold, the lone figure of Scarpia. Her burned face was contorted with hatred and agony. Her blackened arms were raised aloft and there, suspended above her by some unseen force, was one of the giant urns, its orange flames dancing wildly in the breeze, trails of burning oil pouring down its sides and falling about her.

Espen launched himself forward, vaulting with remarkable speed up the steps of the Dirgheon.

"Go!" he cried. "Now!"

For a moment his companions were startled and simply watched him go, but then Sylas started to climb after him.

Naeo reached out and pulled him back. "No!" she screamed. "If we don't get away, it'll all be for nothing."

He tried to pull away. "But we have to help!"

She grasped his tunic and turned him round, glaring into his eyes. "My father's torture would be for *nothing*! All *Espen*'s done will be for nothing!"

He glanced back up at Espen's figure, leaping from step to step, moving with impossible speed and energy, ignoring the pain. Sylas shook his head and looked imploringly at Simia, but found her standing still, her face full of emotion, but firm.

"She's right..." she said. "We can't—"

Her eyes were drawn away, up into the sky. A look of terror formed on her face. The urn of burning oil was hurtling high into the night, travelling in a wide arc, trailing fire in its wake. It was heading straight for them.

As it glided through the air, it was tipping, sending down a shower of flame that cascaded over the steps of the Dirgheon, streaming down the steps towards them. Then they saw Espen, standing directly in its path, his hands already turning and twisting in the air.

"For Isia's sake, go!" he bellowed, never taking his eyes from the sky above.

They looked beyond his flailing arms and saw nothing but the approaching curtain of fire. It seemed hopeless. Sylas wanted to cry out, to do something – but it all seemed too late. And then they heard a new, unearthly sound. At first a low moan, rising to a wail, and then to an ear-splitting scream. It was coming from somewhere near Espen – somewhere directly above him. The urn was sailing over his head now, tipped almost horizontal, gallons of fiery oil plunging down towards him.

But it never reached him.

Suddenly the urn seemed to stop, turn, then twist ferociously in the air, spinning around, flipping over and over, spraying out yet more of the burning oil. But this too was caught by some dark force and hurled around in a wild, swirling vortex. As it spread, it lit up the sky, forming a colossal inverted cone that even at this distance scorched their faces. It was a gigantic, twisting, scalding whirlwind, dancing at Espen's command.

"He'll be all right! We have to go!" shouted Ash suddenly, pointing wildly down the side of the pyramid.

Sylas turned to see that the foremost of the Ghorhund were now just ten steps below them, their bared fangs clearly visible, their yellow eyes glowing in the darkness. Reluctantly he sprinted with Naeo to the other contraption and there he looked at its wings and checked the frame. All was as he hoped.

Without any instruction, Naeo went to the far wing and then, as one, they hoisted it into the air. There they paused, turning to watch Simia and Ash preparing to launch, swaying backwards and forwards, counting down.

The great canvas bird plunged forward. Sylas felt a thrill of excitement as he saw it sweep out into the darkness, the broad wings creaking as they took the strain. It hung for a moment in the air. They heard Simia shriek triumphantly as the wind carried them upwards, but then it tilted forward, slewed to one side and began to gather speed, racing down the side of the pyramid. It dropped out of the sky and pitched towards the stone steps. Sylas watched in horror as the line of approaching Ghorhund began leaping into the air, thrashing their limbs, gnashing their teeth.

"Up!" he cried. "Push on the bar! *Push on the bar!*"

But instead of climbing, the glider seemed to dip even lower, diving into the midst of the Ghorhund, the tip of a wing striking one of the beasts and sending it tumbling down the side of the pyramid. The collision righted it a little and then, as the great wings bowed and the nose lifted, it swooped upwards, slicing miraculously past the leaping Ghorhund and claiming its place in the sky. Ash whooped; his hand was no longer on the bar but in the air, conducting a great updraught of wind, which sent them far out over the city below.

Sylas and Naeo watched it drifting away until it was swallowed by the blackness, then they lowered their eyes to the baying horde, now just moments away. They turned to one another, catching each other's eyes, and smiled.

"Three, two, one..." they said in unison.

They stepped backwards, took two quick steps and threw themselves into the void. For a moment all was silent as if they were floating in nothingness, but then, as they struggled to lift their feet into the sling, they began to fall. Their stomachs turned and the air rushed in their ears as they accelerated: down into the great sea of darkness; down over the ragged stone face, towards the Ghorhund.

One terrace passed below them and then a second and a third. Sylas gasped at the night air, closed his eyes and pushed with all his might against the bar. Suddenly he heard a whip-crack of canvas as it became taught, the creak of timbers as they took the strain. The nose began to lift and then, with a gut-wrenching jerk, they were heaved upwards, gathered by Ash's great current of wind.

They swooped over the clamour of teeth and claws, over the swarming mass of dark, angular bodies, out into the night.

They let out a whoop of triumph as they shifted to one side, changing the balance of the glider and taking them in a long, banking turn. The Dirgheon came back into view, and above it the whirlwind of fire, snaking up into the dark clouds. In its midst they saw the tumbling, glistening urn, whipping around in wider and wider circles as it ascended towards the heavens. Below there was something else, something solid but on fire, long and thin, twisting and flailing as it whirled about in the wind.

It was a human figure, thrashing about as it burned, shrieking as it tried to break free.

"Scarpia," said Naeo, turning her eyes away.

Sylas followed the wretched figure for a moment longer, then winced and drew his gaze back to the Dirgheon. He scoured its surface for Espen, but already it was a hopeless task. The steps where he had been standing were aflame, engulfed by burning oil. Between, above and below, the Ghorhund were now leaping and snarling, clawing at the air. They poured into the openings, charging into the chamber while others turned and swarmed on to the other sides of the pyramid, searching its every crevice, examining every stone. There was no escape.

They watched in silence, saying nothing, their eyes searching desperately, hopelessly. They turned the glider in another wide circle, scything around the Dirgheon one more time. They squinted into the torrents of flame, but could see no sign of him. They let the enchanted winds carry them upwards so they could peer into the openings, but they saw that the lavish chamber was now smothered in black bodies: its hangings torn, its tapestries ripped from the walls. They climbed still higher, spiralling up into the night sky until they were above the army of beasts, until the baying and howls faded far below and they were left only with the wind and stone.

Finally, higher than they would have thought possible, they saw a dark, angular pinnacle: the very top of the pyramid.

There, on a narrow, square terrace, stood a lone figure. It was completely still, a long cloak billowing out behind it, the head turning with the sweep of their glider, following its every move. In that fleeting moment they were filled with hope; their hearts rose and Sylas opened his mouth to cry Espen's name.

But then he stopped. A shiver passed through his body and

a terrible cold flowed into his veins. The figure was not dressed in black, but scarlet; it was not broad, but frail and crooked and stooped. Its shoulders were drawn forward towards its hanging hood and, as the wind lapped at the folds of the gown, he saw the outline of wasted bones and twisted limbs. Suddenly the wind rose a little, lifting the hood just a fraction so that the moonlight slanted inside. There was no face in the shadows. Nothing but a mask of scarlet cloth.

"Thoth," breathed Naeo.

A wave of horror and fear passed through them, drawing the air from their lungs, clawing at their throats. They were seized by terror and despair, as if the night was closing in and pulling them back to earth.

As they rounded the apex of the pyramid, they saw something else. Something lying at Thoth's feet. A large bundle of rags.

It was moving.

"What... what's that?" mumbled Sylas.

But he already knew. He could see the shape of a man's body within the folds of clothing. A hand curled into a fist. A bald head, glistening with sweat, covered almost completely in tattoos.

"No...!" whimpered Naeo, raising a hand to her mouth, her eyes filling with tears.

But then, as they both wavered, as the great canvas bird faltered in the air, Bowe moved. His body straightened, his limbs straining, his back arching. Suddenly he was looking straight at them, his vivid green eyes clear and bright, glistening with the light of the city far below.

His voice came to them on a silent wave. It entered them unexpectedly, powerfully, as though he was speaking at their ear. But his words resonated somewhere deeper, in their minds, their hearts.

"Fly, my child…" he said. "Fly for us all!"

His voice surged through them, lifted their eyes, burned in their veins. Suddenly they came back to themselves, and they knew what they had to do.

Together they pulled on the bar and shifted their weight, banking sharply, allowing the glider to pull them swiftly away. The great frame creaked, the canvas fluttered and moments later they were sailing out across the city, leaving the Dirgheon, Bowe and the terrifying figure of Thoth far behind.

They flew in silence, the image still fixed in their minds: Bowe straining to look up at them and above him, Thoth stooped over his prey. In some ways it was as though they had seen nothing of the Priest of Souls, and yet they felt that they had seen too much: that somehow they had connected with that hollow, broken figure. They felt that they had seen into his blackened eyes and, in the same moment, Thoth had looked into them. He had seen their warmth and their bond; he had seen their hope turning to despair; and in that one glance he had seen Sylas's long journey — the Shop of Things, his passage through the Passing Bell, his flight, the Barrens, Simia, Filimaya…

The glider moved gracefully through the night, borne on magical winds, occasionally turning or tipping slightly on a current, its timber skeleton bending and creaking on eddies of air. And, as they flew, so they were soothed by the gentle motion of the wings, the play of the breeze, the twinkle of torchlight far below.

The cold started to leave Sylas's limbs and slowly, as they came out of their darkest thoughts, he remembered Simia and Ash. They scoured the darkness, hoping beyond hope to see a hardly visible shape, black upon black, turning and swooping at their side.

For some moments they saw nothing, then a dark silhouette shifted in the blackness ahead of them.

For an instant it was gone, but then it reappeared, twisted in the air, then sailed steadily towards them, growing larger and larger. It was too dark to see at first, but then the moonlight caught its wings, its angular shape, its gliding motion. Sylas was about to call out, but his breath caught. He stopped.

Its wings were not fixed and broad like a glider's — they were moving: rising and falling, twisting and tilting in the wind.

It was not a glider at all, but a giant living bird with a proud, angular head, piercing eyes and smooth downy feathers. It was one of the great black eagles he had seen circling the Dirgheon.

It banked, turned and disappeared into the darkness. Even as it did, two others appeared, and then another. Soon they could see six or eight eagles circling and wheeling above the city as though calling them on. And although they took their own path, they did not leave; instead they came together, gathering around them, swooping and turning, diving and climbing. Sylas's heart pounded, blood coursing through his veins. The great birds were flying with them, sharing in their journey. They drew ever closer, the sound of their beating wings floating on the wind, their pale grey eyes shining in the moonlight.

"There!" cried Naeo.

She pointed a short distance ahead of them and there, drifting just below a line of cloud, was the other glider, silhouetted against the lamplights far below.

Sylas and Naeo banked, gathered pace and descended towards their friends, watching as the giant eagles glided ahead of them, behind them, above and below them. They called out to Simia and Ash and their friends yelled their greetings while the great flock looped playfully about them, matching human cries with their own, dancing lightly through the air, welcoming them, leading them.

Simia shrieked with delight and leaned out towards a passing bird, her hand touching the velvety feathers; Naeo and Ash exchanged smiles and looked ahead, across the city to the dark, winding river, the broad estuary and the open sea beyond.

Sylas gazed out at the silent beating wings, at the majestic eagles dancing their dark ballet, and he smiled. He reached out, took Naeo's hand and together they headed out over the carpet of light, flanked by the birds of his dreams.